AF478432

Sex, Race, and Family in Contemporary American Short Stories

SEX, RACE, AND FAMILY IN CONTEMPORARY AMERICAN SHORT STORIES

Melissa Bostrom

Contents

Acknowledgments

The story of this book has been long, and the help I have received has overflowed the bounds of any economy. I thank the many readers who graciously provided feedback at many stages: María DeGuzmán, Linda Wagner-Martin, John McGowan, Laurie Langbauer, Marianne Gingher, Jane Burns, and Bob Johnstone, with a special debt to Tara Powell and Andy Leiter. Thanks to Farideh Koohi-Kamali and Elizabeth Sabo at Palgrave Macmillan for guiding the book, and thanks to Maran Elancheran at Newgen for its design. Funding from UNC's Department of English and Royster Society supported the project at critical junctures.

I have been lucky to have a substantial cheering section of friends behind me: Kim Burton-Oakes, Berenice Cadena Patiño, Mary Cunningham, Brian Dietz, Adam Garratt, Jessica Kem Gorman, Tom Gorman, Jennifer Haytock, Chris Hill, Sharon Joffe, Ann Kakaliouras, Alex McAulay, Lisa McAulay, Fiona Mills, Joy Salyers, Courtney Sears, Cindy Stone, Elaine Tola, Rich Zink, and, above all, Sarah Mazer Zink.

I especially thank my family for lifting my spirits across the miles—my parents, Dave and Kay; my siblings, Lynn and Ben; and my extended family, Andrea Grotenhuis, Todd Grotenhuis, Brian Nowling, Cara Nowling, Paula Nowling, Jo Wier, Jeff Wier, Katie Wier, and Peg Wier. My grandfather, Bob Wier, supported me throughout the work of this project, and we'll all miss him in celebrating its end.

Finally, I would need to write another book to adequately express my gratitude to Krisztian Horvath, whose kindness, sense of humor, intellect, and love have made the journey worthwhile.

Introduction

In the widely acclaimed story "People Like That Are the Only People Here," Lorrie Moore relates the tale of a Mother and a Husband whose Baby has been diagnosed with renal cancer.[1] The story opens with the Mother's discovery of a blood clot in the Baby's diaper and follows the family through his treatment. Moore's story is not a run-of-the-mill family drama, though. The first words the Husband utters in the story follow the Mother's announcement of the Baby's diagnosis; his first reaction is to suggest, "Take notes." Because his wife is a novelist and teacher, he repeats, "Take notes. We are going to need the money" (219). When the Mother, appalled, tells him, "I write fiction. This isn't fiction," he recommends that she write their story as a journalistic report. "Get two dollars a word," he suggests (222). In response to the news that their infant son will need a nephrectomy and chemotherapy at the least, and perhaps the removal of the other kidney and a transplant as well, the Husband immediately focuses on ways to turn this situation into one that is profitable rather than financially draining. Although the Mother resists his advice throughout the story, steadfastly refusing to profit from her Baby's life-threatening illness, she seems to recover from those qualms by the end of the story, when the Baby's cancer has faded into remission. "There are the notes," she writes on the final page. "Now where is the money?" (250).

Moore foregrounds the relationship between the short story and economics here in a way few other writers have done. The Mother's choice to tell the story for money underlines the relationship between writers of short stories and the kind of financial gain they can bring. Originally published in the *New Yorker*—currently the most prominent U.S. magazine printing literary short fiction—this story is particularly important because it was widely anthologized, including in the 1998 volume of the Best American Short Stories series and as the first-prize winner of the O. Henry Awards for that same year. Charles McGrath, the former fiction editor of the *New Yorker*, has speculated that this "knockout" story propelled Moore's collection *Birds of*

America to the *New York Times* bestseller list, a rare feat for any short story collection. The story thus reached a wide audience—wider, perhaps, than almost any other piece of literary short fiction published in the past decade ("The Short Story" E1).[2] The narrative voice of the story, that of the (unnamed) Mother, also sparked speculation by readers and critics that the events related in the story were inspired by Moore's own life. The story's initial appearance in the *New Yorker* fed such conjecture through the contents page, which implied that the piece was a memoir; the first page of the story itself was printed opposite a photograph of Moore (Passaro 83–84). Moore herself was rather coy about the truth of that assumption; her "Contributors' Notes" accompanying the story's publication in the 1998 Best American Short Stories volume say simply, "This story has a relationship to real life like that of a coin to a head. It is dedicated to my son" (291). Even her simile invokes economic terms to explain the story's relation to reality.

Although Moore's story portrays a contemporary example, American women have been writing stories about their families to support them for many decades. The earliest women short story writers in this country turned to the short story after attempting genres such as Sunday School literature, child-rearing and etiquette advice, children's literature, and even the more traditional essays, novels, and poetry (Koppelman, "A Preliminary Sketch" 1). Financially, they found short stories to be the best option for supporting themselves; stories simply sold better and paid more. As Mary Louise Pratt has noted, the story genre is particularly friendly to writers who are new to the literary scene, such as women and minorities, in a way that most other traditional genres are not, allowing a number of new writers to find remuneration and recognition as they launch their careers. Moore herself has remarked that this fact about the story is good for both readers and writers: to have art forms "newly open to people who wouldn't ordinarily have the economic means to write them, is not a bad thing. It allows for voices, and pieces of the world, and life coming into light and play that readers didn't have before" (McGraw, Moore, and Burgin 26). Moreover, as Virginia Woolf observed in *A Room of One's Own*, shorter forms are better suited to women writers, who can constantly be interrupted in their domestic and childcare duties, and fiction requires less concentrated attention than either drama or poetry (Woolf 78, 66). Even contemporary writers find truth in this statement. Sue Miller, in her introduction to the 2002 Best American Short Stories volume, explains that Woolf's dictum held true in her own life: "I wound up writing short stories," she recounts, "because

I didn't feel I had the time or the imaginative energy left to me—after being a mother, having a job, and running a house—to undertake the longer kind of work, the work of the novel, to which I felt more suited" (xiii).

Women writers were not the only ones who discovered the relatively rapid payday possible with short stories. The idea that short stories represented easy money prevailed for many years, reaching its acme during the modernist era, when the number of commercial magazine outlets for stories—and their pay scales—reached their height. John Updike has written nostalgically of this era's importance for some of the greatest American writers of the twentieth century: "For Faulkner, short stories were bread and butter; for Scott Fitzgerald, in the palmy days of the old *Post*, they were an avenue to glamour such as now awaits rock stars" (xiv). Both Faulkner and Fitzgerald sold stories to magazines such as the *Saturday Evening Post* in order to pay the bills while they worked on novels. But writers were not always so happy about the need to write those stories: "Fitzgerald's bitter resentment of the toll in time, energy, emotion, and self-respect taken by the writing of these stories is legendary," remarked Charles R. Hearn (33). "His comment in a letter to Hemingway that 'the *Post* now pays the old whore $4000 a screw' is typical of the self-disparaging remarks he made about the magazine fiction" (33). Moreover, writers' feeling that their art was cheapened by the need to seek a commercial market may also have contributed to a more general impression among the public that the short story was, as Thomas Gullason termed it, a "cheap potboiler" (21). The fact that stories were published side by side with advertisements in those magazines only reinforced that public perception.

The commercial success of short stories was particularly harmful to their status as a genre during the modernist era, since modernists disparaged art that was embraced by the "lowbrow" general public (Ferguson 191). The idea that stories are a source of quick cash has lingered in the public consciousness, despite the fact that, since the 1940s, the market for stories has steadily dwindled to four well-paying, large-circulation magazines and a number of little ones that generally pay nothing, or next to it. In part because of the example of writers such as Fitzgerald and Faulkner, the general public (and some literary critics) has developed the impression that writers use short stories to "practice" their craft until their skills are strong enough to attempt a novel. The idea that short stories are the genre of "apprentice" writers— with novelists the acknowledged masters—has taken hold despite the fact that Faulkner and Fitzgerald, among many others, continued to write stories even after they had mastered the longer form. The rapid growth of contemporary MFA programs in creative writing has helped to substantiate this public impression, for the workshop model these programs employ is much more easily applied to short stories than to novels. Thus our newest writers are, indeed, starting out with short stories as they try to work their way to the more financially lucrative novel. Finally, the idea of the short story as an apprentice genre is reinforced by curricular approaches that present it as appropriate for beginning readers in high school and undergraduate survey literature courses, rather than for advanced study in an upper-level college seminar or graduate school.

The genre's cultural status suffers from a continual comparison with the novel. In a society that celebrates "supersizing," the smaller story is deemed less important, less powerful. Richard Burgin, who writes both short stories and novels, suggests that "this whole size, strength and power thing is so ingrained in us whether it's big cars or big people, big body parts, or big masses of writing" (qtd. in Ferguson 191). Moore calls the story the "Napoleon of the narrative world" whose economy of form has given it both a unique kind of power and a short man's complex (Introduction xviii). Such comments echo those of Edgar Allan Poe, whose criticism of the short story was among the earliest to attempt to delineate critical parameters for the genre. Poe defined a story by its length—readers could finish it in one sitting—and the critics who followed him largely accepted length as the defining characteristic of the genre. Not surprisingly, this criterion proved to be limiting as short story criticism grew; what, for example, was the difference between a long short story and a novella? Critics spun their wheels over such issues, often without significantly advancing the body of short story criticism. In 1963, Frank O'Connor attempted to change the terms of the debate with his book *The Lonely Voice*, in which he characterized the genre by its content rather than by its length. O'Connor described the story as the genre of the loner, the outsider on the fringes of society, and the rebel. The attraction of O'Connor's alternative formulation led most critics to accept his definition without challenge.[3]

By extension of O'Connor's definition, the short story as a genre could be considered a kind of minor literature, according to the criteria of Gilles Deleuze and Fèlix Guattari. In their view, a minor literature is one that exists within the larger body of a major literature. Although Deleuze and Guattari use this term to describe the position of Prague Jews writing in German, such as Kafka, their term might be extended to include the short story, which, as countless critics have noted, is almost always described as smaller and less important than the novel. Minor literature, Deleuze and Guattari explain, is always political: "[I]ts cramped space forces each individual intrigue to connect immediately to politics. The individual concern thus becomes all the more necessary, indispensable, magnified, because a whole other story is vibrating within it" (17). Their description evokes Julio Cortázar's comparison of the short story to a photograph in its portrayal of an image that, by the mere imposition of margins, expands beyond the limits imposed by the form, implying a larger world beyond the borders of the text or picture (246). Through such characteristics, Deleuze and Guattari conclude, minor literature abounds with revolutionary potential.

The story's accessibility to new writers whose cultural participation might be otherwise limited, its relatively low position on the literary totem pole, its portrayal of characters on the edges of society, and its revolutionary promise all suggest that the short story should, as a genre, be better adapted to promoting social change than the novel. Its progressive politics should then be complementary to social movements that wish to alter the status quo, as Deleuze and Guattari suggest. Indeed, feminist theorists who study the way in which women gain knowledge have suggested that the story be used as a metaphor for women's sharing of information between mothers and daughters—that the story serves as a way to explain the empowering knowledge that women share outside patriarchal structures. These theorists, known as feminist epistemologists, aim to fundamentally revise the way Western philosophy conceives of knowledge as independent of knowers; feminist epistemologists argue that factors such as gender, race, and class make substantial differences in the way that people encounter the world and come to know it. Seeing the story as the model of the way that women come to know the world, then, itself represents a tremendous challenge to the status quo.

If short stories, as examples of minor literature, are endowed with revolutionary potential, and the figure of the story passed from mothers to daughters symbolizes a challenge to traditional, masculine-dominated models of knowledge acquisition, then it stands to reason that short stories of mothers and daughters should provide liberating portraits of women who rebel against social constraints. Yet it's not the case. Particularly in stories published since the 1978 appearance of Nancy Chodorow's highly influential book *The Reproduction of Mothering*, mother-daughter relationships tend to depict strict limits on female sexual expression. Ironically, despite the surge in interest in mothering that emerged in the late 1970s with such books as

Adrienne Rich's *Of Woman Born* (1976), Dorothy Dinnerstein's *The Mermaid and the Minotaur* (1976), and Nancy Friday's *My Mother/ My Self* (1977), all of which condemned, in various ways, childcare arrangements that gave mothers the overwhelming majority of responsibility for children, short story writers have continued to create tales that portray mothers and daughters as so close to each other that they have trouble finding separate identities. Such portrayals reinforce the idea that such a relationship is natural and normal. This situation, especially as described by Chodorow, creates what I call an economy of female sexuality: mother and daughter are so closely identified with each other that, for the purposes of sexual expression, they are treated as one person within the family. Only one or the other can find sexual expression at any one time in this zero-sum economy. As Michel Foucault has suggested, the mere act of speaking of sex was once thought to be transgressive, but his analysis has shown that such "transgressions" are merely the reinscribing of networks of power that impact sexuality.[4] Merely writing about sex is not in itself transgressive or rebellious; short stories that portray sexuality are not inherently challenging mores.

By examining short stories' content, and particularly their representation of female sexuality, I argue that the characterization of the genre as inherently revolutionary or, at the least, persistently capable of challenging social norms, is demonstrably false. In fact, the cultural work of the short story is deeply conservative. A close study of stories from the past twenty-five years reveals that not only do they confine female sexuality through rigid economies between mothers and daughters, but they also tend to limit female sexuality differentially based on race. That is, the restrictions demanded by this economy are more powerful the "whiter" the characters are.

Characters of the highest socioeconomic status, those most fully integrated into American life, with the most "normal" sexuality— heterosexuality—experience the greatest limits on female sexuality. Because motherhood can be held literally responsible for the continuation of whiteness, as writers such as historian Anna Davin, philosopher Marilyn Frye, and literary critic Allison Berg have shown, society applies particular pressures to limit it. As the fulcrum on which the future of whiteness depends, motherhood in particular, and female sexuality in general, is the site of special cultural anxiety.[5] This factor helps to account for the conservatism evident in the repeated appearance and working of the female sexual economy.

In itself, however, the cultural anxiety surrounding motherhood is not enough to explain why a genre that has been understood for the past forty years as the voice of the rebel should establish such a consistent pattern of portraying limits on female sexual expression. In the end, it is the short story's relationship to the marketplace, I argue, that determines its cultural role. The virtual disappearance of commercial outlets for the short story, with the notable exception of the *New Yorker*, has significantly narrowed its audience and its cultural importance. While little magazines and literary reviews proliferate, they have such small readerships that, unless a story is collected in one of the annuals such as the O. Henry Prize Stories, the Best American Short Stories, or the Pushcart Prizes, it may reach only a few hundred people. Although Moore suggests that this situation frees story writers from commercial concerns so that they can produce great art (Introduction xv),[6] I contend that the contemporary publishing scene severely narrows the options for writers seeking both a sizable audience and fair compensation. In order to "make it," writers generally need to see their stories printed in the *New Yorker* or another one of the handful of well-paying magazines; success on this scale is often the only way that large houses will bring out story collections by new writers.[7] (Even so, the vast majority of book contracts require the writer to produce a novel as well; publishers are generally skittish about investing in collections.) Instead of creating an environment in which writers are free to express any views they like, even those of characters on the fringes of society, the current literary scene offers a highly limited path to success. The opinion that the short story is a rebel genre can only be held, frankly, by critics who refuse to recognize the importance of economics to the story. This project aims to reinvigorate the field of short story criticism by comparing the theories that have gone largely unchanged in forty years to the realities of practice as shown by the content and context of contemporary stories.

To that end, I begin with a chapter that places criticism of the short story as a genre in dialogue with theories of story in feminist epistemology theory, psychoanalysis, feminist criticism, and deconstruction. I establish that the cultural meanings of *story*, as developed in its relationship to orality and literacy as well as its opposition to history, are crucial for understanding the cultural work of the literary genre of the short story. The second chapter examines the importance and Freudian underpinnings of key mothering texts of the late 1970s, including those by Dinnerstein, Friday, and Chodorow, demonstrating the way in which the economy of female sexuality can be traced to the understanding of the mother-child relationship portrayed in those books. Stories by Ann Beattie, Amy Bloom, and Lorrie Moore illustrate the variety and power of the effects of the female sexual economy on three fictional mother-daughter pairs. In the third chapter, I introduce whiteness as a factor of analysis in order to demonstrate the limits of the sexual economy. After an overview of whiteness studies and its relationship to female sexuality, I examine stories of daughters on the borders of whiteness, by Alyce Miller, Lore Segal, and Achy Obejas, as their contexts and relationships to whiteness shift, resulting in corresponding shifts in the force of the sexual economy. Finally, I close with an exploration of economies of exchange, including alternative accounts of economies by a number of theorists as well as more literal economies that affect the production of and audience for contemporary short stories.

The field of short story criticism is the final vestige of New Criticism in twenty-first-century literary studies. Too long have critics ignored the context of the short story: the changes that have taken place in the material production of the form, the changes in the educational culture (e.g., the rise of MFA programs) that largely produces today's short story writers and their subsequent and requisite participation in the system that produced them. Worse, the field has largely managed to ignore new perspectives on the genre offered by the development of a number of schools of critical theory as well as the shift in the past twenty years toward cultural studies. Short story criticism and theory, in other words, has managed to seal itself in a time capsule as the genre it celebrates becomes less celebrated, less visible, less valuable in American literary life. While this project uses some of the implements from the New Critical toolbox, in particular the strategy of close reading, it expands the realm in which the short story exists, from the pages on which the words are printed to theoretically complex, culturally produced, and culturally limited texts that both reflect and project a world.

Story

The past decade has witnessed a surge of popular and scholarly interest in short stories focused on the family, and particularly on the mother-daughter dyad within that family. One of the earliest anthologies of mother-daughter short stories appeared in 1985, edited by literary scholar Susan Koppelman, and focused on the ties that bind mothers and daughters over many generations; two more collections on similar themes followed over the next six years.[1] Books about the mother-daughter dyad in literature also appeared during the 1980s;[2] by 1993, Susanne Carter had compiled an annotated bibliography devoted to American stories about mothers and daughters. Although scholarly attention to the topic gradually emerged, popular appeal did not immediately follow. Over the next three years, just three more collections of stories were published.[3] Beginning in 1998, however, publications of mother-daughter anthologies grew dramatically: six more collections were published in a three-year span.[4] While some of these collections also include poems and excerpts from longer fiction, the short story is the predominant genre in the anthologies. And although father-son story collections exist, they are considerably outnumbered.[5] Stories of mothers and daughters are apparently more attractive to publishers.[6]

The different collections, understandably, rely on a variety of tactics to sell their respective products. Well-known editors such as Koppelman, Katrina Kenison (series editor of the annual *Best American Short Stories*), and Joyce Carol Oates might attract a prospective buyer. Jill Morgan's anthology confines itself to short stories written by popular mystery, science fiction, and romance authors. Two (Ingman's and Oates/Berliner's) make their claim on readership specifically temporal, calling themselves stories of the twentieth century, presumably to make the stories even more directly relevant to the lives of the buyers. Still others rely on ethnicity as their "hook," as in *Motherland*, a collection confined to the writings of Irish American women, or *Did My Mama Like to Dance?* which devotes much of its space to the writings of women of color.

Not surprisingly, the stories in these collections often share common themes.[7] Some concern a mother and daughter banded together against an external source of tension.[8] Such plots seem to pay homage to Tillie Olsen's 1956 story "I Stand Here Ironing," in which a mother (the narrator) rues the inferior parenting she was able to provide for her oldest daughter, Emily. Because she was poor and abandoned by the child's father soon after her birth, the narrator was forced to leave Emily for long stretches, and when they did have time together, the mother was exhausted. The narrator reflects on her grown-up daughter, recognizing that Emily hasn't received the attention she deserved but attributing this lack of care to the social conditions that force single mothers to work several jobs to make ends meet. Alice Walker's 1973 story "Everyday Use" shares a similar approach, although in this case the external force is the narrator's older daughter Dee, whose arrival pressures the mother and her younger daughter Maggie into closer alliance. Dee decides that her grandmother's quilts would add just the right decorating touch to her new home, but the narrator resists Dee's claim on the quilts, insisting that they're promised to her quiet younger daughter, Maggie. Dee fumes that Maggie doesn't know any better than to put the quilts to "everyday use." But it is Maggie who wins the prized heirlooms, precisely because she knows how to value her family's heritage. The story ends with the narrator and Maggie sitting in peaceful kinship, successful in holding the line against the outside forces that have threatened.

Another common plot is the coming-of-age tale, pitting a daughter against her mother. In Gloria Naylor's "Kiswana Browne," the title character struggles to find her own way as a jobless recent college graduate.[9] When her mother comes to visit her apartment for the first time, Kiswana is defensive, anticipating her mother's criticism at every step. Although much of the plot details their clash over fundamentals such as Kiswana's refusal to sign up for telephone service until she finds a steady job, the story ends with Kiswana realizing that she and her mother aren't so different after all. That this realization is sexually charged—Kiswana sees her mother's painted toenails and recognizes that her father must have a foot fetish, just as her own current lover does—only underscores the daughter's process of maturation. Jamaica Kincaid's "Girl," another coming-of-age tale, follows a mother's oft-repeated instructions to her daughter in a stream of consciousness. The mother reminds her how to do laundry, cook, keep house, walk like a lady, dress like a lady, treat strangers, treat men, and treat babies who were never meant to be begotten. The story does not end as neatly, however, as "Kiswana Browne." The mother fears that, unchecked and unguided, the daughter's sexuality will create trouble for her in the community; at the close of the story, she asks whether her daughter will become the kind of woman "the baker won't let near the bread" (96). In the case of "Girl," sexuality pits mother against daughter rather than bringing them closer together.

The kinds of stories included in mother-daughter anthologies tend toward the "Kiswana Browne" pole rather than that of "Girl." That is, they are generally uplifting in praising the mother-daughter relationship as a source of strength for both participants. (Granted, these examples are among the best-known and most-anthologized stories of the lot.) Few end with outright sadness or bitterness; even the narrator of "I Stand Here Ironing" grasps at the hope that her daughter has had enough attention to bloom a little, even if she doesn't blossom fully. Similarly, "Girl" ends with a question rather than a statement: the relationship is still in progress, and it still offers hope for the girl's proper maturation.

Stories that present what might be seen as more controversial interactions among family members are likely to be omitted from this type of anthology. Take, for example, Flannery O'Connor's "Good Country People." The arrogant and condescending Hulga-Joy gets her comeuppance at the hands of her well-wishing mother Mrs. Hopewell (albeit indirectly). Hulga's disdain for her mother shapes, at least in part, her mother's loneliness and thus her willingness to welcome a traveling Bible salesman. When he lures Hulga to the barn loft with talk of love only to steal her prosthetic leg, he abandons her to her lofty ideals and leaves her stranded with them. Hulga's end is satisfying to readers because it enacts a kind of revenge by her mother, whom Hulga treats with utter contempt. A more literal story of a mother's revenge can be found in Edith Wharton's "Roman Fever," in which two American women reminisce about their courtships as they wait for their daughters to return from romantic adventures of their own. When the women's conversation turns to their long-ago rivalry over a common suitor, Mrs. Slade reveals that she forged a note to Mrs. Ansley, purportedly from the young man. This deception, Mrs. Slade fears, was the cause of Mrs. Ansley's cavorting in the deadly night air of Rome, which led to a protracted illness and eliminated her from competition for the suitor. It is Mrs. Ansley, however, who has carried the more surprising secret all these years; the result of that late-night tryst was her daughter Barbara, fathered by Mrs. Slade's husband just before their marriage. Barbara is living proof of Delphin Slade's love of Mrs. Ansley, a triumph about which Mrs. Slade has known nothing.

While there may be many stories about the mother-daughter dyad that have not been collected in anthologies, the omission of stories such as O'Connor's and Wharton's signals a discomfort with tales that refuse happy endings or that see daughters as instruments of revenge. Tales of incontrovertible differences between mothers and daughters, such as those between Hulga-Joy and her mother, do not make the editors' cut. What, then, according to the philosophy of anthology editors, is a "proper" mother-daughter story? One answer is that such a story portrays a mother passing down wisdom to her daughter; "Girl" is the obvious example, but "Kiswana Browne" operates in a similar way. In "Everyday Use," the narrator has successfully passed on her wisdom as well as her heritage to Maggie even if she seems to have failed Dee; "I Stand Here Ironing" is a mother's lament that she didn't have time to adequately enlighten her oldest daughter. "Good Country People" and "Roman Fever," on the other hand, present no such connection between the generations.

Mother-daughter anthology editors appear to assume that the stories included in their collections should portray a mother educating her daughter. Such an assumption bears remarkable similarity to the theories used in an entirely different realm, by those who study feminist epistemology. Such theorists have used the term *story* as a metaphor to explain the sharing of knowledge among women, particularly to describe the way in which women's knowledge acquisition may challenge dominant male-centered models. Moreover, these writers commonly use the transfer of wisdom from mothers to daughters as the paradigm for all women's ways of understanding the world. In such theory, the "stories" that mothers teach daughters represent the learning patterns of all women. Against the backdrop of feminist epistemology theory, editors' choices of stories that affirm connections between mothers and daughters may seem more logical. The seeming congruence between the anthologized short story and theory is troublesome, however, because the term *story* as metaphor becomes superimposed on the literary genre *story*, without recognizing that the short story as a cultural object has its own history and value independent of its worth as a representation of feminist epistemology.

This intersection between short story theory and feminist theory is just one example of the way in which multiple theories of *story* may be working together—or at odds—in shaping an understanding of the cultural importance of the contemporary short story. Few theorists of the short story have contextualized their work within the larger body of critical theory, of which feminist epistemology theory is one relatively small part. Without exploring the ways in which the two bodies of knowledge might influence one another, theorists of the short story cannot fully account for the ways in which the genre is valued in contemporary literary and popular culture. One of the few critics who has attempted to step outside the rather insular world of short story theory in order to place the work of this world's inhabitants in a larger context is Mary Louise Pratt. Although she identifies herself as an "outsider" to the field, her article "The Short Story: The Long and the Short of It" is the first to extensively consider the ways in which short story theory systematically positions the genre within the culture at large. Since her 1981 article, however, little work has been done to expand her examination. One obvious way to do so is to consider the ways in which *story* functions in other domains of critical theory—not only in feminist epistemology theory but also as the intersection of orality and literacy, history and fiction. Putting short story theory into conversation with other critical approaches helps to reveal the function and value of the short story in U.S. culture.

FEMINIST EPISTEMOLOGY AND *STORY*

Over the past twenty-five years, feminist theorists in several disciplines have turned their attention to the topic of epistemological differences between men and women—that is, differences in the ways in which people acquire knowledge. Their interest stemmed largely from the entrance of women into the academy at an increased rate, combined with the development of academic disciplines and subdisciplines such as Women's Studies, Women's Literature, and Women's History. In order to defend the existence of disciplines that often refused traditional, "male" models of knowledge acquisition, feminists found themselves creating theories of women's epistemology as the foundation for their new approaches. While theorists of feminist epistemology have pursued a variety of justifications for and models of women's ways of knowing,[10] the scholars do share some commonalities. A variety of different approaches to the issue converge on a view of feminist epistemology as many individual threads in a larger tapestry—or many individual stories in a larger anthology—symbolizing the sharing of knowledge between generations of women.

Philosopher Sandra Harding argues that epistemologies are only formed when a hostile environment demands them. These justificatory strategies, she explains, are only necessary when someone calls into question the validity of one's knowledge claims, a difficulty often encountered by feminist thinkers. Sociologist Patricia Hill Collins terms epistemologies "knowledge validation procedures," a term that includes the external pressure of Harding's model; she then spells out the stakes of any alternative epistemology. While alternative knowledge claims by themselves cause little anxiety to conventional knowledge, alternative epistemologies call attention to traditional Western philosophy's assumption of a universal knower, one who is white, bourgeois, and male (to name the most apparent characteristics). As Collins puts it, "[A]lternative epistemologies offer [challenges] to the basic process used by the powerful to legitimate knowledge claims that in turn justify their right to rule. If the epistemology used to validate knowledge comes into question, then all prior knowledge claims validated under the dominant model become suspect" (271). A feminist epistemology, then, has radical potential for disrupting humanism—it strikes at the very roots of beliefs about the culture. Small wonder that such alternative epistemologies are conceived under pressure.

In response to those who ask why feminists need new justificatory strategies, feminist scholar Bettina Aptheker points out that women's experience has been ignored as a possible source of knowledge, because Western philosophy assumes that all knowers are alike. To exclude all experiences that may be pertinent to a gendered existence in the world seems to her deeply unfair. Aptheker constructs a model of tapestries of "dailiness" in women's lives as a feminist epistemology, one that recognizes the patterns in women's everyday experience (even though some of those experiences may share common features with men's experience). She suggests that mapping the commonalities in women's lives may point the way to both recognizing the importance of those experiences (which may be trivialized because of their very dailiness) and creating meaning from those experiences—recognizing that they constitute bases of knowledge claims. She reiterates Alice Walker's idea (from "In Search of Our Mothers' Gardens") that feminists need to think back through their mothers as a way to conceptualize the importance of knowledge gained in women's daily lives. For Aptheker, stories present a way of recording women's experience in the world: "Women's stories locate women's cultures, women's ways of seeing; they designate meaning, make women's consciousness visible to us. Stories transform our experiences into ways of knowing about ourselves as women and about ourselves as women looking at the world" (43).[11] But, she emphasizes, stories are not an end in themselves but are part of a process of dailiness, a process of discovery based on emerging patterns.

While Aptheker's model tends to stress the kinds of knowledge passed on through female family members and received by one or two individual inheritors, philosopher Lynn Hankinson Nelson argues that knowledge is situated in communities. She posits that individuals are not the primary agents of epistemology, for such individuals have already been working within a context of theory and practices. As an example, she cites the discovery of the proton's structure: such a claim could only be made—and, more importantly, validated—in a community that already had a working knowledge of atomic structure and a set of standards for authorizing knowledge claims. For Nelson, the context of knowing is crucial to the validation of knowledge. Such a context thus serves to expand Aptheker's model of knowledge—represented as stories shared between mothers and daughters.

Philosopher Marilyn Frye, in "The Possibility of Feminist Theory," furthers the work of these theorists by explaining why it is important to recognize patterns of experience. She notes that knowledge founded in non-feminist epistemology makes women feel abnormal because their lives often do not fit the model of what Western philosophy has proposed as universal experience. The patterns established by Western inquiry structure its knowledge as normal and even normative, and as such exclude women.[12] Frye proposes a model of patterning, like Aptheker's tapestries, through which women's experience can be traced such that feminists can "remetaphor" the world. Patterns, formed from gendered experiences of the world and thus different from the kind of knowledge affirmed by Western philosophy, allow a visualization of women's experience on a larger scale than simply a set of localized tales. By looking for patterns, theorists look not to create a normative foundation for knowledge but rather to see what has been left out, what has been decentered. Frye advocates that feminists focus on those things that do not fit into the pattern so that they can better understand experiences that have been marginalized or simply ignored. Like a metaphor, one cannot stretch the pattern too far or it will no longer make sense, so Frye suggests thinking of women's experience as an anthology of women's stories, a collection of diverse knowledges that together might begin to constitute women's ways of knowing.

Feminist scholars Nancy Fraser and Linda J. Nicholson have explored the intersection of such epistemology theories with a post-structuralist critique that denies gender (like class, race, etc.) as a category of analysis. They use as one example of postmodern thought Lyotard's rejection of the "grand narrative of legitimation." He does not endorse metanarratives that tell a story of continuous progress over the course of history, because such narratives necessarily ignore historical specificities in their claim to universality. As Fraser and Nicholson point out, however, since both feminist epistemology and postmodernism have as their projects the destruction of the universal subject and universalizing knowledge, one might think that they should be able to find some common ground, despite postmodernism's suspicion of gender as a means of organizing knowledge about the world. As one way of finding that commonality, Fraser and Nicholson look to Lyotard's idea of the "social bond," a kind of tapestry of experience that does not attempt to totalize, but rather has many different threads with no one thread running continuously through it. Each thread in the tapestry can be compared to a mininarrative, local in its specificity and thus avoiding the downfalls of claims to universality. The recognition of mininarratives, or stories, becomes a way to reconcile Lyotard's concerns about ahistorical accounts with the need to value women's experiences (whatever their race, ethnicity, class, age, sexual orientation, etc.).

Trinh T. Minh-ha, in *Woman, Native, Other*, also points to the figure of the story as a way to theorize the foundations of women's knowledge. Trinh, using a vocabulary that echoes that of other thinkers, labels the mininarrative "Grandma's Story." Her theory of story returns to Aptheker's emphasis on the exchange of stories among generations of women while explicitly offering a postmodern critique of it. Stories, says Trinh, are a way of making women's history visible. They are disruptions of the history that patriarchy has legitimated. To illustrate her point, Trinh cites the opening section of Maxine Hong Kingston's *The Woman Warrior*, in which the narrator's mother disrupts the smooth functioning of her culture by repeating the story of her sister-in-law's death. The mother defies cultural codes that dictate that women who do not allow their sexuality to be controlled by the community must not only die for their resistance but also must be erased from history. This aunt does not even have a name, a signal that her identity has been erased for her refusal to submit to community norms. She does not exist—except in the story told by the mother to her daughter. The daughter then continues the disruption by not only retelling the story but also by publishing it, circulating it far beyond the immediate community.[13]

Although the story is a powerful tool for disrupting patriarchy, Trinh argues that feminist epistemologists must be careful about what they value as story in order to avoid excluding what may not fit that formulation. The traditional Western conception of story, for example, includes exposition, rising action, resolution, denouement. But oral traditions or non-Western ideas of story may not fit this formula.

Trinh cites Leslie Marmon Silko's "Storyteller," which speaks to the function of the storyteller who does not fit into Western models of story. In the story, a woman refuses to claim her innocence of a man's death despite her attorney's insistence that she bears no guilt for it. The attorney cannot understand how the woman can claim that she has caused the death of a man who falls through thin ice if she never touched him. The woman, however, knows that she chased the man onto the thin ice, seeking revenge, and feels that his death is her responsibility. The impasse between the woman and her lawyer results from the attorney's inability to grasp that there might be other models of "storyness" that implicate the woman in the man's death, says Trinh. Because of the woman's internal story about the man's death, she claims that she is guilty; her attorney, however, cannot make the woman's explanation square with his own preconceived notions of a "logical" story, and he therefore cannot comprehend her perspective. Although Trinh embraces the concept of the story as a way to value women's experience, she cautions that this model can be limited if feminists impose too narrow a definition on what constitutes a story— a reiteration of the postmodern project. In this way, she sees the "mininarrative" as a way of constituting women's history, of posing women's experience as a disruption of patriarchal models, while noting that even such an epistemological foundation can reify the universal nature of knowledge if feminists don't examine the limits of the model of such knowledge (119–151).[14]

As figured by these theorists, the story or mininarrative becomes a way to represent knowledge transmission from one woman to another (often the passing of wisdom from mother to daughter). Feminist epistemology recognizes that women can have fundamentally different understandings of the world than do the universal knowers postulated by Western philosophy, and feminist theorists value those differing perspectives. This is not to say, however, that all women experience the world in the same way; theorists must value the variety of experiences that women (and, indeed, people) have. Rather than attempting to match these experiences against accepted norms of behavior, feminists should look for patterns and similarities. These patterns may shape themselves into a tapestry of differing threads, to use Fraser and Nicholson's term, or an anthology of women's stories, to borrow Frye's. Collecting women's stories, especially those passed between mothers and daughters, can be seen as a means of validating women's knowledge claims. If such collections only recognize a limited range of women's experiences, however—stories that only portray positive connections between mothers and daughters, for example—then they merely repeat the universalizing errors that feminist epistemologists have worked to undercut.

The Oral and the Written Story

Although both Aptheker and Frye use the metaphor of women's stories to explain their respective theories of feminist epistemology, a tension exists between the two models, for Aptheker's story is transmitted orally, while Frye's paradigm is a collection of stories in an "anthology"—a necessarily written form. Indeed, it is the intersection between these two forms that shapes the short story's function as literary genre. While genre theorists have long recognized the connection between the two modes, little attention has been paid to the way in which cultural treatment of orality and literacy has shaped the significance of the short story, which often acts as a bridge between the two. Understanding the way in which orality and literacy have been approached by critics contextualizes the work of genre theorists who deal with the short story.

The word *story* in English conjures up both the literary genre and the oral form; in fact, Brander Matthews coined the term "short-story" at the turn of the twentieth century in order to address the confusion he saw stemming from the single word's double meaning.[15] Most theorists of the short story claim the genre's origins in orality as a means of establishing its history. Frank O'Connor is a notable exception in this regard; in his view, the short story has a vexed relationship with orality. He prefers to distinguish the literary genre from the oral storytelling tradition, with its "wild improvisation." In O'Connor's view, the short story "began, and continues to function, as a private art intended to satisfy the standards of the individual, solitary, critical reader" (114). Yet O'Connor repeatedly uses the term *storytelling* to describe the process of writing both short stories and novels, calling the former "pure storytelling" and the latter "applied storytelling" (27). Because this term carries connotations of oral as well as literary production—and because O'Connor makes no effort to divorce the term from those meanings—it is difficult to determine precisely how O'Connor sees the short story as separate from the oral tradition. Although O'Connor is never able to settle on a precise explanation of the differences between an oral story and a written one, he is one of the first theorists to remark upon the story's ties to orality.

Several other writers and critics, however, embrace the genre's ties to oral storytelling, often using the terms *story* and *storytelling* interchangeably. Horacio Quiroga, for example, states that "as long as the human language is our preferred vehicle of expression, man will always make stories, because the short story is the one natural, normal, and irreplaceable form of storytelling"(48). Warren S. Walker's study of the genre's ties to folklore reinforces the links between the forms, although Walker acknowledges that the shift to a written form eliminated the flexibility of the storyteller's ability to respond to the audience (e.g., elaborating a funny incident when the listeners are laughing, or abbreviating a tale when the audience seems to lose interest).[16] Noting that Edgar Allan Poe's use of the term "prose tale" (in his review of Hawthorne's *Twice-Told Tales*) differentiated between the oral tradition and the written form, Walker emphasizes that Poe's own stories maintained folkloric elements—he considers the "romantic environment" of Poe's stories, for example, to be rooted in folklore. For Walker, the tie between the oral and the written form has never been severed, and the relationship between storytelling and story writing is crucial to the genre's continued development.[17] (Kincaid's story "Girl," through the mother's narration of instructions to the daughter, demonstrates that the oral nature of the story is still an integral element in shaping the form.)

Pratt, too, values the story's ties to orality but for different reasons. She notes that the novel has traditionally been linked with writing, while the short story carries associations of orality. "The conspicuous tradition in the novel," she writes, "has always been toward writing and bookishness. As is so often observed, the novel was born affirming its own writtenness" (107). These ties to "writtenness" do contribute to the novel's elevation as literary form at the expense of the short story, but they also prevent the novel from acting as an agent of social change in the same way that the shorter genre can. Pratt expresses the genre's potential in this regard:

> The tradition of orality in the short story has special significance in cultures where literacy is not the norm, or where the standard literary language is that of an oppressor. . . . In such contexts as these, the short story provides not just the "small" place for experimentation, but also a genre where oral and nonstandard speech, popular and regional culture, and marginal experience, have some tradition of being at home, and the form best-suited to reproducing the length of most oral speech events. Orality can be counted as one of the important factors behind the flourishing of the short story in the modern literatures of many Third World nations and peoples, where, not incidentally, it is taken much more seriously as an art form than it is elsewhere. (108)

Pratt's evaluation emphasizes the short story's role as a point of entry for writers whose cultures have not traditionally emphasized writing.[18]

The short story can quite literally be the genre of O'Connor's "submerged population group," since it provides a means for new voices to be heard—or read.

According to both traditional theorists of the short story (e.g., Poe and Matthews, whose primary purpose seems to be a defense of the genre against the encroaching power of the novel) and those such as Pratt, who are more concerned with theorizing the cultural work of the genre, the short story has the potential to effect cultural change, although different critics see differing limits to this potential. Extrapolating from Poe and Matthews, the story's creation of a "single effect" offers the opportunity to deeply influence the reader: as Poe puts it, "During the hour of perusal the soul of the reader is at the writer's control" ("Review" 522). Pratt's analysis of the underlying reasons behind this potential points both to one of the genre's greatest strengths and its greatest weaknesses. The short story's ties to orality have made it a welcoming genre to writers who might not otherwise have access to the publication, but they have also, in conjunction with a broader cultural move to value literacy over orality, contributed to its devaluation as a genre. From this set of propositions, then, one could assume that the short story is a left-leaning genre. It should be sympathetic to the case of members of the working classes, people of color, those of nontraditional sexual practices, women—any disenfranchised member of society. The genre provides an opportunity for such people to shape the world in their fictive image.[19]

If "beginning" writers—that is, those making the transition from orality to literacy—can earn esteem and compensation only through publication, then is there a cultural place where oral "texts" might be esteemed? Although some genre theorists run from the oral roots of the short story and others embrace its ancestry, their strong reactions to the link between orality and the story signal that the association carries some stakes. The writings of Walter J. Ong and Jacques Derrida provide an outline of the relative cultural worth of the two states; although the two diverge on many points, they ultimately agree that writing is more valued than oral tradition. Theirs are not the final words on the subject, though. The texts of feminist writers such as Trinh and Hélène Cixous offer ways to envision the relationship between orality and literacy as nonbinary, without privileging one mode over the other.

Ong argues in *The Presence of the Word* that orality is a stage on the way to a culture's path toward literacy, and that while orality does have some positive features (a speaker can be a much more powerful communicator than a writer in some instances, and certain artistic accomplishments are possible only within an oral culture), literacy is necessary in order for culture to flourish, knowledge to be stored, and civilization to progress.[20] From Ong's perspective, literacy (and particularly print and even electronic literacy) is a goal universally to be wished. While primary oral cultures (cultures with limited literate membership) overvalue sound and the power of naming and tend to be conservers of knowledge rather than creators of new knowledge, literate cultures can develop kinds of knowledge that simply aren't possible in an oral system that requires that all information be stored in memory. Writes Ong in *Orality and Literacy,*

> There is hardly an oral culture or a predominantly oral culture left in the world today that is not somehow aware of the vast complex of powers forever inaccessible without literacy. This awareness is agony for persons rooted in primary orality, who want literacy passionately but who also know very well that moving into the exciting world of literacy means leaving behind much that is exciting and deeply loved in the earlier oral world. We have to die to continue living. (15)

Without the powers of writing, says Ong, illiterate subjects are limited in their capabilities to think abstractly (e.g., a circle is a plate, or a square a door, but neither belongs to an abstract category) and have little incentive to remember information that is not directly pertinent to their daily survival (such as the fact that there was a previous ruler of their country). Only the greatest of heroic subjects and the grandest epics are worth remembering; everyday people are forgotten in the need to allocate memory to events and people that are relatively easy to remember. Writing, on the other hand, facilitates a new kind of thought, one that is not reliant on memory for its work since the thinker can record his or her thoughts and follow a direction without the fear of forgetting some part of the path that's been traveled. Books present a forum for knowledge that cannot be disputed with the author, for the author is always removed from the scene of reading, unavailable for argument in the way that a speaker is. According to Ong, literacy confers upon a writer an authority impossible to achieve in a primarily oral culture.

While Ong's argument might draw criticism from poststructuralist theorists such as Derrida for his belief in a universalizing metanarrative (the journey from orality to literacy), the two do share some common ground. Derrida also affirms the primacy of literacy, although he does so in a very different way. [21] Perhaps the iconic moment of Derrida's privileging of writing over speech comes in the title of his article

"Différance," in which the word itself both presents and represents the difference that cannot be recognized aurally. In the earlier book *Of Grammatology*, Derrida lays out the thinking behind this move. Writing is necessarily prior to literacy, for the "exteriority" of language, language as an object, requires that the sign expressed in language refers to a concrete entity (the word on the page). Like Ong, Derrida argues that writing is necessary to the pursuit of knowledge, and that writing can only be the vehicle of such a pursuit because writing precedes language. Without writing, declares Derrida, historicity as a concept could not exist; "writing opens the field of history—of historical becoming" (27). But even while writing facilitates new kinds of understandings of the world, it also marks a move away from language as a possession of the masses toward a point at which language is used as a tool to wield power: "Writing is the very process of the dispersal of peoples unified as bodies and the beginning of their enslavement: 'The body of a nation alone has authority over the *spoken language*, and the writers have the right over the *written* language: *The people, Varro said, are not masters of writing as they are of speech*'" (170). Writing centralizes power in the hands of writers at the expense of speakers. Writing literally confers authority.[22]

Working from either Derrida or Ong, then, one may argue that writing is more powerful than speech. This valuation poses an obvious problem for feminist theorists, however, since female writers have often been cut off from writing (much as their roles as speaking subjects have also been curtailed). How can orality be celebrated when it is a feature of "illiterate"—and thus immature and inferior—cultures and groups? In Cixous's writing, orality and literacy are often so closely intertwined that it is difficult to define the difference; she uses the confusion of speech and writing to avoid reifying the kind of hierarchy that Ong and Derrida establish. Like Cixous, Trinh also tries to keep from privileging one mode over the other, but she more explicitly disentangles speech and writing to address formally the ways in which Western cultures in particular have valued literacy over orality.

In the essay titled "Castration or Decapitation?" Cixous works to topple the binary relationship between speech and writing, although she does so at the risk of merely reversing the hierarchy. She examines the limits of speech when it's attributed to women, explaining that women's speech has not been valued in itself because philosophy has considered it to be mere talking, not speaking. "It is said, in philosophical texts, that women's weapon is the word, because they talk, talk endlessly, chatter, overflow with sound, mouth-sound: but they don't actually *speak*, they have nothing to say" (49). In order to revalue women's speech, she turns to women's writing. The feminine text, claims Cixous, reaches its reader through its "tactility," but for Cixous this is a touch that travels through the ear rather than the fingers. By celebrating the capacity of women's (and feminine) texts to speak (literally) to their readers, she refuses to subordinate speech to writing and valorizes the oral.

In her more famous essay "The Laugh of the Medusa," Cixous further confounds the boundaries between writing and speech even while she affirms that both have radical possibilities for a woman: "She must write her self, because this is the invention of a *new insurgent* writing which, when the moment of her liberation has come, will allow her to carry out the indispensable ruptures and transformations in her history." As Cixous elaborates, this act will be "marked by woman's *seizing* the occasion to *speak*, hence her shattering entry into history, which has always been based *on her suppression*. To write and thus to forge for herself the anti-logos weapon" (250). Women's writing, in Cixous's formulation, is a way to challenge both history's silencing of women through its refusal to hear their voices as well as the rational conventions of patriarchal language. While in this passage Cixous does not limit women's potential to either writing or speech, she is clearly aware that they are different, for on the very next page she declares, "It is time for women to start scoring their feats in written and oral language" (251). She mourns that "woman has never *her* turn to speak—this being all the more serious and unpardonable in that writing is precisely *the very possibility of change*, the space that can serve as a springboard for subversive thought, the precursory movement of a transformation of social and cultural structures" (249). By demonstrating that she recognizes that speech and writing are not identical but also refusing to consistently recognize the boundaries of the terms, Cixous repudiates the primacy of writing.

Trinh, too, refuses boundaries in her use of the terms speech and writing, but this refusal is not her only tactic in addressing the problem of the hierarchy. Like many other theorists of postcolonial literatures, she also explicitly addresses those who treat orality as inferior to literacy in *Woman, Native, Other*, quoting Herman H. Horne and Willa Cather, for example, in discussing the appeal of the "primitive" story to children and "unlettered" peoples.[23] According to these writers, the story, particularly in its oral forms, is only appealing to infantilized audiences; sophisticated, literate readers find nothing of redeeming value in such performances. Storytelling in the West, writes Trinh, has through this line of thinking become appropriated as a form of teaching, but now it's used to "teach children the tales their *fathers* knew"—that is, storytelling has been co-opted by patriarchy and reduced to an educational device. Such a view of the story empties it of the possibility for change that Trinh imagines in the metaphor of Grandma's story. She notes that in the system of story as educational tool, children's stories may have elements of fancy or magic, but they are conveyed in such a way that the young listeners are never confused about what might happen in "real" life. Boundaries must always be kept. In this way, says Trinh, men turn what used to be women's stories into mere lies. Imaginative, fantastic tales that could inspire children are reduced to falsehoods.

Imitating a speaker with such an attitude, Trinh writes, "Living is neither oral nor written—how can the living and the lived be contained in the merely oral? Furthermore, when she [the storyteller] composes on life she not only gives information, entertains, develops, or expands the imagination. Not only educates. Only practices a craft" (126). In such a passage, Trinh seems to be writing in a purposely difficult style. As Herman Rapaport has noted, Trinh's writing tends to fuse orality and literacy, since it is often quite difficult to tell when the voice is hers and when it belongs to an imagined external critic. (Such a difference would be clear were the text an oral one; in this way, her strategy is similar to that of Derrida in "Différance.") Trinh's rhetoric diminishes the argument of those who insist on seeing the story as mere story; she rejects the idea that the only purpose of storytelling is to keep the rational mind well exercised to better serve the purposes of a patriarchal society founded on logical reasoning. For Trinh, storytelling is an act of life; it has magical powers, not just to convey information—but also to imagine and create new worlds.[24]

Trinh is able to capture the magic of writing and speech without reifying a binary relationship between the two. Writing is both speech and not-speech, a listening and a reading, and a breaking of rules:

> Writing, in a way, is listening to the others' language and reading with the others' eyes. The more ears I am able to hear with, the farther I see the plurality of meaning and the less I lend myself to the illusion of a single message. I say I write when I leave speech, when I lose my grip on it and let it make its way on its own. . . . For writing, like a game that defies its own rules, is an ongoing practice that may be said to be concerned, not with inserting a "me" into language, but with creating an opening where the "me" disappears while "I" endlessly come and go, as the nature of language requires. (30–31)

Writing, instead of a being a means of establishing the writer's rational superiority, becomes a way to create community among writers and readers, in which the writer's claims on individuality and authority dissolve into the group of readers. Trinh's vision of writing is thus very much like Walker's description of oral storytelling: the value lies in the community of listeners/readers and the perspectives they bring to the story.

Although Cixous and Trinh offer new ways of valuing orality and literacy, their visions have yet to be implemented on a broad scale, perhaps because to do so would mean finding a way to escape the meanings that have become associated with each of the terms. Despite their work to disrupt the hierarchy between writing and speaking, even these two critics cannot completely escape reinforcing the traditional uses of the terms at stake. Even the writtenness of their thoughts can be seen as evidence that literacy trumps orality. Their work, along with that of Derrida and Ong, is useful, however, in that it provides a context for the theorization of the short story as a literary genre. Because the story is understood to be rooted in oral traditions, it will always seem less important culturally than the novel, which by its very size must be a written work.[25] The story's ties to orality do not completely explain its consistent positioning as lower than the novel in the hierarchy of literary genres, though, and the vast majority of short story critics agree that the novel is persistently more valued. Some critics argue that the lower status is not always a detriment to the genre, however. The lowered expectations for the story created by its diminished status open up the means by which stories can operate in unexpected ways.

GENRE THEORY AND *STORY*

In an oft-quoted 1935 essay, William Saroyan ponders, "What, if anything, is a story? Well, frankly, I do not exactly know, and believe no one exactly knows, and if anyone does exactly know, I believe this knowing isn't so terrifically important, and if it is important at all, I do not believe it is important enough to stand in the way of the growth of art" (qtd. in May, *The Short Story: The Reality of Artifice* 80). Short story theory, although still a relatively young art at the time of Saroyan's essay, has not been able to resolve the question he poses in the nearly seven decades that have followed. Although there is no dearth of short story criticism and theory that attempts to answer the question "What is a story?" very little of it directly addresses the way in which the short story functions as a cultural object. Many genre theorists acknowledge a debt to Cleanth Brooks's and Robert Penn Warren's 1943 textbook *Understanding Fiction* for first drawing serious attention to the theory and criticism of the short story as a genre, but it may well be that the New Critical approach to the story that fathered (so to speak) a renewed interest in the genre also failed to spark approaches that looked beyond the stories themselves. It is only by tracing trends and patterns within a broad range of short story criticism that it is possible to piece together what this field can explain about the story as a cultural object.[26]

Theorists and critics of the short story as genre have often found themselves defending it against what is perceived as the larger and consequently more important genre, the novel.[27] Among its earliest defenders in English is Poe who asserted, "There has long existed in literature a fatal and unfounded prejudice, which it will be the office of this age to overthrow—the idea that the mere bulk of a work must enter largely into our estimate of its merit" (*The Works* 227). As Pratt has more recently noted, the very term "short story" necessarily makes reference to the lack at the heart of the genre—that is, its lack of length vis-à-vis the novel. The relationship between the novel and the short story, according to Pratt, "is not one of contrasting equivalents in a system (separate but equal), but a hierarchical one with the novel on top and the short story dependent." In other words, a short story's very existence as genre depends upon its comparison to the novel.[28] Pratt adds, "Between these paired genres, relations of long to short coincide with relations of unmarked to marked, of major to minor, of greater to lesser, even 'mature' to 'infant'" (96).[29] As she points out, this value system is not inherent in all power relations between genres (if such an idea may exist); for example, says Pratt, the long poem is treated as a variation of the poem, but the ("regular") poem is not devalued simply because it's not long. In part, the short story's position relative to the novel derives from the view that the short story is the genre of an apprentice writer—that is, a writer only writes short stories until she can mature into a fully formed novelist.[30] (Such a view ignores such notable exceptions as Ernest Hemingway, Edith Wharton, Richard Wright, Gabriel García Márquez, and Joyce Carol Oates, to name a few, all of whom continued to write short stories even after they had achieved "mastery" by writing novels.)[31] This treatment of the genre may also have helped to perpetuate the short story's status as a genre appropriate for apprentice readers;[32] high school English classes often focus on short stories rather than expose students to the complexities of the novel. Conversely, very few college-level literature classes—and even fewer beyond the survey for nonmajors—devote themselves to the short story.[33]

In addition to fighting off the short story's devaluation because of its brevity, theorists have also tried to defend the genre by citing its lengthy history.[34] Walker rejects Elizabeth Bowen's appraisal, in her introduction to *The Faber Book of Modern Short Stories*, that "[t]he short story is a young art: as we now know it, it is a child of this century";[35] instead, he wants to demonstrate that the roots of the short story are, in fact, much deeper and older than those of the novel. Walker, a specialist in folklore, noted in the 1980s that many well-known stories are rooted in folklore, a pattern that, according to him, demonstrates that the genre's origins reach back to oral tales.[36] Such a history would set the age of the genre in the thousands of years rather than in the hundreds. Brander Matthews, the second major American theorist of the short story, had similar concerns at the turn of the twentieth century: "In the history of literature the Short-story was developed long before the Novel, which indeed is but a creature of yesterday" (78). Charles E. May, one of the two most important contemporary theorists of the short story, claims that the genre can trace its origins to brief episodic narratives. May says in *The Short Story: The Reality of Artifice* that anthropologists have determined that this type of narrative predates the evolution of the epic, which May identifies as the ancestor of the novel (1). All three critics appear to believe that a long history offers a credibility for the genre unmatched by the novel, and that the short story therefore deserves more critical respect—or, at the very least, the same amount the novel receives.

Another line of defense involves the difficulty involved in producing the story as well as its superior aesthetics. Anticipating critics who believe that the short story is easy to write because of its brevity, Matthews is careful to state that "[t]he Short-story is a high and difficult department of fiction" (75). He continues by noting that while there are almost too many acknowledged masters of the novel to name, there are few great short story writers (in his opinion, only a half-dozen had distinguished themselves by the conclusion of the nineteenth century). The short story is not so simple to write as some might assume, Matthews asserts. Several decades later, Frank O'Connor declares in *The Lonely Voice* that the short story writer must be "more of a writer" and "more of an artist" than a novelist in order to represent a world within the confines of a brief text (22). May likewise grounds his defense of the genre in aesthetics: "The novel exists to reaffirm the world of 'everyday' reality; the short story exists to 'defamiliarize' the everyday" (133). The story, in other words, transforms the everyday into a work of literature with its own aesthetic, apart from that of the novel. Elsewhere, May has paraphrased Elizabeth Bowen in saying that "the short story places human beings alone on that stage which, inwardly, everyone is conscious of occupying alone and that, in this regard, exempt from the novel's often forced conclusiveness, the short story may more nearly 'approach aesthetic and moral truth'" (Introduction xxv). May's position is perhaps the most extreme defense of the short story on aesthetic grounds in his assertion that the genre bests the novel in its approximation of "moral and aesthetic truth." In other words, critics who have not given the short story its due are ignoring the highest form of literary art. May's remarks are the acme (or nadir, depending on one's perspective) of defensive theorization of the genre.[37]

Theorists of the short story, in addition to defending it, are also interested in the form's modus operandi. In particular, they cite the way in which the genre necessarily establishes an intimacy with the reader through the specificity of the story's situation; think of the solidarity (however misplaced) one feels with Sister upon the first reading of Eudora Welty's "Why I Live at the P.O." Because the short story has, by its very nature, little room in which to create its world, it must confine itself to a specific time and place (and, often, to one character). The reader is able to follow the main character's experience quite closely because the form's brevity necessarily limits secondary and tertiary plot lines, such as one might find in the novel. The reading situation created by this economy of form presents an opportunity for a kind of intimacy between reader and character that is unparalleled in the novel; as May puts it, while the novel is a representation of "experience," the short story presents "an experience" (133). The form's length also requires that writers use a kind of shorthand to convey meaning to the readers; think, for example, of Hemingway's "iceberg" principle, more broadly applied.[38] Readers must fill in the blanks, so to speak, based on conventions of reading. As Jonathan Culler states in *Structuralist Poetics*, genre functions as a kind of contract between reader and writer, establishing expectations for their interaction. Clare Hanson puts it a different way: the "[e]llisons and gaps within a text offer a special space for the workings of the reader's imagination," in a way that presupposes a similarity in thinking between the reader and writer (25).[39]

The particularity that facilitates intimacy, however, does not limit the story's application or broader meaning beyond the boundaries of its beginning and end, say critics of the genre. As Pratt has pointed out, many stories present themselves as exemplary through either their titles (e.g., Bharati Mukherjee's "A Wife's Story" or Amy Bloom's

"The Story") or through character names, which are often limited to first names (for instance, Melville's Bartleby has no surname), names that are biblically allusive, or no names at all (such as the Mother, Husband, and Baby of Lorrie Moore's "People Like That Are the Only People Here") (102–103). All of these cases lend themselves to the expansion of each story's meaning from extreme particularity to a broader and more universal meaning. Julio Cortázar has eloquently compared the short story's ability to make meaning to that of the photograph: "cutting off a fragment of reality, giving it certain limits, but in such a way that this segment acts like an explosion which fully opens a much more ample reality, like a dynamic vision which spiritually transcends the space reached by the camera" (268).[40] The carefully chosen details of the short story, then, function to expand its meaning far beyond the specifics of the event it relates.

The growth and development of this genre have been particularly associated with the Americas; perhaps this fact accounts for the defensive impulse in American theorists of the story such as Poe, Matthews, and May. In "Some Aspects of the Short Story," Cortázar stresses to fellow latinoamericanos (Latin Americans), "A discussion of the short story should interest us especially, since almost all the Spanish-speaking countries of America give the story great importance, which it has never had in other Latin countries like France or Spain" (245). While the precise reasons behind this relationship have yet to be established, the association of the short story with the Americas, and with the United States in particular, has been noted by other critics from around the world. Irish short story writer and critic Frank O'Connor has termed the short story America's "national art form" (41). Russian writer B. M. Éjxenbaum notes in his essay on the history of the short story that "[t]he story, precisely as *small form* (short story), has nowhere been so consistently cultivated as in America" (83). Perhaps the development of the form was a declaration of literary independence from England's glorification of the novel,[41] or perhaps it was simply that the magazine culture that evolved in the United States tended to publish short stories rather than serializing novels, as English presses did.[42] Either way, Éjxenbaum asserts at the outset of his essay that

> [t]he novel and the short story are forms not only different in kind but also inherently at odds, and for that reason are never found being developed simultaneously and with equal intensity in any one literature. . . . The novel derives from history, from travels; the story—from folklore, anecdote. The difference is one of essence, a difference in

> principle conditioned by the fundamental distinction between *big* and *small* form. Not only individual writers but also individual literatures cultivate either the novel or the short story. (81)

There is, then, for Éjxenbaum, a fundamental difference between a culture that produces the short story and a culture that venerates the novel. Such a view does little, however, to counter those critics who argue that the short story is a lesser genre, practiced by lesser writers (those who cannot handle the more difficult novel).

If the genre can be associated with a cultural entity such as the United States, might it also serve cultural purposes? While few theorists of the short story have spelled out its social effects in the way that Cortázar has, the subtext of many critics' work implies that the genre does cultural work. Take, for example, Frank O'Connor's famous classification of the short story as the genre of the "submerged population group." He sees the genre as one that can tell the story of alienated loners (Flannery O'Connor's Hulga in "Good Country People" presents an excellent example). While characters on the fringes of society may not make suitable material for a novel, claims Frank O'Connor, the short story elevates them to a central position in the mind of the reader. Because the genre can praise characters who are otherwise ostracized by society, O'Connor's definition lends credence to the possibility that the short story has the potential to make cultural change. The genre's power stems, in part, from its brevity. O'Connor's case owes its foundations to Poe's dictum that any text, in order to preserve its power, must create a unity of impression—"[F]or, if two sittings be required, the affairs of the world interfere, and every thing like totality is at once destroyed" ("Philosophy" 530). Matthews continues Poe's definition some years later: a "Short-story is the single effect, complete and self-contained, while the Novel is of necessity broken into a series of episodes. Thus the Short-story has, what the Novel cannot have, the effect of 'totality,' as Poe called it, the unity of impression" (73).[43] Poe's maxim and Matthews's extension of it refer to the artistic effect of the story, but their assessments could also be applied to the genre's capacity for cultural work.

Pratt, writing a century later, observes that the short story has, in fact, done cultural work: Maupassant's stories, for example, helped to break down taboos regarding social class and sexuality in France, while in Ireland, the short story developed into a kind of national art form that could document modern, everyday life (104).[44] In part, the mere fact that a writer tackles a cause that is not considered proper for literature may lend credibility to the proponents of that cause; and while a novelist would be taking an enormous risk by making such a subject the center of a book, a short story writer (and the prospective publisher, the magazine editor) takes less risk with a shorter piece.[45] Pratt cites, as an example, the fact that childhood experience is often the subject matter for short stories, while, outside the specialized genres for such modes (such as the bildungsroman), the novel offers few cases in which childhood is the central focus. As Pratt puts it, the general exclusion of childhood experience from the novel demonstrates an ideological commitment: "[I]sn't this really a way of saying that childhood experience is not considered normative or authoritative in the society, or that it is considered an incomplete basis for the supposed totalizing vision of the novel?" (106). Much as the short story is considered the genre of apprentice writers, it has also traditionally been seen as the site for experimentation with new subject matter; this view of the genre stems from the short story's status as "lesser" than the novel (97). (Unless one genre is esteemed as "conventional" and thus more conservative, the short story cannot be viewed as experimental.) The freedom to experiment, to portray new kinds of characters and to ask new kinds of questions can be construed as the genre's capacity for effecting change.

This capacity may also be seen in critics' language describing it, particularly that of Éjxenbaum and Cortázar. Éjxenbaum describes the construction of the story as based on "some contradiction, incongruity, error, contrast, etc. . . . By its very essence, the story, just as the anecdote, amasses its whole weight *toward the ending*. Like a bomb dropped from an airplane, it must speed downwards so as to strike with its war-head full-force on the target" (81).[46] Éjxenbaum's metaphor reinforces Cortázar's comparison of the story to the photograph, as a form in which "this segment [the story] acts like an explosion which fully opens a much more ample reality" (246). Cortázar uses another metaphor to describe the power of that "explosion," the philosophy of an Argentinean boxing fan: "[I]n the struggle between an emotive text and its reader, the novel always wins on points, while the story must win by a knockout" (247). For Cortázar, the power of literature lies in its ability to change the opinions of its readers; while the novel can win by the accretion of small points over time, the story can win its reader over much more quickly.[47] The violence of the language in both critics' descriptions underscores their understanding of the short story as a genre that can effect dramatic change and even social transformation.

One reason that the short story has the potential to reach so many readers with its message is the fact of its publication in "popular" forums such as magazines, but this fact is also key to the genre's cultural status vis-à-vis the novel. Because the short story is, by its nature, brief, it is generally packaged with other materials when placed for sale in the publishing marketplace. Usually a story first appears in a magazine or, sometimes, a literary journal, among many other kinds of writing— essays, letters to the editor, and advertisements. The story may even share space on its pages with ads, which helps contribute to readers' perceptions that the story itself is a kind of commodity for sale.[48] More importantly, the story, like the rest of the magazine, is recycled at the end of its usefulness. While some of these stories are eventually compiled and marketed as short story collections, such collections usually owe their existence to stories' initial publication in popular forums such as *Playboy*, the *New Yorker*, or *Redbook*. The association of the story with commercialism is perhaps the genre's greatest detriment in its critical comparison with the novel; to put it another way, the story is to craft what the novel is to art. Pratt states the problem thus:

> [W]hat above all creates the association with craft and skills is clearly the short story's ties to journalism. In the realm of the commercial (as distinct from the literary) magazines, the short story becomes anthema [*sic*] to the art-for-art's sake values that consolidated themselves in the modernist period. In fact, it became exactly what those values are erected against. It is art commodified and commercialized, art one tries to make a living at and (horrors!) possibly even succeeds. (110)[49]

Even though some of modernism's values have lost their luster over time, the vestiges of artistic snobbery remain an impediment to the short story's achievement of full-fledged literary status.[50]

Given the ostensible politics of the short story—its capacity for cultural work, its representation of characters at the margins of society, and its ability to reach popular audiences even at the price of denigration for being popular—one might expect that it would be aligned with movements whose raisons d'être are battles against oppression. Take, for example, feminism: much as women since Simone de Beauvoir have theorized that their oppression under patriarchy stems from their exclusion from the universal (to take Beauvoir's example, women are not included in the "universal" term *man*), proponents of the short story might argue likewise that it has been subsumed under the "universal" term *fiction*, which traditionally suggests *the novel*.[51] The very name of the genre implies an inherent comparison to the novel—the short story cannot be deemed short (and therefore lesser) unless it is compared with something longer.[52]

Moreover, the genre's accessibility to groups of writers who have not traditionally had access to the publishing sphere would appear to make it friendly to feminisms' goals; to revise Virginia Woolf, even without fifty pounds a year and a room of one's own, then, a feminist writer could produce short stories. As Mary Eagleton puts it, "If we are talking about . . . low status then the short story is even . . . lower than the novel. Many critics of the short story have stressed that it is not the primary literary form of our period, that it holds a marginal and ambiguous position in literary culture, and that it is peopled with characters who are in some way at odds with the dominant culture" (62).[53] In other words, the stakes of writing short stories are lower than they might be with more firmly established genres such as the novel, thus inviting writers who do not necessarily see themselves as part of the "dominant culture" to begin publishing their work. With such assumptions in mind, the short story could be viewed in alliance with the aims of liberal feminism—that is, it promotes the entry of women into cultural enclaves traditionally closed to them; encourages women who have faced barriers to their cultural participation because of their racial, ethnic, or sexual identity; and advances women's opportunities for supporting themselves financially.

To put it another way, the short story offers one way for women and other writers who have little access to the publishing sphere to change literary history. By transforming "primitive" oral stories into printed, paid words, such writers can become part of history. Because *history* itself includes the story in its literal appearance on the page, there appears to be a link between the two ideas in English; in French, the association is even closer, since *histoire* means both *history* and *story*. How does the story become part of history, or even become history itself? The writings of Hélène Cixous (in French) and Trinh Minh-ha (in English) help to elucidate the work of the story—particularly the story of someone without power in a writing-centered, patriarchal culture—in the context of history.

(Hi)Story

In the writings of both Trinh and Cixous, the figure of the story is often associated with history, although the two writers approach the intertwining of the terms in different ways. Like the theorists of feminist epistemology discussed above, Cixous is concerned with women's place in history as constructed by Western philosophical discourse. In "Castration or Decapitation?" she finds that women's position in such a history is so obscured that observers must ask themselves, "Where is she? Is there any such thing as woman?" In fact, women who try to find themselves in this kind of history often "feel they don't exist and wonder if there ever has been a place for them" (43). Like Frye, Cixous is concerned that traditional models of the individual's role in history make women seem like abnormalities because such models have no place for gendered experience. Cixous is also concerned with the power of validated knowledge:

> We have to get rid of and also explain what all knowledge brings with it as its burden of power: to show in what ways, culturally, knowledge is the accomplice of power: that whoever stands in the place of knowledge is always getting a dividend of power: show that all thinking until now has been ruled by this dividend, this surplus value of power that comes back to him who knows. (51)

The stakes of alternative epistemology are quite high. As long as only one kind of knowledge is validated, the holder of that knowledge continues to reap the dividends of power. To challenge traditional modes of justifying knowledge claims is thus to challenge those who traditionally hold power.

But in apparent opposition to the theories of feminist epistemology examined earlier, Cixous proposes a model of knowledge validation not only outside the mother-daughter relationship often posited but in fact an extrafamilial, seemingly antifamilial model. In her model, the circulation of knowledge takes place in a context of desire:

> When a woman writes in nonrepression she passes on her others, her abundance of non-ego/s in a way that destroys the form of the family structure, so that it is defamilialized, can no longer be thought in terms of the attribution of roles within a social cell: what takes place is an endless circulation of desire from one body to another, above and across sexual difference, outside those relations of power and regeneration constituted by the family. (53)

While Aptheker, for example, found the mother-daughter bond to be an enabling one, Cixous opposes the restrictions inherent in the family model, particularly in its reification of existing power structures. This attitude seems, however, to be less directed toward the mother-daughter relation in particular than part of an overall attitude regarding the place of women's writing, women's stories, in history. To uphold the family structure of the status quo is to uphold the father's power as a representative of patriarchy; for Cixous, stories have the capacity to upset that power. Women's stories appear, in her writing, to have (at least) a dual nature. History comprises many individual stories—mostly, of course, those of white men who reap the dividends of power. But stories also have a disruptive potential, particularly when they are feminine speeches or texts.[54] Against accepted patriarchal structures such as the heterosexual family, Cixous poses the circulating figure of the story in all its unsettling power.

In Cixous's essays, it is sometimes difficult to tease the story away from history; in such cases, the figure of the story seems to lose its potential for change. For example, in "Castration or Decapitation?" she writes, "The unconscious is always cultural and when it talks it tells you your old stories, it tells you the old stories you've heard before because it consists of the repressed of culture" (52). History here is allied with the "old stories," the "repressed of culture." History is an amalgam, formed by addition, of stories piled upon stories. Even though stories might have revolutionary potential, they sometimes appear to be interchangeable with history. In "Sorties," Cixous imagines that people have discovered that logocentrism (the privileging of reason) exists only to prop up and maintain patriarchal power. At the time of this glorious awakening, she forecasts, "So all the history, all the stories would be there to retell differently; the future would be incalculable; the historic forces would and will change hands and change body" (65). It is the change in history that necessitates the change in stories, and it appears here that the two are no different.

In her most famous essay "The Laugh of the Medusa," she comes closer to untangling the two terms. "In woman, personal history blends together with the history of all women, as well as national and world history" (253). Here "personal history" would seem to be the story, as differentiated from (even while it's assimilated with) national and international histories. The key difference between the terms is the component of imagination, and particularly women's imagination. History is settled, fixed, and stable, but stories are imagined worlds and only become solidified through the processes of history (mastered, of course, by men). When she announces, "The new history is coming; it's not a dream, though it does extend beyond men's imagination," she celebrates women's ability to imagine a new history, to reinvent history through an imaginative act, a new kind of story (253). Without a clear delineation of the difference between the two terms, however, it is difficult to see the story's full potential; by allying it so closely with history, Cixous compromises the ability of the story to transcend history.

Trinh also combines the figure of the story with her conception of history, but in her thinking it is easier to distinguish the role each may play. She calls storytelling "the oldest form of building historical consciousness in community" (148). In contrast to Cixous's perspective, history's foundation in the story means that subversive stories offer disruptive power. The story is also, however, a community's knowledge, a process and circulation that's bigger than one teller. The community must create the story together through shared understanding and memory. Central to this conception of the story is its transmission through generations of women, as Trinh sets forth on the first page of her book:

> The story began long ago . . . it is old. Older than my body, my mother's, my grandmother's. As old as my me, Old Spontaneous me, the world. For years we have been passing it on, so that our daughters and granddaughters may continue to pass it on. So that it may become larger than its proper measure, always larger than its own in-significance. The story never really begins or ends, even though there is a beginning and an end to every story, just as there is a beginning and an end to every teller. (1)

The repetition of the story through these generations is a means of creating a history and also binding women together across time and age.[55]

While Cixous's idea of story often seems to refer to a personal narrative, Trinh's model encompasses a broader scope and questions whether any story is merely personal.[56] She also disrupts the notion that a personal narrative can be *the* story of a person, since the story is larger than any individual. (Here her interest in *The Woman Warrior* is especially fitting, since autobiography in particular is called into question by her model.) Furthermore, Trinh refuses individual ownership of the story, even communal ownership. The story belongs to no particular person, even though it relies on individuals for its circulation: "The story is me, neither me nor mine. It does not really belong to me, and while I feel greatly responsible for it, I also enjoy the irresponsibility of the pleasure obtained through the process of transferring. Pleasure in the copy, pleasure in the reproduction" (122).[57] The individual's pleasure comes from sharing the story rather than asserting ownership; the story defies phallocentric, zero-sum economies—those that would require a limit to pleasure, and particularly women's pleasure—while it valorizes collective repetitions over individual originality and authorship. The fact of the story's repetition, which necessarily entails changes to the story over time, only enhances its value, and this collective story is more powerful than any individual teller: "No repetition can ever be identical, but my story carries with it their stories, their history, and our story repeats itself endlessly despite our persistence in denying it" (122). Finally, the story also serves as a metaphor for the place of the individual in the community: "Each story is at once a fragment and a whole; a whole within a whole. And the same story has always been changing, for things which do not shift and grow cannot continue to circulate" (123). For Trinh, then, the "personal" story seems very different in character than the "personal history" conceived by Cixous.

Although history seems to be imagined in such passages as an accumulation of the circulating story, Trinh marks off a point at which the story and history became antagonistic:

> When history separated itself from story, it started indulging in accumulation and facts. Or it thought it could. It thought it could build up to History because the Past, unrelated to the Present and the Future, is lying there in its entirety, waiting to be revealed and related. The act of revealing bears in itself a magical (not factual) quality—inherited undoubtedly from "primitive" storytelling—for the Past perceived as such is a well-organized past whose organization is already given. (119–120)

At the moment when history began to be constructed in opposition to the story (although Trinh does not identify a specific time), history's fixity took on positive connotations compared to the unstable circulation of the ever-changing story. And from this opposition came a dualism of stable, factual history and unstable, fictional (lying) story.[58] Under these conditions, the story has little power: it is only falsity, merely imagination compared to history's truth. Trinh wants to undo this division, however, for the violence it does to the concept of story. Instead of seeing story and history as opposites, she wants to recognize their differences and value them while avoiding a hierarchical model: "Literature and history once were/still are stories: this does not necessarily mean that the space they form is undifferentiated, but that this space can articulate on a different set of principles, one which may be said to stand outside the hierarchical realm of facts" (121). The story is thus a liberating force, one that doesn't have to conform to the reality of the observable world; literature can be revolutionary where history cannot. For Trinh, the story is the emblem of literature's radical potential in the face of historical conservatism.

Thus while Cixous tries to untangle the story from history, Trinh celebrates their affinities while acknowledging that history and literature need to be defined as separate but interdependent domains. Both Cixous and Trinh imagine that challenges to history will come from women's stories—feminine texts or Grandma's story. Eagleton speaks to the appeal of the form in this respect: "Perhaps for some women writers their interest in this form has arisen, not from their belief that it is known and safe, but from their hope that the flexible, open-ended qualities of the short story may offer a transforming potential, an ability to ask the unspoken question, to raise new subject matter" (65). In each case, however, these visions of the story's ability to disrupt systems of authority could well be extended to any storyteller who is not at the top of the hierarchy of power; they are not limited solely to women writers of feminine texts. Given the thinking of Cixous and Trinh, one can see that to completely divorce the story from history would remove its ability to effect change; yet it must remain outside "the realm of facts"—historicity—in order to imagine a different conclusion to history.

The Story Behind the Story

In an article elucidating the process of choosing eighteen stories for her 1985 mother-daughter story anthology, Susan Koppelman asserts that "the mother/daughter relationship was the single most frequently portrayed relationship in and subject matter of short stories written by women between 1826 and the present" ("Between Mothers and Daughters" 47). Such a statement invites the question, Why would women writers choose to address the mother-daughter relationship in so many stories? Perhaps it is because this relationship is unique to women's experience, and because few male writers had attempted to describe it in their own stories. What seems an even more important question to address, however, is why publishers found the mother-daughter relationship to be such an appealing subject in short stories written by women. Did publishers think that the mother-daughter relationship was the most appropriate subject matter for short stories by women and thus print those stories more often than other kinds of stories? As Suzanne Ferguson points out, the preservation (in published form) of texts is a signal that a portion (usually the upper class) of a culture finds them important (177–178). Such stories are only available for Koppelman's selection process because the "culture"—in the persons of individual publishers—has found them important enough to preserve by printing them.

The answers to these questions lie, at least in part, in the cultural function of the short story. Although theories of feminist epistemology appeared long after the earliest stories in Koppelman's collection, the idea that knowledge among women is passed down orally from mothers to daughters is hardly a radical one. It isn't illogical, then, that the story might have seemed, even in the early nineteenth century, an appropriate venue for putting down in type mothers' advice to their daughters, albeit in a fictionalized form. Moreover, because the short story is a transitional form that allows its tellers to move from orality to literacy, it is a reasonable choice for women writers, and particularly the earliest ones, who were entering the realm of print for the first time. The story's rapid remuneration, at least relative to the novel, could well have made it an attractive form for such writers. Because of the genre's ability to do cultural work, it may well have seemed the appropriate form in which to present women's lives, particularly mothers' and daughters' lives. And although publishing stories of women's relationships with each other might have represented a small disruption of a history that had not consistently valued women's stories, stories as a genre are not as important culturally as the novel, and therefore not as disruptive as a novel with the same subject matter would be.

While these reasons may have held true for stories published in the early nineteenth and even the early twentieth centuries, why have publishers over the past two decades become so enamored of the mother-daughter story anthology? Collecting a group of stories about mothers and daughters, written largely by women, is more risky, culturally speaking, than printing a single story as only one part of a magazine, especially when that story is nestled among advertisements and can itself be viewed as a kind of commercial product. But if the majority of the stories in mother-daughter collections merely affirm cultural assumptions about the relationships between mothers and daughters—that mothers pass on wisdom to their daughters, as just one example—don't these collections effectively empty the stories of their potential to do cultural work? The act of printing a group of mother-daughter stories may be the biggest risk that publishers are willing to take; including stories that challenge readers to reexamine their assumptions about mothers and daughters in those collections may be too far for publishers to go.

In other words, the publications of mother-daughter story anthologies that have only praise for these relationships compromise the promise of the story as expressed in the work of feminist theorists of epistemology as well as Cixous and Trinh in their examination of the story's links to orality and history. The work that the mother-daughter story could accomplish in its celebration of women's different ways of knowing, in its praise for disruptions of patriarchal power in a literacy-based society, in its ability to acknowledge history while imagining a different future for it—all of these opportunities are negated by editors' choices of stories that only envision mothers and daughters fitting into one kind of behavior pattern. Further, such stories, read alone, imply that mothers can only pass on knowledge to their daughters in one mode—in positive, oral methods rather than, say, providing negative role models—thus ignoring alternative possibilities for feminist epistemology. It would, it appears, be too risky to include in such anthologies stories such as Wharton's or O'Connor's, in which a daughter's connection to her mother is not purely positive, in which a daughter and her mother may actually be in conflict, in which a mother may use her daughter as an instrument of revenge. None of these collections pose significant challenges to popular conceptions of mother-daughter relationships such that the members of, say, Oprah's book club would take offense.[59]

In discussing her choices of stories for her 1985 anthology, Koppelman says that she wanted to publish stories that represent the lives of "real" women. She cites as a particular influence on her choices the media attention that Nancy Friday's *My Mother/My Self* (1977) was receiving in 1983. Koppelman says she found the book "a sustained act of female self-hatred, a kowtowing to the patriarchy." When she asked other women what they thought of the book, she found that they agreed with her assessment. Based on this common reaction, she says, she sought stories that "reflect real women's lives as mothers and as daughters and their common struggles in a world hostile to their survival as independent and inter-dependent, self-defining and woman identified" (51). In other words, Friday's portrait of conflict and strain between mother and daughter made Koppelman so upset that she deliberately chose stories that would counter Friday's account.

While Koppelman's strategy for selecting stories may have been philosophically sound, given the state of American feminism at the time, more than two decades have passed since then.[60] Yet little change has taken place in the types of stories that are anthologized, even as recently as the year 2000. Because the story, given its association with orality and with history, is not unlimited in its potential to effect cultural change, it is not altogether surprising that some stories represent relatively conservative cultural values—that is, they celebrate traditional, happy, and relatively uncomplicated mother-daughter relationships. Are these collections, however, representative of the larger body of stories on the same subject? The next chapter will consider the cultural work of mother-daughter short stories, particularly that of stories written in the decades following the publication of Friday's book and other theories of mother-daughter interactions. Examining more closely the workings of relationships between mothers and daughters, and particularly their individual abilities to pursue sexual happiness, is one way to test the theorization of the story against its practice.

CHAPTER 2

The Female Sexual Economy

Responding to critics who believed that the short story had peaked in the nineteenth century, Bonaro Overstreet, writing in 1941, predicted a hopeful future for the short story in the coming years. Overstreet's hope for the recovery of the story in the twentieth century lay in the genre's burgeoning interest in the workings of the human mind:

> It seems to me that the short story, today, far from being in a state of decline, is approaching a state where it can rightly mean more than it has ever meant. As it becomes increasingly deft in its power to portray our individual and social complexity, it will offer a veritable treasure house of insight-materials not only to lay readers whose main preoccupation is living with their human fellows but to sociologists and psychologists. At a time when an understanding of human behavior seems the only alternative to racial suicide, we can thank our lucky stars that our short-story writers, with full sincerity, are at the job of trying to understand. (90–91)

For Overstreet, the short story was not only a literary form but also a means by which people could understand the world around them, an almost scientific perspective on the human condition. Stories were both reflections of the world that exists and projections of possible worlds—reasons to be hopeful about the future of humanity. Overstreet's emphasis on the short story as a tool for insight into human psychology foregrounds the genre's association with loners and outcasts, a link that would later be established by Frank O'Connor in his 1963 study *The Lonely Voice*.[1] According to O'Connor, the short story is the genre most appropriate to the portrayal of those on the fringes of society—presumably the very people whose behavior psychologists and sociologists, not to mention lay readers, would find most interesting. The story can portray "submerged population groups," as O'Connor termed them, because, in Overstreet's words, it has the "power to portray our individual and social complexity."

While O'Connor found the short story suited to telling the tale of the outsider, more recent critics have pointed to the genre as particularly suited to tale tellers who are themselves outsiders in a patriarchal society. Women writers, for example, have found the genre welcoming because, for one thing, there are fewer established "masters" of the short story than there are of, say, the novel.[2] Although women writers may have become interested in the genre because it offered a relatively open playing field in this respect, another factor may be the opportunity to present characters and situations that are not traditionally valued in literature—for example, the everyday domestic work of women in the home.[3] Mary Burgan, as one proponent of this view, describes the tradition of American women short story writers as one that seeks "ways to recover some kind of personal identity for characters" who have been "forced . . . to dismantle the past and then challenged . . . to put it back together again in a revisionary way" (271). Her description of women short story writers' attempts to recover identity for their characters implies that these are characters who were not previously portrayed as complete, three-dimensional people. Burgan's account, furthermore, underlines the genre's depiction of people who create new futures for themselves out of the detritus of the past. Her assessment echoes the hopeful attitude of Overstreet's evaluation.

Women writers who began writing short stories brought with them a new focus to the genre: the relationship between mothers and daughters. This subject was so appealing to women short story writers, in fact, that Susan Koppelman found it the most frequently portrayed relationship in short stories written by women between 1826 and 1993 ("Between Mothers and Daughters" 47). Although it is impossible to know exactly why these writers chose to portray mothers and daughters in so many of their stories, one explanation is that the subject is a realm of knowledge generally restricted to women. Mary Helen Washington, discussing black women writers, suggests that such women "have found in their mothers' legacies the key to the release of their creative powers" (351–352)[4]; her sentiment echoes that of Alice Walker, who finds spiritual and artistic inspiration in the creativity of her foremothers. Linda Wagner-Martin observes that it may be impossible for women writers to escape the influence of their mothers, for "at least one of the dominant voices in their lives—perhaps the voice that literally gave them language—was their mother's" (94). And Judith Kegan Gardiner agrees that the mother-daughter relationship is crucial to women writers' output; in her view, the fictional characters produced by such writers can be seen as the metaphorical daughters of their creators. In other words, the heroes of women's texts are ultimately representations of the writers' daughters. Gardiner bases this claim on her assertion that women's identities are primarily formed through the mother-daughter relationship; the force of such relationships on women's identity formation is so powerful that it must necessarily shine through the writings women create.[5]

Theories such as Gardiner's grew out of the explosion of inquiries into the mother-child and, more specifically, mother-daughter relationship during the late 1970s in the United States.[6] Some of the most prominent books to emerge from this period include Adrienne Rich's *Of Woman Born* (1976), Dorothy Dinnerstein's *The Mermaid and the Minotaur* (1976), Nancy Friday's *My Mother/My Self* (1977), and Nancy Chodorow's *The Reproduction of Mothering* (1978), which not only earned cultural currency at the time of their publication but have since proven their staying power—all four have been reissued recently, with twentieth anniversary editions published for Rich, Dinnerstein, and Chodorow, and Friday's book reprinted in 1999.[7] Using a variety of methodologies, each of these authors explored the personal and cultural meanings of mothering. Although the preponderance of such studies fell within the domain of the social sciences, literary scholars and presses soon took notice, stimulating the publication of short story anthologies about mother-child and, more specifically, mother-daughter relationships, as well as scholarly considerations of them.[8] As Adrienne Rich explained in her social history of the institution of motherhood, it's not surprising that this relationship ignited the interest of women short story writers: "The cathexis between mother and daughter—essential, distorted, misused—is the great unwritten story. Probably there is nothing in human nature more resonant with charges than the flow of energy between two biologically alike bodies, one of which has lain in amniotic bliss inside the other, one of which has labored to give birth to the other" (225).[9]

Not only does the work of story writers reflect interest in mother-daughter relationships, but it also echoes the influential theories of the late 1970s. Specifically, I argue that stories written in the past twenty-five years portray mothers and daughters as so closely identified with one another that it is difficult for daughters to break away from their mothers—an overriding theme of Friday, Dinnerstein, and Chodorow's studies. As a result, mothers and daughters are so closely associated with one another in these stories that, for the purposes of sexual expression, they are treated as one person: at any given time, only one of them can experience a fulfilling sexual relationship. This limit on female sexuality within the family that constrains sexual expression to either mothers or daughters is a zero-sum economy I term the *female sexual economy.*

Generally speaking, daughters' overidentification with their mothers stems from the daughters' failure to break their original attachment to their mothers. One problematic result of the overly close relationship between mothers and daughters is often a competition between them for male sexual attention, a conflict dramatized in the opening of Joyce Carol Oates' story "Where Are You Going, Where Have You Been?" The first paragraph explains that fifteen-year-old Connie's mother "hadn't much reason any longer to look at her own face" because of her advancing years. Connie, on the other hand, is confident—perhaps overly so—about her appearance: "[S]he knew she was pretty and that was everything. Her mother had been pretty once too, if you could believe those old snapshots in the album, but now her looks were gone and that was why she was always after Connie" (118). Because Connie's mother is now battling Connie for sexual attention, she takes revenge against her daughter in the only way she can: by nagging at her. While this story ends with Connie paying the ultimate price for flaunting her sexuality, it is not alone in making ominous predictions for the outcomes of mother-daughter sexual competition. Stories written later present various results of such rivalries, but those results are rarely positive for both the mother and daughter or for their relationships. Despite the fact that these stories have appeared in the quarter-decade since the explosion of mother-daughter studies, they largely fail to move beyond the restrictive patterns described and critiqued by Friday, Dinnerstein, and Chodorow.

Because psychoanalysis is the foundation for these three theorists' arguments, I return to the Freudian theories that undergird these texts,[10] despite the fact that the Freudian psychoanalytic model of female development is peppered with problems[11]—not the least of which is a failure to theorize the psychic development of homosexual and bisexual individuals. While Dinnerstein and Chodorow question the underlying assumptions of Freud's approach (Friday is much less explicitly critical), they also ultimately adopt much of his perspective in their treatment of the mother-daughter relationship.[12] Stories written since the late 1970s that treat the mother-daughter relationship tend to do so through echoes of the mothering texts, themselves an echo of Freud. The sometimes unusual (and occasionally bizarre) theories proposed in the mothering books reappear as embodied behaviors in the female characters of contemporary short stories. The principles Freud elucidates (or obscures, depending on one's point of view)—particularly as filtered through texts such as *The Reproduction of Mothering*—help explain the logic behind family limits on female sexuality portrayed in contemporary short stories.

THE FATHER OF MOTHER-DAUGHTER THEORIES

A woman is *her mother / That's the main thing.*

—Sexton 48

The centrality of the mother-daughter relationship in Freud's theories of female psychosexual development is remarkable because almost nowhere else in them does the mother take on such importance. In Freud's model of male development, for example, it is the all-important father who frightens the boy out of his attachment to his mother and forces him to look outside the family for love-objects. The mother is merely the vessel (rather literally) for the boy's earliest development, but his later personality definition takes place through the mediation of the father. The mother's comparatively prominent role in Freud's understanding of female development is not as positive as that of the father in the model for boys, however. Daughters' relationships with their mothers are the cause of psychosexual confusion, competition over the father, intense jealousy, and even extended erotic attachments to their mothers when girls fail to move beyond their mothers in seeking love-objects. The unique bond between the female members of a family creates much more turmoil—and many more possibilities for girls to stray from the track of "normal" heterosexual development—as girls mature into women.

Although he was the most influential theorist of the mother-daughter relationship, Freud devotes relatively little time to addressing it. In many of his essays, Freud uses boys as the models in his theories of psychic development, assuming that girls develop the same way. In fact, in his earliest work, Freud treats girls and boys the same way when thinking about their relationships to their mothers.[13] According to these early essays, both boys and girls progressed through the Oedipus complex, shifting their initial love-object (the mother for boys, the father for girls) to the opposite parent; they then were frightened out of desiring that particular parent by the castration complex, which forced them to move to representatives of the appropriate sex other than their parents. As Freud later realized, the problem with this conceptualization of children's development is that the mother is the first love-object for both girls and boys. Somehow, then, he had to explain how girls made the initial shift in love-object to their fathers.

In the essays "Femininity" (1905) and "Female Sexuality" (1931), Freud develops various explanations for the girl's move from her mother as love-object to her father. In one account, Freud posits that the daughter resents the mother for weaning her from the breast when a younger child arrives, causing her to discard her mother as love-object and turn toward her father. In a second explanation, Freud proposes that the mother (or the child's nurse, the mother's proxy) was probably the first to stimulate the girl sexually in the act of changing her diapers, but the mother was probably also the parent who made masturbation taboo. The inherent contradiction in such behavior is cause enough for the girl to rebel angrily against her mother as love-object, thereby shifting her affections to her father. Freud's third explanation is that once the girl discovers her lack of a penis and realizes that this grave deficiency is suffered by all those of her sex, she blames her mother for sending her out into the world without this necessary equipment and shifts her attachment toward her father.[14] Perhaps Freud offered so many explanations because he recognized that they had such weaknesses; in the first two cases, for example, boys would be subject to the same treatment as girls—being weaned and having their diapers changed—yet they do not shift their affections to their father as love-object as a result. The third account contradicts some of Freud's other theories of development; for example, in boys, the castration complex occurs when they see their mother's genitals and assume that their father has castrated her; they don't blame their mother for women's "lack" of a penis. Finally, in all three versions, Freud's explanation of the progression of events for girls virtually overturns the developmental course prescribed for boys. That is, while boys pass through the Oedipus complex first and the castration complex second, girls' development reverses the process— their resentment at castration drives them into the Oedipus complex. Yet should these processes fail to force girls to shift their affections to a male love-object, they will experience paranoia and hysteria in later life, according to Freud.[15]

One interesting element of these explanations is that the girl must experience jealousy of her mother in order to shift toward her father. Those girls who successfully renounce their mothers find themselves intensely jealous of them, for their wish for the penis is converted into the wish to have the father's child, Freud explains in "Some Psychical

Consequences of the Anatomical Distinction between the Sexes" (1925).[16] In "Female Sexuality," he asserts that girls who experience a strong attachment to their fathers also experience a strong attachment to their mothers. It would follow, then, that the strength of the girl's attachment to her mother determines both the degree of her attachment to her father and the intensity of her subsequent jealousy of her mother. It is the unfortunate girl who has a strong attachment to her mother, for she will later be jealous of her; of course, a girl in the opposite condition suffers from a weak attachment to her father—perhaps one so weak that her commitment to heterosexuality is less than robust. Only the lucky Goldilocks, it seems, can survive penis-envy with much hope for a properly heterosexual future.

Thus, after passing through the castration complex via penis-envy (which is then converted into the wish to bear the father's child), the girl arrives at the Oedipus complex. In Freud's words, "[T]he girl is driven out of her attachment to her mother through the influence of her envy for the penis and she enters the Oedipus situation as though into a haven of refuge" ("Femininity" 129). Provided that the girl completes this final stage successfully, she will have accomplished an orientation toward male love-objects other than her father. (If she remains in the Oedipal phase too long, however, she will retain her attachment to her father rather than becoming erotically interested in men outside the family.) Even after the many opportunities for the girl to fall by the wayside of "normal" development during these stages, peril still lies ahead in the reemergence of the Oedipal complex during her pubescent years.

Freud identifies this stage as pivotal in one of the few essays in which he treats female homosexuality in-depth, "The Psychogenesis of a Case of Homosexuality in a Woman" (1920). Responding to the pleas of a young woman's parents to reform their daughter's obsession with an actively bisexual woman, Freud attempts to understand the reasoning behind the daughter's choice of a female love-object. He traces the daughter's particular interest in young mothers back to her attachment to and subsequent jealousy of her mother, brought about by the resurgence of the Oedipus complex. Just as the daughter was experiencing the wish to bear her father a child, her mother did exactly that: "It was not *she* who bore the child, but her unconsciously hated rival, her mother. Furiously resentful and embittered, she turned away from her father and from men altogether. After this first great reverse she forswore her womanhood and sought another goal for her libido" (157). Paradoxically, the girl's great jealousy of her own mother resulted not in an intensified wish for her father but in her pursuit of other young mothers.

Although this particular woman chose other women as love-objects, the case itself dramatizes Freud's theories of jealousy and, indeed, competition between heterosexual mothers and daughters. Just at the point when daughters reach sexual maturity, their mothers are often reaching middle-age, setting the stage for conflict between them:

> In such circumstances mothers with daughters of nearly a marriageable age usually feel embarrassed in regard to them, while the daughters are apt to feel for their mothers a mixture of compassion, contempt and envy which does nothing to increase their tenderness for them. . . . The [mother], still youthful herself, saw in her rapidly developing daughter an inconvenient competitor; she favoured the sons . . . and kept an especially strict watch against any close relation between the girl and her father. (157)

The jealousy that begins, for girls, with penis-envy during the castration complex is thus reciprocated by the mother when the girl matures into a young woman. The basis of this competition is entirely sexual; it is the implicit threat in the girl's (hetero)sexuality that causes the mother to take precautions to protect her territory, so to speak. Luckily for this particular mother, her daughter became so disgusted with her own parents that she turned to female love-objects outside the family; mothers of daughters who desire heterosexual objects must remain vigilant as long as there is a chance of competition for the father.

According to Freud, then, girls face a multitude of obstacles to their "normal" development into heterosexual women who desire men other than their fathers. The first hurdle they must overcome is their initial attachment to their mothers. While Freud proposed three possible mechanisms by which girls might turn away from their mothers toward their fathers, his explanations leave much to be desired—so much that it seems possible, and even likely, that some girls will not progress through the castration complex as Freud sees it. Here is the first chance for girls to deviate from "normality"—by failing to shift their attachments from their mothers to their fathers. Those fortunate girls who are successful at this stage must then experience penis-envy, which is converted into a desire to bear their fathers' children. Because of the implicit competition for the father's love between the daughter and her mother, even the "normal" girl feels herself in a constant rivalry with her mother. While the Oedipal complex does resolve during childhood, it reemerges as the girl enters puberty, at the very moment when her mother begins to question her own sexual desirability—despite the fact that, according to Freud, the girl has now shifted her attentions to male love-objects other than her father. Based on Freud's theories of development, then, girls either remain strongly attached to their mothers as love-objects or compete with their mothers for the affections of men.[17] Either way, girls' sexual identities are irrevocably tied to their mothers.

FREUD'S DAUGHTERS: FRIDAY, DINNERSTEIN, AND CHODOROW

Mothering is an "extraordinary condition which is almost like an illness, though it is very much a sign of health."

—Winnicott 15

Freud's theories, developed largely during the first three decades of the twentieth century, reemerged with a vengeance in the 1970s. The reawakened interest in female sexuality stemmed from the sexual revolution in the United States during the 1960s. (Friday's previous two books, for example, focused on female erotic fantasies.[18]) Dinnerstein, Friday, and Chodorow, in their respective texts, all represent themselves as engaging in scientific or scholarly inquiry into the limits placed on female sexuality. The three authors use psychoanalysis to varying degrees to support their arguments about the ramifications of then-current mother-child, and especially mother-daughter, parenting arrangements, with Friday acknowledging the least debt to psychoanalysis, and Dinnerstein and Chodorow relying increasingly heavily on it.

In *My Mother/My Self*, Friday attacks the mother-daughter relationship for the detrimental impact that its intimacy has on the daughter's sexuality. While she acknowledges that the relationship has tremendous potential for closeness—more so than a mother has with her son—that intimacy can also be constraining:

> [W]hen one woman gives birth to another, to someone who is like her, they are linked together for life in a very special way. Mother is the prime love object, the first attachment for both male and female infants. But it is their sex, their sameness that distinguishes what a mother has with her daughter. No two people have such an opportunity for support and identification, and yet no human relationship is so mutually limiting. (20)

In particular, Friday accuses all mothers of repressing their own sexuality rather than demonstrating the possibility of mothering behavior balanced with a healthy sexuality. Such an attitude, says Friday, leaves daughters believing that "ladies" do not engage in sex. This deception causes several problems in the relationship, according to Friday. First, because adolescent girls sense that their mothers are hiding something, they begin to doubt their mothers' trustworthiness as guides. Second, girls who are too close to their mothers interpret any sexual expression of their own that takes place outside marriage as an irrevocable break with their mothers. If the daughter can find peace with her own life without guilt, says Friday, "she can learn to enjoy and be proud of her sexual self. But the symbiotically tied girl picks up on her mother's fear or dislike of sex. She is afraid to enjoy these new feelings; they would mark her as *different* from mother, separating her from the only source of love she has been taught she can depend on" (72). The girl who is too closely tied to her mother—and for Friday, this definition includes the vast majority of girls—depends so much on her mother for emotional security that she does not feel that she can risk her mother's disapproval by expressing herself sexually.

The closeness in the mother-daughter relationship also creates an atmosphere of competition for the father's affections: "In mother's earliest and usually unconscious efforts to handle feelings of competition with her daughter, she teaches the little girl not to expect too much physical attention from daddy. 'Come away. Daddy has important papers to go over'" (44). Not only does the little girl learn that she should expect affection from her mother, but she is also taught that her father is off-limits as a source of emotional support. Paradoxically, the daughter reacts to her mother forcing her away from her father by identifying with her mother even more strongly:

> [T]his denial of our bodies, desires, and independence is not based on love for mother. It is a reaction formation, in which we disguise what we really feel and act out its opposite. It is a form of "protesting too much": "Oh, no, I'm not mad at mommy for keeping daddy away from me, and telling me there's something wrong and dangerous about what I feel in my body. In fact, mother is the one I want to be close to all my life long." (89)

Even marriage, which would seem to be the ultimate break with the mother in the daughter's affirmation of her independent sexuality, finally strengthens the daughter's identification with her mother—confirming that she is, indeed, the "nice girl" that her mother always hoped for, a woman who limits her sexuality to marriage, and who keeps it invisible even then. In Friday's view, daughters are fated to rebel against their mothers' attitudes toward sexuality, marriage, and mothering—even if, in the end, the daughters repeat their mothers' behavior. Even those who say that they were closer to their fathers than their mothers, for example, are simply deluding themselves into believing that fewer fights with their fathers—who were rarely present in the home, at best—translates into greater closeness. Such women, despite their affirmations of strong father-daughter relationships, still act like their mothers (238–240).

After establishing that women should blame their mothers for any failings they may have, Friday briefly suggests, about halfway through the book, that the solution is for daughters to face their anger at their mothers. "We may say, 'I'm not angry at my mother!'—but why do we go into such a rage when our daughter doesn't clean up her room, or our husband is late? The fury is not appropriate. It has been displaced from mother onto someone 'safer'" (224). Facing this anger, Friday asserts, will free daughters to go on living their adult lives without an undercurrent of irrational fury that stems from their relationships with their mothers. Friday congratulates herself that, thanks to her advice, women everywhere can confront their resentment of their mothers.

While Friday's book reads as a kind of hate letter to her mother that, in the very last pages, admits to a catharsis accomplished by writing a 400-page book, it exhibits some important psychoanalytic foundations—the daughter's lasting identification with the mother, the competition between the two (presumably heterosexual) females for the affections of the father, the daughter's deeply held resentment of the mother and its ties to her sexuality. Although Friday occasionally cites Freud (her scant footnotes mention two Freud essays), it is difficult to determine the extent of Freud's influence on her writing; the bibliography lists only the entire *Standard Edition* rather than individual essays. Friday would like her readers to believe that she has taken a scientific approach to the topic through interviews with therapists, but, conveniently, none of them contradicts her own views. Marianne Hirsch has characterized this methodology as a "highly questionable and embarrassingly simplified use of theoretical and interview sources" ("Mothers and Daughters" 212).[19]

In addition, Friday opens each chapter with a lengthy autobiographical tale, usually related to her own sexual development and the way in which her mother (or her mother's surrogate) has thwarted it. At best, Friday's book is a thinly veiled narrative of her own sexuality, with a supporting cast of therapists who help her to "interpret" her feelings toward her mother. Friday presents her own story as that of women everywhere, presenting her book as a scholarly approach, when in fact she makes little attempt to consider any sources but her own memories. The worth of Friday's book, however, lies in two areas, according to Hirsch: first, it is the book that inaugurated popular interest in the subject of the mother-daughter relationship; second, it exemplifies the standpoint that the relations between mothers and daughters are fixed and impossible to change ("Mothers and Daughters" 212). Such an attitude may help to account for the longevity of literary ideas about the stifling closeness of the mother-daughter bond.

Compared with Friday and Chodorow, Dinnerstein's *The Mermaid and the Minotaur* represents a middle ground in late 1970s approaches to the topic of the mother-child relationship. She explicitly eschews the limitations of a scholarly approach in her preface, saying that the book "makes no effort to survey the relevant literature" because to do so would violate her "principles. I *believe* in reading unsystematically and taking notes erratically" (ix). Any discomfort the reader feels at her arguments, she continues, stems not from a lack of evidence for her arguments but rather from the reader's own defensiveness against the painful truth of her assertions. Like Friday, Dinnerstein offers few footnotes. Still, the foundations of her book lie in such creditable texts as Simone de Beauvoir's *The Second Sex*, Solomon Asch's *Social Psychology*, Norman O. Brown's *Life against Death*, and Freud's "Civilization and Its Discontents" and "The Future of an Illusion."

Dinnerstein's argument centers on her call for mothers' roles in parenting to be decreased. She claims that the extraordinary power mothers hold over their children causes a backlash in the broader culture, which then anoints men as leaders in order to combat the near omnipotence of the mother. Reducing mothers' responsibilities as caregivers would thus lessen the need to reject maternal power through patriarchal structures. Failure to do so has apocalyptic consequences: humans' "survival on earth" depends on distributing parenting responsibilities more equitably; without such a change, Dinnerstein characterizes humanity's trajectory toward the future as "suicidal," because we will ultimately take out our aggressions toward powerful mother figures on Mother Earth (9, 110). She challenges the assumption that woman-centered parenting arrangements are natural, asserting that, under the status quo, the men who make public policy are emotionally out of touch with "survival-essential considerations," while the women who do have experience with them lack the power to make policy (82). In Dinnerstein's view, a rearrangement of parenting responsibilities would have far-reaching consequences that would ultimately alter all facets of American society.

On a smaller scale, mothers' power over their children impedes their maturation into independent adults. For boys, this problem stems from their childhood experience of their mothers as omnipotent beings; according to Dinnerstein, this early impression leads them to generalize that women are more powerful than men. Such boys never mature into self-confident men, since they question their own abilities. The situation for girls, however, is much more dire. Because, like boys, girls experience their mothers as "magically" powerful, they also question their own self-efficacy. At the same time, however, girls and their mothers may experience a closer bond than boys and their mothers do: the mother "is likely to experience a more effortless identification, a smoother communication, with a girl baby than with a boy baby" (68). Through this strong identification, girls can see in their sex and in themselves the possibility of magic, even while they view their mothers as much more powerful:

> The woman feels herself on the one hand a supernatural being, before whom the man bluffs, quails, struts, and turns stony for fear of melting; and she feels herself on the other hand a timid child, unable to locate in herself the full magic power which as a baby she felt in her mother. The man can seem to her to fit her childhood ideal of a male adult far better than she herself fits her childhood ideal of a female adult. (85)

At the same time, paradoxically, Dinnerstein claims that "mother-raised" women, by virtue of being women, experience themselves as more self-sufficient than "mother-raised" men (42). Because, during childhood, people see their mothers as deeply powerful, "the threat to autonomy which can come from a woman [when they become adults] is felt on a less rational, more helpless level, experienced as more primitively dangerous, than any such threat from a man" (112).

In Dinnerstein's view, contrary to Friday's, the father is not the source of competition between the mother and daughter for male affections but a daughter's welcome respite from the demands of the intimidating mother. In the father, the daughter "gains a less equivocal focus for her feelings of pure love, and feels freer to experience her grievances against her mother without fear of being cut off altogether from the ideal of wholehearted harmony with a magic, animally loved, parental being" (51–52). Because the daughter feels less threatened by her father—through no fault of her mother's, but merely her presence as caregiver during childhood—she focuses her love on him: "A father can be quite tyrannical, then, and still be felt as in some sense a refreshing presence. His power is more distinct and clearly defined than the mother's, his wisdom less eerily clairvoyant" (176). Later, the daughter's unequivocally affectionate feelings toward her father are then transferred to appropriate male sexual partners (through a mechanism that doesn't appear to interest Dinnerstein).

Even in the realm of sexual intercourse, the power of the mother intrudes. For both men and women, sex is mediated through the infant's original relation to the mother; each tries to repair the original break with the mother through intercourse.[20] Because the pleasure of each participant is directly proportional to his or her ability to re-create the original connection with the mother, the woman experiences less pleasure during sex: "She is the one whose physique more closely resembles the physique of the first parents, and who is likely to have incorporated this parent's attitudes more deeply; he is therefore apt to be the one who can more literally live the infant experience of fulfilling primitive wishes through unqualified access to another body" (61). In fact, the woman's power is so strong, as a representation of her lover's mother, that she "can . . . re-evoke in him the unqualified, boundless, helpless passion of infancy. If he lets her, she can shatter his adult sense of power and control; she can bring out the soft, wild, naked baby in him" (66).

Dinnerstein's interpretation of sex as an attempt to rejoin with the mother has two other important ramifications. First, under such an assumption, women's sexual creativity is seriously curtailed; a woman who behaves in a way that the man does not expect interrupts his fantasy of reunion with his mother and therefore decreases his pleasure by reminding him of the original separation. Women's sexual pleasure is, in Dinnerstein's model, forever constrained as a result of the infant's early relationship with the mother; she even says that women describe the self-imposed limits on their pleasure as "the gift of the mother" (64). Second, the combination of the sexual constraints created by the original closeness to the mother and the societal double standard concerning men and women's promiscuity threatens the monogamous relationship between women and men, encouraging men to stray. This system benefits men by giving them even more chances to experience imagined reunions with their mothers, but, according to Dinnerstein, it also benefits women: "[T]he owned woman [the wife] can enjoy this opportunity vicariously, imagining how he feels, how it is for him to own her and still be free; at the same time she can enjoy through him access to another woman, to a body like the one she herself loved at the beginning" (238). Still, the most important benefits of the system Dinnerstein outlines are enjoyed by men: they are limited neither in their sexual creativity nor in their range of sexual partners, even when married. Only by ending the reign of the mother over the infant by reforming childcare arrangements, implies Dinnerstein, can this situation be revised to offer more equitable sexual opportunities for women.

As does Friday's, Dinnerstein's book suffers from its pseudo-scholarly approach to the mother-child bond. Rather than attempting to support her arguments with "interviews," as Friday does, Dinnerstein relies on emotional appeals to the reader. She frames her book so that no matter how the reader reacts, Dinnerstein proves herself correct: if the reader buys her argument that patriarchal structures result from the threatening powers of the mother, then Dinnerstein is right, and if the reader feels defensive at Dinnerstein's assertions and tries to refute them, then it's also, conveniently, because she's correct—the reader has so deeply absorbed the cultural hatred of the mother that he cannot see Dinnerstein's point. With few footnotes and minimal use of scholarly sources, she tends to use personal experience as the litmus test of her statement: if we have ever noticed male domination in any form, then we must agree with her. Of course, readers who are not already convinced that current gender arrangements will be the cause of humans' eventual extinction will have a difficult time finding Dinnerstein's arguments convincing; in fact, she introduces the book by saying that she assumes that her readers are already convinced of this point (4).[21]

Dinnerstein's argument anticipates that of Chodorow in *The Reproduction of Mothering* in its call for a shift in parenting responsibilities in order to limit the incredible power of the mother over children. Chodorow's book, however, offers a scholarly and methodical investigation of the reasons that women (and particularly white, middle-class Western women) have traditionally mothered, as well as a review of the consequences of this practice. While a good deal of biological and evolutionary research has demonstrated that infants and children need close relationships with a small number of adults in order to thrive, says Chodorow, it hasn't demonstrated that those adults must necessarily be mothers. Further, she questions women's supposed biological predisposition to mothering; even if mothering developed as an evolutionary adaptation to women's nursing capabilities, they are now beside the point, since the development of infant formula, for example, has eliminated the necessity for mothers to be the adults responsible for feeding babies. Even in turning to sociology and anthropology to explain mothering trends across cultures, Chodorow finds no convincing explanations of why women mother—in fact, she notes, sociological theories are generally tautological in nature: women mother because women have always mothered. Her book is an attempt to explain how mothering comes to reproduce itself.

To do so, Chodorow turns to psychoanalysis, relying on Freud's developmental essays but filtering them through the object-relations tradition. Psychoanalysis, she says, "provides a systemic, structural account of socialization and social reproduction. It suggests that major features of the social organization of gender are transmitted in and through those personalities produced by the structure of the institution—the family—in which children become gendered members of society" (39). Her argument incorporates the traditional psychoanalytic model that sees individual development as the result of drives, but her use of object-relations psychology revises that trajectory to recognize that development is not a one-size-fits-all mold but rather the effect of drives in the context of relationships with others.[22] Those relationships shape the way that drives manifest themselves and are resolved as a child matures. Because relationships are so important to the psychic growth of human beings in the object-relations perspective, relationships between children and their adult caregivers can take on special importance as those children mature. In Chodorow's view, industrial capitalism has disrupted traditional childcare arrangements that once included extended family and community members as parents. Increasingly, mothers have become the primary caregivers for children, and their influence over their children, particularly in the earliest years, is no longer diluted by the presence of grandparents, aunts and uncles, or other interested adults. Because social arrangements have evolved, mothers' power over their children is greater than ever before, and their relationship takes on special meaning as children develop psychologically.

Chodorow's account also owes a special debt to Gayle Rubin's formulation of the sex/gender system and the ways in which cultural economics shape parenting responsibilities. According to Rubin, every society has its own cultural definitions of sex and gender, and every society has its own sex/gender system, which she defines as "a set of arrangements by which the biological raw material of human sex and procreation is shaped by human, social intervention and satisfied in a conventional manner, no matter how bizarre some of the conventions may be" (165). Rubin bases her argument on Lévi-Strauss's observations of the way in which exchanges of women for goods facilitate social bonds; according to Lévi-Strauss, for example, heterosexual unions developed as a social institution because of gendered divisions of labor—women needed men's hunting skills for meat, while men needed women's housekeeping and gathering skills to survive. Chodorow expands this argument to contend that women's roles as primary childcare providers are similarly socially instituted, and she follows Rubin's lead in looking to psychoanalysis for an understanding of the ways in which individuals assimilate social assumptions about sex and gender in forming their own identities.

While the primary contribution of Friday's book was to demonstrate that competition necessarily arises between mothers and daughters, and Dinnerstein's was to show that maternal influence was so threatening that it led to patriarchal structures and might spell the end of humanity, Chodorow's book explains how parenting arrangements are perpetuated psychologically through generations. Chodorow argues, like Friday and Dinnerstein, that exclusive mothering has harmful consequences. The infant sees the mother as so powerful that he feels threatened by his sense of dependence on and merged identity with the mother; even as an adult, the individual may be hesitant to enter another close relationship: "When a person's early experience tells him or her that only one unique person can provide emotional gratifications—a realistic expectation when they have been intensely and exclusively mothered—the desire to recreate that experience has to be ambivalent" (79). Further, as they grow older, boys and girls begin to see women as self-sacrificing, caring, and nurturing, but they also associate women with their own powerlessness as infants; children of both sexes then begin to idealize fathers as individuated people, not merged with the mother, who represent growth and the world outside the home (83). "For children of both genders," Chodorow asserts, "mothers represent regression and lack of autonomy" (181).

Daughters in particular are harmed by mothers' exclusive parenting, but they are also the people who reproduce parenting arrangements when they become mothers themselves. Chodorow revisits Freud's developmental schemas, emphasizing the differences between girls and boys. Because boys experience their mothers as their initial love-objects and then eventually shift their affections to other women, they consistently find themselves attracted to women (at least in "normal" development). Mothers are also the initial love-objects for girls, and although heterosexual girls eventually shift toward men as they mature, even they never completely abandon their initial attachment to a woman. Working from Helene Deutsch's theorization of this relational triangle,[23] Chodorow asserts that girls and women have a more complex relationship to the world because of their psychic development: they maintain a strong emotional tie to women even as they are attracted to men. Because their bond with other women is so strong, women's sexual relationships with men can never be completely fulfilling; this state of affairs leaves them searching for powerful connections that they ultimately find in their children: "Women come to want and need primary relationships to children. These wants and needs result from wanting intense primary relationships, which men tend not to provide both because of their place in women's oedipal constellation and because of their difficulties with intimacy" (203). Because the connection between mothers and their female children most closely approximates the mother's own preoedipal experience of a powerful love, the relationships between mothers and daughters help to begin the cycle again, setting in motion the strong attachment to women that will lead to the daughter's own ambivalent relation to men and the search for connections with other females.

Although Chodorow's argument has a well-researched basis in psychoanalysis and is willing to embrace complexity rather than brush over it, making it a much more convincing account than either Friday's or Dinnerstein's, the book is not without its flaws. One of the problems in Chodorow's formulation is that it assumes a middle-class nuclear family structure of a mother who stays at home with her children and a father who goes out into the working world, which, even in 1978, was not so universal as Chodorow's explanation would have readers believe. In large part, this limitation is due to her argument's basis in psychoanalysis, which makes similar assumptions about the configuration of the family. She also acknowledges at a few points that lesbian mothers might well turn her claim on its head, but she never follows through with possible corollaries to such situations. Moreover, like Dinnerstein, she asserts that one goal of heterosexual intercourse is to reclaim each partner's relationship to the mother. Because Chodorow carefully dissects and critiques psychoanalytic perspectives at many other points in her argument, it's unusual that she accepts this particular scenario whole. Finally, and most importantly, Chodorow proposes that the solution to the problems she elucidates in the book is for fathers to take a significantly more active role in parenting. Such a change, she says, would result in a diminished fear of mothers' power and thus a less patriarchal society as a backlash against that power.

Because the foundation of her explanation lies in psychoanalysis, a relatively unchanging road map for human psychic development, however, it is difficult to see how a shift in childcare responsibilities would alter, for example, the daughter's strong connection to her mother, which lies in their shared sex rather than necessarily mothers' exclusive parenting.[24] To put it another way, as Judith Lorber does, "[I]f most men have developed nonaffective personalities and strong ego boundaries, where are you going to find enough men with psychological capabilities to parent well and thus break the general pattern of the emotional primacy of the mother?" (Lorber, Coser, Rossi, and Chodorow 485).[25] While her book provides a careful reinterpretation of the importance of the mother in early childhood and the consequences of that relationship in adult situations and social constructs, Chodorow's reliance on psychoanalysis is both the fruitful explanatory mechanism and the Achilles's heel of her argument.[26]

Ultimately, Friday, Dinnerstein, and Chodorow represent, despite their considerable variation, three accounts of the same phenomenon: the effects of a stiflingly close relationship between mothers and daughters. All agree that this bond creates both a strong affection between the two as well as a deep resentment and fear on the part of the daughter; constraints on heterosexual intercourse that limit each partner's participation to a kind of recreation of the birth scene; an idealization of the father, and, in turn, men in general, as the representatives of independence and ambition; and a cultural fear of maternal omnipotence that leads to a patriarchal power structure as a means of retaliating against the mother's powers. Although the approaches to changing this situation differ significantly—for Friday, individual women confronting their mothers will allow them to move forward, while Dinnerstein and Chodorow seek to shift parenting responsibilities on a large scale toward a more equitable male-female balance—in each case, the writer recognizes the dramatic cultural consequences of the mother-daughter relationship, and the immense scope of the solution that must be put into place to address them.

While significant weaknesses undercut some of these writers' arguments, it is important to recognize that their books are the best-known examples of the surge of interest in mother-daughter relationships during the late 1970s. Their interpretations of Freudian and object-relations theory are the filter through which many readers—and writers—have come to understand psychoanalytic models of female sexual development. While Dinnerstein and Chodorow in particular claim that the problems they document in mother-child relationships lead to broad societal harms, all three writers also record ways in which individual daughters are injured by the closeness of their bonds with their mothers. They paint a picture of daughters who hate their mothers, who find themselves stymied sexually and unfulfilled by sexual relationships with men, who can never fully break free of their original attachments to their mothers, and who, try as they might, are never able to experience themselves as distinct individuals, separate from their mothers. This image haunts the literary portrayals of the generation of short story writers to follow.

THE NEXT GENERATION: STORIES OF MOTHERS AND DAUGHTERS

There is no more personal claim than that for sexual freedom and at no point has civilization tried to exercise severer suppression than in the sphere of sexuality.

—Freud, "Jokes and Their Relation to the Unconscious"

Mothers and daughters in contemporary short stories often appear to reflect the views of these mothering theorists. Fictional depictions include tensions between the generations, competition for the father's attention and affections, and even thwarted sexual expression in the daughters, á la Friday. The bond between mothers and daughters, although usually close, is also the source of conflict; daughters try to escape the trajectories of their mothers' lives, attempting to create themselves in their own images, rather than their mothers'. Despite the daughters' struggle for autonomy and the right to self-definition, however, the daughters often fall into a pattern that draws them into even closer comparison with their mothers. That closeness becomes identification—in spite of the daughters' best efforts—within the context of the stories. While the daughters and mothers remain discrete characters for the purposes of fiction, sexually speaking they seem so closely fused that they become one person. That identification creates powerful limits on sexual expression for these characters, for, as one person, they are allowed the sexual appetites of only one person—that is, either the mother or the daughter may express herself sexually at any one time, but never both simultaneously. The female sexual economy restricts sexual expression within the family unit, limiting female sexuality so that its power is in check, so that it cannot take on the force of overwhelming maternal omnipotence.[27] Virtually any short story published in the past twenty-five years that deals with the mother-daughter bond as a central theme (and especially so when the women involved are white and upper-middle-class or upper-class, as I shall argue in the next chapters) fits into this model.

Often, the female sexual economy appears as a situation in which the daughter finds her own sexual expression deadened by the discovery of her mother's sexuality, as in Ann Beattie's "Find and Replace." Amy

Bloom's "When the Year Grows Old" presents the opposite case, in which the daughter begins to experience herself as a sexual being as a result of her mother's loss of sexual autonomy due to mental illness. A more surprising variation of this model, seen in Lorrie Moore's "Which Is More than I Can Say about Some People," is the implication of erotic love between mother and daughter in the interests of regaining the prenatal experience of oneness, a portrayal that seems directly influenced by the theories of Dinnerstein and Chodorow. Even this modification, however, maintains a limit on female sexuality, for as long as the mother and daughter are erotically engaged with one another, they do not seek sexual expression with anyone outside the family. In fact, this model represents the ultimate incarnation of the female sexual economy. In their variety, these three stories present the valences of the female sexual economy in its stifling consequences for both mothers and daughters.

These three authors are a sample of contemporary short story writers who have earned critical accolades. Although all three happen to be women, I have selected these stories not because of the writers' sex but because they exemplify the way in which mother-daughter relationships have been portrayed in a variety of stories published in the past twenty-five years. (There are precious few stories by male authors in which the bond between the mother and daughter is more than tangential to the plot.) All of these writers have placed stories in the U.S.'s most prestigious publications; have earned recognition for their stories in the Best American Short Stories series (in fact, Beattie and Moore have both served as annual editors, and both of them earned a place in John Updike's *Best American Short Stories of the Century*) and the Prize Stories: The O. Henry Awards series; and have won several awards. Moore, who teaches at the University of Wisconsin at Madison, lists a Guggenheim Fellowship, an NEA (National Endowment for the Arts) fellowship, and the PEN/Malamud Award for excellence in short fiction among her honors. Bloom, a trained psychotherapist, also teaches writing at Yale; she was nominated for the National Book Award for her first short story collection *Come To Me*; her second, *A Blind Man Can See How Much I Love You*, was a nominee for the National Book Critics Circle Award. Beattie has won an award in literature from the American Academy of Arts and Letters and, like Moore, earned a Guggenheim Fellowship and the PEN/Malamud award. Beattie is the best established of the three writers and has received the most critical attention, in part because she is the oldest of the group (born in 1947, whereas Bloom was born in 1953 and Moore in 1957). Though these three writers were born across the span of a decade, they are part of a generation that may well have encountered the theories of Friday, Dinnerstein, and Chodorow as young women. Regardless of whether they actually read the books, the influence of these theories clearly emerges in their writings.

Ann Beattie's "Find and Replace," published in the *New Yorker* in 2001 and collected in *Follies* in 2005,[28] presents the paradigmatic case of the female sexual economy: the daughter, horrified by her mother's pursuit of a new sexual partner soon after her father's death, finds herself unable to pursue sexual fulfillment because of her mother's behavior. On the surface, mother and daughter are linked by a common interest in writing; middle-aged Ann, who freelances to finance her work on the "Great American I Won't Say Its Name," travels the globe on assignments through her cousin's ad agency, while her retired mother is characterized as a compulsive note writer who would "probably send greetings on Groundhog Day, if the cards existed" (84).[29] Although their shared interest in writing offers them a common ground, Ann finds her mother's habit silly; she indulges her mother's requests to write condolence notes upon the demise of friends' pets. The context of the story speaks volumes to Ann's actual connection to her mother: she is returning home to memorialize her father seven months after his death. The fact that Ann has not only missed her father's funeral but has avoided her mother for seven months afterward, offering no assistance in settling her father's affairs or emotional support during what undoubtedly was a difficult time, shows Ann in all her solipsistic glory.[30]

Even so, it is Ann's relationship to her mother that determines her behavior in the course of the story. Ann's own immaturity is highlighted repeatedly, particularly in contrast to her mother's grown-up conduct. For example, when Ann mocks her mother's note-writing obsession, she says, "She keeps the greeting-card industry in business," but she also mentions that "no one ever seems to disappear from her life (with the notable exception of my father)." To Ann, her mother is characterized by her long-standing friendships—even to the extent that "[s]he still exchanges notes with a maid who cleaned her room at the Swift House Inn fifteen years ago—and my parents were only there for the weekend" (84). That the mother is never identified by name further emphasizes the fact that she is defined by her relationships to others. Ann's closest friend, on the other hand, appears to be the cousin who keeps her occupied with freelance jobs—and he is mentioned only once in the course of the story. When Ann sarcastically impugns the social skills of her mother's romantic interest, her mother retorts, "You might ask yourself why you've had fallings out with so many friends." While Ann verbally defends herself against her mother's question, she also admits to herself, "She was right, of course: I had left too many friends behind. I told myself it was because I traveled so much, because my life was so chaotic. But, really, maybe I should have sent a few more cards myself" (86). Ann's mother is shown to be both chronologically and emotionally more mature than her daughter through her ability to maintain relationships. The end of the story confirms this impression: Ann has had offers of communication from two men—the young man at the car rental and the cop who pulled her over for speeding—yet she chooses isolation over any attempt at forming new relationships.

Ann often reverts to childish behavior during the course of the visit. When she returns her rental car, for example, the young man at the desk, a trainee, mistakenly offers her a special on a Mustang, as if she had come in to rent a car rather than return one. When a supervisor overhears this exchange, Ann rents the Mustang impulsively to keep the trainee out of trouble—despite the fact that her mother thinks she has returned to New York, and she no longer has a place to stay. Ann finds herself attracted to young Jim Brown, the trainee, who has recently been diagnosed with ADD for his own impulsive behavior. We don't, however, know just how young Jim is until near the end of the story, when Ann admits, "He was probably twenty-five years, maybe thirty years, younger than me" (89). Her choice of the Mustang itself seems symbolic of her yearning to return to a time when she was Jim's age, since she had owned one back then. She tells the cop who pulls her over for speeding (stereotypically a young person's crime) that the car brings back memories of the one her father bought her as a bribe to keep her in college, and her story is sympathetic enough that the cop not only reduces her violation to a warning but also offers his phone number. Ann's impulsive choice to drive a car reminiscent of her college years and her attraction to a young trainee emphasize her immaturity.

In part, Ann's childish behavior can be seen as a reaction against her mother's decision to move in with her neighbor Drake Dreodadus. Moreover, she paradoxically believes that she is playing her father's role in attempting to thwart this relationship. In fact, her reaction to the news that Drake has proposed cohabitation to her mother is unusually formal. When her mother confesses that Ann may find her response to the proposition surprising, Ann replies, "The only surprising thing would be if you'd responded in the affirmative." When Ann's mother hoots, "'Responded in the affirmative!' Listen to *you*," she confirms the reader's sense that this is unusual behavior for Ann (85). As she continues to discuss the idea with her mother, Ann sits in her father's chair, quite literally taking his place.[31] When she finds herself unable to talk her mother out of moving into Drake's house, Ann fantasizes about murdering him to stop her mother, a thought that is so powerful that it colors her interactions with others. Upon discovering that the cop has given her his phone number rather than a ticket, Ann remarks to herself, "[I]f I kill Drake, the number might come in handy" (89). Rather than being intrigued by the prospect of a liaison with this man, her thoughts immediately turn to his usefulness in an official capacity, should she choose to eliminate her mother's lover.

Ann's erratic behavior might be explained by the fact that she is returning home to face the death of her father, an event that she has psychologically avoided for the past seven months. Her perception of her father's death reflects her self-centered thinking: "I'm superstitious. For example, I thought that even though my father was doing well, the minute I left the country he would die. Which he did" (84). From Ann's point of view, she was the cause of her father's death—despite the fact that he was in a hospice, a signal that he was seriously ill well before her departure. Despite this sense of guilt, Ann spends very little time actually mourning her father—her greatest energies on this account are spent in dissuading her mother from moving in with Drake. She is, however, clearly working through his death on a subconscious level, and it is this emotional work that leads to her impulsive rental of the Mustang. She has an obvious connection to a Mustang because it was the car her father bought her to convince her to stay in college, but something about Jim Brown also triggers a connection to her father. When he mentions his diagnosis with ADD, Ann associates the name of the disease with the ALS patient who was her father's friend in the hospice. The highly tangential nature of this association demonstrates the workings of Ann's mind far beneath the surface of her interactions with Jim Brown. Although she does not seem to recognize the connections herself—she brings up her college Mustang only in an effort to weep her way out of a speeding ticket— Ann has clearly been deeply affected by the loss of her father, and she sees in her mother's choice of a surrogate the threat of her own replacement.

Ann's sense that she, as a surrogate for her father, has been found and replaced pervades the story—although to Ann, what matters is the replacing rather than the finding. The title "Find and Replace" refers to Ann's career writing "[s]tuff that really happens," and simply "program[ming] the computer to replace one name with another" to protect herself against emotional reactions by the subjects of her writing (88). Ann also finds the "find and replace" strategy handy in her personal life. After meeting Jim Brown, for example, she imagines that she replaces her (age-appropriate professor) ex-boyfriend with the new (much younger rental agency employee) man. Similarly, when the police officer stops her for speeding, she tries to excuse her actions by pleading that her mother is dying. She justifies the substitution to herself: "After all, it was a terrible situation. The easiest way to express it had been to say that my mother was dying. Replace 'lost her mind' with 'dying'" (89). Ann and her mother seem very much alike in this respect, for of course from Ann's perspective her mother has found and replaced her father with a new dad—Drake Dreo*dad*us. Ann is troubled to see this occurrence even on a symbolic level: her mother has used the memorial candles meant to honor her father to make a romantic champagne toast with Drake in celebration of their new life together.

Although Ann and her mother are portrayed as very different personalities, both are engaged in quests to find and replace. Ann uses this technique to avoid any deep emotional connection to people, whereas her mother finds and replaces in order to maintain a sense of connectedness after she loses her husband. The most significant difference between them lies in the mother's fundamental success in replacing her late husband with a new love, whereas Ann merely fantasizes about replacing her ex-boyfriend with Jim. When, at the end of the story, she has the opportunity to reach out to either Jim or the cop, she chooses isolation instead of taking action that could make her feel connected to another person: "I realized that there was someone waiting to hear from me: possibly two people—the kid *and* the cop. . . . I could have made a phone call, had the evening go another way entirely, but everyone will understand why I decided otherwise." Ann's justification of her actions rings hollow, yet she claims that her readers "can't help understanding" her decision: "[f]irst, because it is the truth, and, second, because everyone knows the way things change." These vague statements in fact do nothing to demonstrate that the reader would instinctively understand her plight; they are, instead, pleas for understanding. When Ann says "everyone knows the way things change," she is apparently talking about herself: perhaps this statement means that as she grows older, she is less likely to strike up a romance with a stranger, far from home. It seems more plausible, however, that her flickers of romantic interest are dampened by the changes in her mother's life: she has just returned to her mother's street only to see Drake open the door and escort her mother into the house. She realizes that there is no chance for her to change her mother's mind: "There was nothing I could say. It had all been decided. There was not a word I could say that would stop either one of them" (89). In the face of her mother's sexual autonomy, Ann finds herself impotent.

The relationship between Ann and her mother exemplifies the female sexual economy, for Ann is unable to find sexual expression precisely because her mother can. The similarity between the two characters in their efforts to find and replace is so strong that, for the purposes of the story, they are treated as one unit within the family. Only one of the two is allowed to individuate herself through sexual expression. The sexual economy conserves that sexuality, meting it out one at a time. In this way, "Find and Replace" echoes much of the work of the mother-daughter theorists of the late 1970s. The mother's chilling effect on Ann's sexuality, albeit inadvertent in this story, seems a subtle variation of Friday's rant against mothers' influence on their daughters. Moreover, Ann's age-inappropriate behavior—driving a convertible reminiscent of the one she owned during college, flirting with much younger men—echoes the conflict that is the subtext of the story, that is, the earliest conflict between daughter and mother. The fact that Ann interprets her relationship with her mother as a kind of competition over her father deepens the story's ties to mother-daughter theory. In the end, this story demonstrates a perfect maintenance of female sexuality.

Amy Bloom's "When the Year Grows Old," first published in *Story* in 1992 and collected a year later in *Come To Me*, is a story in which the disappearance of the mother's ability to express herself sexually works to facilitate the daughter's maturity—the reverse of the situation in "Find and Replace." Bloom's tale presents a much younger mother-daughter pair in Laura and her fourteen-year-old daughter Kay; over the course of the story, Kay sees her mother drift progressively further away as bipolar disorder takes hold. Kay's loss is ironic, however, because the woman who emerges in her mother's manic state allows Kay to develop a sense of self that was submerged when her mother was healthy. When Kay first notices a change in her mother, she is disturbed by this strange woman's violations of the limits that used to define her mother: she is clad in black and pads barefoot around the basement, where she has taken up residence. She has also acquired a pet cat and started smoking. When Kay asks in disbelief whether there is truly a kitten in the basement, a pet her father has specifically forbidden, her mother responds in what Kay considers an alarming fashion: "Kay's mother giggled. The giggle was more frightening than the cigarettes. Kay's mother did not giggle; she smiled pleasantly at her husband's elaborate puns, and she pretended not to hear Kay's rude remarks" (147). This hippie creature who seems to have taken over Kay's mother's body is at first frightening to Kay precisely because she bears such a physical resemblance to the mother who is always in the kitchen promptly at 5 p.m., preparing dinner in time to teach English as a Second Language in Adult Education. This new mother is alarming because she has made the familiar strange: "Kay was having trouble with the idea that this weird beatnik knew everything her mother knew and seemed to be able to make use of it, in ways her mother was never able to manage" (148). Watching her mother's transformation, Kay sees an opportunity to change herself, to grow beyond the limitations by which she has been confined.

Part of Kay's growth naturally involves her developing sexuality, which she begins to realize with the help of Laura. One afternoon, she comes home "crying because she was fourteen and four inches taller than the only boy who was even a little bit nice to her" (154). Her mother comforts her:

> My God, you got so beautiful this year, every time I look at you now I think, "The brightness of her cheek would shame those stars, / As daylight doth a lamp; her eyes in heaven / Would through the airy region stream so bright / That birds would sing and think it were not night." You are really just the Juliet. Romeos are a little hard to find in ninth grade, though.

Kay is thrilled by this poetry-quoting mother, a contrast to the woman "who used to tell her she really could be cute if she smiled more"; this new mother talks "in this quirky, husky voice, a voice of lovers remembered, disappointments survived" (155). By linking Kay's sexual promise to her own sexual history, Laura connects herself with her daughter in their potential. Through Laura's words, Kay begins to see the sexual identity that binds them together, and it is through this connection that the bond between mother and daughter deepens. Recognizing her mother's sexuality is key to Kay's understanding of her own.

With these recognitions, however, comes Kay's desire to keep her mother's attention for herself. She faces a challenger for these attentions in her father, though. Kay's unspoken thoughts about her father, narrated in a style of free indirect discourse, are so intensely hateful that they evoke the narrator of Sylvia Plath's "Daddy."[32] All that Kay and her father seem to have in common is her mother, his wife—and it is the competition for her attention that appears to be at the core of Kay's abhorrence of her father. We first witness the acrimony between

Kay and her father in the present tense of the story. The first time Kay returns from school to discover that her mother is not in her usual place, she fantasizes that Laura's been murdered by an anonymous criminal, then revises that wish: "Even better, murdered by her father, who will rot in jail and Kay will change her name and never, ever visit him" (146). That evening, Martin, baffled by Laura's descent into the basement,[33] tries to maintain a sense of normalcy by asking Kay to set the table for dinner. When his daughter responds with "No problem," he scolds her for sounding like a gas station attendant and informs her that the proper response to his request is a polite "That will be fine." The narrator tells us that Kay complies with his wishes, echoing his statement in her coldest voice, then thinks to herself, "And I hate you, you fat, fat, evil pig, and I hope you die" (149). Her response seems entirely out of proportion to the dimensions of her father's request— even for a rebellious teenager. Similarly, when, later in the story, Martin asks his daughter to go upstairs so that he can talk to his wife in private, the tone of his request does not seem out of the ordinary. The narrator's intrusion, however, tells us otherwise: "He sounded the way he always did when he talked to her, as though they were strangers forced to share a seat on a terrible train ride" (156). Kay's perceived animosity in her relationship with her father clearly colors her interpretation of his interactions with her.

As the story continues, we learn that their relationship has not always been so strained. "When Kay was born," we are told, "she could barely stop crying long enough to eat, and Martin would walk her all night, up and down the apartment stairs, while Laura put her head beneath two pillows and cried until dawn. For six months, they all slept on wet sheets. The only picture he had ever carried was of Kay, four months old" (156). Their earliest interactions, then, forced Martin into a mothering role—one he cherished, as evidenced by the wallet picture, but one that he was not able to maintain as Kay grew beyond infancy. As an apparent consequence of this early bonding, however, Martin is unable to see his adored daughter as anything but the helpless infant; he is not able to recognize that cherished child in his hateful adolescent daughter.

As a small child, Kay's relationship with her father seemed blissful. She would walk to his office every day after school, and her father would let her drink cocoa from her favorite mug, swinging her legs seated atop his desk:

He introduced her to all the pretty girls who came in and out, and they all smiled at her in a nice way and played with her hair and stood very close to her father. When she was ten, he started locking the office door, and then he said she was old enough to walk straight home by herself. Kay thought he was ashamed of her, and she was ashamed too. She wrote terrible things about him on the wall behind her dresser, but it didn't help. (159)

The narrator intimates that sex has brought an end to the close relationship between father and daughter. Perhaps Martin felt that, by age ten, his daughter might have found something unseemly in his relationship with the "pretty girls" at the office, and he thought that he was protecting her from uncomfortable suspicions by shooing her away. Even more likely is the possibility that Martin was having an affair with a coworker and hid his infidelity from his wife by barring his daughter from witnessing any untoward behavior. Kay does not appear to recognize either of these explanations as feasible, however; she reads the lock on the office door as a rejection of her affection. Just at the moment that Kay's affections toward her father should be paving the way for future sexual attraction to other men, she finds her desire for her love-object thwarted. She does the only logical thing she can, psychoanalytically speaking, at such a point: she returns to the figure of her mother as love-object.

Kay's love for her mother at this stage moves beyond mere identification because of a shared sex: she sees herself as the white knight rescuing her mother, the damsel in distress. When Kay senses that her father may assert his authority and send her mother away, she becomes anxious:

> "What are you going to do?" Kay asked [him], feelings of power, of supernatural strength, surging through her chest. She will rescue her mother the way policemen shimmy through traffic to rescue toddlers, the way acrobats catch each other at the last, impossible half-second. She will swing past her father, leaving him fat and clumsy on the ground, and she and her mother will whirl through light-filled air, landing softly, not even breathing hard, on their own tiny platforms. (156–157)

Kay's wildly romantic imaginings are, first, out of proportion to the threat of the situation: Martin is acting to restore his wife's mental health by sending her to an institution where she can receive appropriate care, not threatening her with physical or verbal abuse. Second, Kay's projected selves in this passage are both, interestingly, male: she becomes a policeman and then a male acrobat who catches his female counterpart as they swing through the air. While it may well be that

Kay has internalized her household's power dynamics to assume that men are the only people capable of powerful action, her vision of herself also suggests that she could be a romantic rival to her father (although obviously more so in the case of the acrobats than in the policeman-toddler scenario). Kay's reverie demonstrates her fear that her father, by imposing the boundaries of "normality," of mental health, will remove her mother from her sphere of desire and replace her with a desexualized automaton.

As it turns out, her fears are well founded. When her mother does return from hospitalization and treatment, Kay longs to once again elicit the woman who spoke in a voice of loves remembered, to win her back from the man who has stolen her away. She wishes she could use her rival's tools, proven so effective at taking her mother away, to triumph in her mother's love: "Kay wants to speak softly, to use her father's basement voice to win her mother back; they will read poetry and eat pizza, and in the end he will shrivel up and blow away, leaving nothing behind but his dorky black shoes. They will be fine then" (161). The pubescent Kay, straddling the borders of childhood lore and adult sexuality, sees her father as an oddly masculine Wicked Witch of the West, an omnipotent force that can only be destroyed by fortuitous, indeed magical, circumstances.[34] Against his powers, she is helpless to regain her mother's love.

Kay's developmental story exemplifies what can go wrong in the psychoanalytic schema. First, she is estranged from her mother at birth because of Laura's severe postpartum depression. Although her father lovingly takes over the "mothering" responsibilities for the infant, he seems fundamentally unable to reconnect with his daughter when she moves beyond the stage of helpless childhood into a growing independence. Kay's explosive and illogical anger at her father, however, is of the same ilk that Friday describes in the resentment of daughters toward their mothers. In this case, the father's early role as surrogate mother seems to have taken hold in Kay's psyche, and her reactions to him in adolescence are those Friday associates with mothers. A second obstacle to Kay's "normal" psychosexual development is posed by her father when he bars her from his office. At age ten, on the cusp of puberty, Kay should be transferring her affections from her father to nonfamilial male love-objects, according to Freudian psychoanalytic theory; instead, she feels herself shut out from her father's love and turns toward her mother. Although the context for Kay's development is in each case the reverse of the ideal Freud envisioned, there is hope for her yet, ironically enough, because of her mother's illness. In this context, Kay fills the void left by her mother by developing into a sexually mature woman herself. The story offers little hope for the recovery of Laura's formerly vibrant self, but Kay can carry on her sexual torch as she dons the mantle of womanhood. To facilitate Kay's individuation, her mother's must be subsumed, much as Dinnerstein and Chodorow theorized.

In Lorrie Moore's "Which Is More than I Can Say about Some People," which first appeared in the *New Yorker* in 1993 and was later included in her collection *Birds of America* (1998), the economy of female sexuality reaches its peak in that neither mother nor daughter is allowed sexual expression outside the family. The story is framed by the daughter Abby's dismay at her promotion from analogy writer to a kind of traveling ambassador for her standardized-testing company, in spite of her worse-than-deathly fear of public speaking. Both to gain confidence in her eloquence and to escape her troubled marriage, she flees to Ireland, believing that kissing the Blarney Stone will provide the antidote to her professional fears, if not her marital woes. She invites her widowed mother on the journey only because rental cars with standard transmissions are cheaper than automatics, and Abby can't drive a stick. If the fact that Abby's mother is accompanying her out of economic necessity rather than a genuine desire for her company signals that there may be trouble to come, Mrs. Mallon's initial appearance in the story only reinforces the reader's sense of apprehension. When Abby informs her mother of her promotion, she laments that she will have to be a people person. Mrs. Mallon replies, "A *peeper* person?" (27). This misunderstanding foreshadows many more to come in the course of the story. The one positive omen for the trip is the fact that it represents a return to Mrs. Mallon's heritage—she's one-sixteenth Irish, she proudly reminds Abby. Thus conjoined, the two embark on a trip to the mother's one-sixteenth motherland.

At first glance, sexuality does not appear to be an important theme in the story. This description is especially true of Abby's character, who appears less turned on by sex than by the analogies she creates for standardized tests. For Abby, the trip is motivated by her desire to avoid her husband. It's not altogether surprising that the relationship is in trouble, since Abby married Bob primarily to assuage her grief over her dog's death. "She had begun to keep him as a kind of pet," the narrator tells us, and when Abby thinks of him, she imagines him sitting on the rug in front of the fireplace, exactly where her dog used to sit (27). Although Abby's feelings toward Bob are described as a "mix of loneliness and lust and habit . . . the mix that was surely love," Abby clearly needs to convince herself that this combination does spell love. Worse, it's more than a little troubling that Abby's sexual partner is a surrogate for her late dog; sexuality seems, for Abby, to be subsumed by affectionate attachment. Abby's attempts to find fulfilling heterosexual partners include a failed affair: she seeks out the town's token bachelor, but when he tries to seduce her, she responds to his words with confusion and exits hastily. After this failure, she returns to her husband, who exclaims, "Honey, you're home!" (28). (He lacks only a lolling tongue and wagging tail in his excitement at her return.) Abby can bear the homecoming for only a week before she books a trip to Ireland to escape.

Through much of the story, Abby feels herself regressing into childhood. From the minute she gets into the rental car in Ireland, she becomes aware that she is no longer in control of her situation: "[S]itting on what should be the driver's side but without a steering wheel suddenly seemed emblematic of something" (28). The sensation of childishness is both terrifying and freeing, but it also leads her toward childish behavior. On the first day in Ireland, she thinks to herself, "Ireland was a trip into the past of America. It was years behind, unmarred, like a story or a dream or a clear creek. I'm a child again, Abby thought. I'm back. And just as when she was a child, she suddenly had to go to the bathroom" (29). For Abby, childhood is not only an idealized era when life was simpler but also a time of heightened awareness of bodily needs. On the trip, her physical bravery is a constant cause for dispute with her mother. When Abby characterizes their visit to preaccord Northern Ireland, with its armed men on each side of the street, as "a little scary," her mother attacks her: "If you get scared easily." Abby recognizes that daring has become their central conflict: "That Abby had no courage and her mother did. And that it had forever been that way" (30).

Abby's physicality and her courage are also foregrounded in the story's most dramatic episode: the kissing of the Blarney Stone. In order to reach the stone, Abby sees, one must hang backward from a ledge, anchored only by a surly "leprechaun" who holds the visitors' legs. Although the pilgrimage to the Stone was her original reason for making the trip, once she approaches her turn, Abby becomes hesitant and begins to whine "I can't." She has turned into a child completely, and her mother bullies her: "But you came all this way! Don't be a ninny!" Such provocation, Abby knows, "never gave her courage; in fact, it deprived her of courage. But it gave her bitterness and impulsiveness, which could look like the same thing" (41). Although Mrs. Mallon's nagging ultimately succeeds in motivating Abby to kiss the Stone, it is because Abby's thinking and behavior have reverted to a childish state, not because she is acting as an adult.

The power relation between mother and daughter is not uniform throughout the story, however. The kissing of the Blarney Stone represents the turning point of the story: Abby realizes that she and her mother have reversed roles, and she has become the mature one in the pair. Prior to the Blarney Stone episode, Mrs. Mallon prods Abby about her marital troubles, declaring, "Women of your generation are always hoping for some other kind of romance than the one they have" (36). This type of statement typifies Mrs. Mallon's feeling of superiority over Abby as part of a wiser generation. Similarly, the title of the story comes from Mrs. Mallon's repetition of the phrase "which is more than I can say about some people," always obliquely referring to Abby's behavior in comparison with her own or that of her other daughter, Theda, whose Down syndrome is treated as a kind of relentless cheerfulness rather than as a disease.[35] Abby, Mrs. Mallon constantly points out, does not live up to the ideal behavior of these standard bearers. This phrase disappears from the story, however, after Mrs. Mallon nearly loses her balance after kissing the Blarney Stone. The disappearance signals a shift in the relationship between mother and daughter. Abby realizes her own strength lies in her unique perspective on the world when she says to herself, "[I]t was a ruse, all her formidable display. She was only trying to prove something, trying pointlessly to defy and overcome her fears—instead of just learning to live with them, since, hell, you were living with them anyway" (43). The fact that Abby begins to understand how to handle her own fears on a trip motivated by terror of public speaking signals her own emotional growth spurt, in which she surpasses her mother.

Although Mrs. Mallon at many points in the story seems determined to lord her age and wisdom over her daughter, she paradoxically also wants to consider herself Abby's generational equal. At the beginning of their trip, for example, Mrs. Mallon announces that they will tour the island completely, drive over every inch, "because that's just the kind of crazy Yuppies we are" (29). While this statement may be another of Mrs. Mallon's misunderstandings (along the lines of *peeper* person), it also demonstrates that she puts herself in the same age group as Yuppies, who are, by definition, young—a qualification Mrs. Mallon, at sixty, possesses perhaps in relation to octogenarians. Later, as the two drive by Limerick, they make up their own song: "There once were two gals from America, one named Abby and the other named Erica." This moment is notable because it's the only point in the story at which the mother's first name appears; at all other times, she is Mrs. Mallon, a title that clearly marks her as a generation separate from her daughter. Here, in this moment of childlike delight, the two are on equal footing. Similarly, in a moment of excitement, Mrs. Mallon calls the two of them "Playgirls of the Western World!" (40).[36] Mrs. Mallon wants to see herself as her daughter's equal in age, but her choice of epithet may actually highlight the differences between them, since Synge's play dramatizes conflict between the generations (in this case, father and son) rather than harmony.

The psychological foundation for Mrs. Mallon's efforts to liken herself to Abby seems to lie in a comment she makes after Abby catches her behaving in a childlike way. Because she was the oldest child, Mrs. Mallon reveals, she never really had a childhood of her own, for her mother treated her as a confidante. By the time Mrs. Mallon was an adult, she had real adult responsibilities—a husband and two children, one of whom, Theda, needed special care. Abby, with her solitary spirit, was the only one who demanded little of her mother. Mrs. Mallon says to Abby, "But then there was you. You I liked. You I could leave alone" (39). Treating Abby like a fellow adult, Mrs. Mallon found, was the way to achieve her own contentment, and her sentiment that they are more like sisters than mother and daughter eventually seems to rub off on Abby. Near the end of the story, Abby concludes, "It was really the world that was one's brutal mother, the one that nursed and neglected you, and your own mother was your only sibling in that world" (46). This statement apparently sums up the meaning of the story for Abby—that mother and daughter can repair their relationship, no matter how shredded, by a metaphorical rebirthing process that makes them sisters, that equalizes and neutralizes the power relation between them.

The story's seeming position that the sibling relationship is superior to a mother-daughter bond is enhanced by the womb imagery that pervades the story. While the womb is usually perceived as deeply comforting and restorative, here it is threatening, stifling, and even a bit repugnant. At one point in their journey, Abby thinks to herself, "[H]ere she and her mother were, sharing the tiniest of cars, reunited in a wheeled and metal womb" (37). Although initially the womb seems merely confining, it also takes on valences of destructive power. When Abby and her mother visit an ancient grave tunnel, it's described as having a "floor plan like a birth in reverse, its narrow stone corridor spilling into a high, round room" (32). Although the tour guide proudly trumpets the antiquity of the grave, Abby wishes he would address what, to her, seems its most salient and important feature: "its deadly maternal metaphor" (32). Abby's reverse tracing of the birthing process leads her not into amniotic tranquility but toward anxiety and dread. The association of death and birth returns at the

Blarney Stone. Although she has bullied Abby into kissing the Stone, Mrs. Mallon is terrified when her own turn comes. Her fright is so strong that she cannot get up from her position on the rock floor: "[W]hen she struggled to come back up, she seemed to be stuck. Her legs thrashed out before her; her shoes loosened from her feet; her skirt rode up, revealing the brown tops of her panty hose" (43). The reader's view in this image is directed downward to the struggling woman and directly under the mother's skirt, between her thrashing legs. This image is repulsive rather than comforting, and the view is coupled with the threat of annihilation, since Mrs. Mallon's struggle is not simply to right herself but to keep from falling off the rock to her death.

In a paradox like the one created in Mrs. Mallon's insistence on both her motherly superiority and her sisterly relationship to Abby, the story's imagery establishes the danger of the maternal body while also conferring on that body a tinge of eroticism. "When Abby was a child," the narrator informs the reader, "her mother had always repelled her a bit—the oily smell of her hair, her belly button like a worm curled in a pit, the sanitary napkins in the bathroom wastebasket, horrid as a war" (36). The characteristics that Abby found so disgusting signaled her mother's sexual maturity—oily hair, like menstruation, is a trait of the postpubescent body, a body endowed with sexual possibility, while the belly button is both the sign of Mrs. Mallon's bodily connection to her own mother and a feature commonly displayed for its sexual allure. Abby's recollections then move to an incident when, as a child, she burst into an unlocked ladies' room stall and saw her mother "sitting there in a dazed and unseemly way, peering out at her from the toilet seat like a cuckoo in a clock." For the child Abby, the scatological and the sexual are linked, and bodily functions, no matter their purpose, are repulsive. "There were things one should never know about another person," Abby decides (37). Yet the journey has forced the two characters into uncomfortable proximity, riding in a wheeled and metal womb, "sharing small double beds in bed-and-breakfasts, waking up with mouths stale and close upon each other, or backs turned and rocking in angry-seeming humps." This account, if taken out of context, would appear to be a description of two longtime lovers waking up together. In this single sentence, the characters are both ensconced in a womb (which paradoxically contains the mother and her daughter) and awakening in a conjugal situation. The narrator continues, "Talk of Abby's marriage and its possible demise trotted before them" (37). The juxtaposition of these situations highlights Abby's failure in her heterosexual relationship and her current state, sleeping with a woman who also happens to be her mother.

The sexually charged nature of Abby's relationship to her mother is enhanced by the context of their trip: Mrs. Mallon has joined the trip because of her dexterity with a stick shift, and the two are journeying to kiss a giant stone. The subtle phallic allusions are confirmed by Abby's embarrassment when, told by an innkeeper that the name of the bread they are eating is Curranty Dick, her mother responds, "Don't I know it" (40). Abby only needs to be embarrassed about her mother's remark if there is something sexual about the food's name. Her situation with her mother is clearly given erotic overtones, a fact that is emphasized near the end of the story when Abby thinks of a test-analogy to describe their trip: "*Blank* is to childhood as journey is to lips" (46). While lips are associated with speech and eating, those activities would be more closely linked to *mouths*; lips, however, are allied with erotic acts. The sexual character of this relationship is given its final weight in the last sentence, just after Abby has toasted her mother: "[Mrs. Mallon] had never been courted before, not once in her entire life, and now she blushed, ears on fire, lifted her pint, and drank" (46). Mrs. Mallon's interpretation of the toast as a kind of wooing confirms that she, too, sees an erotic component to her relationship with her daughter.

The story presents two predominant images that appear deeply contradictory: a struggle for power between an aging mother and her younger daughter, and a mother who wants to see herself as the contemporary of that daughter, for whom she is an object of erotic desire. The apparent incongruity of these images can be resolved through psychoanalytic theory, particularly as it emerges through the filter of mother-daughter theory. Abby's attachment to and desire for her mother are those of every young girl's relation to her first love-object; her feelings of childishness in the face of her mother's superiority represent not only a power struggle between the two but also a recollection of Abby's earliest love. While this situation directly echoes Freud's theories of female psychosexual development, other features of Abby's relationship with her mother have no clear parallel in Freud. The image of Abby and Mrs. Mallon sleeping in a marital bed, for example, in the same sentence in which they are presented in a womb-like car, could be straight from Dinnerstein or Chodorow: Abby is in bed with her mother because she cannot find heterosexual satisfaction with her husband (or even an attempted affair with the town bachelor). Although men find heterosexual intercourse satisfying because the act allows them to re-create their earliest connection with their mothers' bodies, according to Dinnerstein and Chodorow, it can never be as gratifying for women; on the most basic level, men's bodies bear little resemblance to the mother's, and penetration by a sexual partner hardly seems an acceptable substitute for reentry into the womb.

Even more important is the spirit of competition that pervades the relationship between Mrs. Mallon and her daughter. According to the triumvirate of mother-daughter theorists, this rivalry is not only natural (in fact, it seems tame compared to the portrait Friday paints) but is the result of patriarchal arrangements resulting from the child's earliest feelings of threatening dependence on the mother. In order to assert her independence and individuate herself, according to psychoanalytic theory, Abby must defy her attachment to her mother and desire men instead. Ironically, however, Abby's rebellion leads her into an unsatisfying marriage, which pushes her back toward her mother. Moreover, neither of these women experience sexual fulfillment in the course of the story. Abby cannot find sexual satisfaction even when she attempts an affair, and Mrs. Mallon's widowhood precludes any sexual activity on her part. Despite the erotic overtones of the interactions between mother and daughter, there is never any actual sexual contact between them, and the phallic imagery of the story (the stick shift, the magnificent stone to be kissed) hints that both women seek heterosexual satisfaction. This story offers less sex than either Bloom's or Beattie's, for here the economy of female sexuality is at its culmination: neither mother nor daughter is allowed sexual expression outside the family. Instead, the identification of mother with daughter becomes so close that they are portrayed as generational equals, pushed back into the womb together. For Abby, overcoming her mother's power over her merely means that her mother is reduced to a sibling, rather than achieving sexual maturity.

Other Mothering

Writing in 1980, Susan Contratto Weisskopf noted that cultural and scholarly assumptions supposed motherhood and sexuality deeply contradictory—that once a woman became a mother, her sexuality became so buried beneath her responsibilities as a mother that it effectively disappeared.[37] Weisskopf acknowledged that she was indebted to the writings of Rich and Chodorow for pointing out that sexuality and motherhood were not mutually exclusive. Even so, Rich's portrait of her own struggle to maintain a sense of self and writer apart from her role as a mother was hardly an optimistic perspective on the balance between motherhood and sexuality, and Chodorow's book, though it did attempt to attend to the mother, is more focused on the daughter's psychic and sexual development, as she later admitted.[38] Neither book is a shining example of the ways in which women can maintain a sense of their own sexuality while mothering.

Weisskopf's observation that motherhood was usually considered asexual prefigured the ways in which the mothering theories of the late 1970s, from which she took her inspiration, would appear as later literary themes. In the short stories by Beattie, Bloom, and Moore, motherhood is usually portrayed as asexual. In Beattie's "Find and Replace," the mother's reclaiming of her sexuality interrupts her daughter's ability to find sexual fulfillment of her own; Ann is so horrified by her mother's sexual involvement with Drake that she ignores the romantic overtures of two sexual prospects, choosing isolation and asexuality. Bloom's "When the Year Grows Old," on the other hand, presents a sexualized portrait of the mother Laura, but her overt sexuality is portrayed as a symptom of her mental illness rather than as the attribute of a healthy woman. Although she is able to encourage the blossoming sexuality of her daughter Kay, Laura's own is eventually deadened by medication and institutionalization. Asexuality takes hold of both mother and daughter in Moore's "Which Is More than I Can Say about Some People," in which Abby and Mrs. Mallon undertake a quest shaded by phallic undertones but never find sexual fulfillment. The erotic intimations of the story portray a mother and daughter unable to move beyond their earliest relationship as parent and infant, confined to a womb that will not allow them to experience themselves as separate and sexual individuals. Mothers are either satisfyingly asexual or threatening in their sexuality, and their expressions of sexuality shape the ways in which their daughters can approach their own sexual identities.

These stories appear deeply imbued with the mothering theories of Friday, Dinnerstein, and Chodorow in the way they treat the possibilities for sexual expression in mothers and daughters. The economy of female sexuality within the family is maintained—no matter the cost to mother or daughter. The treatment of female characters in these stories is deeply conservative—that is, sexuality is literally conserved and restrained. Further, these literary portrayals fail to move beyond the restrictions on mothering portrayed by theorists of the 1970s, despite the fact that these stories were published well after those theories had their heyday. The stories hearken backward in time in their images of female sexuality, rather than pushing forward and imagining fewer constraints on women. In this way, they are also culturally conservative. Rather than being literary forms "increasingly deft in [their] power to portray our individual and social complexity," as Bonaro Overstreet had hoped back in 1941, these stories return female sexuality to the state of the late 1970s. Such portrayals are particularly distressing because, according to theorists of feminist epistemology, "the story" is a metaphor for the empowering way in which mothers pass on knowledge to their daughters.[39] The knowledge—messages about proper female sexuality—communicated in these stories acts not to free or empower the daughters (and, sometimes, the mothers), but to limit and control them.

Because these stories portray white women of high socioeconomic status, they invite further analysis in their presentation of a metaphorical economy. The next chapter examines increasing pressures on the economy of female sexuality in order to demonstrate that this trend in contemporary short stories is focused on white families. Women who do not fit comfortably within this category are not as constrained in their sexual expression, as I will argue, while those who meet this description are the most likely to be limited by the sexual economy. Through this analysis, we can begin to understand the reasoning that underlies the apparent literary anxiety about unchecked female sexuality, and the way in which it is particularly marked when characters occupy the highest tiers of American racial status.

Economies of Whiteness

While the female sexual economy is powerfully at work in the stories by Beattie, Bloom, and Moore, elsewhere it seems to disappear. Those three stories portray mother-daughter relationships in which either mothers or daughters can find sexual expression, but not both at the same time. In Gloria Naylor's "Kiswana Browne," on the other hand, both mother and daughter enjoy a sense of sexual fulfillment, a commonality that actually helps to bring the characters together by the end of the story. In the course of the story, readers witness the conflict between twentysomething Kiswana and her mother as she moves into her first apartment and looks for her first job. Although mother and daughter disagree on several issues—the suitability of Kiswana's apartment, her choice to forego phone service, her decorating choices, and, most importantly, her decision to renounce her given name, Melanie, for the African Kiswana—the story ends not with conflict but with a sense of mutual understanding. The key to the ceasefire between them is Kiswana's recognition that both she and her mother have lovers who find erotic delight in painted toenails. Rather than constraining the characters so that either mother or daughter can find sexual satisfaction, this story not only allows both women to express themselves sexually, but it even celebrates their parallel sexual experiences.[1] What could account for the differences? One factor is that the characters in Beattie, Bloom, and Moore's stories are white and those in Naylor's are black. While this statement is an oversimplification, it also foregrounds a trend: the whiter the characters, the more the sexual economy works to constrain them. This pattern raises two important questions: first, what counts as whiteness, and second, why might there be more sexual limits on white characters than on black ones? To answer both of these questions, I turn to critical race theory and, more narrowly, whiteness studies.

In the United States, whiteness generally refers to a quality possessed by people with white skin, defined as those who have no ancestors of color (as in the one-drop rule that, for decades, defined blacks on the basis of having one drop of "black blood"). Valerie Babb notes that the definition of whiteness as the absence of nonwhite ancestors—a term defined by the lack of its opposite—is one that underscores the complexity of whiteness:

> Part of the difficulty in characterizing whiteness lies with its having no genuine content other than a culturally manufactured one, developed unevenly over a period of time, influenced by and responding to a variety of historical events and social conditions: among them, the need to create a historical past, the need to create national identity, and the need to minimize class warfare. As whiteness evolved in response to these demands, it did so in no linear or orderly fashion, had no single abiding vision that created it, had no single source from which it sprang. (16)

The evolution of whiteness means that it is historically contingent; depending on the national moment, the beneficiaries of whiteness vary. The historical development of whiteness has meant that "being white [has become] synonymous with being American" (2).[2] Not only are whites considered Americans, though; Americans are also thought of as white. Once a group of people becomes integrated into the United States, they become Americans and thus white. (Of course, only particular kinds of people qualify for full integration.) Books such as Noel Ignatiev's *How the Irish Became White* and Karen Brodkin's *How Jews Became White Folks* testify to the process of whitening among two immigrant populations, demonstrating that social conditions rather than ancestry or phenotype (appearance) have generally determined the meaning of whiteness.

To some extent, this view of whiteness conflates race and ethnicity.[3] After all, Irishness, for example, would seem to be an ethnicity that falls under the umbrella term "white." Yet as Ignatiev has demonstrated, in the early years of the United States, "Irish were frequently referred to as 'niggers turned inside out'; the Negroes, for their part, were sometimes called 'smoked Irish.'" (41). In other words, ethnicity's relationship to race is historically determined. In the early nineteenth century (and in some cases, up through the Civil War), Irishness as an ethnicity fell under the umbrella term of blackness rather than whiteness. Groups that eventually became white did so, in fact, at the expense of blacks, as Ignatiev documents; through organized violence and refusals to work with blacks, the Irish were eventually recognized as "white" by whites who were secure in their racial identity. This theme emerges in the whitening of many different populations, including Jews, eastern and southern European immigrants, and the working class.[4] In *Playing in the Dark*, Toni Morrison has suggested that blackness is essential to the creation of literary whiteness, but her characterization might well be applied to the whole process of racial formation[5] in the United States.

Because whiteness is not a fixed concept, and because it operates only in relation to nonwhiteness, "whiteness" as a racial term is not always useful—despite the fact that the first use of the term *white* to refer to race occurred in the North American colonies and thus has a distinctly American provenance (Dyer, *White* 66). Although the United States is wedded to a paradigm of two races, one black and one white, the very simplicity of this model is also its weakness.[6] Without blacks, whites would have no racial identity; one is dependent on the other for meaning. Similarly, this system deals only in absolutes; those who do not precisely fit into either category are left in a sort of limbo that must be resolved through identification as either black or white. Importantly, it is not the individuals themselves who can resolve the problem; this ability lies with those who are secure in their whiteness. As Marilyn Frye has put it, "Whites exercise a power of defining who is white and who is not, and are jealous of that power" ("On Being White" 115). While the "whites" Frye refers to as making decisions about whiteness are phenotypically white—that is, they bear the visible markings of what's considered white in contemporary American culture, such as appropriate skin color, facial features, and hair texture— the fact that some people can judge other people who are borderline cases to be white undermines the very idea of stable whiteness.

If whiteness cannot be defined as race, then what might it be? Barbara J. Fields has suggested that race can be most usefully treated as ideology rather than biology:

> The very diversity and arbitrariness of the physical rules governing racial classification prove that the physical emblems which symbolize race are not the foundation upon which race arises as a category of social thought. That does not mean that race is unreal: All ideologies are real, in that they are the embodiment in thought of real social relations. (151)

Kalpana Seshadri-Crooks, thinking in a similar way, suggests that race is "a regime of visibility that secures our investment in racial identity" (21). Within her framework, whiteness, because it cannot be pinned down in language, creates anxiety that motivates people to seek affirmation of its existence through visual stimuli. Whiteness becomes the central signifier in the chain of racial terms; even though there is no concrete signified, everything refers to whiteness. Eric Lott uses the metaphor of nineteenth-century American minstrelsy practices to refer to the emptiness of whiteness, explaining that blackface can be thought of as internalizing the other, and that whiteness operates through images and fantasies of black men in the same way that blackface operated by projecting black men over white faces. Whiteness, in other words, becomes itself an "impersonation" (491). And as Richard Dyer observes, "[W]hite is not anything really, not an identity, not a particularising quality, because it is everything—white is no color because it is all colors. This property of whiteness, to be everything and nothing, is the source of its representational power" ("White" 7). In short, whiteness, even if not a race, is a source of cultural power in both its visibility and invisibility, a ubiquitous presence even when absent.

Whiteness, then, refers to the power and social access afforded to people who are determined to be white by those who are most secure in their whiteness—even though it is impossible, as the critics above demonstrate, to be "fully" white. Whiteness is always contingent, and the tautology that maintains it makes the category seem paradoxically both impregnable and flexible. Importantly, whiteness works at varying levels; unlike pregnancy, it is possible to be a little bit white. As Mab Segrest has put it, "If whiteness is a signifier of power and condition of access in U.S. culture, then women are less white than men, gay people less white than straight people, poor people less white than rich people, Jews less than Christians, and so forth" (45). Whiteness can also change its intensity in different times and contexts. Troy Duster has suggested the metaphor of H_2O to describe the fluid functioning of race in America; in his model, race can simply be something in the air (a gas) or a free-floating term (water), but there are moments at which it crystallizes, hardening into ice. His language could well apply to whiteness, too, for there are times at which whiteness seems diffuse and almost meaningless, but given a particular context, the force of its operations becomes hardened and clear as ice. John Hartigan, Jr., for example, has charted the ways in which working-class "hillbilly" whites living in urban Detroit, a predominantly black city, tend to downplay their whiteness at home, even in their mixed-race neighborhoods, but recognize that their whiteness is heightened when they leave their areas and enter the projects (192). As Harryette Mullen points out, Ralph Ellison plays on this idea in *Invisible Man* through the scene in the paint factory, in which the narrator is required to add ten drops of black paint in order to create a paint that is the whitest white, Optic White (44). Whites become whiter in the presence of blacks; without the contrast, their color fades nearly into neutrality.

Although whiteness cannot simply be defined by phenotype, it is associated with certain values and behaviors that help to uphold it. Culturally, whiteness is associated with civilization (as the opposite of barbarism), education, morality, and financial security. Charles Chesnutt, in the essay "Race Prejudice," ironically comments that blacks can most effectively counter discrimination by becoming whiter: "Thus our savage has become civilized, our heathen Christian, our foreigner a native, our slave a citizen, our Negro a man of mixed blood, our pauper a land owner. The prejudice against him has decreased" (87). Similarly, Frantz Fanon writes of the colonized black man who has adopted the occupier's values as "becom[ing] whiter as he renounces his blackness, his jungle" (18). The more a black man absorbs the colonizer's values, the more he begins to believe that "one is a Negro to the degree to which one is wicked, sloppy, malicious, instinctual. Everything that is the opposite of these Negro modes of behavior is white. . . . In other words, he is Negro who is immoral. If I order my life like that of a moral man, I simply am not a Negro" (192).[7] Maureen T. Reddy, writing of more contemporary phenomena, notes that the media periodically report on black students who characterize academic achievers among them as "acting white," suggesting that those who value education are implicitly whiter than their peers (95–96). And Frye describes "whitely" behavior—the behavior of white people acting white—as prizing propriety, manners, abiding by the rules, and following procedures ("White Woman Feminist" 155).[8] In short, almost any mode of behavior that could be described as positive, mature, refined, or logical is associated with whiteness.

Central to whiteness are values of restraint and control, as Dyer has explained. Yet, logically speaking, whites must also engage in sexual reproduction in order to perpetuate the white "race"—and that heterosexual contact must be limited exclusively to white partners. The conflicting agendas of whiteness' need for order and reason on the one hand and its need to reproduce itself on the other result in a paradox, writes Dyer: "Our minds control our bodies and therefore both our sexual impulses and our forward planning of children. The very thing that makes us white endangers the reproduction of our whiteness" (*White* 27). Heterosexuality, then, is the site of the greatest anxiety about race; it offers both the opportunity to further whiteness through biological reproduction and the most powerful danger to it in the form of interracial sexual relationships.[9] Because white women are quite literally the mothers of the "race," they become the focus of special attention.[10] In contrast to white men, who are supposed to feel conflicted about the opposition of their sexual drives (their "dark" nature) and their need to maintain control over their bodies, according to Dyer, white women are not supposed to have any sexual drives. These attitudes are problematic, since unless white women engage in heterosexual intercourse, there is little chance of having future generations of white children. As Dyer points out, the model of whiteness for white women is the Virgin Mary, who was able to conceive without the mess of sexual congress (*White* 29). The unfortunate difficulties inherent in following this model for white women do nothing to decrease its cultural resonance.

White women could well be seen as the apotheosis of whiteness, since they are the mothers of the "race" and the ultimate objects of desire at the same time that they are supposed to be the asexual bearers of the standard of whiteness. Dyer notes that this paradoxical, flexible character of whiteness is precisely what sustains it. Because white women are the iconic bearers of whiteness, there is special pressure, much as Frye points out, for them to conform to whiteness' rules of order. The hopes of whiteness are invested in them, a fact revealed by the persistent portrayal of white women as whiter than their male counterparts in popular culture, as Dyer convincingly demonstrates in *White*. Weddings present the best examples of the association between whiteness and white women as its mode of reproduction, for brides are dressed in a way that accentuates white skin as well as symbolizing their purity, their lack of sexual contamination (particularly the "dangerous" heterosexual contact with nonwhite lovers) (76). These values are codified in the image of Barbie, the doll whose plastic image of perfection has often stood in for the ideal female body in American popular culture. Barbie's enduring sex appeal comes not only from her large breasts and disproportionately small waist, but also her tanned but decidedly white skin and her straight blonde hair. Barbie, as Rhonda Lieberman points out, was actually invented by a Jewish woman, who, rather than endowing Barbie with traditionally Jewish features, made the doll "the ultimate *shiksa* goddess" by projecting onto Barbie what is considered sexually appealing in American culture (108).[11] The acme of white womanhood, Barbie, is visibly white and visually sexy but finally (literally) frigid to the touch. Her sterile sexuality is the epitome of whiteness.

Because white women are in many ways the pinnacle of whiteness, they bear a special responsibility for maintaining its control. This is the point at which whiteness intersects with the female sexual economy, the constraint that either mother or daughter can find sexual expression, but not both at the same time. White women represent both the supreme objects of male heterosexual desire and the chaste mothers of the race. They embody the paradoxical nature of whiteness, and it is their sexual choices that will determine the future of whiteness. While white women must have (heterosexual) sex to sustain the white race, they must be selective in their partners, both to ensure the whiteness of the offspring and to demonstrate white values of self-control, reason, and restraint. Although whiteness can and must tolerate female sexual activity up to a certain point, it must also regulate that activity, ensuring that it does not exceed the limits of what constitutes white (or whitely) behavior: the cultivation of civilization rather than barbarism. The sexual economy ensures that whiteness can continue through sexual reproduction, but it limits female sexual expression in order to keep a family's women within the boundaries of acceptably white behavior. It is no mistake that the origins of the sexual economy can be traced to the writings of Nancy Friday, Dorothy Dinnerstein, and Nancy Chodorow: all three assumed a Western, middle-class, nuclear—white—family for their models of mothering.

Whiteness constitutes a form of power and social access for those who are deemed to possess it. Despite its association with the absence of color, whiteness also possesses shades and shadows. A woman who is white among her neighbors may be less white in a different context; among upper-class women, or, if she is Jewish, among Christian women, for example, she is no longer as white. These kinds of shifts in whiteness affect the functioning of the sexual economy. The whiter the woman is in her context, the more she is constrained by the economy. Women who are on the borders of whiteness, who deviate slightly from the ultimate whiteness, are particularly susceptible to a changing enforcement of the sexual economy. When they are defined (or, occasionally, define themselves) as nonwhite, outside the boundaries of whiteness, they are freed from the economy's constraints, but when they seek white identification, the family must operate within the economy.

Stories exemplifying this dynamic run the spectrum from a biracial daughter in the 1970s Midwest negotiating an identity between her black and white parents in Alyce Miller's "A Cold Winter Light" (1994) to a mother-daughter pair of Austrian Jewish immigrants working to adapt to New York's Upper West Side in the 1940s in Lore Segal's "Burglars in the Flesh" (1980) to a Cuban woman reflecting on the influence of her arrival in Miami in 1963 on her subsequent life in Achy Obejas's "We Came All the Way from Cuba So You Could

Dress Like This?" (1994). In each case, race is flexible and depends on the characters' context for definition; their racial identities can change over time—and sometimes merely in a matter of minutes, depending on their situation. All three stories have been anthologized in collections focused on the portrayals of the characters' ethnicities: Miller's in *Crossing the Color Line: Readings in Black and White*, Segal's in *Her Face in the Mirror: Jewish Women on Mothers and Daughters*, and Obejas's in both *Cubana: Contemporary Fiction by Cuban Women* and *Cuba*.[12] I have chosen these stories because they have already earned some critical recognition by virtue of their selection for anthologies in which they serve as exemplars of stories about interactions between blacks and whites, or Jewish women, or Cubans. Moreover, the fact of their anthologizing makes them more readily accessible and more likely to be familiar to a larger audience.

The range of the stories' content, style, and presentation of race as a fluid subject offers a glimpse into the complexity of the operations of race when it comes to female sexuality within the family. From Miller's story, which initially tests traditional racial classification but ends by reinforcing stereotypes about blackness and whiteness, to Segal's, which demonstrates some opportunity for immigrants to move toward whiteness at the cost of blacks who cannot, to Obejas's, which offers the strongest means to challenge whiteness and the sexual economy, these stories represent several approaches to the sexual economy as they reveal both the workings and the slippages of race in the United States. These stories also, however, reveal the force of both whiteness and the sexual economy on the women they portray. The whiter the characters are, the more they are subject to the constraints imposed by the sexual economy. In each case, the stories show themselves to be essentially conservative, reinforcing notions of proper sexual behavior associated with race.

All three authors were born abroad, a commonality that might account for their sharp interest in the functioning of race in the United States. Alyce Miller, who has garnered the least amount of critical attention of the trio, was born in Zurich, Switzerland, but grew up in the San Francisco Bay Area. She characterizes her writing as "deal[ing] with the complicated dynamics of race and gender and the ways they inflect the lives of ordinary people" ("Alyce Miller"), and her collection *The Nature of Longing* (1994), in which "A Cold Winter Light" appears, is no exception. The volume won the Flannery O'Connor Award for Short Fiction; Miller has also earned the *Kenyon Review* Award for Literary Excellence in Fiction and the Lawrence Prize for Fiction from the *Michigan Quarterly Review*. She currently teaches in the creative writing program at Indiana University.[13]

Lore Segal's early childhood was rather more dramatic than Miller's. In 1938, when she was only ten years old, Segal fled the encroaching Nazi presence in Vienna, her birthplace, for England under the auspices of the Kindertransport. Her best-known work is *Other People's Houses* (serialized in the *New Yorker* beginning in 1961 and published as a volume in 1964), an account of her experience living with strangers during this period. She has received acclaim for her short stories, earning inclusion in both the O. Henry Awards Prize Stories and The Best American Short Stories. She is also a prize-winning children's author whose honors include a Guggenheim Fellowship and grants from the National Endowment for the Arts. Segal taught in the United States from 1968 until 1996, when she retired from the faculty of the Ohio State University.[14]

Achy Obejas, who has lived much of her life in the Midwest, was, like the heroine of "We Came All the Way from Cuba So You Could Dress Like This?" born in Cuba. In 1962, at age six, she and her parents moved to the United States following the Cuban Revolution; she was raised in Michigan City, Indiana, and eventually moved to Chicago. As a journalist, she has been a member of a Pulitzer Prize-winning team; she currently is a cultural writer for the *Chicago Tribune*. Her creative writing has also earned such honors as two Lambda awards and an NEA fellowship for poetry, and her novel *Days of Awe* was singled out for recognition as a best book by the *Los Angeles Times* and the *Chicago Tribune*.

The stories by Miller, Segal, and Obejas exemplify the fluid functioning of race. Their texts make plain the shifting operations at work in whiteness and demonstrate that it is anything but a stable entity. In each case, it is possible to witness alterations from nonwhiteness to whiteness and vice versa. For example, the biracial daughter in Miller's story shifts her identification from white to black over the course of the tale, a choice that allows her to exceed the boundaries of the sexual economy by refusing whiteness and its limits. In Segal's story, the main character is a fugitive from the Holocaust living in New York in the late 1940s. Although her Jewishness is highlighted by her personal history, it fades into the background when she is set against her African American boyfriend; while this character should have been considered nonwhite because of her Jewishness in this time and place, she is whitened through her affiliation with her lover. By becoming whiter, she invokes the power of the sexual economy. Obejas's story presents the most complicated portrait of race and sexuality, for her protagonist lives not only on the border between black and white as a Cuban émigré, but her bisexuality presents a challenge to the sexual economy. In each case, the reader must understand the social and historical context of the story to understand the operations of race within them and to appreciate the ways in which race interacts with the forces of the sexual economy.

BETWEEN BLACK AND WHITE: ALYCE MILLER'S "A COLD WINTER LIGHT"

Miller's story portrays a young woman who is literally on the border between black and white. The story is part of Miller's 1994 collection *The Nature of Longing*, which won the Flannery O'Connor Award for Short Fiction; like O'Connor in "Everything That Rises Must Converge," one of Miller's interests lies in the interaction between blacks and whites. In Miller's story, sixteen-year-old Olivia is the daughter of a white mother and a black father, and until the beginning of the story, she has felt little pressure to choose an identification with one racial category or the other. This particular winter, however, Olivia learns that her father is having an affair with a black woman, and the emotional turmoil generated by this discovery initially helps her recognize her implicit identification with her white mother, but she ultimately embraces a sexuality she associates with blackness. The story refuses blackness and whiteness as terms identified only with skin color, enlarging their definitions to include other physical features as well as behavior. It complicates the use of these words as labels and provides a glimpse of the ways in which blackness and sexuality may be aligned against imagery of whiteness and purity.

The accumulation of meanings around blackness and whiteness in Miller's story can be best understood in the context of writings on black-white relationships and the children produced by those relationships. In the story, Olivia lives near Elyria, Ohio, around 1970. Her racial situation seems relatively uncommon; in the course of the story, she identifies only one other family in town with parents of two different races. Her experience seems borne out by the facts of the real-world United States of 1970. According to Ruth McRoy and Edith Freeman, only 62,500 American black-white marriages were documented in 1970 (164). The majority of these relationships appear to have consisted of an African American husband and a white wife.[15] The relationships themselves violated a number of deeply held taboos in American culture, even while confirming stereotypes about black men's sexuality. In addition, the marriages often produced children who encountered their own questions about racial identity unique to a U.S. system that insists on categorizing people as either black or white.

Maureen T. Reddy, a white writer who married a black man near the time at which Miller's story is set, has noted in her book *Crossing the Color Line: Race, Parenting, and Culture* that most outsiders (both black and white) regard such relationships as "sick," seeing the black spouse's choice of a white partner as an internalization of a white supremacism that dictates that everyone should want a white sexual partner, and the white spouse's choice as merely a search for the "exotic" (10). She points out that under South African apartheid, the white spouses of blacks were reclassified as blacks themselves, and she suggests that in some ways this process is also in effect for white spouses of black partners in the United States, who, to find acceptance, often find themselves disconnecting from white culture, which rejects them, to embrace black values. "The process does not work the other way, however," observes Reddy. "The black partner does not become white, does not acquire white privilege, does not describe that feeling of masquerade, has *always* been a spy in the enemy's country. The color line is permeable in one direction only" (23). Reddy's intuitions about the treatment of white women married to black men, or even in relationships with them, demonstrate that race can operate fluidly (even if she believes that it is subject to certain limits).

Reddy's recounting of her experiences as the wife of a black man, which she published in the 1990s, are merely a recent installment in the ongoing tale of American anxiety concerning relationships between black men and white women. Charles Chesnutt, an American lawyer, essayist, and fiction writer who was himself the product of racial mixing (visibly white, he chose to identify as African American), noted that Mississippi's 1880 legal code declared black-white mixed marriages "incestuous and void"; as a result of these laws, Chesnutt concluded, it was necessary to assume that any black person with a white or nearly white complexion was "the offspring of a union not sanctified by law"—in other words, a bastard ("What Is a White Man" 30, 31). While these laws have slowly disappeared, their effects remain: children who are visibly biracial (black-white) face discrimination. Indeed, as Ruth Frankenberg observed more than 100 years after Chesnutt's essay, marriages between whites and men and women of color have been either illegal or without constitutional protection for the vast majority of the past 400 years of American settlement (72).

Frantz Fanon, a black psychiatrist from the Antilles, sought to understand the psychology shaping the taboos against sexual relationships between blacks and whites when he published *Black Skins, White*

Masks in 1952.[16] The combination of black men and white women is particularly troubling to white society, Fanon suggests, because of stereotypes of black men as highly sexualized beings who are superior lovers to their white counterparts. Whites think that Negroes always operate "on the genital level," says Fanon, and he mockingly outlines white stereotypes about black men: "As for the Negroes, they have tremendous sexual powers. What do you expect, with all the freedom they have in their jungles! They copulate at all times and in all places. . . . Be careful, or they will flood us with little mulattoes" (157). The conflict between white and black men centers on sexuality, writes Fanon, with each side treating the black man's sexuality as a weapon (159).[17]

Fanon observes that sexual relationships between black men and white women have their own special set of meanings. While a white man, particularly in the kind of colonial or even postcolonial society that Fanon describes, can easily sleep with many women, including black women, that behavior is often interpreted as a "seizing" of the sexual partner. But, he notes, "when a white woman accepts a black man there is automatically a romantic aspect. It is a giving" gesture rather than one of being taken by force (46)—an understanding of the relationship that runs counter to popular stereotypes. Moreover, through this relationship, the black man becomes whiter: "By loving me she proves that I am worthy of white love. I am loved like a white man." Imagining himself to be the black man in an interracial marriage, Fanon writes, "I marry white culture, white beauty, white whiteness. When my restless hands caress those white breasts, they grasp white civilization and dignity and make them mine" (63).[18]

Ruth Frankenberg used interviews rather than psychological theories to attempt to understand white women's attitudes toward race in her 1993 book *White Women, Race Matters*; she found social taboos against relationships with black men were among her respondents' most strongly held convictions about race. After interviewing white women married to black men, Frankenberg concluded that social perceptions of such relationships also begin to equate the white partner with sexual stereotypes about black men: "[W]hite women who choose interracial relationships are presented as sexually 'loose,' sexually unsuccessful, or (at the least negative) sexually radical" (77). Such a sentiment explains Jennifer A. Reich's observation that white mothers who are seen with children of mixed race are assumed to be adoptive mothers rather than the biological parents of such children (181–182). Presumably, it's more socially polite to assume a stranger's child is adopted than it is to assume that she was sexually intimate with a black man.

As Frankenberg found in her research, the result of these opinions about interracial relationships is generally that the children produced by such unions can never fit into American society. While this sentiment is often used to justify racist attitudes toward black-white relationships, its prevalence also shapes the way that biracial children feel about themselves. McRoy and Freeman explain that these children are caught between one highly valued social group and a denigrated[19] one, and "they learn to calculate quickly the social mathematics of being black versus being white" (165). The difficult choice of identifying with one group or the other, indeed, with one parent or the other, is often made harder by a society that wants to categorize race neatly as black or white.[20] Adrian Piper, herself biracial, has explained that her "white" appearance has prohibited her acceptance by blacks, but she has also found that whites don't welcome a person with known black heritage among their ranks, for such an inclusion cheapens the value of whiteness (21). "[B]lacks and whites alike," she writes, "seem to be unable to accord worth to others outside their in-group affiliations without feeling that they are taking it away from themselves" (16–17). This economy of racial self-worth becomes a kind of zero-sum game that is impossible for a biracial person to win. As Harryette Mullen puts it, "'Pure' whiteness has actual value, like legal tender, while the white-skinned African-American is like a counterfeit bill that is passed into circulation, but may be withdrawn at any point if discovered to be bogus. The inherited whiteness is a kind of capital, which may yield the dividend of freedom" (50).

In Miller's story, Olivia initially seems to identify as white, without much questioning her racial identity; even her best friend is white. The narrative suggests this identification most strongly through Olivia's comparison with her thirteen-year-old sister Pam. Although she is three years younger than Olivia, Pam engages in much riskier behavior than her sister. When Olivia discovers that Pam has been sneaking out at night to see her boyfriend, she confronts her sister the next morning with a hissed warning: "You better not get pregnant, girl." Pam retorts, "You don't even know what you're talking about, Miss Whitegirl" (66). By telling her sister to stay out of trouble, Olivia is acting like a white girl, according to Pam. Ironically, however, Pam is "lighter than Olivia, with skin the color of shredded wheat." It is Olivia's behavior that makes her "whiter" in Pam's eyes, even though it is Pam whose skin is actually whiter. Skin color, however, is not the whole story. The narrator continues to describe Pam: "[H]er features were broader and her hair was naturally nappier though, like Olivia, she had a perm and wore her hair in a shoulder-length pageboy" (66). While skin color and features may seem to be in conflict in identifying Pam racially, it is her behavior that confirms her blackness against Olivia's relative whiteness: "Pam was only thirteen, but she tried to act grown, wearing her skirts so short there wasn't much left to the imagination. Now she was going with a twenty-year-old hoodlum. . . . Imagine, in the eighth grade, with a grown-up boyfriend! Old fast yellow Pam, calling herself slick, walking downtown and swinging her hips with her big chest poked out" (65).

Olivia's sexual conservatism—her unwillingness to engage in the kind of promiscuous behavior she suspects of Pam—is generally associated with whites, as Dyer and Frye have explained. Olivia displays what Frye terms "whitely" behavior: prizing propriety, manners, abiding by the rules, and following procedures. In Miller's story, whiteness is equated with proper behavior, respect for one's parents, and working to maintain the bonds of family. For example, her mother's best friend tells Olivia, "You're a good girl. . . . And getting so grown-up too!" This remark praises Olivia for her choice to stay out of (sexual) trouble even as she gets "so grown-up." Olivia's mother remarks that her older daughter is her "dependable one. I don't know what I'd do without her" (69). Olivia's dependable behavior is characteristic of the values of whiteness—restraint and control—as Dyer notes. And her anxiety about Pam's intimacy with a "hoodlum" typifies white apprehensions about sex with possibly nonwhite partners.

In part because Olivia's father does not strongly identify as black, she experiences little conflict about her racial identity until her father's behavior changes—or rather, she makes a discovery about her father. The story opens as Olivia finds a hidden Polaroid in the back of her father's desk drawer. Secreted in a dark corner of the basement, the snapshot reveals "a tall, dark black woman [who] stared back coyly, the way subjects do when the photographer knows them intimately." Olivia initially recognizes that the woman is beautiful, but she also notes that the woman is "what her father's mother would call '*too* black'" (61). As Olivia continues staring at the picture, she sees that the woman, whose name she will soon learn is Wilma, "wore a short red leather skirt that hugged her hips and a see-through black blouse with lace on the wide collar. From her earlobes dangled large silver hoops that reflected light" (62). Her clothes connote an explicit sexuality. The tight skirt that reveals the woman's legs, made of an animal skin that emphasizes her sensuality, is red, a color traditionally associated with sexual promiscuity; her gauzy blouse is black, and the skin revealed through it is likewise black, heightening her blackness. The silver hoop earrings contrast this ensemble by reflecting light and showing whiteness against the woman, against which she and her clothing appear even darker. As the narrator reports, "Down to the last detail, this woman was the exact opposite of Olivia's small, white, red-haired mother" (62). Wilma's outfit, together with Olivia's suspicion of this woman's illicit sexual behavior, reinforces her tenuous association of dark-skinned women with heightened sexuality.

Moreover, the unidentified woman's blackness makes Olivia's father blacker by association. On the back of the photograph, Olivia reads the inscription "Merry Christmas to my Chocolate Santa" (62). The Polaroid leads Olivia to become suspicious of her father's recent change in appearance: she has noticed that "her father had skipped several shaves and his hair was lengthening into a natural" (64). Olivia later spots her father with his mistress, and she notices that instead of the Russian hat with ear flaps that he normally wears to protect himself from the cold, he is wearing the black beret that Olivia gave him for Christmas. Her father had always refused to wear the beret on the grounds that he looked like a Black Nationalist, despite Olivia's protest that French people wear berets. Now that he is seeing a black woman, however, his reservations about the beret's meaning seem to have either faded away or become more consonant with his own philosophy. Olivia observes her father's behavior and, furious with him for cheating on her mother, yells after him as he pulls out of the driveway: "You know how I hate your lyin' ass. . . . It's a little late to try to get black on us now!" (71).

Whiteness and blackness become even more complex in Olivia's relationship to her best friend, a white girl named Tonya. For Tonya and her mother, the most important aspect of Olivia's racial heritage is her blackness. As the story progresses, Tonya's mother becomes overprotective of her daughter in Olivia's presence; she asks whether there will be boys present whenever Tonya asks permission to go out. Olivia knows that Tonya's mother is not simply afraid of boys; she intuits "exactly what kind of boys Tonya's mother meant. Black boys" (72). To Tonya's mother, Olivia's blackness is associated with the threat of black male sexuality against her white daughter. Those fears have some foundation in fact: what Tonya's mother doesn't realize is that her daughter seeks out black boys rather than the other way around. On one excursion to a convenience store, for example, the girls are approached by three black boys in a car. When the driver invites Olivia and Tonya to join them at the roller rink, Tonya begs Olivia to agree, squealing that the driver is cute. Olivia rejects this idea, telling Tonya that "[t]he driver was a white-girl lover" (76). Fed up with Tonya's pleading, Olivia finally says, "I can't get you in with black kids, Tonya. I have my own troubles. You're on your own" (77). Clearly Olivia feels that Tonya is leveraging their friendship as a means to meet cute black boys. In Tonya's mind, much as in her mother's, then, Olivia's blackness provides a conduit to black men—and their sexual promise (or threat).[21]

In her research on nonfictional daughters of white mothers and black fathers who lived in largely white suburban neighborhoods, France Winddance Twine found that, despite some visibly black features, these girls were able to identify as white with relatively few challenges to their racial identities until puberty. (One signal that the girls identified as white was that they did not feel the need to censor themselves around whites; people who identify as black generally self-monitor during communications with whites.) More importantly, though, Twine determined that the girls' economic class allowed them to see themselves as, at worst, racially neutral rather than black—until they began dating. In order to be accepted by her peers as fully white, a young woman must be the "legitimate romantic partner" of a white male, according to Twine's research (232). When these girls found themselves rejected by white boys, they turned to dating men who identified as African American. This change signaled to their friends and parents that they had begun identifying themselves as biracial or black, and it tended to create a gulf between the girls and their white mothers. They began to feel that their mothers could not understand them as biracial or black, and the daughters changed the way they interpreted their interactions with their mothers. As one respondent put it, she no longer saw her mother as "culturally competent" to carry on conversations that addressed racial identity and racism (238).

Because her father is a professor at the local university, Olivia as a character fits precisely into the demographic Twine studied. In fact, her father's status as a professor on campus helps to catalyze Olivia's transformation in identification. Toward the end of the story, Olivia's father is twice characterized as an Uncle Tom figure; black students at a protest rally attack him as "an Uncle Tom, the white administration's puppet, married to the oppressor, hired to appease, and an enemy to the struggle" (78). Olivia, hearing these charges against her father, begins to defend him, now that she knows about his affair with a black woman. Olivia tells her best friend Tonya, "My father's decided to try being black after years of being an Uncle Tom" (74). This recognition is the first time that black identification takes on a positive valence for Olivia. She later tells Tonya, "My mother needs to dump his ass. She sacrificed everything to marry him and now look at how he's acting." The narrator adds, "She said it as if the events signaled some fault of Tonya's" (74). Of course, none of this situation is Tonya's fault, but the fact that Olivia blames Tonya, a white girl, for this issue indicates that, although Olivia is sympathetic with her mother's plight to some extent, she blames her mother for letting her husband cheat on her. This sentiment takes on new force when the girls arrive home and Tonya complains that her own mother never lets her have any freedom to go where she wants, as Olivia does. Olivia's mother responds, "I don't know if it's so much freedom. . . . I guess I just try to take into consideration that my children are, well, half black, and these are difficult times." Olivia listens in astonishment, thinking that "[s]he hated her mother's small, thin mouth, so smugly set in the shape of those words." Her mother continues justifying her decision in what the narrator characterizes as a "new voice of betrayal" by saying that she would be stricter too if her children were white (82–83).

This is the first time in the story when Olivia's mother acknowledges her racial difference from her daughter, and Olivia seems to interpret this statement as her mother's disassociation with her, in treating her differently because of her blackness. Suddenly, Olivia perceives herself as quite separate from her mother and Tonya, imagining that snow begins falling through the roof and onto the kitchen table; she sees the two of them as "two strangers suddenly lit up in the cold winter light. Slowly they disappeared into the whiteness, indistinguishable from all the other white people she knew" (83). At this moment Olivia rejects the light that is part of her own physicality—her mother's white skin.

Olivia chooses to echo her father's sly behavior, solidifying her identification with blackness. When her father arrives home from what she knows to have been a visit to his mistress, Olivia takes advantage of the situation. Instead of showing restraint and obeying the rules of civility—acting whitely, as Frye would put it—Olivia drops the Polaroid of the mistress down the basement stairs, where it lands face-up on the bottom step, waiting for her father to spot it and recognize that she has discovered his infidelity. She imagines "the tremendous changes that lay ahead. They began with her descent into the wintry night, leaving Tonya in her place. From now on, regardless of the lateness of the hour, the changing months, the shift of seasons, the occasions that would mark her growing up, she, Olivia, would come and go in the Corvair as she pleased, unhurried and unquestioned" (86). Like her father and Pam, who are able to sneak out of the house relatively easily, Olivia envisions herself leaving with little interference.

The context of the passage makes it clear that Olivia is not leaving the house just to get a little air: she is out to find some boys for herself, perhaps the same boys she ran into earlier that afternoon with Tonya. Her knowledge of her father's affair makes feasible—or at least facilitates—her own sexual experimentation. Through her behavior, through her choice of action over uncertainty, and through her choice to express her sexuality without limitations, Olivia demonstrates that she has opted out of whiteness and chosen blackness instead.

The story's equation of blackness with sexuality and rule-breaking and whiteness with chastity and rule-abiding behavior re-creates the female sexual economy, but in a new way. As long as Olivia identifies as white, with her mother, the female sexual economy is maintained. Their whiteness and sexual purity are preserved, while only the "blacker" Pam, among the women of the family, finds sexual expression. When Olivia repudiates her mother and her whiteness by choosing to act in a way that she associates with blackness, however, she exceeds the female sexual economy. With Olivia's choice, two women in the family find sexual expression, repudiating the economy. It is only once she decides to identify with her blackness rather than whiteness that Olivia is able to escape the constraints imposed on her to be a "good girl," a white girl, an asexual girl. Olivia's choice to affiliate with blackness enables the thwarting of the sexual economy for her family.

Miller's story, through its careful attention to Olivia's attitudes about race and identification, provides a useful perspective on the ways in which individuals are affected by a racist society that wants to insist on either blackness or whiteness. It is also troubling, however, in its reinforcement of stereotypes about whiteness and blackness. The story could have challenged preconceptions about race through its revelation of the processes of racial identification; instead it associates whiteness with "good" and "moral" behavior, education, civilization, and the upholding of the family unit, while it suggests that blackness is properly associated with immoral and unrestrained sexuality, disdain for the integrity of the family, lying, and cheating. Although Olivia's youth might otherwise excuse her simplistic understanding of race in the story, one of the things that Miller's story accomplishes is the exposure of Olivia's thought processes about race and the way they are shaped by her interactions with other people in a racist society. Moreover, the freedom Olivia gains at the end of the story is tainted by the reader's sense that she is embarking on a campaign of self-destruction. Because she is mimicking her father's behavior and Pam's, it is difficult to see how breaking away from the sexual economy could be construed as positive. On the whole, while the story offers a means for refusing the sexual economy, it suggests that the kind of unrestrained sexual behavior that Olivia, Pam, and their father exhibit is harmful both to its practitioners and to those around them. In other words, the story reinforces white norms regarding proper (sexual) behavior.

Jews Become White Folks: Lore Segal's "Burglars in the Flesh"

Segal's story, first published in the *New Yorker* in 1980, demonstrates the way in which Jewish immigrants can become whitened in the presence of blackness. In this story, Ilka Weissnix, a twenty-two-year-old Austrian Jewish woman who has been living in New York for a year, tries to help her mother, Flora, a recent arrival to the United States, acclimate to her new living situation. With the help of Ilka's cousin Fishgoppel, a student at Yale who speaks only Yiddish and English, the German-speaking Ilka and her mother attempt to adjust to life in the United States after leaving Vienna. Flora is haunted by the memory of Nazi persecution in her native land, and her conversations with her daughter revolve around the resulting nightmares. In many ways—their language, their misapprehensions of American culture, the reason that they have left Vienna for the United States—Ilka and Flora are portrayed as outsiders to white life in the United States. In this story, whiteness is equated with assimilation into American culture— whiteness as Americanness. As immigrants who are not yet fully white, the Weissnixes should not be as influenced by the familial sexual economy as whiter characters would be; against the presence of Ilka's boyfriend, who is black, however, the characters gain in whiteness. As in Ralph Ellison's metaphor of Optic White paint, Segal's story demonstrates that one drop of black makes what is somewhat white into glaring whiteness.[22] Against the blackness of Carter Bayoux, Ilka's boyfriend, Ilka and Flora's whiteness solidifies, and the constraints on their sexual behavior increase. The "flesh" of the story's title is the key to the workings of this story, both in terms of the color of that flesh and in terms of the sexual expression allowed it.

The story's time and place are crucial to understanding the role of Flora and Ilka's Jewishness. While in twenty-first-century America we may consider Jewishness a characteristic of culture rather than of race, Jews were still commonly labeled a separate race into the 1940s.[23] As recently as 1968, Leonard Fein could remark in "Israel's Crisis," "The fact of the matter is that Jews, however much we have accumulated the trappings of American success, are not white. We are not white symbolically, and we are not white literally. . . . We are too much an oppressed people, still, and too much a rejected people, even in this country, to accept the designation 'white'" (qtd. in Jacobson 274). Similarly, James Baldwin, writing in 1984, asserts that Jews' whiteness is historically conditioned:

> It is probable that it is the Jewish community—or more accurately, perhaps, its remnants—that in America has paid the highest and most extraordinary price for becoming white. For the Jews came here from countries where they were not white, and they came here, in part, *because* they were not white; and incontestably—in the eyes of the Black American (and not only in those eyes) American Jews have opted to become white, and this is how they operate. (2)

In this statement whiteness operates both as a racial term and a marker of cultural assimilation, as it does throughout the history of Jews in the United States, as Karen Brodkin and Matthew Frye Jacobson argue. Jews' identity in the United States has been formed in part by their status as immigrants (most come from southern and eastern Europe) and by their religious and cultural differences as Jews. In turn, their racial formation has been influenced both by their class status as immigrants, particularly in the early decades of the twentieth century, and by the pseudoscientific and sociopolitical discourses that linked Jews to Africans and blacks.

Brodkin, in *How Jews Became White Folks*, argues that many of the reasons that Jews were considered what she terms "off-white" or "not-quite-white" stem from their position in the labor market as newly arrived immigrants. Despite the fact that many Jewish immigrants were highly skilled in the garment trade before coming to the United States early in the twentieth century, for example, they could find only unskilled garment jobs upon their arrival. (They were, at the same time, prevented from entering other industries by white labor unions who insisted on whiteness as a precondition of employment.) Brodkin explains that this phenomenon occurs again and again when a new group (immigrants, blacks, women) enters the workforce of almost any industry. Jobs that were formerly considered skilled are suddenly downgraded to unskilled work, but these laborers are expected to reach a new level of intensity, maintaining productivity at the previous rate. Employers could thus pay their employees less without sacrificing their levels of output.

Because the jobs were filled with what were seen as undesirable employees, the characteristics of the kinds of jobs these groups were able to fill became associated with the groups themselves. Thus immigrants (or blacks, or women) were seen as fit to work only in unskilled positions that kept them from moving into the middle class, reinforcing notions that they were lazy and suited for little else. The association between immigrant groups and common occupations bled into social conceptions of the members of that group. Thus, comments Brodkin, "because African American and eastern and southern European immigrants did dirty jobs" in Pennsylvania's steel industry, "this was often proof enough that they too were dirty" (57). Rhetoric that separated these immigrants from "white" Americans was not confined to stereotypes about labor, however. Early twentieth-century censuses used categories for native versus nonnative immigrants, even within the white race. Because immigrants from northern and western Europe were more likely to have arrived in the United States a generation earlier, they could thus classify themselves as "native" immigrants, whereas southern and eastern Europeans were shunted into the nonnative category (60). Further, the 1924 Johnson-Reed Act imposed quotas on immigration from Asia and the less desirable countries of Europe (i.e., mostly eastern and southern nations). Governmental policy until the early 1940s reified the division between "real" whites and the immigrant populations that included most Jews.

In these ways, according to Brodkin, class and race became conflated. Because of the confluence of these two factors, and because race in the United States is traditionally conceived of in terms of duality—white and black—immigrants on the borders of whiteness became socially constructed as black. Writes Brodkin,

> Jews, Puerto Ricans, Irish, and African Americans appeared as different constructions on a rainbow of state-sanctioned not-whitenesses. Although the stereotypes that were applied to them varied in their particulars, the spectrum was still assigned common cultural attributes: men and women alike were characterized as dirty, lascivious, immoral, and either knaves or fools. And the men, whether hypermasculine or effeminate, all lusted after white women. (85)

Stereotypes that Americans commonly held about blacks were, through the process of equating class with race, transferred to immigrant workers.[24] Unflattering portraits of these groups emerged from their work in undesirable jobs. The threat that these groups posed to "true" whites became not only economic, in the sense that "true" whites feared that these not-whites would take their jobs, but also statistical in terms of reproduction. "Real" whites, afraid that immigrants would reproduce so quickly that they would outpace the white population, conceived of these groups in hypersexual terms. As Brodkin puts it, "When immigrants were seen as a necessary part of that working class which did the degraded and driven labor, they were constructed with stereotypes of blackness—stupid, shiftless, sexual, unable to defer gratification" (71). The highly sexualized portrait of "off-white" immigrants that Brodkin paints suggests that Jews, as part of the denigrated immigrant groups, would have been seen in much the same terms.

In part, social discourse that equated Jews with blacks stemmed from earlier preconceptions, often generated by pseudoscientific writings, that the two groups shared common ancestry. Robert Knox, in his mid-nineteenth-century *Races of Man*, described the Jewish race's physical traits:

> Brow marked with furrows or prominent points of bone, or with both; high cheek-bones; a sloping and disproportioned chin; and elongated, projecting mouth, which at the angles threatens every moment to reach the temples; a large, massive, club-shaped, hooked nose, three or four times larger than suits the face—these are features which stamp the African character of the Jew, his muzzle-shaped mouth and face removing him from certain other races. (qtd. in Jacobson 180)

This "African character" could, in 1850, serve as grounds to justify unequal treatment of Jews. Sander L. Gilman notes that the (supposed) likeness of Jewish noses to those of Africans has served as a visible marker not only of race but also of the psychology of the nose bearer:

> The Jew's nose makes the Jewish face visible in the Western Diaspora. That nose is "seen": as an African nose, relating the image of the Jew to the image of the Black. It was not always because of any overt similarity in the stereotypical representation of the two idealized types of noses, but because each nose is considered a racial sign and as such reflects the internal life ascribed to Jew and African no less than it does physiognomy. (71)

Belief that Jews and Africans sprang from the same line was so widespread that newspaper critics reviewing *Porgy and Bess* in 1935 could casually link "George Gershwin's talent for 'American-Negroid music' to the 'common Oriental ancestry in both Negro and Jew'" (Jacobson 5). The perceived link between the black race and Jews underlined the conception of Jews as a race separate from whites. Jacobson cites, for example, headlines of newspapers such as the *Baltimore Sun* and *Detroit Free Press* during the 1930s and early 1940s dealing with Nazi policy, referring to the Nazis' efforts to solve the "race problem" or efforts to exterminate the "Jewish race" (187).

One other factor that may have contributed to fear of and discrimination toward Jews is the fact that, paradoxically, Jews look distinctively Jewish and yet look like everybody else, as Gilman points out.[25] In part, efforts to link Jews to blacks may have functioned to keep Jews at a remove from other whites. While Jews were assumed to look different from non-Jews for a thousand years, Gilman writes, it was such an intangible difference that it often had to be signaled through concrete identifiers, such as the "Jew's cap" or "Jew's badge," the cordoning of Jews in ghettos during the Middle Ages, and even the tattoos in Nazi concentration camps. The need to mark Jews off from other whites, to indicate the very difference that was supposed to be physically obvious, demonstrates a powerful psychological need for non-Jewish whites to separate themselves from Jews. Gilman comments on this mysterious power of Jews to look both Jewish and non-Jewish at the same time: "While Jews were understood to be different, one form of that difference was their uncanny ability to look like everyone else (that is, to look like the idealization of those who wanted to see themselves as different from the Jew)" (70). The schizophrenic definition of Jews as both white and black—just like other whites and simultaneously utterly distinct—speaks to the level of anxiety about identifying Jewishness in the United States.

By the 1940s, the decade in which Segal's story is set, competing forces were at work in shaping Americans' attitudes toward Jews. Charles E. Silberman cites polls conducted between 1940 and 1945, indicating that from one-third to half of Americans would have "sympathized with or actively supported" an anti-Semitic politician's campaign; only 30 percent would have opposed it (57). Even as the war progressed, anti-Semitic feeling failed to wane: between 1940 and 1944, the number of Americans who saw Jews as "a menace to America" actually increased from 17 to 24 percent. (Compare the latter number to the percentage who saw German Americans and Japanese Americans as a similar menace—6 and 9 percent, respectively.) And, notes Silberman, Jews perceived anti-Semitism as so strong even after the war that they Anglicized their names. In the late 1940s and early 1950s, at the peak of the trend, approximately 40,000 Jews each year filed to change their names through state courts. They comprised 80 percent of the total number of Americans who applied for such changes during this period (59).

During roughly the same time period, however, Franklin Roosevelt's New Deal programs began to consolidate social welfare to benefit whites at the expense of African Americans, according to Jacobson: "[I]n part *because* of the centrality of 'Negro-white' relations beginning with the New Deal, many other races were forgotten, too . . . the problematic Letts, Finns, Hebrews, Slavs, and Greeks of 1924 [the Reed-Johnson Act] became ever more 'white' as the politics of segregation overwhelmed the national agenda" (246).[26] Jews became whiter in comparison with the increasingly disenfranchised African American population. Both Brodkin and Jacobson mark the end of World War II as a turning point in the discourse of Jewishness as race. Even though the term *white Jew* had currency during the 1940s— a term that emphasized that the association of whiteness and Jewishness was the exception, not the rule—attitudes were slowly beginning to change, in large part because of the revelation of the Holocaust in Europe.[27] Jacobson describes 1945 as a historical moment "when 'racial' Jewishness was still a live, yet a newly intolerable, conception" (176). Brodkin agrees but notes, "This is not to say that anti-Semitism disappeared after World War II, only that it fell from fashion and was driven underground" (87).

"Burglars in the Flesh" is thus set on the brink of receding anti-Semitism, and while Ilka and Flora do not arrive in the United States at the peak of anti-Jewish feeling, their Jewishness is nonetheless notable when they arrive during the late 1940s.[28] Further, their status as immigrants would have made their social position even less stable. While they hail from Austria rather than one of the less desirable eastern or southern European nations, social attitudes blurring the distinction between Jews from western Europe and those from other sectors would likely have made them targets of some discrimination. Ilka and Flora thus have very slight claims to whiteness in this story; their status is qualified once by their Jewishness and again by their immigrant-ness. It is only against the background of the blackness of Carter, Ilka's boyfriend, that they are rendered discursively white, to paraphrase Robyn Wiegman.

Details of the story help to identify Ilka and her family as outsiders, not yet assimilated into America. Cousin Fishgoppel's unusual name, for example, which translates roughly as "fish fork," and her ability to speak Yiddish immediately mark her as distinctive among the general American population. Fishgoppel's uniqueness even extends to the character of her apartment: on her first morning in the United States, Flora breakfasts in her niece's "sausage-shaped kitchen." The fact that Flora perceives the kitchen as sausage-shaped suggests that she comes from a culture very familiar with that food. At the time, Flora is wearing "her tasseled jacquard dressing gown—a survivor, too, from pre-Hitler mornings of coffee and buttered rolls in Vienna" (32). This passage establishes the time of the scene through the reference to Hitler, but it also emphasizes Flora's origins as generally European and specifically Viennese. A few moments later "Ilka watched her mother pour herself a cup of American coffee, taste it, and grimace" (32). Flora is clearly unaccustomed to American tastes, a fact of which readers are constantly reminded by her continuing complaint that Americans don't know how to cut up chickens properly for goulash. This refrain maintains the gap between Flora and an assimilated American.

While details of dress and taste in food are small reminders that Ilka and Flora are not yet fully American, the difficulty of stumbling through their dialogue reminds us as readers that they are new arrivals. Although Ilka has been in the United States for about a year before her mother's arrival at the beginning of the story, her English is not letter-perfect. She tells Carter that her mother repeats the story of fleeing from the Germans because "my mother enjoys to convict herself" (36). Flora's English is even less comprehensible. Her efforts to communicate to Carter the tale of her flight are so convoluted that they're almost funny, despite the tragedy that underlies her words: "Evei were it, every Sunday, something with my foots, my shoe, never the daddy, Ilka, isn't it? But before Oberpest has he already fevered. How comes it I have farther gone?" (35). Moreover, Segal's story emphasizes that Flora and Ilka are not just any Europeans, and not just any Jews, but Jews persecuted by Hitler's regime. Their Jewishness makes them different, and it is the reason they have undergone such suffering.[29]

While Flora isn't always able to articulate her ideas in English, she is able to express to Ilka in German the force of her constant nightmares. Her recounting of the nightmares establishes the importance of black and white imagery to the theme of the story. The dreams are rooted in three major sources: the clanging of the radiator on winter nights, Flora's excruciating back pain, and her memory of leaving her dying husband on the road to Oberpest on a death march in the final days of the war. These three ideas are expressed, however, in nightmares of ant-like men breaking into the kitchen, banging around trying to assemble a burglaring tool, and stabbing Flora with a knife: "And they walk inside and they start to grow, and they grow and they grow and stand upright, and they are really men except they are ants—you know how ants have shiny black sections, head, middle, and tail end, like three shiny black beads, like black patent leather" (33). Another night, we learn more details of Flora's nocturnal visions: "[T]he two burglars rummaged in their black bag" (33). The association of the nightmare burglars with blackness continues even after Flora revises her original conception of them later in the story: "[T]hey are made out of something completely different [than flesh], not like black beads so much—and nothing *like* patent leather, as I thought at first . . . more like the shiny black parts of a motorcycle" (41). And in her final semilucid words of the story, as she lies in the hospital waiting for tests to determine the cause of her agonizing pain, she declares to Ilka, "The black is their uniform! They are three policemen. That is the real horror" (42).[30]

Flora's conceptions of the "burglars" who cause her so much anguish change with time, but they are always perceived as black. Their evil nature is expressed, for her, in their loud banging in the night (the sound of the radiator, translated into a dream), their sharp knives plunging into her flesh (her back pain), and, worst of all, their affiliation with the police who, in her mind, are equated with the German soldiers who occupied her country and forced her and her husband out. Although all of these associations are negative, there is one point early in the story when Flora believes that the burglars have some potential for upstanding behavior. She explains to Ilka,

> The biggest of the ants must be the father, because he makes them wash up. He asks Daddy where they can wash their hands, please—perfectly polite—and Daddy, very polite, too, bowing, nodding, shows them behind this white sort of folding screen and I'm surprised—this is so peculiar, *in the dream* I am surprised—that there is this row of bowls in the kitchen and they wash their hands and the father makes them *dry* very thoroughly. (32)

In Flora's explanation, the Daddy ant is the force imposing civilization on the younger ones. Whereas the ants' usual behavior consists of loud clanging, moving around behind her back to attack her, and giving her generally menacing looks, in this dream Flora sees the ants behaving almost as if Miss Manners were directing them—asking polite questions, washing up, and drying their hands thoroughly. Importantly, in this passage Flora mentions nothing of the ants' blackness. In fact, their polite behavior occurs mostly behind the shield of a white screen. From Flora's perspective, the ants' blackness is hidden by the screen, which blocks her direct view of them. It is thus only while the ants are whitened by the intervening screen that they behave as civilized beings, that they can represent positive values and demonstrate the potential to change their wicked ways.

The image of black ants behind a white screen is only one of several juxtapositions of the two colors. In other cases, however, the images are usually positioned against Carter's blackness. For example, when Ilka is preparing her mother for Carter's visit, she asks Flora not to tell any of her stories, which, she claims, would only repeat what's been all over the newspapers and radio. When her mother protests, Ilka becomes frustrated and says, "The point is, Carter is a Negro and they have their own stories" (34). Against the relief of Carter's stories, Flora's become not just Jewish or European but white. This contrast reappears when Carter tells Ilka about his first marriage: "Bonnie was my first wife, a white girl—when we were just out of high school. She used to love my dad's slave stories. I tell you my dad was born a slave?" (36). The fact that Carter's father was a slave makes him even blacker, an idea that is presented together with the fact of his first wife's whiteness. In fact, it was her fascination with his father's blackness that was, from Carter's perspective, her primary attraction to him.

Stories are not the only illustrations of such a contrast between whiteness and blackness. Some of Carter's other comments also help to establish a pattern of ideology that associates whiteness with intellect and blackness with the body. Flora, anxious to distance herself from the responsibility for decorating their apartment when Carter is visiting, tries to communicate that the furniture was chosen by Fishgoppel. Carter, catching her meaning, replies, "I have met Fishgoppel, and I'd guess her mind works at such a white heat it would shrivel away any thoughts of furniture" (35). Fishgoppel's brilliance is not simply Carter's perception; the narrator notes a few pages later that "Fishgoppel had done well—had done spectacularly—on her examinations" (37). A graduate student at Yale, she is clearly the most intellectual of the four characters; of the three family members, she is also the most Americanized, and thus the whitest. Carter, on the other hand, recognizes that he bears associations with corporeal matters, and not simply because of his corpulence. On another occasion, Carter tells Ilka that one of his friends proposed a way to solve the "Negro problem" once and for all: "Get it disseminated to all white folk: We don't do it so good either."[31] Carter acknowledges that he may attract white women simply because of the color of his skin and a stereotype that black men possess unusual sexual prowess.[32] In fact, Carter has had so many wives—has been so magnetic in his sexuality— that he confesses to Ilka that he's ashamed of himself, and he refuses to tell her the precise number.

By giving Carter a slave ancestor and highlighting his sexual abilities, the narrator completes the image of Carter as possessing many of the stereotypes of black men. Moreover, Carter is an alcoholic, and one of his binges results in his being carted off to the asylum. His disease also apparently prevents him from maintaining a stable job, since he normally lives in a hotel, and the narrator never mentions what Carter does for a living. Fit together, these elements characterize Carter as a sexual predator, a relatively uneducated drunkard, and the son of a slave who can't hold down a job or keep a wife.[33] No wonder, then, that Fishgoppel thinks of him (and the narrator refers to him several times) as the "wrongest man in America." In the abstract, Carter's description could be seen as a stereotype taken to the level of caricature. Such an image matches up well with the emphasis on Ilka and Flora as Jews fleeing the Holocaust, the quintessential image of Jewishness at that time. Ilka's remark to her mother that she needn't tell any more Jewish stories, that "[t]hey've been in the papers, they've been in the newsreels at the movies, on the radio" (34), demonstrates the saturation of American media with the stories of Jewish refugees.

Taken together, the powerful blackness imagery associated with Flora's nightmare "burglars" and Carter's racial blackness suggest that Carter himself might be a "burglar in the flesh." Read this way, one possible interpretation is that Flora objects to Carter stealing her child.[34] Flora's imagined association between the burglaring ants and the police in their black uniforms and the repeated labeling of Carter as the "wrongest man in America" suggests that he is himself a kind of burglar. Yet Flora's behavior belies this sentiment. At the end of Carter's first visit, she invites him to visit again, offering, "I will make you a goulash, but not like by us! In America knows nobody how cuts one properly up a chicken" (36). Her enthusiasm for Ilka's relationship with Carter is expressed later in the story when she asks her daughter, "Why don't you marry him?" Flora says this not in a teasing way, but because, she adds, in a rare moment of linguistic clarity, "I understand that you like him. . . . I understand it is not good for a man like that to live alone" (40). Flora clearly not only approves of the relationship but also shows insight into his character.

Flora may understand Carter because the two of them are so similar: although Flora is portrayed in the story as a very thin, very Jewish invalid who acts quite aged, she actually has quite a lot in common with the portly black Carter. For example, the two share a fear of New York City, baffling to Ilka. While Flora's fear of the city, and the subway in particular, is the newcomer's dread of unfamiliar places, Carter's is the learned fear of a city dweller. The two are also the same age, a surprising fact that we learn only at the very end of the story. Flora and Carter both have a propensity for craziness as well. While Carter's stems from his alcoholism—after a particularly rough binge the police take him "[t]o the nuthouse" (40)—Ilka believes that her mother is going crazy because she is so haunted by what seem to her irrational dreams: "Ilka yearned to lay her head down on her mother's lap and say, 'Help me. If you are going crazy, I won't know what to do'" (39). The story ends with Flora in the hospital, telling Ilka that the ant-men are going to cut her and that they must because it is the law. Her last words to Ilka are a response to the doctor's conversation with Ilka, which, because it is in English, she does not understand. She conflates the doctor with the ant-men of her dreams: "*Now* are they going to do it? I don't understand what is happening" (42). Those last words cause us as readers, much as Ilka does, to question her sanity in the face of such extreme pain.

Flora's commonalities with Carter, especially because they are emphasized at the end of the story, make this story in some ways the tale of Ilka falling in love with a black male version of her mother. From a psychoanalytic perspective, Ilka can be seen as stuck in a pre-oedipal attachment to her mother, which is expressed in a more appropriate form (albeit only slightly more appropriate, from Fishgoppel's point of view) as her affection for Carter. This interpretation makes sense, given that at many other points in the story, Ilka acts in a rather childish manner. She gets fed up with her mother's extended recounting of her nightmares, prompting her mother to hurry up and continue every time she takes a breath with "And . . . ." When she is unable to reach Fishgoppel to share her worries over her mother's sanity, she riffles through the phone book aimlessly rather than taking any other sort of action, until, a few days later, she is fairly well convinced that her mother is going crazy. Despite this realization, when Carter calls to invite her to visit him in the Connecticut countryside, Ilka immediately abandons her mother. Her mother is so ill, however, that Fishgoppel calls Ilka within a matter of hours to return to New York and take her mother to the hospital. Ilka's immature behavior and impulsiveness emphasize her status as the child of the story. Her immaturity relative to her mother is further stressed through Flora's behavior, because she acts far older than her chronological age. The normal temporal gulf between mother and daughter is increased by Ilka's acting like a young child and Flora's acting like a much older woman.

This situation also highlights the sexuality—or apparent lack thereof—of the characters. Ilka's sexuality evokes the unhampered eroticism of a child: she is free to sleep with even the "wrongest man in America." Her mother, on the other hand, presents herself as an invalid, rarely straying from the apartment, perpetually weary and always complaining about ailments physical and psychological. Ilka's lover is a man portrayed in a highly sexualized light, while Flora, wasting away, is entirely desexualized; her only encounters with men are with Carter and the Polish refugee who works at the butcher's, who she hopes will be able to cut up a chicken properly. Yet the sexualities of mother and daughter in this story are exactly the opposite of traditional Jewish norms of sexual conduct for unmarried and married women.

As Brodkin explains, Jewish communities in the United States generally had few restrictions on unmarried women but carefully regulated married women's sexuality. Unmarried daughters were presumed to be virgins and therefore unaware of sexual pleasures, so they "were not seen as sexual beings in need of social and/or ritual regulation" (114). Instead, the energies of the community were focused on married women: "Because a woman became sexually wise once she married, she could not then go about so freely in public. If she were to attract the attentions of other men, she would threaten her husband's honor. . . . In Jewish culture, married women were potential seducers whose behavior needed to be regulated socially and ritually" (115). The community had strict regulations meant to maintain married women's purity and to neutralize their ability to attract the sexual attentions of men who were not their husbands. For example, women's hair was believed to arouse men, so women shaved their heads and wore wigs; women also were required to take ritual baths each month after their periods before resuming sexual contact with their husbands. Indeed, it seems that society's energies were so focused on reining in the sexuality of married women that it tended to overlook the possible sexual impulses of the daughters, as Brodkin comments. Jewish daughters were portrayed in literature by Jewish authors as intelligent and ambitious, she notes, but fictional accounts had little to say about their quests or even longing for sexual love. Even in feminist writing, Brodkin notes with surprise, she "found scarcely anything about sex and the Jewish girl!" (130).

The contrast between usual norms for female sexuality in the Jewish community (of which Segal would presumably be aware) and those expressed in this story reinforce the way in which Ilka and Flora are comparatively whitened—Americanized—through Carter's presence. While married women like Flora, who had already experienced sex, were seen as likely seductresses if left free of the checks of community regulation, in this story middle-aged Flora is the least sexy person possible—barely alive, and hardly a danger to other women's husbands. Ilka, on the other hand, who should be innocent of sex because she is not married, indulges in sex at every opportunity—so many times that her mother begins counting the number of times she leaves the house to see Carter. As women whose racial identities are moving toward whiteness, Ilka and Flora are constrained by the sexual economy. This fact holds true despite the fact that Ilka's relationship with Carter both whitens her in comparison and keeps her on the edges of whiteness because of her choice of a black sexual partner.

Flora and Ilka's status as Jewish refugees should thwart their identification as white Americans, but when they exist in the relief of Carter's blackness—a man who, like other African Americans of the time, was only barely American himself in terms of social acceptance and civil rights—they become comparatively white. Like other immigrants, they find social mobility at the expense of blacks; as critics including Brodkin, Jacobson, and David R. Roediger have shown, groups that have become whitened in America have found social mobility at the price of leaving blacks at the bottom of the social pecking order. Without Carter's shadow shifting their whiteness into relief, Ilka and her mother (in her middle-aged sexual prime) might have each had the freedom to pursue sexually fulfilling lives outside the sexual economy, since by the standards of 1940s America they are only barely white. The end of the story provides hope (if that's the word for it) that Ilka might eventually find herself fully Americanized: the story's continued comparisons of Carter and Flora suggests that, much as Flora seems to be failing by the final words, Carter may not have much longer to live either.[35] If Ilka can only end her fascination with black men as sexual partners, she will continue her progress toward whiteness. Her victory, should it be achieved, will not come without a price: assimilation into America will require the loss of sexual freedom (if not the loss of life) for her mother and the loss of her first love in her new country.

Cuban Cross-Dressing: Achy Obejas's "We Came All The Way From Cuba so You Could Dress Like This?"

Obejas's story also tells the tale of an immigrant family in the United States. In this case the family hails from Cuba and the year is 1963. The story, originally published in *Michigan Quarterly Review* and collected in an anthology of the same title in 1994, portrays a narrator and her family who live on the edges of whiteness. This tale demonstrates the possibility of some flexibility in the female sexual economy as a consequence of the family's ethnic and racial positioning in the United States, since Cubans as a group already exist on the borders between white and Latino identity. The sexual economy is also complicated by the narrator's sexual behavior, since she chooses to sleep with both women and men. Because the founding texts of the female sexual economy (by Friday, Dinnerstein, and Chodorow) presuppose heterosexuality, this situation presents a challenge to the functioning of the economy even while it in many ways merely shifts the terms of the identification equation from mother-daughter to father-daughter to explain the narrator's choices. Although at the beginning of the story both mother and daughter are endowed with sexual potential, once the narrator begins to assimilate into American culture—that is, once she begins to become white—we find that the sexual economy reappears.[36] Like Ilka and Flora, the whiter the narrator becomes, the less freedom she and her mother have to find sexual expression. The more closely the narrator approaches whiteness, the more she is constrained by the economy; her rebellion against it through her sexual behavior and her return to her Cuban roots offers her the possibility of reprieve from it.

The family's Cuban origins place them in the racial borderlands of the United States. Because of their unique history and situation, Cubans are a minority even within the Latina/o category: according to Richard Delgado and Jean Stefancic, they comprise only five percent of the total U.S. Latina/o population (xvii). In fact, Cubans are so marginal to this group's experience that Delgado and Stefancic's anthology *The Latino/a Condition* includes only three mentions of Cuba in its 700 pages. Berta Esperanza Hernández-Truyol, in one of those three references, testifies to Cubans' rhetorical exclusion from the category Latina/o, confirming their marginal position: a "Cuban was not deemed not to be one of 'us,' even among a group of Latinas/os . . . sometimes the first wave of Cuban refugees, because of their education and professional status, are viewed more like the majority, the privileged" (27). Obejas's fictional family, part of this initial wave of Cuban émigrés, fits this description, placing them near, but not quite within, the category reserved for native-born white Americans. As Miguel Gonzalez-Pando has noted, U.S. media have created an image of Cubans as a homogenous group, "glamorizing the Cuban exiles as model émigrés—white, well educated, and enterprising" (x). Moreover, because many Cubans consider themselves political exiles rather than immigrants, they have rhetorically refused to be assimilated into U.S. racial categories. In short, Cubans are not easily defined as a racial group in a country whose population prefers the simplicity of black or white.

The history of Cuba has itself contributed to the precarious status of Cuban arrivals to the United States. Cuba has had a complicated relationship with its mix of races.[37] Antonio Benítez-Rojo notes that Cuba had a unique racial constitution in the eighteenth century, with a relatively small ratio of slaves to free blacks rather than large numbers of slaves and only a handful of freedmen, as in other Caribbean nations (68–69, 320). Moreover, only Haiti was more influenced by African cultures than Cuba among Antillean nations. The strong African influences and sizable black population may have contributed to a delay in seeking national independence; as Benítez-Rojo explains, many of Cuba's nonblack inhabitants feared that the country's independence would have meant the end of slavery, resulting in a free population that was 60 percent black (122). Yet Jose Martí's nineteenth-century revolutionary rhetoric that Cuba should be a nation "with all and for all" helped to subsume such racial anxieties, sending them underground. Alejandro de la Fuente suggests that since the late nineteenth century the ideal of *cubanidad* (Cubanness) has downplayed racial differences by suggesting that they threaten national unity ("The Resurgence" 30). Yet this attitude has acted more to silence public discourse on racism than to effect the end of discrimination, de la Fuente adds.[38]

In the early decades of the twentieth century, U.S. attitudes toward Cuba were largely founded on perceptions of the island's races. As Lisa Brock and Bijan Bayne point out, between 1900 and 1930 "the Caribbean and Latin America as a whole were largely cast as 'black' and 'female' as justification for U.S. penetration and domination: They were too Indian, too mestizo, too black, too female, and too childlike to join the world of white masculine nations" (187). Cuban intellectuals, and particularly those who were part of the Afrocubanista cultural movement, responded to what they perceived as racist North American attitudes by continuing to encourage *mestizaje* (racial mixing) during the late 1920s and early 1930s, according to Alejandro de la Fuente (*A Nation for All*).[39] This notion became so tied to the idea of *cubanidad* that flagrant acts of discrimination were treated as sources of national shame (15–16). Cuba's pride in its history of *mestizaje* can be seen, as Evelio Grillo recounts, in the custom of Cuban men calling their female lovers *mi negrita* (my little black one), a tradition that has carried on from the Spanish occupiers of the island, who took black women as their concubines or wives. Grillo remarks that this pet name is applied to women both black and white and comments that "[i]t is a term of endearment which is considered a special part of love-making" (11). The net effect of these attitudes was that, by the late 1920s, despite government efforts to "whiten" the population by attracting European immigrants, Cuba could no longer claim to be white (de la Fuente, *A Nation for All* 177). *Mestizaje* had taken hold of the island.

In the decade surrounding the revolution, Cubans witnessed dramatic social and economic changes. As Louis A. Pérez, Jr., explains, the 1950s were a time of tension for the population, as all social classes suffered from an increased cost of living combined with an increase in unemployment (175). Most Cubans found that they could no longer maintain the quality of life to which they had become accustomed. The anxiety of the middle class, especially the white middle class, only grew when Fidel Castro took power in 1959. According to de la Fuente, rumors circulated at the time that Fulgencio Batista, the deposed dictator, had been supported mostly by blacks because of his mestizo (mixed-race) ancestry; whites, therefore, were hopeful that their situation might improve under Castro. Castro, however, recognized that he could make ideological progress against the United States by combating racism in his own country, thereby gaining the support of other nations. By framing the issue as one of class privilege that the revolution would eliminate, Castro claimed that Cuba would be able to rid itself of racial discrimination. He called for a series of national debates on racism that would free the island of its influences; more than ever, instances of racism became cause for national embarrassment (*A Nation for All* 18, 266). By 1962, Cuban public officials were already talking about racism and discrimination in the past tense, and the Second Declaration of Havana, issued in February 1962, declared that Castro's revolution had "eradicated discrimination because of race or sex" (de la Fuente, "The Resurgence" 31). Public discussions of racial inequality were silenced; there was no need to debate what no longer existed.[40]

For many middle- and upper-class Cubans, Castro's coup represented the end of their hopes for affluence, and large numbers of mostly white Cubans—including the family in Obejas's story—departed the island for Miami in the years immediately following 1959 (de la Fuente, *A Nation for All* 276).[41] The United States that they encountered, however, often refused to recognize them as white; it had historically treated Cubans as black. For example, Brock and Bayne, in their study of Cuban baseball players in U.S. leagues, found that most Americans considered Cubans blacks, no matter how white they may have looked, prior to the 1950s' integration of black and white teams (184). Even players who looked white enough to be included on major league teams faced racial slurs; Brock and Bayne cite player Ossie Bluege, who recalled, "In those days, all Cuban ball players were called niggers" (185). De la Fuente notes that Cubans were the target of segregationist practices in the United States just as African Americans were: in 1915, a Tampa beach sported a billboard reading "Cubans not admitted" in 1915; around 1920 a Virginia governor banned Negroes, "China men," and Cubans from "official institutions" (*A Nation for All* 177). Similarly, Gonzalez-Pando interviewed one émigré who recalled signs in Miami reading "No Cubans, no pets, and no children" (37).

This treatment was particularly surprising to the recent Cuban émigrés because many of them had long considered themselves friends of the United States. Gonzalez-Pando notes that some of the émigrés were quite familiar with U.S. culture already; as well-off Cubans, they would have vacationed in nearby Florida (90). Pérez remarks, "Vast numbers of Cubans had redefined themselves and in varying degrees identified with ways and things North American . . . no other attribute characterized large sectors of the Cuban upper and middle classes more than their identification with the United States" (176–177). The earliest groups of émigrés were, as Gonzalez-Pando has stated, generally well-educated professionals and visibly white, within the boundaries of Cuban society, but the United States had a legal and social tradition of treating those with one drop of "black blood" as black.

Social treatment of the first wave of Cuban immigrants differed dramatically from official governmental support. Cuban refugees fleeing Castro's revolution served U.S. ideological interests during the Cold War era, and the American government supported them to an unprecedented degree, as Linda Martín Alcoff has described. These immigrants benefited from language training, loans for education and business, assistance in locating jobs, housing allocations, and legal recognition of their professional degrees from Cuba "to an extent other Third World immigrants still envy" (36). President Johnson's Great Society programs, begun in 1965, further increased government assistance to Cuban immigrants (36). Finally, the Cuban Adjustment Act of 1966 allowed Cubans in the United States to become American residents or naturalized citizens without going through the same process that refugees from other countries had to endure (Gonzalez-Pando 45). U.S. governmental treatment of refugees from the Cuban Revolution is unique in our history.

In part, those refugees were treated so well because their departure from Cuba was motivated not by a desire for improvement in economic status but by a fear of what they'd lose under Castro's government; their racial characteristics and socioeconomic status, however, undoubtedly contributed to their treatment. Later waves of

Cuban immigrants, less white and less financially secure, faced a very different reception. Those who arrived as part of the Mariel Boatlift in 1980, commonly called the Marielitos, were forced to live in refugee camps for months; the lucky ones who were not deported were finally released into U.S. society with almost no governmental assistance. They joined the workforce at the level of other working-class Hispanic immigrants, such as Puerto Ricans and Dominicans (Alcoff 36). In contrast, Cubans and Cuban Americans who had arrived in the earliest waves of immigration during the 1960s had firmly established themselves economically by the 1980s: their average household income was nearly equivalent to the national norm, and over one-fifth of households reported incomes of $50,000 or more—roughly double the national average for Hispanics at the time (Gonzalez-Pando 125).

The influx of immigrants from Latin America and the Caribbean into the United States triggered a national debate about how to categorize these new residents. Starting in 1980, the Census Bureau included new ethnicity options for the racial category "white": Hispanic and non-Hispanic. This change was an attempt to recognize that Hispanics could be white; as Neil Foley puts it, "Hispanic identity thus implies a kind of 'separate but equal' whiteness—whiteness with a twist of salsa, enough to make one ethnically flavorful and culturally exotic without, however, compromising one's racial privilege as a White person" (49). (Although first-wave Cuban immigrants are generally accepted within the category *Hispanic*, according to Suzanne Oboler, their inclusion as part of the group *Latino/a* is more contested.) Although the new Hispanic category was meant to defuse the racialization of immigrants, it instead seems to have encouraged a profusion of new racial categories. Alcoff cites a study of SAT scores reported in the *Chronicle of Higher Education* that breaks down students' performance across a number of discrete "racial" categories including Hispanic, Mexican American, and Puerto Rican (33). Clearly, efforts to recognize a Hispanic ethnic dimension as an overlay to racial categories have not entirely succeeded.

Because of the confusion that surrounds the racial categorization of Hispanic immigrants and the further confusion that accompanies Cuban immigrants' racial and ethnic inclusion in that category, contemporary Cuban Americans still face challenges in identifying themselves within the contradictory grammar of race in the United States. Maria de los Angeles Torres, for example, writing in 1995, says of her travels between Cuba and the United States: "I am 'white' when I wake up in Havana, but I am 'other' because of my migratory experience.

I am again 'other' when I journey the thirty minutes through airspace to Miami, because I am no longer 'white.' . . . I arrive in Chicago, and again I am other, now because I am Latina in a city which is defined in black and white" (36). Flavio Risech echoes her when he writes in the same year: "In a sense I and others like me change race when we cross this border: only a profoundly coded *cambio de piel*—a kind of cross-dressing involving shifting between two very different social constructs of race—could make it possible for me to be a *blanquito* there and a latino and therefore something of a 'person of color' here" (58–59).

The narrator in Obejas's story finds herself in a similar position, caught between her native Cuban culture and the racial attitudes of the United States. She recounts the story of her family's beginnings in the United States from the perspective of an adult who has now acculturated herself to her new home but who poignantly recognizes the ways in which she was on the fringes of society as a child. Her arrival in the United States in 1963 as a Cuban immigrant places her very much in what Gloria Anzaldúa has termed "the borderlands": most saliently to the narrator's childhood self, she cannot speak the dominant language, she is not familiar with the economic structures of the new country (represented by a baffling trip to an overwhelming array of options at the grocery), and she is an observant Catholic rather than a majority Protestant. As the story unfolds, it reveals that she is also positioned outside the sphere of dominance through her poverty, her ethnicity, and even her age.

In her first few hours in the United States, the narrator experiences the power of assumptions about her identity. For example, the Hungarian INS worker constantly draws attention to her own hatred of the Communists in her homeland, hoping to create an affinity with the new immigrants. The INS officer assumes that they share a common loathing for Communism everywhere, and she communicates with the family on this basis. An even more provocative example of this attitude occurs during the family's wait at the processing center. To make the young narrator feel more comfortable, a volunteer locates a Colombian woman who can speak with her. Again, although the two people share only a language, they are assumed by the volunteer to be kindred spirits. Yet even the Colombian woman makes her own assumptions about the narrator. When the woman pulls out a Bible, the narrator tells her that she is Catholic, and the Colombian woman says that "well, she was once Catholic, too, but then she was saved and became something else. She says everything will change for me in the United States, as it did for her" (116). This woman predicts that the narrator, too, will be "saved" from Catholicism and convert to the normative Protestantism of the United States.[42]

Even more unsettling is the fact that the Colombian woman, after only a few minutes with the girl, claims to recognize that the ten-year-old narrator, like herself, must suppress her attraction to women. "She says there's . . . a problem, an impulse, which she has to suppress by reading the Bible. She looks at me as if I know what she's talking about" (116). The woman begins reading from her Spanish Bible: "Your breasts are like two fawns, twins of a gazelle that feed upon the lilies. Until the day breathes and the shadows flee, I will hie me to the mountain of myrrh and the hill of frankincense. You are all fair, my love; there is no flaw in you" (116–117). This erotic passage from Song of Solomon, spoken by a lover to his beloved, is a peculiar choice of reading given that the listener is sitting at a government processing center, across from her parents. That the poem is read by one female to another disrupts the assumed heterosexuality of the loving pair in the biblical text, and the Spanish language serves as a cover for the Colombian woman's erotic impulses toward the child narrator; she uses their common language to explore her assumptions about the girl. The reader's reaction to this scene may be like that of the narrator's mother: when the narrator reports to her that the Colombian woman read sections of the Bible, the account "makes my mother shudder" (120).

Despite the fact that other characters make assumptions about her similarities to them, the narrator is sensitive to her difference from others. Her consciousness of her status as an outsider in this new country is particularly pronounced in her awareness of race in the people she sees around her. At first glance, her observations seem to be objective descriptions of her surroundings. For example, when her family arrives at their first American lodging, a hotel, the narrator describes it as having "a view of an alley from which a tall black transvestite plies her night trade" (122).[43] Years later, as an adult she goes to the Cuban Interests Section in Washington, DC, to apply for a visa to visit Cuba and speaks with "a golden-skinned man with the dulled eyes of a bureaucrat" (125). The narrator also repeatedly mentions two notable blond lovers throughout the story, pondering, "I wonder, if we'd stayed [in Cuba] then who, if anyone—if not Martha and the boy from the military academy—would have been my blond lovers, or any kind of lovers at all" (125). Clearly her awareness of race is tied up in her identification with Cuba, since she would not have had the opportunity to find many blond lovers had her family remained there. The narrator's heightened consciousness of race is that of a person whose affinity with whiteness is contested, not someone who is secure in her white privilege. Her awareness of racialized bodies hints that her own racial identity may be in question.

Two incidents in the story extend the narrator's examination of race beyond the cursory, deepening our understanding of the marginal position that she and her family occupy. The first event takes place on the first day of the family's arrival in the United States, while they are waiting in the processing center. A volunteer from Catholic Charities spots the young narrator and offers her three gifts: "oatmeal cookies, a plastic doll with blond hair and a blue dress, and a rosary made of white plastic beads" (114). These gifts serve to demonstrate the narrator's relationship to whiteness, which here is equated with (U.S.) Americanness. The doll, as it turns out, is the most lasting of the three gifts. The fact that the narrator takes note of the doll's blonde hair and blue dress (in contrast to her own green sweater, which shares no colors with the American flag) signals the doll's difference from her own appearance and underlines the recurrence of blond lovers throughout the story. The plastic doll, like the plastic rosary beads, might seem manufactured for obsolescence, but in fact it becomes a permanent reminder of this day. The narrator recalls an image of herself upon leaving the processing center that day: "I'm still clutching the doll, a thing I'll never play with but which I'll carry with me all my life, from apartment to apartment, one move after the other. Eventually, her little blond nylon hairs will fall off, and, thirty years later, after I'm diagnosed with cancer, she'll sit atop my dresser, scarred and bald like a chemo patient" (115). The narrator never identifies with this doll in the way that young girls are supposed to; instead, the doll becomes a fixture, a decoration. It is only when the doll's blond hair falls out, in seeming solidarity with the narrator's own experience of treatment for cancer, that the narrator feels some sense of identification with her.[44] This change signals the adult narrator's recognition of her own integration into white American culture, even if it is at the price of baldness.

The narrator's mother dreams of a whiter life for her daughter, a life that matches the narrator's eventual identification with the doll. The narrator describes her mother's wishes for her future:

Here's what my mother dreams I will be in the United States of America: The owner of many appliances and a rolling green lawn; mother of two mischievous children; the wife of a boyishly handsome North American man who drinks Pepsi for breakfast; a career woman with a well-paying position in local broadcasting.

> My mother pictures me reading the news on TV at four and home at the dinner table by six. She does not propose that I will actually do the cooking, but rather that I'll oversee the undocumented Haitian woman my husband and I have hired for that purpose. She sees me as fulfilled, as she imagines she is. (117)

The life that the narrator's mother imagines for her daughter is founded on American material culture. The "rolling green lawn," the many time-saving appliances, and the ocean of Pepsi her husband will consume—all of these are, to her mother, symbols of success and, in America, symbols of middle-class whiteness.[45] The career that her mother imagines for her in local broadcasting might be the life of a Latina woman who embraces her ethnic roots, especially in a major city like Miami or Chicago (the two locales in which the story is set), but it is pointedly contrasted against the life of the "undocumented Haitian woman" who serves the family dinner. In comparison with this woman, the narrator gains in relative whiteness: her professional employment, legal refugee and middle-class status, and Cuban ethnicity trump the Haitian woman's illegal presence in the country as she works for poverty-level wages. To use Troy Duster's metaphor, in the presence of the imagined Haitian woman, the narrator's normally fluid racial status hardens into a block of comparatively white ice. The "boyishly handsome North American" husband completes the picture of white suburban bliss, confirming the narrator's status as white through heterosexual marriage.

While the gifts from the Catholic Charities volunteer and her mother's dreams for her illuminate the narrator's racial marginality, her father's dreams for her future demonstrate how gender and sexuality operate to further complicate her position. Her father, says the narrator, imagines that she will be a lawyer and judge in the United States. She qualifies that statement immediately afterward, however: "Not that he actually believes in democracy—in fact—he's openly suspicious of the popular will—but he longs for the power and prestige such a career would bring, and which he can't achieve on his own now that we're here, so he projects it all on me" (117). Moreover, her father's vision for her future has none of the familial accoutrements that his wife pictures for their child. "My father," notes the narrator, "does not envision me in domestic scenes. He does not imagine me as a wife or mother because to do so would be to imagine someone else closer to me than he is, and he cannot endure that. He will never regret not being a grandfather; it was never part of his plan" (117). Her father's ideal career is one that is usually associated with whiteness, much as her mother envisions her in a life inflected by whiteness, but more than that, it is a life that stereotypically belongs to white men. The existence the narrator's father imagines is not one of balancing work and family in an idyllic suburb but rather one solely focused on work, and specifically work that allows her to attain power and prestige in the United States. Sexuality is completely absent from his vision; it is as if, for him, the ultimate whiteness—the ultimate success—is completely abstracted from embodied desires.

The parents' dreams demonstrate their wishes for their daughter to become whiter—richer, more powerful—versions of themselves. The narrator says of her mother's dream, "She sees me as fulfilled, as she imagines she is." While the mother's dream for her daughter improves on her own lot in several important ways—her daughter has a career as a TV news anchor rather than a hotel maid, is released from the drudgery of domestic chores through the assistance of the undocumented Haitian woman, and is blessed with two boys rather than one girl[46]—her dream reflects her own life through its combination of work and family. The narrator's father, on the other hand, is desperately unhappy with his identity as a worker in the United States, and he therefore projects his desire for career fulfillment onto his daughter. While the narrator reveals that her mother worked as a maid in a luxury hotel in the United States, we know only that her father worked at a bank—nothing of his position. The father's investment in work as a form of identity is underlined when the narrator, as a college student, accuses her father of using her merely as an excuse for emigration: "Look, you didn't come for me, you came for you; you came because all your rich clients were leaving, and you were going to wind up a cashier in your father's hardware store if you didn't leave, okay?" Her father responds with startling violence to the charge that he has displaced his own desires onto her: "And then my father will reach over my mother's thin shoulders, grab me by the red bandanna around my neck, and throw me to the floor, where he'll kick me over and over until all I remember is my mother's voice pleading, Please stop, please, please, please stop" (121).

This incident highlights the father's deeply embedded identification with his daughter. When the narrator tries to break with it by pointing out that he had separate motives for leaving than simply her own well-being, he brutally rejects her attempt to separate from him, even if her effort is merely verbal. He imagines his daughter as a successful lawyer who takes all the satisfaction of her life from her job and has no outside passions. Moreover, when the college-aged narrator expresses to her parents her wish to visit Cuba, the land of her birth, her father declares that she will make the trip "[o]ver [his] dead body" (125). When the narrator later learns that she must find her old Cuban passport in order to make the trip and asks her parents if she can have it, her father responds, "Do you think I would let you betray us like that?" (126). To her father's way of thinking, her attempt to claim an identity that he has now set aside, much as he has set aside the family's passports in the safe deposit box, represents a rejection of his choices.[47] Ironically, the father was the one member of the family so distraught over his inability to return to Cuba safely that he tried to take his own life.

Although the narrator outwardly tries to break away from her father, she is also deeply ambivalent about their relationship. For example, she says of her father's impending death, "When my father dies, I will feel sadness and a wish that certain things had been said, but I will not want more time with him" (127). While she experiences loss at his death, her remark carries none of the sense of affinity with her father that he clearly felt with her. Yet her behavior belies any total rejection of identification with her father, for at the memorial service, she finds herself mimicking him: "I'll be in the lobby smoking a cigarette, a habit I despised in my father but which I'll pick up at his funeral" (128). It's as if she has taken up her father's place by carrying on his torch, so to speak. Similarly, his death frees her to return to Cuba, which, while clearly against her father's wishes, also fulfills one of his deeply held aspirations. After the funeral, the narrator discovers that he had kept a list of things to take back to Cuba, stored with other cherished possessions such as his university diploma and a newspaper clipping from the day of the family's arrival in the United States. The faded list is testament to her father's undying desire to return to his homeland. By traveling in his place, the narrator manages both to defy her father and continue his legacy.

The narrator's sexual choices combine the same respect for her father's wishes with her rebellion against them. Although she remains childless, it is not out of any repression of sexuality; the story is peppered with memories of her lovers. Even when she was only ten years old, she drew the erotic attention of the Colombian volunteer, a sign of things to come. Near the beginning of the story, she remembers,

> For all the blond boyfriends I will have, there will be only two yellow-haired lovers. One doesn't really count—a boy in a military academy who subscribes to Republican politics like my parents . . . who will try, relatively unsuccessfully, to penetrate me on a south Florida beach. I will squirm away from underneath him, not because his penis hurts me but because the stubble on his face burns my cheek. (115)

This is the narrator's only mention of a male sexual partner, despite the fact that the memory of the blond boy is prefaced with a statement indicating that she had a number of other blond boyfriends. Among her female lovers, she recalls a Cuban political writer, a blonde "gold digger" named Martha, and "all the girls before and after her here in the United States" (115, 126). The most important of them, the lover who earns the most thorough account of the relationship, is a fellow Cuban woman, "a politically controversial exile writer of some repute" (126). Whereas the narrator's previous lovers (who are blond and thus presumably white) have responded with "oh baby baby" or "ooohhh ooooohh-hhh" during sex, this woman cries, "*Aaaaaayyyyyyaaaaaaayyyyaaaaay*" (126). The relationship with the writer is the only one whose end is not mentioned, suggesting that it is the most lasting, and that their shared Cuban background is the basis for its success. Although the narrator has no dearth of lovers, her involvement with them does not violate her father's wishes for her. She knows that he could not endure the thought of her being closer to another man or even a child than she is to him, and, by becoming neither a wife nor a mother, she fulfills his hopes. By finding her most fulfilling relationships with nonwhite lovers, however, she also challenges his wish for her to become white.

Together with her ambivalent identification with her father, the narrator's behavior, whether it is construed as bisexuality or lesbianism, presents a challenge to the sexual economy.[48] She offers the possibility that the female sexual economy could be disrupted; indeed, since the principles of the female sexual economy derive from Freud's descriptions of "normal" heterosexual development—overidentification with the mother, which causes the daughter to break away and begin to desire a male love-object—any course of development that fails to achieve prescribed heterosexuality could represent a challenge to the economy. Further, at the beginning of the story's chronology, both mother and daughter are endowed with erotic potential, a fact that would further appear to thwart the economy's control. The narrator recounts that on their first night in the United States, her parents acted like young lovers when the realization that they had escaped sank in: "[M]y mother runs her fingers through his hair and nods, and they both start crying, quietly but heartily, holding and stroking each other as if they are all they have" (130). On that same day, the ten-year-old narrator encounters the Colombian woman, who reads her a sexually charged biblical passage and who suggests that the narrator, like herself, has erotic impulses that she cannot control. At this point both the mother and the daughter are offered the potential for sexual expression, in violation of the sexual economy.

As the narrator and her mother age, however, the daughter's sexual opportunities increase while the mother's fade away, apparently in accordance with the economy. Five years after the narrator observes her parents passionately embracing, their relationship no longer seems so adoring: when the narrator's father makes an infuriating remark, she remembers that "[m]y mother will ask him to please finish his *café con leche* and wipe the milk moustache from the top of his lip" (119). Her refusal to dignify her husband's ridiculous remark with a response is akin to parents ignoring a child's temper tantrum, and her gesture is more like that of a mother wiping milk from her child's face than a lover's caress. The affection that the childhood narrator witnessed between her parents appears to have dissolved by the time she's a teenager. As time goes on, the narrator witnesses even fewer interactions between her parents; they seem to have drifted further apart. When the narrator's father physically attacks her after she accuses him of leaving Cuba out of self-interest, her mother can only plead with him to stop. Her father's anger grows over the years, until he dies of a heart attack while driving, yelling at someone. The few details the narrator provides about her parents' relationship suggest that they become distant, so that by the time of her father's funeral, her mother does not even try to catch a final glimpse of her husband before his casket is closed. "I couldn't leave, it wouldn't have looked right," she tells her daughter. "But thank god I'm going blind" (128). By this time the passion that once existed between the parents has disappeared completely.

The apparent working of the sexual economy in this case might be explained by the aging process: as the daughter ages, her sexuality is foregrounded while her mother's naturally fades into the background. Yet other stories, particularly those under examination in chapter 2, do not follow this pattern. In Amy Bloom's "When the Year Grows Old," for example, the pubescent daughter grows in her nascent sexuality at the cost of her middle-aged mother, but Laura's loss of sexual expression is the result of overmedication for her bipolar disorder rather than any natural process. Lorrie Moore's "Which Is More than I Can Say about Some People" presents Abby and Erica, in whom all heterosexual impulses are reduced to the dynamics of either a mother-infant relationship or to the bond between sisters. Neither woman finds any successful form of sexual expression. And in Ann Beattie's "Find and Replace," it is Ann's widowed and elderly mother who finds sexual fulfillment with Drake Dreodadus, not the middle-aged Ann. There is, therefore, no predetermined pattern to the sexual economy that would explain the gradual loss of sexual expression by the narrator's mother in Obejas's story.

A more compelling explanation is that the daughter becomes whitened over the course of the story, and that, as a white woman, she is bound by the sexual economy. In her first days in the United States, both she and her mother are nonwhite: they do not speak the language, their Cuban ethnicity is constantly highlighted, and they do not fit into the Protestant model of white America. The family faces discrimination in housing and even at the hairdresser's. As the narrator grows up, however, she begins integrating into U.S. culture. She learns English—well enough to earn an optometry scholarship to Indiana University—and she joins in antiwar and consciousness-raising movements. Her adoption of the hippie dress code, in fact, stirs her father to respond, "We left Cuba so you could dress like this?" (121).[49] In short, as she grows up, the narrator is fulfilling the Colombian woman's prediction that everything would change for her in the United States. The narrator's similarity to the blonde doll she received upon her arrival grows as time passes, until the two resemble one another almost perfectly just before the narrator's death from cancer. The narrator's assimilation into white U.S. culture brings with it some privileges, but it also incurs a demand for her family to comply with the sexual economy.

The narrator's integration into American culture can also be indexed through the green sweater she wears on the day her family arrives in Miami, which becomes an important symbol of her relationship to whiteness. The story begins with the words, "I'm wearing a green sweater. It's made of some synthetic material, and it's mine. I've been wearing it for two days straight and have no plans to take it off right now" (113). The narrator, at this point ten years old, sees the sweater as her tangible link to her Cuban past. When a volunteer at the INS processing center tries to get her to trade in her sweater for "a little gray flannel gym jacket with a hood and an American flag logo," she responds by "wrap[ping] myself up tighter in the sweater, which at this point still smells of salt and Cuban dirt and my grandmother's house" (114–115). Although the young narrator resists this attempt at conformity with American dress, the importance of her choice in garments is underlined by the story's title, "We Came All the Way from Cuba So You Could Dress Like This?" By the time she is in college, she recalls, the green sweater has been left behind in the closet of her childhood bedroom, and it is her dressing like a hippie, in a fringed suede jacket and bell-bottom jeans, that raises her father's ire. Her dress code signals her politics—her participation in antiwar demonstrations, consciousness-raising groups, and gay liberation meetings—as well as her integration into the fabric of American life.

As an adult, the narrator encounters the green sweater again when her mother wraps family mementoes and her Cuban passport into it after her father's death. The return of the green sweater facilitates her return to Cuba, this time as an American.

Although the sweater symbolizes her ties to Cuba, the narrator holds the power to determine whether to identify with her Cuban roots, and how deeply. Flavio Risech has characterized Cuban Americans' ability to move between cultural affiliations as a kind of cross-dressing, and his description fits the narrator's position in Obejas's story: "In the metaphor of cross-dressing, I suggest that we of the Cuban-American second generation have at our disposal a wide array of identity 'garments,' the specific cultural, political and social attributes that we have acquired by virtue of having lived in the distinct communities of Cuba, exile Miami, and other U.S. cities, and that taken together make up who we are" (57). Although the narrator is a first-generation Cuban American, Risech's description aptly describes her position and her ability to take the green sweater on and off, depending on her desire to assimilate.

Her choice to "dress" as Cuban or as American offers the narrator the chance to challenge her whitening, and thus to challenge the sexual economy. While she has put the green sweater away through much of the story, she is able to reclaim it when it is time to return to Cuba. Her whiteness, her assimilation into the United States, becomes a kind of uniform she can choose to wear—or not. In large part, her ability to challenge her status as white stems from her sexual behavior; her refusal to obey the norms of heterosexuality already places her on the margins of whiteness. To paraphrase Segrest, white women are less white than men, and gay people and lesbians are less white than heterosexuals. Moreover, the narrator's Cuban status, already on the edge of both Latina/o identity and whiteness, offers her the chance to move between the two more fluidly than is possible for many people. Although the female sexual economy is in effect while the narrator is "wearing" whiteness, Obejas endows the narrator of her story with options for thwarting it that have simply not been available to other characters.

Becoming White, Becoming American

These three stories, taken together, portray both the operations and the limits of the female sexual economy. In Miller's story, Olivia is able to escape the constraints of the economy by embracing blackness, even though that gesture is troubling in both its motives and its reification of stereotypes about blacks and whites. In "Burglars in the Flesh," Ilka and Flora find themselves becoming whiter in comparison with Carter's blackness, although Ilka's sexual relationship with a black man keeps her on the borders of whiteness. Obejas's story, in contrast, presents opportunities for thwarting the economy through the narrator's ability to "dress" as white, a situation that offers her both many of the privileges of whiteness without its costs. The latter two stories in particular affirm Babb's assertion that being white is synonymous with being American; as the characters progress in their assimilation as Americans, they become whitened. Olivia, in contrast, like other African Americans, is cut off from the chance to become fully American by her biological race and appearance.

One element of whiteness has been left largely unexamined so far: the association between whiteness and economic success. As the editors of *White Trash* point out, the label *white* presumes a certain socioeconomic status; those who do not meet that criterion are then identified in a way that sets them off from other whites, as "white trash." Although the dreams of the narrator's parents for their daughter in the Obejas story perhaps most clearly demonstrate the equation of whiteness with financial success, there are also hints of the relationship between the two in the other stories. In the Miller story, Olivia's father finds promotion to the local college from his secondary school teaching job to be an indicator of achievement, but the college students accused him of being an Uncle Tom for taking the job. His economic prosperity and improved social standing make him whitened in the eyes of his daughter. Similarly, Segal's story portrays the three family members on a scale of assimilation and projected socioeconomic status: Flora, the most recent arrival, has no job and few prospects for finding one, given her poor English; Ilka, who has been in the United States for a year before her mother arrives, has slightly more success but is still limited to employment opportunities directed toward immigrants rather than native-born Americans; while cousin Fishgoppel, who has lived in the United States the longest, is on her way to, at the least, middle-class status and a certain level of social standing through her education at elite Yale University. And in all three of the stories considered in chapter 2, the families are, at minimum, solidly middle-class and often working their way up the socioeconomic ladder.

The final chapter will examine more fully the implications of economics for the functioning of both whiteness and the sexual economy. Because higher socioeconomic class is associated with whiteness, the better-off the characters, the whiter they appear. For this reason, the sexual economy is associated with a very literal economy that increases in strength the whiter (and thus more American) the women are. In the next chapter, I explore alternative models of economy as a counterpoint to the operations of the sexual economy. In addition, I investigate the material conditions of the short story's publication in an effort to understand the way in which market economic forces might influence the content of stories.

Exploring the ways in which economics, both literal and metaphorical, influence and inform the production of stories, which by their very nature function in their own economy of form, offers a deeper insight into the reasons that short stories consistently portray limits on female sexuality, mediated by race and class.

Economies

As the stories in the previous chapter demonstrate, whiteness as a racial label is neither simple nor straightforward. Whiteness shifts depending on context: Ilka's Jewish "race" is whitened when she is around Carter, her black boyfriend, in Lore Segal's "Burglars in the Flesh," for example. As each of those stories illustrates, the whiter the women become, the more they are constrained by the female sexual economy that limits sexual expression to either mother or daughter. The female narrator of Achy Obejas's "We Came All the Way from Cuba So You Could Dress Like This?" is the only character who effectively challenges the sexual economy through her choice of both women and men as sexual partners. Her sexuality disrupts the ideals of whiteness, particularly by challenging its reliance on heterosexuality for the continuation of the race.

Obejas's narrator, and indeed all three protagonists in these stories, exemplifies the way in which whiteness is not simply one shade but rather a range of possibilities, each of which may involve a different kind of access to social power. So far, however, my discussion of whiteness has been limited largely to the interplay of ethnicity, national origin, language, and biological race. But whiteness is also a socioeconomic marker in the twentieth- and twenty-first-century United States. National discourse on welfare, for example, carries an undercurrent of racism, for the label of "welfare queens" used by welfare's opponents is a kind of code for African American women, people often (and wrongly) assumed by the American public to be the major beneficiaries of welfare.[1] In the minds of many Americans, the poor are equated with nonwhites, so much so that whites who are poor are referred to as "white trash," a label that separates them from other whites (who are, through their higher socioeconomic standing, presumably not trash). As Annalee Newitz and Matt Wray, the editors of the collection *White Trash*, point out, "[T]he term *white trash* reminds us that one of the worst crimes of which one can accuse a person is poverty. If you are white, calling someone 'white' is hardly an insult. But calling someone 'white trash' is both a racist and classist insult" ("What Is 'White Trash'?" 170). The term functions to exclude certain people who, although their skin may appear white, do not possess the socioeconomic qualifications of whiteness. In part, the meaning of success in the United States—and thus the meaning of whiteness, for full integration of any outside group into the dominant culture is signaled by that group's inclusion in the term "white"—has been associated with the myth of the American dream. Dreams of becoming financially prosperous are integrally connected to dreams of fitting into the culture at large.

While the previous chapter examined characters who were moving toward whiteness from its margins, either through biracial heritage or immigrant status, some poor whites may also desire standing as "fully" white rather than "white trash." Many of the characters in Dorothy Allison's collection *Trash*, for example, are labeled "white trash," either by their community or by themselves—or by Allison, through their inclusion in a collection with this title. In most of these cases, the female sexual economy does not apply: the daughters, who often narrate the stories, find fulfilling romantic (often lesbian) relationships while their mothers seek financial security through sexual relationships with men. In other words, both mother and daughter find sexual expression simultaneously. These exceptions to the limits of the sexual economy might be explained by the fact that the daughters are usually lesbian, for, as in the case of Obejas's narrator, sexual choices that do not comply with the strict heterosexuality necessitated by whiteness offer female characters the opportunity to escape the economy's constraints. In several of Allison's stories, however, daughters have sex with men (although often by force or through necessity) as do their mothers (and, in some particularly disturbing cases, with the same men). In these situations, however unsettling readers may find them, the sexual economy is exceeded. For the purposes of whiteness, it does not matter how much or with whom these "trash" characters engage in sex, for, by virtue of their socioeconomic status, they will not be the parents of future whites.[2] These characters are not bound by the same limitations that "true" whites would be.

The importance of sexual activity to the class status necessary for inclusion in whiteness is demonstrated, in Allison's stories, by characters who desire to rise above "trash." In "'The Meanest Woman Ever Left Tennessee,'" Shirley Boatwood fantasizes that she will one day be accepted as something other than trash—even if she has to leave her family behind to do so. Shirley hates her husband, hates fulfilling her conjugal duties to him, and hates the products of those unions, the children who will not stop coming. She believes others recognize "quality" in her, an attribute she thinks distinguishes her from her trashy family. In Shirley's mind, proper behavior includes not just a decent job and work ethic but also a restrained sexuality. In one scene, she compares herself favorably to her coworkers, who often waste time talking or dreaming but have the nerve to complain about how poorly they're used. "Trash," Shirley proclaims, "don't know the meaning of use. Just like you kids." Neither group, to Shirley's thinking, appreciates the value of a good day's work and a good day's pay. When she comments that her kids eat boiled rice like they don't know its value, her daughter Mattie pipes up, "Two cents a pound." Shirley responds to this impertinent answer by telling Mattie, "You little whore. . . . You an't worth two cents a night yourself " (26). For Shirley, Mattie's presumptuous attempt to raise herself to the level of her mother only confirms her status as trash, a class synonymous with loose sexuality. The cheapness Shirley assigns as Mattie's sexual worth underlines the link in her own thinking between economics and sexual behavior. As Newitz and Wray point out in their introduction to *White Trash*, the phenomenon Allison illustrates in her stories exemplifies the association of the label "white trash" with sexual behavior outside the bounds of "proper" whiteness (171).

Allison's stories illustrate the way in which the category of whiteness excludes those whose class status does not meet its stringent requirements. In the case of Allison's characters, the sexual economy is irrelevant; the women in these families (albeit in a limited way, especially given the examples of rape and incest related in the stories) are free to pursue their sexual interests. These characters' relative sexual freedom stands in contrast to the sexual economy that is in effect most stringently for the women of Ann Beattie's "Find and Replace," Amy Bloom's "When the Year Grows Old," and Lorrie Moore's "Which Is More than I Can Say about Some People," the three stories examined in the second chapter. In those stories, all the characters occupy at least middle-class status: Ann, the narrator of the Beattie story, is a freelance writer who makes enough money to travel internationally and rent convertibles on a whim; the family in Bloom's story includes a manager-father and a mother who teaches at a community college; and the events in Moore's story are occasioned by the daughter's promotion at a job that pays well enough that she can finance a spur-of-the-moment trip to Ireland. In each of these cases, the sexual economy constrains the women's sexual opportunities. These characters possess few of the qualifications that might keep them on the margins of whiteness—nonwhite parents, language barriers, immigrant origins, or "white trash" status—and they therefore cannot exceed the economy as Obejas's narrator or Allison's characters do.

The collections in which stories such as Obejas's and Allison's appear are relatively unusual themselves on the literary scene, for neither *Trash* nor *We Came All the Way from Cuba So You Could Dress Like This?* includes a story that was originally published in one of the four major American magazine outlets for literary short fiction—*New Yorker*, *Esquire*, *Atlantic*, and *Harper's*. Each was published by a relatively small press (Allison's by Firebrand Books, which specializes in feminist and lesbian authors, and Obejas's by Cleis Press, devoted to sexuality and gender studies as well as gay and lesbian studies) rather than a large house. Like the stories they contain, these collections have found homes on the margins of the larger literary market; by targeting specific audiences, these collections find limited economic success. The stories by Beattie, Bloom, and Moore, in contrast, have followed a more conventional trajectory: Beattie's and Moore's stories were initially published in the *New Yorker*, and Bloom's first appeared in *Story* magazine, an outlet once recognized for publishing important new writers that folded (for the second time) in 1999;[3] their collections were brought out by houses such as HarperCollins and Knopf. In these cases, the stories that have enjoyed the most economic success portray the sexual economy at its most limiting for female characters. For this reason, it is important to examine the meaning of the term *economy* in the context of its broader meaning of exchange and commerce, for the economics of the short story—a genre defined by its economy of form—appear to affect not just its status in the literary realm but also its content. Writing on Henry James, Philip Horne has suggested, "There are conflicting economies in the world of literature, and the poetic economy of art has to operate, for the professional writer, within the larger, more prosaic business of earning a living" (7). His words are no less applicable to the contemporary literary scene.

In the previous two chapters, I have focused on the content of contemporary short stories, and thus far, I have used the term *economy* with reference to the female sexual economy to refer to a closed-system, zero-sum structure in which one character can find sexual expression only at the cost of the other (at least in the case of the whitest characters). Economies do not always take this form, however; they can also involve uneven exchanges, expenditure, and excess with no particular purpose other than the fact of exceeding the system. Throughout this chapter, I explore the work of a number of writers whose works appeared in English during the past twenty-five years, but whose models of economy have had little effect on the contents of stories, which I argue are fundamentally conservative. In the following section, I explore the work of such theorists as Luce Irigaray, Hélène Cixous, and Georges Bataille, who argue that these new forms of economy represent the potential for revolutionary change. Irigaray and Cixous in particular see the possibility of unlimited outflow of female sexuality as a utopian economy that would bring about a new society, while Bataille perceives expenditure, broadly conceived, as a necessary and positive means of establishing and maintaining the fabric of social life. These visions of an economic system that functions not by constraint and control but rather through spending without thought of repayment provide a liberating counterpoint to the portrayal of the female sexual economy, a fundamentally conservative proposition. They help to illustrate, through their contrasting images of revolution, just how devoted the sexual economy is to preserving the status quo, and serve to confirm my argument that the short story is, in its content, a conservative form.

In the second section of this chapter, I suggest that this conservatism is due in large part to the tremendous economic constraints on the short story as genre. Through an examination of the market for contemporary short stories, I expose the contradiction between Frank O' Connor's famous characterization forty years ago of the short story as the voice of the loner on the fringes of society and the need for current short story writers to find success by appealing to the greatest possible target audience. With a better understanding of the ways in which short stories and the tales they tell reflect and interact with the economy of culture at large, I hope to reconcile short stories as a practice with their theorization. Finally, I propose in the third section that Pierre Bourdieu's formulation of cultural, symbolic, and economic capital, among others, provides a way to account for the short story's cultural work over the past twenty-five years.[4]

ALTERNATIVE ECONOMIES: ABUNDANCE, EXCESS, EXPENDITURE

Irigaray and Cixous share an interest in economies, especially as they relate to issues of female sexuality. Irigaray's interest in economy seems to originate with her understanding of the mother-daughter relationship as an economy of one, a constraining relationship that refuses to recognize each woman as an individual. Cixous is interested in mothering, although she sees in the love relationship between mother and child a model for revising economic systems. Both envision new kinds of economies that shatter masculine traditions of calculation and accounting, alternative economies that disrupt history and signal revolution. Bataille sees the act of understanding economies in a new way as a revolutionary act through his formulation of a general economy, one that is not limited merely to exchange and trade between human beings but one that expresses the relationship between people and the social and natural world they inhabit. The works of these three writers were translated into English during the twenty-five-year period since the publication of *The Reproduction of Mothering*, but these visions of alternative economies have made little difference in the portrayal of the economy of female sexuality as it appears in short stories of the same era. By comparing these theories with the practice as I have traced it in the previous two chapters, I argue, the conservatism of the short story as a genre becomes apparent.

Irigaray has described the traditional mother-daughter relationship as one of stifling closeness that prevents women from experiencing a sense of individuality—precisely the issue that drives the female sexual economy. Her narrative "And the One Doesn't Stir Without the Other," first published in French as *Et l'une ne bouge pas sans l'autre*, appeared in 1979, just a year after Chodorow's *The Reproduction of Mothering* was issued in the United States. While Chodorow's book focused on the psychological and sociological conditions that create the cycle of overmothering for daughters, Irigaray explores the impact of that problem on an imagined daughter who narrates the piece. The daughter asks her mother to step backward, to let her have her independence, so that each of the two can find an individual self: "Keep yourself/me outside, too. Don't engulf yourself or me in what flows from you into me. I would like both of us to be present. So that the one doesn't disappear in the other, or the other in the one" (61). The daughter's feeling that she cannot separate from her mother is caused, says the narrator, by society's definition of women as "[t]rapped in a single function—mothering" (66). Without an available social identity outside motherhood, women cannot separate themselves from their maternal role without losing themselves. The situation is not only harmful for the daughter, however; it has grave consequences for the mother as well: "When the one comes into the world, the other goes underground. When the one carries life, the other dies" (67). The narrator wishes that there were a way for both of them to exist as distinct individuals, each enjoying her own life without the necessity of eliminating the other: "And what I wanted from you, Mother, was this: that in giving me life, you still remain alive" (67).

Irigaray's strategy in the narrative, as the translator Hélène Vivienne Wenzel notes, is one of subtly overturning Freudian approaches to female sexuality.[5] Where Freud saw women as essentially lacking (namely, a penis), Irigaray refigures the image of woman in this text to one of plenitude. The abundance of affection that the mother shares with her daughter has become poisonous, however, in a patriarchal society that sees women only as mothers, without offering them any alternate avenues for expression. When female sexuality is limited only to motherhood, mothers become harmful to their daughters, and the daughters' very existence has a kind of lethal power over their mothers. Plenitude becomes an important theme in Irigaray's later writings as well, where she uses the language of excess to contradict Freud's idea of lack and thereby to envision women who move beyond any zero-sum economy into a realm of unfettered and unquantifiable sexual expression for women. For Irigaray, as well as Cixous, the recognition of women's pleasure is a necessary step in challenging the existing social order.

Her best-known essay, translated as "This Sex Which Is Not One," exemplifies this strategy in its imagery of limitless female sexuality. Irigaray refuses the Freudian position that woman's genitalia is counted as a lack and instead calls for an understanding of women's genitals as two lips that are constantly touching, such that they are not either one or two but rather plural (101, 102). This new calculation of women's plural sex disrupts a binary Freudian economy that gives men a value of one but women a zero. Particularly in the context of an industrialized nation, "a culture that claims to enumerate everything, cipher everything by units, inventory reverting by individualities," Irigaray's new math renders a woman who is *neither one nor two. . . . She renders any definition inadequate*" (103). This multiplicity has ramifications beyond merely the sexual, though. Irigaray specifically relates women's plurality of pleasure to traditional conceptions of economy: "Woman enjoys a closeness with the other that is *so near she cannot possess it, any more than she can possess herself.* She constantly trades herself for the other without any possible identification of either one of them" (105).[6] More than simply a challenge to masculine mathematics, Irigaray uses the expansion of women's pleasure through constant genital contact to pose a challenge to men's economies. Once a woman becomes the subject of her own pleasure rather than an object of men's, she interrupts the exchange of women on the market. No longer merely goods to be circulated, no longer quantifiable merchandise that can be counted in an inventory, women's recognition of the plurality of their pleasure represents the first step in creating a viable challenge to masculine economies.[7]

In "Women on the Market" and "When the Goods Get Together,"[8] Irigaray takes issue with Lévi-Strauss's formulation of kinship relations, the theory that the exchange of women in marriage cements social relationships and founds the incest taboo.[9] From Irigaray's perspective, this system circulates women's bodies as a kind of social currency that enables the continuation of life and culture, but without being recognized for their contribution. Women, she argues, are the laboring (in both senses) class whose exploitation is necessary for the smooth functioning of relationships between men. Proper compensation for women's work would expose the double system that sees women as exchange-value but men as the exchangers. Irigaray suggests that one way to accomplish this disruption would be for women to establish trade relations with each other out of the sight of men, refusing to be traded themselves in an "[e]xchange without identifiable terms of trade, without accounts, without end—Without one plus one, without series, without number. Without a standard of value. . . . Where use and exchange would mingle" ("When the Goods Get Together" 110). In this "economy of abundance," as Irigaray terms it, all the calculations would shift. Rather than focusing on value, on requiring an equivalence of exchange, the economy among women would ignore the worth of objects as assessed by men and celebrate the act of trading—or, more accurately, giving—itself. In this utopian vision, "[n]ature would spend itself without exhaustion, trade without labor, give of itself—protected from masculine transactions—for nothing; there would be free enjoyment, well-being without suffering, pleasure without possessions" (110). In the ideal world she imagines "[h]ow ironic calculations, savings, more or less ravishing appropriations, and arduous capitalizations would be!" (110). The new order would liberate women and their pleasure.

Cixous's writing, like Irigaray's, is infused with a desire to overturn a social order that fails to value women's pleasure. The very act of women's writing, she affirms in "The Laugh of the Medusa," challenges the masculine economy: "Because the 'economy' of her drives is prodigious, she cannot fail, in seizing the occasion to speak, to transform directly and indirectly *all* systems of exchange based on masculine thrift. Her libido will produce far more radical effects of political and social change than some might like to think" (252). For Cixous, women's pleasure exceeds what men can understand and is in itself revolutionary. This pleasure, or *jouissance*, offers a way to escape masculine economies. To embrace women's libidinal economies that know no bounds, she argues, is to embrace a new political economy as well, one in which value is no longer determined solely by men. This action works to disrupt the trajectory of history and tradition, for those are founded on a masculine economy: "All history is inseparable from economy in the limited sense of the word, that of a certain kind of savings. Man's return—the relationship linking him profitably to man-being, conserving it. This economy, as a law of appropriation, is a phallocentric production."[10] She sees masculine economies as characterized by endless consumption, as in the case of Don Juan's parade of amours, but without providing any kind of compensation for the women ("Castration or Decapitation?" 47). Like Irigaray, Cixous sees women's appropriation as objects for exchange as part of a masculine economy that must be overturned in order for women to be recognized as subjects themselves.

Cixous takes particular offense at Nietzsche's characterization of woman as what she terms the "gift-that-takes," and one part of her project is revising this type of economics. Only men who want to take everything themselves, she remarks, could think about women in this way ("The Laugh of Medusa" 259). Women, as Cixous imagines them, are constantly in a state of giving rather than taking; moreover, they give with no regard for what they might receive in return. The female economy is no economy at all but a constant gift giving and is in many ways linked to women's ability to mother. The gift of life, or at least the possibility of this gift, is one that only woman can provide; this is why women are worth even more, according to Cixous's calculations, than men.[11] The taboos associated with pregnant women, she writes, are driven by the fact that during these nine months women double their value within the masculine economy but also that each woman "valorizes *herself* as a *woman* in her own eyes, and undeniably takes on weight and sex," rather than understanding herself merely as an object for exchange ("Sorties" 90). The fact of motherhood in itself upsets masculine modes of accounting, for it is a kind of giving without expectation of return on investment. Woman's generosity shares abundance without thought for recompense, without a masculine consideration of the economic benefits of the gift: "She doesn't 'know' what she's giving, she doesn't measure it. . . . She gives more, with no assurance that she'll get back even some unexpected profit from what she puts out." As Irigaray does, Cixous envisions the kind of gift-economies associated with women as shattering all masculine notions of economy, as rendering economic terms irrelevant ("The Laugh of Medusa" 264).

Rather than using the term *economy*, then, Cixous shifts the terms of the equation by modeling her utopian system of exchange on love, a gift given without expectation of profit. This model changes all previous understandings of masculine exchange: "Wherever [woman] loves, all the old concepts of management are left behind. At the end of a more or less conscious computation, she finds not her sum but her differences" ("The Laugh of Medusa" 264). Moreover, because love cannot be quantified or calculated, it cannot be repaid exactly, to erase the debt of love. This model invalidates old ideas of exchange, writes Cixous ("Castration or Decapitation?" 48).[12] Importantly, the use of love as the paradigm of giving requires a recognition and a knowledge of the other as a subject rather than an objectification of people for the purposes of exchange.[13] Rather than increasing financial resources, Cixous's vision of love would cause an increase in knowledge and understanding as well as delight in discovering the other. She uses as an exemplar of this system of love Shakespeare's Cleopatra, whose enormous wealth was nothing compared to the love she shared with Antony:

> Absolute queen of several countries, she can give more than anyone. . . . [She and Antony] do not take all this for something, they reduce it, with a kiss, to the nothing that it has never ceased to be, save in the eyes of beings who know nothing of love, that is to say, everybody. At no moment do all these glories, all these treasures, for which men make peoples kill each other, make them bat an eye. ("Sorties" 127)

Cleopatra valued love over untold treasures, says Cixous, and represents the ideal of the "economy" of love for which she argues. Further, because history itself is a kind of economy—one of saving—Cixous states that her revision represents a challenge to the way the past is understood. Love as a mode of exchange interrupts what she terms the logic of the same in favor of a recognition of differences.

Cixous and Irigaray share a belief that a change in human understanding of economies could be revolutionary. Both writers develop their theories based on their interpretations of female sexuality (the libidinal economy for Cixous, women's genitals for Irigaray), seeing women's recognition of their own subjecthood as key in overturning masculine economies that refuse to see them as anything more than objects to be exchanged. For each of them, abundance and excess offer means by which straightforward accounting can be disrupted. In this belief, they share an approach with Bataille, whose concept of the gift provides the potential for a wholly new understanding of economy, neither capitalist nor communist, but rather one based on the principles of ancient peoples, such as the Aztecs or Native Americans. In contrast to Irigaray and Cixous, however, Bataille is not interested in associating different kinds of models with gendered distinctions. His approach is that of a general economy, not limited to merely trade or sexuality, but rather an overarching theme of free expenditure that makes human life worthwhile and (re)connects it to the universe.

Like Irigaray and Cixous, Bataille's approach to economics could never be reconciled to the academic discipline of the same name. As Bataille describes it, he sees his project as revising what he calls the political economy.[14] Rather than understanding exchanges between human beings or groups of human beings in isolation, Bataille's theory of general economy, as described in *The Accursed Share*, strives to situate human beings in the context of their surroundings. He sees "a need to study the system of human production and consumption within a much larger framework" that takes into account the workings of the natural world as well as the implications of exchange and trade for social relations between people (*The Accursed Share* 20). Within the broad category of consumption, he explains in the early essay "The Notion of Expenditure," there are two types: the first is what is required for the continuation of life and productive work in society, but the second type involves unproductive expenditures, activities that have no end in themselves (at least, he qualifies, in primitive cultures). Examples of the second type include mourning, games, art, and war; these events and acts represent no immediate gain for those involved in their production or consumption. In the case of nonproductive expenditure, Bataille says, the "*loss* . . . must be as great as possible in order for that activity to take on its true meaning."[15] In the natural world, Bataille sees the processes of unproductive expenditure constantly at work: "The very principle of living matter requires that the chemical operations of life, which demand an expenditure of energy, be gainful, productive of surpluses" (*The Accursed Share* 27). If this is the natural order of the world around us, reasons Bataille, then shouldn't human behavior also produce such surpluses?

In primitive societies, Bataille argues, this principle guided social rites and relationships. Among the Aztecs, for example, the sacrifice of healthy, young citizens who could otherwise have contributed to the production economy of the state symbolized a kind of unproductive expenditure. Drawing particularly on Mauss's work on the gift, Bataille noted that North American Indians, too, celebrate feasts called potlatches, lavish spreads of food and gifts that share the amassed treasure of the host. While, among Native Americans, the extravagance of each host's potlatch was a challenge to his rivals to reciprocate the act of generosity, Bataille envisioned the unanswered potlatch as the ideal of unproductive expenditure or *dépense*, the free gift, as Michèle Richman defines it (3).[16] Without the rise of capitalism and the Protestant work ethic, Bataille believes, these economies of unlimited giving might have continued, but their developments encouraged the accumulation of wealth for accumulation's sake, rather than seeing treasure as a communal property to be shared for the good of the society. Capitalism created an artificial desire to store up money and property that defied the natural human desire to share the surplus in a magnificent manner and without a purpose beyond the joy of sharing, notes Michael Richardson (71). It also condemned forms of sexuality that did not lead to productive reproduction, celebrating instead sobriety, hygiene, and duty (Botting and Wilson 23).

By refusing to recognize the need for unproductive expenditure, capitalism creates what Bataille terms the "accursed share." In this form, capitalism transforms what were once rites that cemented society's celebration of the sacred into pollution, nuclear accumulation, global warfare, and massacres, writes Richardson. "As it gave a value to accumulation," he continues, "so capitalism introduced rational calculation based upon a principle of growth. In the process it broke man's relative equilibrium with the environment and served to estrange us from our sense of ourselves in the world" (76). Through his formulation of the general economy, Bataille proposed a restoration of what he saw as fundamental human values embodied in the *dépense* of the Aztecs and Native Americans, reestablishing a harmonious relationship with the natural world and rejecting the cold calculations of capitalism.[17] As Richman notes, Bataille did not want his ideas recognized simply as a general principle that could be applied to human life, but rather as a complete divergence from the principles of traditional economics (6). For Bataille, the liberation of expenditure represents a kind of revolution, concludes Allan Stoekl (xvii). To return to what Bataille regarded as original human ethics, to live according to his theory of the general economy, would not be to work within a closed system but to celebrate the reopening of opportunities for celebration and social cohesion in a radical change.

Irigaray, Cixous, and Bataille all imagine revolutionary change through models of expenditure and excess. All three refuse the kind of zero-sum economy that, I have argued, characterizes the female sexual economy. In the case of Irigaray and Cixous, that type of economy is described as specifically masculine; as feminists, they reject it. Bataille, too, saw limits on sexuality as negative for humans; in his opinion, the Protestant influence on capitalism created a societal condemnation of sexual practices that did not lead directly to (re)production. For each of these writers, limits on human productivity, including sexual expression, provide an important impetus for revolution.[18] Despite the fact that most of the writers whose stories I have examined have explicitly identified themselves as feminists, their work in the short story is far from it. The contrast between the alternative economies imagined by Irigaray, Cixous, and Bataille and the existence of the female sexual economy underlines the way in which the short story does little to advance social revolution; it is, rather, more invested in maintaining the status quo, even if that involves masculine and conservative economies.

TAKING THE STORY TO MARKET

Moving from economies in the abstract, as they influence the content of short stories, to the particular, I would now like to examine the context in which stories appear: the marketplace. As I established in the first chapter, short stories' status in the literary hierarchy of genres is diminished by their appearance as parts of magazines and journals rather than as books unto themselves. This fact highlights the nature of the short story as a commercial object, one that is purchased like any of the commodities for sale in the advertisements that often surround it in such publications. Indeed, as Thomas Leitch found in his study of the *New Yorker*, the most important publisher of short stories over the past twenty-five years, that the magazine's design has been predicated on a smooth integration of complementary advertising and content, such that the two begin to merge into one another.[19] The editors are unusually selective about the kinds of products advertised in the *New Yorker's* pages as well the tone of those ads for its readers, Leitch notes. "Moreover, the advertising is often designed as a complement to the editorial material, with words and pictures sometimes supplied by, or in close imitation of, the magazine's contributors" (135). This situation does nothing to dispel the reader's perception that the stories printed within the magazine have any more staying power than the ephemera printed alongside them.[20] John Edgar Wideman compares the experience of reading short stories in magazines to watching TV dramas; both, he says, are "embedded in a collage of advertisements, news stories, simulations, editorial voice-overs, station breaks, logos, appeals subtle and not so subtle for direct audience interaction with the medium (phone numbers to call, perfume to sniff, calendars, coupons). Story is fractured, infected, less and less distinguishable from the marketing collage" (xix). For readers who encounter stories in magazines like the *New Yorker*, fiction may seem like just another product for sale.

In order for stories printed in magazines like this to survive long enough to warrant critical attention[21] and economic success, not to mention the more literal kind of survival—preservation beyond the recycling bin—they generally must find at least one more publication: either collection in a single-author volume or inclusion in an anthology such as the annual O. Henry Prize Stories or the Best American Short Stories.[22] (Either way, the best way to achieve a second appearance is to make sure the first occurs in a major venue, since, as Susan Rochette-Crawley points out, the editors of multiauthor "prize" anthologies rely on the prior judgment of the editors of prestigious magazines to narrow the pool of worthy selections, for it is becoming increasingly difficult to read every one of the small journals and magazines.[23]) Even getting published by a major house almost always requires the inclusion of a novel in the book contract; editors and their bosses are reluctant to bring out story collections alone, because they don't sell.[24] The only recent literary short stories to appear on the *New York Times* bestseller list belonged to Adam Haslett, whose *You Are Not a Stranger Here* was a Today Show book club selection; Lorrie Moore, whose *Birds of America* sold largely on the strength of the powerful "People Like That Are the Only People Here"[25]; and Melissa Bank's *The Girls' Guide to Hunting and Fishing*, which grew out of the title story, commissioned by Francis Ford Coppola for the first anniversary of his magazine *Zoetrope*. (Bank's collection earned a phenomenal $275,000 advance, spent fourteen weeks on the bestseller list, and vaulted *Zoetrope* into the big leagues of short fiction publications. It clearly represents an exception rather than the rule.)[26]

The rules that govern the road to financial success and eventual inclusion in the canon for the short story are very different than those for the novel, and they hinge on economic considerations. Yet critics of the genre have traditionally preferred to ignore those factors, stuck in a modernist notion of pure art divorced from the marketplace. Such critics seem to have reversed the philosophy that celebrates lack of financial success as evidence of high art in order to interpret short stories' low sales figures as proof of their lofty aesthetic status. Those who ignore the short story's position as a commodity miss both the external pressures on its appearance (in magazines, journals, collections, and short story annuals[27]) and its content.

Changes in the publishing scene, particularly for magazines and literary journals, have made a great impact both on the availability of short stories for readers and the market for their writers. The turn of the twentieth century saw a boom in periodical publishing in both the

United States and Britain, and, by 1903, each illustrated magazine was publishing some sixty stories a year (Horne 3). By the 1920s and 1930s, there were enough well-paying outlets that writers could feasibly finance their novel writing by selling short stories. F. Scott Fitzgerald, for example, earned most of his income this way from the 1920s until 1937, when he went to Hollywood to work on screenplays. In 1925, the year *The Great Gatsby* was published, Fitzgerald made almost twice as much selling five stories ($11,025) as he did from royalties and advances for his novels ($6,245.25). Fitzgerald could do so well selling stories because there were so many popular magazines at the time that published short fiction, including *Redbook, Ladies' Home Journal, Woman's Home Companion, Vanity Fair, McCall's, Collier's, Liberty Magazine, Smart Set, Scribner's Magazine, Hearst's International Magazine*, and, most importantly for writers, the *Saturday Evening Post*. This lucrative outlet, which also provided a home for many of William Faulkner's stories, as well as those of other well-known novelists, was paying Fitzgerald as much as $4,000 per story by 1929, and it provided a readership of some two and a half million (Hearn 33).[28]

Over the years, however, the field of periodicals publishing short stories has changed substantially. The post-World War II scene saw many changes, not the least of which was the advent of television, which co-opted the audience of both movies and magazines. By the early 1950s, critics were bemoaning the dearth of outlets for short fiction.[29] Small magazines that had previously been outlets for fiction either folded or were bought up by entertainment conglomerates (Bishop 287). Among larger magazines, several disappeared (some, in the case of *Vanity Fair*, for example, reappearing later), and the remaining ones published far fewer stories than before. *The New Yorker*, for example, which first appeared in 1925, published as many as three stories a week in the 1950s. Even in the 1980s, the magazine printed two stories per issue; currently, it averages one story per issue. And the *Atlantic*, once a reliable monthly outlet for fiction, announced in the spring of 2005 that it would only publish stories in its annual fiction issue, an act that has "ghettoized" fiction, according to Rachel Donadio (27). The combination of the dwindling number of magazines publishing stories and the diminishing number of stories they publish has created the dismal present-day market for short fiction. Today, there are between four and six major magazines left (depending on which critic one asks) that regularly publish literary short fiction, and altogether they may print some 100 stories per year.[30] For their work, writers can earn somewhere between $1,500 and $2,000 on the low end of the scale up to $10,000 in an unusual case. Compare these figures to Fitzgerald's compensation of $4,000, which, adjusted to today's dollars, would be the equivalent of $48,000 (Passaro 92). John Updike, reflecting on these momentous changes, has remarked, "Fifty years, in sum, have seen the number of general magazines that publish fiction greatly shrink, and the field of weekly national magazines that print fiction shrink to one. I wonder, could any young writer now support himself or herself and a family, as I did in my twenties, by selling six or so short stories a year?" (xiv).[31]

Moreover, the women's and men's magazines that writers, in previous decades, could often count on as markets for their stories have published fewer and fewer stories over the course of the past half-century. Among men's magazines that publish fiction, *GQ, Esquire*, and, as Pearl K. Bell terms it, "that peculiar Janus-head of porn and culture called *Playboy*" (42) are the most prominent. They also, as Alice Adams observes, pay extremely well (xiv). Over the past twenty-five years, *Esquire* has been the outlet for the most-recognized fiction, rarely going more than a few years without a story included among at least one of the story annuals, and *Playboy* stories have been so honored seven times over those years (most heavily in the O. Henry Prize stories). *GQ* was a relative newcomer on the scene, with one story apiece included among the 1997 and 2000 Best American Short Stories[32]—but *GQ* stopped publishing fiction in 2003. And William Abrahams, editor of the O. Henry Prize stories from 1978 to 1996, observes a decline in the number of quality stories offered in *Esquire* in particular. In his introduction to the 1979 volume, he notes that *Esquire* publishes fewer stories, perhaps because the editors believe that their readership is less interested in fiction than in fact. Although he singles it out, Abrahams acknowledges that "*Esquire* is not alone in this turn against fiction. It has made the most dramatic countermove, and so is the most immediately noticeable" (10).[33] Indeed, the situation has only grown worse in the years since his observation, and especially since 11 September 2001. Rachel Donadio quotes Adrienne Miller, the literary editor of *Esquire*, in 2005: "We're in a dark cultural moment. I think people seem to feel more comfortable with nonfiction. . . . Fewer and fewer people seem to believe fiction is still essential for our emotional and intellectual survival" (27).

Among women's magazines, the drop-off has been even more precipitous. *Godey's Lady's Book*, one of the earliest women's magazines in the United States, was one of several regular outlets on which female short story writers could rely for a targeted audience (Koppelman, "A Preliminary Sketch" 4). Over the years, women's magazines including

Redbook, *Mademoiselle*, *Cosmopolitan*, *Glamour*, and *Mirabella* have printed stories among their pages, and in the past quarter-century each of them has published fiction recognized in one of the two short story annuals.[34] The last story from a women's magazine to be included in either the Best American or O. Henry Prize collections, however, was in 1995, and they are only sparsely represented after 1987. Both the frequency and the quality of the fiction being printed have diminished.

This situation is emblematic of a larger trend, according to Abrahams. As early as 1979, he laments the lack of stringent standards for the fiction published by the women's magazines, which, he says, have targeted themselves toward "young homemakers, young suburbanites, and young swingers" rather than young readers (11). By 1984, he is already writing an obituary for serious fiction in these publications: "[T]he women's magazines are sinking, where fiction is concerned, to abysmal depths" (xi). He continues,

> These magazines, self-proclaimed to be in the forefront in their attention to "today's woman"—so brilliant at home and in the office, so interested in interior decoration, microwave cooking, the latest in manners and morals—evidently think their readers too simpleminded to recognize the astonishing achievements, the esthetic sensibility, the wit, the virtuosity of style, the depth of feeling, the grasp of the complexities of contemporary life represented by women writers of our day. The magazines that pass them by are quite simply anachronisms: they belong for all their free-flowing sexuality and pop psychologizing to the 1950s. (xii)[35]

Alice Adams, writing seven years later, concurs with Abrahams's judgment, concluding that women's magazines no longer publish anything close to the amount of quality fiction that they once did and that editorial condescension toward the audience has significantly worsened: editors at these magazines, she says, "have always wanted stories, and especially the endings of stories, to be spelled out, explained, as though the women who read these magazines are wholly uneducated and/or mildly retarded, incapable of appreciating a subtle or, God help us, an ambiguous ending." She characterizes her own attempt to place a story in such a magazine as "so appalling" that she finally withdrew the submission (xiv).

With some commercial outlets publishing fewer stories, and some disappearing altogether, literary journals and small magazines printing stories have proliferated. Abrahams, in his 1979 introduction to the O. Henry Prize volume, comments that these small-circulation outlets used to be the places where beginning writers found homes for their first stories as they worked their way up to the more prestigious big magazines. Although this fact is not in itself troubling, Abrahams writes, the fact that quarterlies often lack sufficient funding and therefore tend to disappear rather quickly (and even more quickly in times of economic recession, such as the late 1970s and early 1980s) bodes ill for the future of short story writers. "The signs suggest," he predicts, "that we are entering a bleak period, after a relative and extended heyday, for the short story in magazines that aim at reaching a wide public" (10).[36] Edward Bishop, in his history of little magazines, defines them as "magazines that do not make money; they are trying to promote new ideas or forms of art, rather than sales." For this reason, Bishop says, the magazines' funding comes from a few supporters and a handful of subscribers who want to see an outlet that fills a niche not served by the current periodical culture. "The little magazine," remarks Bishop, "is always in an adversarial position with regard to the dominant culture, and when it loses that adversarial edge, or the enthusiasm of its backers, it dies. Thus most little magazines have a very short run" (287). Yet by 1993 Abrahams was convinced that writers will become more and more reliant on these financially unstable outlets as commercial magazines publish fewer stories each year (xii).

Because the number of well-paying options for story writers have narrowed considerably since Fitzgerald could earn $4,000 per story, many writers must turn to little magazines and quarterlies to publish not only their first stories but also those written throughout their career. With precarious finances, these magazines cannot afford to pay their writers much, or sometimes anything. The *Kenyon Review*, for example, paid ten dollars a page for its stories until 2004, when, in an editorial effort to better remunerate its writers, it tripled that rate (Lynn 1). Others cannot afford even that, compensating their writers with merely a subscription to the magazine. As a result, writers have had to turn elsewhere to finance their habit, and the rise of creative writing programs in the United States has helped to fill the gap. Positions teaching the next generation of writers in MFA programs pay current writers the money they might have earned by selling stories fifty years ago. (And they thereby create a market for their own work, for students in those programs feel the need to stay current with contemporary writing and purchase little magazines and new collections [Feldman 27].) Abrahams writes in 1986 that the result of this shift is to create a large number of good writers who then reproduce their style by teaching the next generation, a situation he views with some alarm (x). And Updike notes that, rather than financing a writer's writing, publishing short stories in magazines now accredits writers as able to teach fiction in creative writing programs. The result is a popular suspicion that "short fiction . . . has gone from being a popular to a fine art, an art preserved in a kind of floating museum made up of many little superfluous magazines" (xiv–xv). This cycle is perpetuated by the lack of commercial magazine outlets for fiction, which, as they dwindle, force more writers into the academy and the little magazines.

With the decline in the number of stories printed in men's and women's magazines and in large-circulation commercial magazines more generally, the one outlet that has remained fairly steadfast in regularly paying well for and publishing fiction over the years has been the *New Yorker*.[37] Although some critics bewail the decrease in the number of stories the *New Yorker* now prints (down from three per issue in the 1950s to an average of one a week today), the magazine is nearly universally acknowledged as the most influential outlet for present-day story writers.[38] John Updike characterizes it as "the publication that has come to dominate the short-fiction market" (xiv); Martin Arnold calls it "the premiere showcase for short fiction" ("Story Ideas from Coppola" E3); and Abrahams in the 1993 volume of the O. Henry Awards series says of the magazine, "[Y]ear after year, week after week, stories of outstanding merit have appeared on a scale . . . unrivaled by any other magazine intended, as it is, for a large readership" (Introduction xiv).

Indeed, a look at the contents of the two annuals devoted to the short story over the past twenty-five years reveals the *New Yorker* as the leading publisher of quality fiction. In the case of the O. Henry Prize stories, there are no more than two consecutive years during which the *New Yorker* is not the source of one of the top three winners; so regular is its appearance among the prize winners that in 1998 and 2000 it was the source for two out of the three. The Best American Short Stories series, which favors stories from the *New Yorker* even more heavily (despite the fact that, since 1978, the stories have been selected by a rotating guest editor), often contains eight or nine *New Yorker* stories out of a total of twenty. Given that this series, which sells about 100,000 copies of its annual, regularly outperforms the O. Henry Prize stories and even most single-author collections (Arnold, "A Big Anomaly in Short Stories" E3), short story readers among the general public are likely to conclude that the *New Yorker* dominates the short fiction market. When Updike served as guest editor of the *Best American Short Stories of 1984*, he was so aware of the magazine's primacy in previous years that he set a quota for himself on the number of *New Yorker* stories he could include (xiv). So important has the *New Yorker* been on the story scene that critics and reviewers often refer to "the *New Yorker* story" as a type, even when they're talking about stories that never appeared in the magazine, and even though they recognize that the species is now extinct.[39]

Overall, then, the erosion of commercial outlets for stories through both the decrease in the number of magazines publishing stories and the number of stories they publish, together with the resulting reliance of the story marketplace on little magazines that pay little or nothing to their writers, have combined to produce a literary scene dotted with creative writing MFA programs that support most writers. For such writers, publication in the *New Yorker* often represents the pinnacle of achievement in the short story world, a signal that a writer has arrived and a boost to any author's bid to publish a story collection with a major house. Now that there are so few well-paying vehicles for story writers, though, it would seem that the pressure on writers to craft the kinds of stories that might appeal to the fiction editors of commercial magazines should have disappeared. As Lorrie Moore puts it, "Having long lost its ability to pay an author's rent . . . the short story has been freed of its commercial life to become serious art, by its virtually every practitioner" (Introduction xv). What Moore suggests is that the freedom produced by the lack of a market for short stories has opened the field for the production of high art rather than merely popularly (and financially) successful texts. Even if the status of "serious art" is the destiny of the contemporary short story, though, the story will still need a market, however narrow, in order to achieve recognition.

The Field of Short Story Production: The Economic World Reversed?

At this point Bourdieu's theories of capital may be helpful in understanding the situation.[40] Bourdieu, like Moore, has characterized the field of literature as one that reverses the rules of the economic world: texts that are financially successful generally earn critical recognition from literary scholars in an inverse pattern.[41] Best sellers, works by popular writers such as John Grisham and Jackie, generally don't get taught or studied by literary scholars (except, perhaps, under the rubric of Cultural Studies). Texts that sell well are not generally included in the category "artistic," or, in the case of short stories, literary. William O'Rourke, writing of the short story genre in particular, notes that the more the commercial market and general readership for stories shrinks, the more they are valued by scholars and reviewers (199). For this reason, Bourdieu observes, the cultural meaning of each text is made twice over: once by the author, and once by the society into which it is delivered ("A Sociological Theory" 224). Reception of the work therefore becomes as important as the ideas put forward in it.[42]

In the case of short stories, the packaging is an important component of determining what ideas are put forward in the text. I'm not just talking about stories' appearance in magazines or anthologies; the very compactness of the text—its economy of form—creates particular limitations on both the writer and the reader. Rather than being a genre appropriate for apprentice readers, as many teachers and critics have assumed, the short story presents necessarily dense and compressed information that very well may not prove accessible to readers without the educational background (what Bourdieu would call educational capital) and aesthetic experience to "decode" it ("Field of Cultural Production" 220).[43] The brevity of the form does not allow for the kind of scene-setting exposition common to the novel; writers must often rely on a few carefully chosen details to telegraph the time and place of the story,[44] and sometimes even the topic of dialogue, as in the case of Hemingway's "Hills Like White Elephants." (My own experience teaching such a story is that nonmajor undergraduates—apprentice readers—need a great deal of help in contextualizing and understanding the conversation that takes place.) The kind of short stories that might constitute "high art" to Moore can thus be appreciated only by those with the educational capital to apprehend them, or else the habitus[45] (set of practices) of a family in which broad reading is encouraged, along with the leisure time and financial status to undertake it.[46] In either case, the reader is likely to possess not only educational or cultural capital (a family that prizes cultural appreciation, for example) but economic capital as well to facilitate the endeavor.

As O'Rourke points out, the intensive nature of reading a short story is also true of the writing process. His approach is based on the value of time, for both readers and writers. He draws a distinction between popular forms, which are labor-intensive for writers, and what he calls "fashionable" forms, which are capital-intensive. Although the short story is no longer popular, says O'Rourke, it is now fashionable. That's because the writers' time, which is very valuable, is used sparingly in the communication of dense material in a short amount of space and time. "Time," he writes, "is conserved and capital investment (education, formal training) increases in the production (and consumption) of the densely structured, written short story. Romance novels," in contrast, "are the popular literary form; they are read by people who in essence want to *kill* time—those whose time is much less valued" (202–203). O'Rourke reads the rise of small presses and the increase in creative writing programs as logical outgrowths of the prizing of capital-intensive institutions related to the short story. Labor-intensive popular forms, then, are accessible to large audiences, but they require little investment of capital by either their writers or their readers; capital-intensive art forms like the story conversely require substantial amounts of educational and cultural capital.

Related to these factors in the field of short story production is Bourdieu's understanding of taste, what he calls distinction. Where O'Rourke argues that readers whose own time is valuable will themselves privilege the short story, Bourdieu formulates (and demonstrates through considerable data) that the relationship between readers and taste is one based on negativity and rejection. That is, one group of readers—what he would call a class of readers, although he is not using the term in a strict Marxist sense—chooses the objects it will value by the fact of another class's rejection of them.[47] "In matters of taste, more than anywhere else," Bourdieu writes, "all determination is negation; and tastes are perhaps first and foremost distastes, disgust provoked by horror or visceral intolerance . . . of the tastes of others" (*Distinction* 56). In the case of photography, for example, itself a genre only on the margins of Bourdieu's definition of art, working-class viewers are much less likely to value photography for photography's sake—perhaps an image that makes a comment on the art of photography—than a picture of a field of flowers, a concrete object. They define themselves not just by their economic status but by their taste in art, which they establish by rejecting the art of the bourgeoisie. Conversely, then, the bourgeois class distinguishes itself by refusing that which is esteemed by the working class. By the accounting of either O'Rourke or Bourdieu, then, the short story has become a genre of the bourgeoisie, read mainly by those with the cultural and educational capital to find it (for who else has time to locate and read the many small magazines and literary reviews in which short stories now appear?) and appreciate it.[48]

As Paul DiMaggio argues, however, these dualist views of the world of art ignore the very real impact of "middlebrow" producers. In the case of the short story, such producers would include the men's and women's magazines that used to be regular publishers of "fashionable" rather than "popular" fiction, to use O'Rourke's terms. To ignore the marketing of "high culture" to the masses is to miss a crucial level in the hierarchy of art forms, contends DiMaggio. "[T]he very process of definition of a dominant high culture in the arts," he writes, has "relied upon the assistance of commercial enterprises in packaging for middle-class consumption an institutionally authorized mix of prestigious cultural goods, much of which had been part of a general popular culture less than a century earlier" (141). In the short story field, such an example might include the short story annuals, which cull from the small presses and larger commercial magazines the best of the year's lot (at least as determined by that year's editor). In terms of the larger cultural field, these annuals mark for the petit bourgeoisie, those who desire to move up in the hierarchy of classes, the stories and writers that represent the taste of the highest class.

The fact, however, that these annuals, despite their efforts at including a broad range of small outlets, tend to reproduce the editorial choices of the large commercial magazines means that the short story market continues to be dominated by these magazines, and the *New Yorker* in particular. The present state of affairs creates the opposite of the situation Moore describes: with so few paying outlets, writers who want to achieve the kind of success that a collection from a large publishing house can bring are driven to write the kinds of stories that they think editors of high-circulation publications will select to print for their readers. This narrowing of options limits rather than expands the kinds of stories that writers choose to work on. It also limits the field of quality fiction writing to those who can either afford to publish in nonpaying magazines or those who are willing to negotiate with what may be condescending editors in order to earn a fair return on their labor. In short, this situation produces the kinds of stories that are limited by cultural anxieties about female sexuality and race, because it targets those readers[49] who are most likely to be racially and socioeconomically white—that is, those readers who have the greatest power and social access. It is precisely this cycle that preserves the conservatism in the stories I have analyzed in the second and third chapters.

ECONOMIES OLD AND NEW

As I have argued throughout this book, the state of the contemporary American short story is complexly but certainly related to the state of its market. Its economy of form has important implications both for the kinds of readers it attracts and for its place in the hierarchy of literary genres. Its publication in magazines rather than in dedicated volumes contributes to the denigration of the genre as merely another kind of advertisement to be recycled when the reader is through. And its shrinking outlets contribute not to an opening up of topics for writers but rather a spreading conservatism when it comes to issues of great cultural anxiety such as female sexuality, motherhood, and whiteness. It is no accident that I first discovered economies of female sexuality in short stories; in fact, they are the genre best suited to portray them.

What might the future hold for the short story, then? In an era when leisure time is becoming increasingly scarce, many critics have forecasted a resurgence of the story from its alleged renaissance in the 1980s, arguing that the shorter form should fit better into Americans' hectic schedules. Barbara Kingsolver's remarks are representative of this sentiment:

> I have always wondered why short stories aren't more popular in this country. We Americans are such busy people you'd think we'd jump at the chance to have our literary wisdom served in doses that fit handily between taking the trash to the curb and waiting for the carpool. We should favor the short story and adore the poem. But we don't. Short story collections rarely sell half as well as novels; they are never block-busters. They are hardly ever even block-denters. From what I gather, most Americans would sooner read a five-hundred-page book about southern France or a boy attending wizard school or how to make home decor from roadside trash or *anything* than pick up a book offering them a dozen tales of the world complete in twenty pages apiece. (xiii)

But Ann Beattie rejects the logic of reading shorter works in shorter amounts of time. "It's often been said," she writes, "that short stories are so popular now because they are an ideal form for our time. This is said in the same spirit, it seems to me, as announcing that finger food that can be eaten in one bite is preferable at cocktail parties" (Introduction xi). Rather than serving the economy of time that is the outcome of current trends in professional and family life, in which Americans work many hours with so few left over to devote to family and cultural pursuits, it seems as if the short story could merely fall by the wayside.

Moreover, and more troubling, this attitude seems to have perme-ated the circles of literary scholars. In an era of ever-multiplying approaches to literature through critical theory, short story criticism, often stuck in the mud of New Critical methods from the 1950s, has failed to develop. With few exceptions, critics are no longer interested in the short story or the genre theory that applies to it. As a result, E. L. Doctorow can complain, as recently as 2000, that the genre lacks a "proprietary critic," as lyric poetry has Helen Vendler (xiii). This is in part because the genre's most prolific critics, Susan Lohafer and Charles

May, have now either moved into researching the psychological processing of the story (Lohafer) or retired (May). *Studies in Short Fiction*, the journal that for years was a stalwart outlet for critics of the short story, produced its last issue in 1999. Theory and criticism of the short story are quickly disappearing.

In her introduction to the 2006 volume of the Best American Short Stories, Ann Patchett writes an impassioned plea for the short story's survival:

> The short story is in need of a scandal.
>
> The short story should proclaim itself to be based on actual events and then, after a series of fiery public denials, it should hold a press conference in Cannes and make a brave but faltering confession: None of it actually happened. It was fiction all along. Yes, despite what's been said, it has always been fiction and it is *proud* to be fiction. The short story should consider staging its own kidnapping and then show up three weeks later in *The New Yorker* claiming that some things happened that cannot be discussed. Or perhaps the short story could seek out the celebrity endorsement of someone we never expected, maybe Tiger Woods, who could claim that he couldn't imagine going out to the ninth hole without a story in his back pocket. They are just the right size for reading between rounds of golf. It doesn't really matter what the short story chooses to do, but it needs to do something. The story needs hype. It needs a publicist. Fast. (xv)

Patchett, a writer best known for her work in other genres, cleverly describes the plight of the contemporary story as well as her acute discomfort at its lack of attention. Her characterization of the genre's troubles, though witty, sums up the painful state of the short story's popular profile. Much as the short story seems to be in failing health in Patchett's description, criticism of the genre is practically on its deathbed. My project represents an intervention in the field, a new way of interpreting both the impact of late 1970s mothering texts on literature and the cultural work of the short story. Through a sustained engagement with critical theory rather than an insistence that its influence remains outside the realm of short story criticism, this project signifies what I hope is resuscitation of the field. I caution new practitioners, though, that they must be attentive to not only the content of the stories themselves but also the cultural context in which they appear. Only through this approach, I believe, can those of us interested in continuing to work in this genre make the case that our commitment has significant cultural consequences.

Notes

Introduction

1. The use of roles rather than names to differentiate among the characters is a technique common to the short story, where the generality functions to make the meaning of the story more universal, as Mary Louise Pratt has noted in "The Short Story: The Long and the Short of It" (*The New Short Story Theories*, ed. Charles E. May [Athens, OH: Ohio UP, 1994, 2–3]).

2. The only writers of story collections to regularly appear on the best-seller list are Louis L'Amour and Stephen King, as McGrath notes.

3. One exception is E. L. Doctorow, who writes in the introduction to *The Best American Short Stories 2000* (eds. E. L. Doctorow and Katrina Kenison [Boston: Houghton Mifflin, 2000]) that "O'Connor's attempt to differentiate the short story as a genre by virtue of its sociology doesn't hold up under examination." But, he notes, it is possible to turn O'Connor's definition into an insight rather than a rule: "The story as a particular kind of fiction may not be definable by its construction or its length, but what *is* critical is its scale. Smaller in its overall dimensions than the novel, it is a fiction in which society is surmised as the darkness around the narrative circle of light" (xiv). Even in this case, one of the few explicit rejections of O'Connor's approach, Doctorow chooses to preserve O'Connor's understanding of the story's relationship to the society it represents— but, interestingly, his criticism returns to the length criterion that O'Connor wanted to avoid.

4. Foucault has argued for a reconceptualization of power in both his two-volume *The History of Sexuality* (New York: Vintage, 1990) and in his essay "The Subject and Power" (*Critical Inquiry* 8 [1982]), in which he asserts that "what defines a relationship of power is that it is a mode of action which does not act directly and immediately on others. Instead, it acts upon their actions" (789).

5. There is a strong cultural tendency to see motherhood as asexual, despite the fact that such a view is utterly illogical, as a study by social scientists Ariella Friedman, Hana Weinberg, and Ayala M. Pines ("Sexuality and Motherhood: Mutually Exclusive in Perception of Women," *Sex Roles* 38 [1988]: 781–800) and a survey of mothering literature by Nancy Chodorow and Susan Contratto (later Weisskopf)

("The Fantasy of the Perfect Mother," *Rethinking the Family: Some Feminist Questions*, eds. Barrie Thorne and Marilyn Yalom, rev. ed. [Boston: Northeastern UP, 1992]) attest. No less compelling, however, is a corresponding desire to see childhood, including adolescence, as asexual; as Ann duCille illustrates in "The Shirley Temple of My Familiar" (*Transition* 73 [1997]), audiences were horrified when a nineteen-year-old Shirley Temple, arguably the oldest American girl, wed Ronald Reagan in the 1947 film *That Hagen Girl*.

6. Moore's argument that the freedom of content choice produced by the lack of commercial outlets for the short story does have some basis in history, if it can be illustrated by an opposing case. According to Bill Mullen ("Marking Race/Marketing Race: African American Short Fiction and the Politics of Genre, 1933–1946," *Ethnicity and the American Short Story*, ed. Julie Brown [New York: Garland, 1997]), in 1945, near the height of the short story's market, a group called the Writers' War Board issued a report on literary portrayals of racial and ethnic minorities. The most sympathetic genre was determined, by a survey of recent literature, to be drama, which provided honest portrayals of minority characters; it was followed by novels, the movies, radio, comics, the Northern press, and advertising. Last, and, the report said, "most heinous," was the short story. The Board found that this genre was the worst offender in terms of its reliance on stereotypes.

7. McGrath in fact comments that a cynic might believe the ideal composition of a story collection would include six stories from the *New Yorker*, two from a women's magazine, and one from another commercial venue such as *Vanity Fair*. McGrath's comments, quoted in 1987, are even less realistic now, since fewer women's magazines than ever (with the exception of *Ms.*, which is noncommercial) publish quality literary fiction (Gayle Feldman, "Is There a Short Story Boom?" *Publishers Weekly* 25 December 1987: 26).

I STORY

1. Susan Koppelman, ed., *Between Mothers and Daughters: Stories across a Generation* (Old Westbury, NY: Feminist, 1985); Christine Park and Caroline Heaton, eds., *Close Company: Stories of Mothers and Daughters* (New York: Ticknor and Fields, 1987); Irene Zahava, ed., *My Mother's Daughter: Stories by Women* (Freedom, CA: Crossing, 1991).

2. These include monographs such as Marianne Hirsch, *The Mother/ Daughter Plot: Narratives, Psychoanalysis, Feminism* (Bloomington: Indiana UP, 1989) and collections such as Cathy N. Davidson and E. M. Broner, eds., *The Lost Tradition: Mothers and Daughters in Literature* (New York: Frederick Ungar, 1980).

3. Geeta Kothari, ed., *Did My Mama Like to Dance?* (New York: Avon, 1994); Katrina Kenison and Kathleen Hirsch, eds., *Mothers: Twenty*

Stories of Contemporary Motherhood (New York: North Point P-Farrar, Straus and Giroux, 1996); Faye Moskowitz, ed., *Her Face in the Mirror: Jewish Women on Mothers and Daughters* (New York: Beacon, 1994).

4. Jill Morgan, ed., *Mothers & Daughters: Celebrating the Gift of Love with 12 New Stories* (New York: Penguin, 1998); Alberto Manguel, ed., *Mothers & Daughters: An Anthology* (San Francisco: Chronicle Books, 1998); Jill Morgan, ed., *Mothers & Daughters* (New York: Signet, 1999); Heather Ingman, ed., *Mothers and Daughters in the Twentieth Century: A Literary Anthology* (Edinburgh: Edinburgh UP, 1999); Caledonia Kearns, ed., *Motherland: Writings by Irish American Women about Mothers and Daughters* (New York: HarperCollins, 1999); Joyce Carol Oates and Janet Berliner, eds., *Snapshots: 20th Century Mother-Daughter Fiction* (Boston: David R. Godine, 2000).

5. For example, Alberto Manguel, editor of *Mothers & Daughters: An Anthology*, also collected the texts in *Fathers & Sons: An Anthology* (San Francisco: Chronicle, 1998).

6. One reason for publishers' apparent preference for stories focused on mothers and daughters over those of fathers and sons may well be that men are less likely to read fiction than are women. One demographic study quoted on the NPR program *The Connection* ("Buy the Book") found that only 44 percent of men read fiction, compared with 77 percent of women. Assuming that mostly women will buy mother-daughter stories and mostly men will buy father-son stories, the former have almost twice the built-in market of the latter.

7. For the sake of the reader's familiarity with the works, the stories discussed here are also commonly collected in literary anthologies (i.e., Heath, Norton, etc.).

8. Perhaps the most commonly cited example of this type of plot comes from a novel rather than a short story—Toni Morrison's *Beloved* (New York: Plume-Penguin, 1987). The circumstances of the external tension are, of course, much more complicated in the novel-length treatment.

9. "Kiswana Browne," while it is capable of standing alone, also functions as part of a short story cycle, a group of tales linked by common characters, places, or themes. For more on the importance of this form, especially in its relation to writers of color, see James Nagel, *The Contemporary American Short-Story Cycle: The Ethnic Resonance of Genre* (Baton Rouge: Louisiana State UP, 2001). Maggie Dunn and Ann Morris (*The Composite Novel: The Short Story Cycle in Transition* [New York: Twayne, 1995]) argue that the short story cycle might more productively be termed a "composite novel," to acknowledge its affinities with the longer form. For a broad overview of the form, its history, and analysis of representative works, see Susan Garland Mann, *The Short Story Cycle: A Genre Companion and Reference Guide* (New York: Greenwood, 1989). In order to comprehensively address the theorization of the independent short story, this project does not take up the theorization of the short story as part of a cycle, which has its own, separate body of theory.

10. For a broad spectrum of approaches to the problem, see Linda Alcoff and Elizabeth Potter, eds., *Feminist Epistemologies* (New York: Routledge, 1993).

11. Margaret Atwood, in her 1989 introduction to the Best American Short Stories volume, has suggested that women's stories are often the inspiration for story writers of both sexes: "Our first stories come to us through the air. We hear voices. Children in oral societies grow up within a web of stories; but so do all children. . . . Traditionally, both the kitchen gossips and the readers-out-loud have been mothers or grandmothers, native languages have been mother tongues, and the kinds of stories that are told to children have been called nursery tales or old wives' tales. It struck me as no great coincidence when I learned recently that, when a great number of prominent writers were asked to write about the family member who had the greatest influence on their literary careers, almost all of them, male as well as female, had picked their mothers" (xv).

12. As one example, consider the medical profession that, for years, understood human health as men's health. Medical studies used only men as their subjects. Thus medical knowledge of heart disease, for example, was understood to be universal until scientists began to investigate women's differing experiences and risks.

13. The mother's insistence that this is not a story to tell again is much like the narrator's insistence in Morrison's *Beloved* that "this is not a story to pass on"—that is, it functions to necessitate the story's circulation.

14. While Trinh wants to give value to the mininarratives of women, many of her arguments could be applied to the stories of men who are not part of the dominant power structure—that is, men of color, gay or bisexual men, men who are not at the upper stratum of socioeconomic success, etc.

15. Ian Reid, in *The Short Story* (London: Methuen, 1977), notes that the first appearance of the term *short story* meaning a kind of literary product was in the 1933 OED supplement (1). While the association between the literary genre of the short story and the oral form of the story may seem to be a whimsy of the English language, Mary Louise Pratt ("The Short Story: The Long and the Short of It," *The New Short Story Theories*, ed. Charles E. May [Athens, OH: Ohio UP, 1994]) notes that in some languages the terms for "story" as tale and the genre of the short story are interchangeable—for example, in Spanish, *cuento*; in French, *conte* (94).

16. Walker's comment echoes Twain's advice to the teller of the humorous tale in "How to Tell a Story." Twain directs the storyteller to capitalize on carefully placed pauses to keep the audience's attention and to punctuate the punch line. Twain emphasizes the interaction between teller and audience in making the delivery of the humorous tale as effective as possible.

17. An excellent example of the oral tradition in American literature is provided by Joel Chandler Harris's Uncle Remus tales (*Nights with Uncle Remus: Myths and Legends of the Old Plantation* [Boston: James R. Osgood, 1883]); Charles Chesnutt later played on the Uncle Remus trope in his short story collection *The Conjure Woman* (Boston: Houghton Mifflin, 1899).

18. William O'Rourke ("Morphological Metaphors for the Short Story: Matters of Production, Reproduction, and Consumption," *Short Story Theory at a Crossroads*, eds. Susan Lohafer and Jo Ellyn Clarey [Baton Rouge: Louisiana State UP, 1989]) is the sole dissenting voice on this matter: he asserts that the sermon is the more logical transitional form between orality and literacy.

19. While producing texts in exchange for both monetary compensation and cultural recognition may subtly shift an author's subject-position (thereby perhaps bringing him/her closer to privileged status), this risk is necessary in order to empower new writers as well as the readers who find characters similar to themselves in the stories created by such writers.

20. In fact, Ong goes so far as to compare stages of literate development to the psychosexual stages of Freudian theory; in his paradigm, orality corresponds to the oral stage, print to the anal, and the evolution of electronic media to the genital. He notes that under such a pattern, humanity can be said to have only recently approached maturity (*The Presence of the Word Some Prolegomena for Cultural and Religious History* [New Haven: Yale UP, 1967], 103).

21. Derrida is addressing writing in particular, while Ong's use of the term *literacy* frequently encompasses manuscript writing, the technology of print, and electronic forms. While Ong claims, in *Orality and Literacy: The Technologizing of the Word* (New Accents Series. London: Methuen, 1982), that Derrida's formulation applies to print rather than manuscript writing, this distinction is not important for the purposes of my argument.

22. O'Rourke's remarks in his own essay ("Morphological Metaphors for the Short Story: Matters of Production, Reproduction, and Consumption," *Short Story Theory at a Crossroads*, eds. Susan Lohafer and Jo Ellyn Clarey [Baton Rouge: Louisiana State UP, 1989]) seem to echo Derrida's; he goes so far as to characterize writing as the appropriate medium for art, while oral forms are good merely for popular consumption: "The mass audience finds most of its entertainment in forms that are overwhelmingly oral (television, movies, and popular literature). One of the requirements of the oral form is not stopping and thinking about what has been said (or read), lest we lost the thread of the narrative, miss what is said next. The written form allows readers to influence the space-time equation: to think, reflect, ponder, if they choose" (199–200).

23. Literary historian Lionel Stevenson ("The Short Story in Embryo," *English Literature in Transition* 15 [1972]) makes much the same suggestion about the short story as genre when he says that short narratives expand when a culture becomes more complex, in order to better reflect the greater cultural complexity. Appreciation of a "simple" story, then, implies that one comes from a "simple" culture.

24. Although Trinh doesn't mention it, an excellent example of story-telling's magical powers can be found in the character of Uncle Julius in Chesnutt's *The Conjure Woman*.

25. This is not to say that novels cannot be presented in oral modes. Charles E. May opens *The Short Story: The Reality of Artifice* (New York: Twayne, 1995), in fact, with the assertion that while the short story has developed from oral storytelling, the novel is the descendant of the epic—apparently willing to ignore the fact that the epic originated as an oral form. Most short story theorists assert, however, that the story has closer ties to orality in its history and development than does the novel.

26. Because a detailed history of short story theory is not the aim of this project, some texts will inevitably be omitted from the discussion. For a good starting bibliography of short story theory, see Charles E. May, ed., *The New Short Story Theories* (Athens, OH: Ohio UP, 1994). Book-length studies from the last twenty years include Valerie Shaw, *The Short Story: A Critical Introduction* (London: Longman, 1983); Susan Lohafer, *Coming to Terms with the Short Story* (Baton Rouge: Louisiana UP, 1985); May, *The Short Story: The Reality of Artifice*. A useful collection of essays can be found in Susan Lohafer and Jo Ellyn Clarey, eds., *Short Story Theory at a Crossroads* (Baton Rouge: Louisiana UP, 1989). For a broad range of short story writers' comments on the writing and criticism of the genre, see Ann Charters, ed., *The Story and Its Writer: An Introduction to Short Fiction*, 6th ed. (New York: Bedford, 2003).

27. Sometimes even the titles of short story critics' writings betray their defensiveness: see Thomas H. Gullason's "The Short Story: An Underrated Art," *Studies in Short Fiction* 2 (1964).

28. Although almost every short story theorist relies on comparisons with the novel in order to define the short story, theorists of the novel are under no such obligation. Novel theory seems perfectly able to function without any mention of the short story. See, for example, Edgar Allan Poe, *The Works of E. A. Poe*, ed. John H. Ingram, Vol. IV (London: A. & C. Adams, 1901); Ian Watt, *The Rise of the Novel: Studies in Defoe, Richardson, and Fielding* (Berkeley: U of California P, 1957). For a notable exception, see George Lukács, *The Theory of the Novel*, trans. Anna Bodtock (Cambridge: MIT P, 1971).

29. Interestingly, Pratt also notes that this relationship between the two genres exists even in those languages where no such linguistic relationship between the two words presupposes that the short story will be compared to a longer genre.

30. William Faulkner took the opposite view—that one only became a novelist after failing as a short story writer: "Maybe every novelist wants to write poetry first, finds he can't, and then tries the short story, which is the most demanding form after poetry. And, failing at that, only then does he take up novel writing" (qtd. in Fredrick L. Gwynn and Joseph L. Blotner, eds., *Faulkner in the University* [New York: Vintage, 1965], 207).

31. F. Scott Fitzgerald, in fact, was spurred to success in publishing short stories *after* his first novel was accepted (Arthur T. Vanderbilt II, *The Making of a Bestseller: From Author to Reader* [Jefferson, NC: McFarland, 1999], 5).

32. No one has advocated the genre's appropriateness for apprentice readers and writers more forcefully than Herbert Ellsworth Cory ("The Senility of the Short-Story," *What Is the Short Story?* eds. Eugene Current-García and Walton R. Patrick, rev. ed. [Glenview, IL: Scott, Foresman, 1974]). According to Cory, the short story's "technique is so much less difficult than that of the essay that high-school teachers find it facile material for their students. Nothing is more insidiously easy in America to-day than to become a popular teacher with the short-story as your medium. It is so much easier to write than the essay and so much more obviously attractive that hundreds of grub-streets supply an artificially simulated demand, obtuse undergraduate students of composition plunge their teachers into a premature literary dyspepsia, hundreds of languid and day-dreaming women make it possible for quack teachers to earn with private classes a plausible semblance of an honest living" (63).

33. Susan Lohafer writes in *Coming to Terms with the Short Story*, "Probably every teacher and professor of English has taught a short story—once. But stories, as a rule, turn up in the curricula for beginners and 'nonmajors,' and hardly anyone who teaches graduate students teaches stories—*as such*" (134).

34. This is such an important rhetorical strategy for critics of the short story that most book-length studies written before 1980—and, in the case of Charles May, even as late as 1995—open with a statement about the short story's lengthy history. See, for example, H. E. Bates, *The Modern Short Story: A Critical Survey*, 2nd ed. (London: Michael Joseph, 1972); Reid, *The Short Story*; May, *The Short Story: The Reality of Artifice*.

35. Elizabeth Bowen's assessment probably refers to what critics variously label the modern or lyric short story as opposed to earlier forms, which more closely resemble the tale (Introduction, *The Faber Book of Modern Short Stories*. London: Faber & Faber, 1936. Rpt. in *The New Short Story Theories*, ed. Charles E. May [Athens, OH: Ohio UP, 1994]).

36. Most other historians of the genre would agree that the short story's roots are in folklore, fables, and other traditionally oral forms. See, for example, Bates, *The Modern Short Story*; Walter Allen, *The Short Story in*

English (Oxford: Clarendon, 1981); Gordon Weaver, ed., *The American Short Story, 1945–1980: A Critical History* (Boston: G. K. Hall, 1983); Philip Stevick, ed., *The American Short Story, 1900–1945: A Critical History* (Boston: G. K. Hall, 1984).

37. In "The Nature of Knowledge in Short Fiction," May comments in a similar vein that the novel is "primarily a social and public form" while the short story is "mythic and spiritual" (133). Although he is sometimes defensive about the short story's treatment at the hands of literary critics, May, with perhaps the exception of Susan Lohafer, is the most important contemporary advocate of the short story. The original publication of his *Short Story Theories* in 1976, notes Lohafer, was a critical moment in the development of short story theory. Of the collection, Lohafer says in *Coming to Terms with the Short Story* that "there is no more valuable source" as a introduction to the breadth of theory (32). May's revision of that collection, *The New Short Story Theories*, published in 1994, represents a significant advance in the field. Because May's scholarly work as both writer and editor has made the texts in this collection key to the ongoing conversations in short story theory, the articles collected there are also critical to the arguments advanced in this chapter.

38. John Gerlach puts the idea thus in his article "The Margins of Narrative" (*Short Story Theory at a Crossroads*, eds. Susan Lohafer and Jo Ellyn Clarey [Baton Rouge: Louisiana State UP, 1989]): "[A] story is an invitation to construct explanations, explanations about causality, connections, motives. When we feel we are constructing them significantly . . . we sense story" (80).

39. Of course, this supposition can also be seen as a drawback to the form: if a reader is not on the same wavelength as the writer, understanding and appreciation of a story may be lacking.

40. Valerie Shaw has also linked the short story with visual texts in *The Short Story: A Critical Introduction*, arguing that the short story's development has been guided by advances in painting and then photography and that the short story collection is the print equivalent of an art exhibition (13–17).

41. Although Washington Irving is widely considered to be the "father" of the American short story, Éjxenbaum ("O. Henry and the Theory of the Short Story," trans. I. R. Titunik, *Readings in Russian Poetics: Formalist and Structuralist Views*, ed. Krystyna Pomorska [Cambridge: MIT P, 1971]) argues that Irving's tales owe more to the English sketch than to an independently evolved short story. Éjxenbaum does not, however, name any particular author as the progenitor of the American form.

42. Ferguson agrees in "The Rise of the Short Story in the Hierarchy of Genres" (*Short Story Theory at a Crossroads*, eds. Susan Lohafer and Jo Ellyn Clarey [Baton Rouge: Louisiana State UP, 1989]): "The fact of serial publication, and the popularity of serialized novels among the

English middle classes, inadvertently gave the short story its break. In addition to the serialized novels which presumably kept the reader coming back week after week, many short stories were published by magazines" (182).

43. Norman Friedman, in "What Makes a Short Story Short?" (*The Essentials of the Theory of Fiction*, eds. Michael J. Hoffman and Patrick D. Murphy, 2nd ed. [Durham: Duke UP, 1996]), disputes the use of the "single effect" as the characteristic marker of the short story, arguing, "there is certainly no reason why a short story should have more unity than a novel" (101). He continues, refusing to recognize the traditional separation between novels and short stories, by claiming that "the materials and their organization in a short story differ from those in a novel in degree but not in kind" (101).

44. It seems ironic that Pratt, an American critic, sees the short story as the Irish national literature, while the Irish O'Connor bestows that honor upon the United States.

45. Susan Koppelman, in "A Preliminary Sketch of the Early History of U.S. Women's Short Stories" (*Journal of American Culture* 22.2 [1999]), notes an exception to this rule: collections of stories published as serial remembrance books (such as *The Atlantic Souvenir*, *The Token*, and *The Gift)* were not only useful gifts of friendship but sometimes helped raise funds for causes such as abolition and temperance movements (3).

46. Éjxenbaum's assessment of the story, focusing, as it does, on the stories of O. Henry, may not seem as applicable to contemporary writings as it does to those of the earlier part of the century. This theoretical stance, however, could well have helped to reinforce critical assessments of the story as the genre of the immature reader, for it is one that provides the reader with relatively immediate gratification, rather than the postponed and repostponed pleasures of the novel.

47. Cortázar's essay ("Some Aspects of the Short Story," *The New Short Story Theories*, ed. Charles E. May [Athens, OH: Ohio UP]) includes an extensive consideration of the potential of literature as a tool of social revolution. Interestingly, he does not see the necessity to dilute the message of "popular" literature to make it accessible to the masses. "Watch out," he warns, "for the facile demagogy of those who demand a literature accessible to everyone!" (253). Cortázar takes the position that, for the writer with a revolutionary commitment, any kind of writing can be revolutionary—it has no particular subgenre (science fiction, murder mystery, or fantasy may all prove useful options, even if they are not usually considered radical forms). But such writers need not "dumb down" their artistic works in order to have political power. "You do the people no favors if you offer them a literature which they can assimilate without effort, passively, like those who go to the cinema to see cowboy movies" (254). In Cortázar's view, the only truly revolutionary literature is that which challenges the public to think in new ways.

48. Falcon O. Baker, in "Short Stories for the Millions" (*What Is the Short Story?* eds. Eugene Current-García and Walton R. Patrick, rev. ed. [Glenview, IL: Scott, Foresman, 1974]), inadvertently documents this problem in his praise for the availability of good fiction in the early 1950s: "Even in the most surprising places good fiction sometimes crops up. *Woman's Day* is found at seven cents a copy sandwiched between loaves of bread and canned vegetables in the A & P grocery" (121).

49. Pratt's point is buttressed when considering that William Faulkner and Elizabeth Bishop (to name merely two examples), both authors best known for their work in other genres, wrote short stories when they needed to make money quickly. On Bishop, see Brett Millier, *Elizabeth Bishop: Life and the Memory of It* (Berkeley: U of California P, 1993). On Faulkner, see Donald Kartiganer, "An Introduction to the Last Great Short Story" (*The Oxford American* May/June 1995).

50. Ferguson concurs with this explanation: By the early decades of the twentieth century, "[r]ejection by the lowbrow became a touchstone of high modernist art, and to be too popular . . . was to court critical deprecation. Appreciation of the short story, along with that of other modernist art forms, became connoisseurship . . . the pre-eminence of the short story as a modernist genre grew out of the modern highbrow audience's acceptance of fragmentation as an accurate model of the world. . . . The brevity that marked 'minor' to earlier generations became a badge of the short story's superior representational capacity" (191).

51. Again, Pratt's essay provides a detailed history of the comparison of the short story to the novel. She does not go so far, however, as to compare the short story's position with that of women in patriarchal society.

52. Interestingly, Pratt points out that even in languages in which the term for the short story does not imply its brevity, the usual critical approach to the genre consists of comparing it with the novel (94).

53. Mary Eagleton ("Gender and Genre," *Re-Reading the Short Story*, ed. Clare Hanson [New York: St. Martin's]) breaks with the majority of short story theorists, who cite a lengthy history for the genre, by claiming a longer history for the novel; this piece of evidence, in her argument, is additional reason that the short story is an opportune genre for women writers.

54. Cixous uses the term *feminine* in "The Laugh of the Medusa" (trans. Keith Cohen and Paula Cohen, *New French Feminisms: An Anthology*, eds. Elaine Marks and Isabelle de Courtivron [New York: Schocken, 1981]) to refer not only to texts written by women but all those who disrupt patriarchal authority: "It is impossible to *define* a feminine practice of writing. . . . But it will always surpass the discourse that regulates the phallocentric system; it does and will take place in areas other than those subordinated to philosophico-theoretical domination. It will be conceived of only by subjects who are breakers of automatisms, by peripheral figures that no authority can ever subjugate" (253).

55. Trinh's vision of stories that can transcend history echoes Walter Benjamin's account of the difference between story and history in "The Storyteller: Reflections on the Works of Nikolai Leskov," trans. Harry Zohn, *Illuminations*, ed. Hannah Arendt (New York: Schocken, 1968): "The value of information does not survive the moment in which it was new. It lives only at that moment; it has to surrender to it completely and explain itself to it without losing any time. A story is different. It does not expend itself. It preserves and concentrates its strength and is capable of releasing it even after a long time" (90).

56. Trinh notes elsewhere that no story can be universal or all-encompassing in scope; despite the boundless fluidity she often ascribes to her model, a story without an end, middle, or beginning would simply be "the vision of a madwoman" (123). The story must have an end, even if that end is temporary and only necessary in a transition from one speaker to another, for without an end, there is no way to talk about the story as object.

57. Here Trinh appears to posit a model of orality in repetition (with a difference) of Barthes's *The Pleasure of the Text*, trans. Richard Miller (New York: Hill and Wang, 1975).

58. John Edgar Wideman (Introduction, *The Best American Short Stories 1996*, eds. John Edgar Wideman and Katrina Kenison [Boston: Houghton Mifflin, 1996]) commented on the effect of this opposition between fact and fiction on the contemporary short story: "Mainstream culture systematically trivializes fiction by opposing it to other modes of representation deemed 'true.' We co-opt and corrupt the art of storytelling by enlisting it in the service of journalism and the big lie of advertising. Our fear and distrust of fiction reflect America's unfinished business of coming to terms with difference, our national reluctance to give full and equal credit to the *other* story—the woman's story, the black story, the immigrant story, the homeless story, our own story reimagined, the daunting freedom and responsibility that a reimagined self would demand" (xvii).

59. Although Oprah's book club has been a fascinating enterprise to observe, Oprah's choices have been almost exclusively novels. (The other choices have been memoirs.)

60. In fact, the state of American feminism in the early 1980s, particularly in literature departments, was such that Toril Moi's 1985 accusation that it was too uncritically positive—for its unquestioning praise of women writers and their texts, and for the critics who advanced this agenda—was met with outrage. For most American feminists in literary studies, truly critical analyses of texts written by women were anathema. For the original comment, see Toril Moi, *Sexual/Textual Politics: Feminist Literary Theory* (London: Routledge, 1985). Moi's account of the incident, and her response, appears in *What Is a Woman? And Other Essays* (Oxford: Oxford UP, 1999).

2   THE FEMALE SEXUAL ECONOMY

1. For a more thorough discussion of the theorization of the short story, see chapter 1.

2. Mary Eagleton, in "Gender and Genre" (*Re-Reading the Short Story*, ed. Clare Hanson [New York: St. Martin's, 1989]), suggests that the "newness" of the short story form relative to the novel makes it particularly inviting to women writers who are intimidated by a tradition of "great masters" (60). Julio Cortázar ("Some Aspects of the Short Story," trans. Aden W. Hayes, *The New Short Story Theories*, ed. Charles E. May [Athens, OH: Ohio UP, 1994]) agrees that the short story has few "great masters," although for different reasons—he asserts that writing short stories is more difficult than writing novels, a fact demonstrated, he says, by the much smaller number of masters of the short story compared to the novel.

3. Of course, modernism cannot be discounted as an influential force in the shift toward the portrayal of ordinary life in literature; the novels of Virginia Woolf, as only one example, provide a glimpse into the everyday, ordinary life of characters in a way that was uncommon prior to the modernist era.

4. Mary Helen Washington, ed. (*Invented Lives: Narratives of Black Women 1860–1960* [Garden City, NY: Anchor-Doubleday, 1987]) continues, "Maybe it is the educated daughters' need to open the 'sealed letter' their mothers 'could not plainly read,' to have their mothers' signatures made clear in their work, to preserve their language, their memories, their myths. Before these signatures can be read clearly, we will have to free the mother from the domination of the daughter, representing her more honestly as a separate, individuated being whose daughters cannot even begin to imagine the mysteries of her life" (351–352).

5. Similar views are expressed about women's biography and autobiography by Lynn Z. Bloom and Bell Gale Chevigny. Lynn Z. Bloom, in "Heritages: Dimensions of Mother-Daughter Relationships in Women's Autobiographies" (*The Lost Tradition: Mothers and Daughters in Literature*, eds. Cathy N. Davidson and E. M. Broner [New York: Frederick Ungar, 1980]) argues, "[I]n women's autobiographies the author, in recreating and interpreting her childhood and maturing self, assumes a number of the functions that her own mother fulfilled in the actual family history" (292). Bell Gale Chevigny, in "Daughter's Writing: Toward a Theory of Women's Biography" (*Between Women: Biographers, Novelists, Critics, Teachers and Artists Write about Their Work on Women*, eds. Carol Ascher, Louise DeSalvo, and Sara Ruddick [Boston: Beacon, 1984]), uses Chodorow's theory to construct a model of women biographers' relation to their subjects: "Women writing about women, I am persuaded, are likely to move toward a subject that symbolically reflects their internalized relations with their mothers and

that offers them an opportunity to re-create those relations" (375). While this is certainly not the only model for understanding autobiography, it seems to be a common thread running through feminist conceptions of women's autobiography, and its basis in the mother-daughter relationship signals the importance of this bond to feminist theorists, particularly during the 1980s.

6. Gardiner is particularly indebted to Chodorow's model of the mother-daughter relationship for her theory.

7. While there were other important studies of the mother-child relationship published during the same era, none has proven as influential in academic studies, both literary and otherwise, in the period since. For a sampling of the range of articles on the subject appearing in the 1970s, see Rachel Blau DuPlessis, ed., *Toward a Feminist Theory of Motherhood*, spec. issue of *Feminist Studies* 4.2 (1978): 1–202; Lee Chambers-Schiller, ed., *Mothers and Daughters*, spec. issue of *Frontiers* 3.2 (1978): 1–80; E. M. Broner and Cathy Davidson, eds., *Mothers and Daughters in Literature*, spec. issue of *Women's Studies* 6.2 (1979): 123–234. For monographs, see Edith Neisser, *Mothers and Daughters: A Lifelong Relationship*, rev ed. (New York: Harper & Row, 1973); Jessie Bernard, *The Future of Motherhood* (New York: Dial, 1974); Signe Hammer, *Daughters and Mothers. Mothers and Daughters* (New York: Quadrangle, 1975); Jane Lazarre, *The Mother Knot* (New York: Dell, 1976); Judith Arcana, *Our Mothers' Daughters* (Berkeley, CA: Shameless Hussy, 1979).

The interest in mothering that emerged from the 1970s has had an enormous impact on the appearance of mothering texts in the decades since. It would be impossible to list even the monographs that have been published in the past twenty-five years, not least because the list would immediately be outdated. Instead, I provide here a selection of some of the types of approaches inspired by writers such as Friday, Dinnerstein, and Chodorow. For sociological perspectives, see, for example, Ruth Wodak and Muriel Schulz, *The Language of Love and Guilt: Mother-Daughter Relationships from a Cross-Cultural Perspective* (Amsterdam: John Benjamins, 1986); Barbara Katz Rothman, *Recreating Motherhood: Ideology and Technology in a Patriarchal Society* (New York: Norton, 1989); Jacquelyn S. Litt, *Medicalized Motherhood: Perspectives from the Lives of African-American and Jewish Women* (New Brunswick, NJ: Rutgers UP, 2000). Psychological and psychoanalytic approaches include Jane B. Abramson, *Mothermania: A Psychological Study of Mother-Daughter Conflict* (Lexington, MA: Lexington Books-D. C. Heath, 1987); Nini Herman, *Too Long a Child: The Mother-Daughter Dyad* (London: Free Association, 1989); Naomi Ruth Lowinsky, *Stories from the Motherline: Reclaiming the Mother-Daughter Bond, Finding Our Feminine Souls* (Los Angeles: Jeremy P. Tarcher, 1992). Cross-disciplinary works include Ann Dally, *Inventing Motherhood: The Consequences of an Ideal* (London: Burnett,

1982); Shelley Phillips, *Beyond the Myths: Mother-Daughter Relationships in Psychology, History, Literature and Everyday Life* (London: Penguin, 1991); Sara Ruddick, *Maternal Thinking: Toward a Politics of Peace* (Boston: Beacon, 1995). For self-help orientations, see Roni Cohen-Sandler and Michelle Silver, *"I'm Not Mad, I Just Hate You!": A New Understanding of Mother-Daughter Conflict* (New York: Viking, 1999); Paula J. Caplan, *The New Don't Blame Mother: Mending the Mother-Daughter Relationship* (New York: Routledge, 2000); Sheila Schuller Coleman, *Between Mother and Daughter* (Old Tappan, NJ: Fleming H. Revell, 1982). (Coleman's book is, even more narrowly, an example of Christian self-help by the daughter of evangelist Robert Schuller.)

8. See chapter 1 for a more complete list of such works.

9. The term *cathexis* derives from Freudian psychoanalysis and is defined by Jean LaPlanche and J.-B. Pontalis in *The Language of Psych-Analysis* (New York: Norton, 1973), as an "[e]conomic concept: the fact that a certain amount of psychical energy is attached to an idea or to a group of ideas, to a part of the body, to an object, etc." (62).

10. As Marianne Hirsch has persuasively argued in *The Mother/Daughter Plot: Narratives, Psychoanalysis, Feminism* (Bloomington: Indiana UP, 1989), an understanding of psychoanalysis is crucial to appreciating literary portrayals of mothers and daughters, too.

11. Although the critique of Freud that follows has been formed over many years of reading, I am most indebted to the following sources for my perspective: Gayle S. Rubin, "The Traffic in Women: Notes toward a 'Political Economy,'" *Toward an Anthropology of Women*, ed. Rayna Reiter (New York: Monthly Review, 1975); Nancy J. Chodorow, *The Reproduction of Mothering: Psychoanalysis and the Sociology of Gender*, 2nd ed. (Berkeley: U of California P, 1999); Adrienne Rich, "Compulsory Heterosexuality and Lesbian Existence," *Powers of Desire: The Politics of Sexuality*, eds. Ann Snitow, Christine Stansell, and Sharon Thompson (New York: Monthly Review, 1983); Luce Irigaray, "This Sex Which Is Not One," trans. Claudia Reeder, *New French Feminisms: An Anthology*, eds. Elaine Marks and Isabelle de Courtivron (New York: Schocken, 1981); Julia Kristeva, "Stabat Mater," trans. Arthur Goldhammer, *Poetics Today* 6 (1985); Judith Butler, "Gender Trouble, Feminist Theory, and Psychoanalytic Discourse," *Feminism/Postmodernism*, ed. Linda J. Nicholson (New York: Routledge, 1990); Julia Kristeva, "Motherhood according to Giovanni Bellini," *The Portable Kristeva*, ed. Kelly Oliver (New York: Columbia UP, 1997).

12. Dorothy Dinnerstein (*The Mermaid and the Minotaur: Sexual Arrangements and Human Malaise* [New York: Harper & Row, 1976]), for example, acknowledges that there are problems in Freud, but proclaims, "Feminist preoccupation with Freud's patriarchal bias, with his failure to jump with alacrity right out of his male Victorian

skin, seems to me wildly ungrateful. The conceptual tool that he has put into our hands is a revolutionary one. If we are afraid to use it—and using it is frightening—we have only ourselves to blame" (xi).

13. See, for example, the self-conscious revision of Freud in "Some Psychical Consequences of the Anatomical Distinction between the Sexes" (*The Standard Edition of the Complete Psychological Works of Sigmund Freud*, ed. James Strachey, vol. 19 [London: Hogarth, 1968], 249).

14. These explanations are most fully described in "Femininity" (*The Standard Edition of the Complete Psychological Works of Sigmund Freud*, ed. James Strachey, vol. 22 [London: Hogarth, 1968]), although they warrant brief summary in the earlier essay "Female Sexuality" (*The Standard Edition of the Complete Psychological Works of Sigmund Freud*, ed. James Strachey, vol. 21 [London: Hogarth, 1968]). Freud takes up penis-envy in greater detail in "Some Psychical Consequences of the Anatomical Distinction between the Sexes."

15. He links the period of attachment to the mother (usually prior to age four) with the origins of hysteria: it "is not surprising when we reflect that both the phase and the neurosis are characteristically feminine, and further, that in this dependence on the mother we have the germ of later paranoia in women. For this germ appears to be the surprising, yet regular, fear of being killed (? devoured) [*sic*] by the mother" ("Female Sexuality" 27). While Freud here equates the failure of the girl to transfer her affections to her father with illness as an adult, it is not clear that he means that homosexual object-choice (the logical result, according to his theory, of a failure to shift from mother to father) is an illness of the same category as paranoia and hysteria.

16. As Freud puts it, "She gives up her wish for a penis and puts in place of it a wish for a child: and *with that purpose in view* she takes her father as a love-object. Her mother becomes the object of her jealousy. The girl has turned into a little woman" ("Some Psychical Consequences of the Anatomical Distinction between the Sexes" 256). And earlier in this essay Freud asserts, "Even after penis-envy has abandoned its true object, it continues to exist: by an easy displacement it persists in the character-trait of *jealousy*. Of course, jealousy is not limited to one sex and has a wider foundation than this, but I am of the opinion that it plays a far larger part in the mental life of women than of men and that that is because it is enormously reinforced from the direction of displaced penis-envy" ("Some Psychical Consequences of the Anatomical Distinction between the Sexes" 254). In "Femininity," Freud suggests that women who have not moved beyond penis-envy to envy of their mothers suffer greatly. Such women may eventually end up in analysis, where, even if they cannot get a penis, they can at least expect to restore themselves to the "capacity . . . to carry on an intellectual profession" (125).

17. While I am simplifying matters somewhat, Freud's prescriptive theories tend to recognize two major paths of sexual development for children—the normal, and everything else.

18. Nancy Friday, *My Secret Garden: Women's Sexual Fantasies* (New York: Trident, 1973); Nancy Friday, *Forbidden Flowers: More Women's Sexual Fantasies* (New York: Pocket-Simon & Schuster, 1975).

19. Nancy J. Chodorow and Susan Contratto, in "The Fantasy of the Perfect Mother" (*Rethinking the Family: Some Feminist Questions*, eds. Barrie Thorne and Marilyn Yalom, rev. ed. [Boston: Northeastern UP, 1992]), sum up Friday's book thus: "It speaks to the daughter in all women and tells them that their problems are not political, social, personal, or, heaven forbid, caused by men; their problems are caused solely by their mothers" (205).

20. Dinnerstein does not discuss lesbian or gay sexual relationships. She does recognize, however, that her argument is "frankly ethnocentric" in terms of focusing on middle-class nuclear families (40).

21. For other examples of criticism of Dinnerstein, see Hirsch, *The Mother/Daughter Plot*, and Chodorow and Contratto, "The Fantasy of the Perfect Mother"; for a condemnation of Dinnerstein's hetero-sexist assumptions see Rich, "Compulsory Heterosexuality and Lesbian Existence."

22. Chodorow relies most heavily on the works of Melanie Klein, Michael and Alice Balint, W. R. D. Fairbairn, and Harry Guntrip in her understanding of development through the object-relations perspective.

23. See Helene Deutsch, *The Psychology of Women: A Psychoanalytic Interpretation*, vol. I (New York: Grune & Stratton, 1944).

24. In her preface to the second edition, Chodorow pointedly acknowl-edged this shortcoming: "I am noting that the call for equal parenting, while supported by my argument linking mothering and male domi-nance, was contradicted in consequential ways by my accounts of maternal subjectivity and its centrality for women and of the corre-spondingly distinctive character of the mother-child bond" (*The Reproduction of Mothering* xvi).

25. This article (Judith Lorber et al., "On *The Reproduction of Mothering*: A Methodological Debate," *Signs* 6: 482–514) presents responses from scholars in several different fields to Chodorow's book, as well as Chodorow's replies to them, and is thus a useful primer in critical response to the book.

26. Because Chodorow's book has been so influential (as the cover of the twentieth anniversary edition trumpets, *Contemporary Sociology* named it one of the ten most influential books of the past twenty-five years), it has drawn a vast array of comment, of which these criticisms are merely a sample. Rosemary Putnam Tong's *Feminist Thought: A More Comprehensive Introduction* (Boulder, CO: Westview, 1998) provides a useful overview of the kinds of criticisms leveled at

Chodorow (145–150). Most critics have focused on Chodorow's use of psychoanalysis as the foundation of her study, but their objections have ranged widely. Nina Baym ("The Madwoman and Her Languages: Why I Don't Do Feminist Theory," *Tulsa Studies in Women's Literature* 3 [1984]: 45–59) condemned Chodorow, and indeed all other psychoanalytic feminists, for her appropriation of Freud, saying, "To my perception, there is manifest in the feminist theorist's obsession with Freud precisely that masochism that Freud and his followers identified with the female. We are most 'daddy's girl' when we seek—as Jane Gallop not long ago expressed it—to seduce him" (51–52). Parveen Adams, in "Mothering" (*m/f* 8 [1983]: 40–52), argued that Chodorow's reliance on psychoanalysis reduced the complexities of the social world down to the relative simplicities of a psychic one, and E. Ann Kaplan (*Motherhood and Representation: The Mother in Popular Culture and Melodrama* [London: Routledge, 1992]) expanded that argument to say that Chodorow confused psychic mothers with social ones. Marianne Hirsch, in *The Mother/Daughter Plot*, took Chodorow to task for founding her theory on the androcentric writings of male writers such as Freud and Lacan, noting that such a framework erases the subjectivity of the mother. Nancy Fraser and Linda J. Nicholson expressed a postmodern suspicion of psychoanalysis as a metanarrative that ignores historical and local specificity and addressed Chodorow's work from this perspective, in "Social Criticism without Philosophy: An Encounter between Feminism and Postmodernism" (*Feminism/Postmodernism*, ed. Linda J. Nicholson [New York: Routledge, 1990], 19–38).

27. Only one literary critic has approached limits on female sexuality in a similar manner, although her remarks are confined to the novels of Jane Austen and isolated from the theoretical context of the mothering texts I examine. Susan Peck MacDonald, in "Jane Austen and the Tradition of the Absent Mother" (*The Lost Tradition: Mothers and Daughters in Literature*, eds. Cathy N. Davidson and E. M. Broner [New York: Frederick Ungar, 1980]), comments that in order for the girls of Austen's novels "to mature as successfully independent adults—and in order for the novels to focus centrally upon them—the most powerful outside personality, the person who could best facilitate the adolescent's social rites of passage, but who could in doing so upset the balance of the adolescent's precariously sought selfhood, the Mother must be kept at some sort of distance. By this distancing the daughter is allowed to fulfill the potential passed along to her by her mother; she recreates her mother's life, preserving what is best in it and avoiding its failures. While the absence or failure of her mother appears to threaten the daughter, the stronger, hidden threat is that she will become too like her mother and not a strong enough individual in her own right. She must therefore be distanced either physically or psychologically in order to create herself and in so doing to fulfill her inheritance from her mother" (68–69).

28. The story was quickly collected in the latest edition of *The Story and Its Writer* (6th ed., ed. Ann Charters [New York: Bedord, 2003]). In many ways, "Find and Replace" (*New Yorker* 5 November 2001: 84–89) is typical of Beattie's stories, as critics have considered them: its narcissistic narrator misses the point of the story she's telling, and tries to find freedom in an American car. See Barbara Schapiro, "Ann Beattie and the Culture of Narcissism," *Webster Review* 10.2 (1985); Susan Jaret McKinstry, "The Speaking Silence of Ann Beattie's Voice," *Studies in Short Fiction* 24 (1987); Steven R. Centola, "An Interview with Ann Beattie," *Contemporary Literature* 31 (1990); James Plath, "My Lover the Car: Ann Beattie's 'A Vintage Thunderbird' and Other Vehicles," *Kansas Quarterly* 21.4 (1989). Beattie's style here enhances the economy of the subject matter through its "economy of exposition in narration, an economy of which Beattie's stories are exemplary," according to Carolyn Porter in "Ann Beattie: The Art of the Missing" (*Contemporary American Women Writers: Narrative Strategies*, eds. Catherine Rainwater and William J. Scheik [Lexington: UP of Kentucky, 1985], 12).

29. The fact that the narrator and the author share a first name, as well as the first-person narration, might lead readers to believe that the author is actually telling her own story. The story's framing by truth-claims would seem to support such an interpretation: it opens with the words "True story" and closes with a justification of Ann's decision to remain alone by saying that the audience will understand her choice "because it is the truth." In fact, however, the theme of "find and replace" undercuts any such notion of stable, objective truth, since Ann later describes her writing as nonfiction with the names changed: "[I]n the final version, every time the word 'Mom' comes up it's replaced with 'Aunt Begonia,' or something." Such a characterization leads the reader to question just how limited Ann's habit of finding and replacing the truth might be. It is a particularly unusual element of a Beattie story, since Beattie admitted in a 1997 interview, "[G]enerally I'm not taken with metafiction at all" and, in the same interview, noted, "I'm not trying to have, à la Philip Roth, a character named Philip Roth standing there in my work, but I'm more willing to show my hand." Robert W. Hill and Jane Hill, "Ann Beattie," *Five Points* 1.3 (1997): 43, 28.

30. Because the story is told from Ann's point of view, it offers little direct evidence that would condemn Ann for her behavior. Beattie's minimalist style, however, encourages the reader to read between the lines, so to speak, to understand the context for Ann's conduct.

31. John Gerlach, in "Through 'the Octascope': A View of Ann Beattie" (*Studies in Short Fiction* 17 [1980]), comments that it is common for Beattie to "twist the roles traditionally assigned to the sexes while

maintaining traditional values" (489), but his assessment is that Beattie generally uses this technique for comic effect. In "Find and Replace," however, the effect of Ann's gender-role reversal is more tragic.

32. The resemblance is solidified in a later comment about Kay's father, who refuses "to sit by while his wife act[s] like some second-rate Sylvia Plath" (150). Such a comment strengthens the sense of identity between Kay and Laura, since Kay speaks in the tones of Plath's narrator, while Martin compares his wife to Plath herself.

33. Laura's descent into the basement may be a symbolic move into the realm of the id, a metaphorical rejection of the influence of the external world as represented by Freud's diagram in "The Ego and the Id" (*The Standard Edition of the Complete Psychological Works of Sigmund Freud*, ed. James Strachey, vol. 19 [London: Hogarth, 1968], 12–66). She is, however, duly disciplined for this rejection.

34. Her father's monstrosity looms so large in Kay's mind precisely because of his unreadable gender in this passage. Only the image of her father, crushed (ironically enough) by the traditionally feminine domestic space of the home, serves as an imagined reassurance. As Judith Halberstam argues in *Female Masculinity* (Durham: Duke UP, 1998), masculine women (such as the Wicked Witch of the West) present a particularly threatening aspect to a society in which reading gender at a glance is highly valued. The inversion of gender in Kay's father, then, is especially grotesque when he takes on the form of this allegedly female character.

35. Theda's character, because of her illness, represents no threat to the sexual expression of either her mother or her sister. For the purposes of the story, she is treated as a sexual nonentity—she is a perpetual child. In this way, her character maintains the female sexual economy within her family.

36. The reference is to J. M. Synge's *The Playboy of the Western World* (Dublin: Maunsel, 1907).

37. A study by Israeli researchers published in 1988 found empirical support for Weisskopf's observations; their results demonstrated that participants did not associate mothers with sexuality, nor did they associate what they characterized as "sexual" women as mothers. Ariella Friedman, Hana Weinberg, and Ayala M. Pines, "Sexuality and Motherhood: Mutually Exclusive in Perception of Women," *Sex Roles* 38 (1988).

38. "*The Reproduction of Mothering* is written from the daughter's point of view more than that of the mother, even as the kernal [*sic*] of the mother's viewpoint, in the psychological capacities, desires, and identities whose development it describes, can be elicited from within it." Nancy J. Chodorow, "Reflections on *The Reproduction of Mothering*—Twenty Years Later," *Studies in Gender and Sexuality* 1 (2000): 348.

39. See chapter 1 for a detailed discussion of this perspective.

3 ECONOMIES OF WHITENESS

1. Another powerful, but less well-known, example can be found in Sherley Anne Williams's "The Lawd Don't Like Ugly" (*Between Mothers and Daughters: Stories across a Generation,* ed. Susan Koppelman [Old Westbury, NY: Feminist, 1985]), in which young Q.T. finds a surrogate mother in Miss Ead. Although Q.T. sees Miss Ead as her role model and depends on her to help negotiate the world of the projects, she is stunned when Miss Ead, who has promised to find her money for school clothes, fulfills her promise by arranging for Q.T. to sleep with her own boyfriend in exchange for a new dress. This story's ending is, of course, much less positive than Naylor's.

2. Babb's comments echo W. E. B. DuBois's analysis of blacks' experience of double consciousness in America in *The Souls of Black Folk: Essays and Sketches* (Chicago: A. G. McClurg, 1903).

3. Critics vary widely on the dividing line between race and ethnicity. Dalton Conley ("Universal Freckle, or How I Learned to Be White," *The Making and Unmaking of Whiteness,* eds. Birgit Brander Rasmussen et al. [Durham: Duke UP, 2001]), for example, suggests that individuals can choose their ethnicities but that their choice must fall into the racial category into which others place them; in other words, people choose their ethnicities, but the world around them determines their race (37). Stuart Hall, in "New Ethnicities" (*Black British Cultural Studies,* eds. Houston A. Baker, Jr., Manthia Diawara, and Ruth H. Lindeborg [Chicago: U of Chicago P, 1996]) defines *ethnicity* as acknowledging "the place of history, language, and culture in the construction of subjectivity and identity, as well as the fact that all discourse is placed, positioned, situated, and all knowledge is contextual" (378). This statement, however, is no less applicable to race than to ethnicity. Is it fair to see ethnicity as a subset of race? Harlon Dalton ("Failing to See," *White Privilege: Essential Readings on the Other Side of Racism,* ed. Paula S. Rothenberg [New York: Worth, 2002]) says that "[e]thnicity is the bearer of culture" (16). Noel Ignatiev ("The New Abolitionists," *Transition* 73 [1997]), however, claims that there is no overarching whiteness that includes ethnicities under its umbrella, arguing that there is no culture of whiteness—only specific cultures associated with ethnicities (199). In the face of these disputes, and in the context of American national discourse that much more often hinges on the term *race* than *ethnicity,* I choose to focus my attention in this chapter on race.

4. See Karen Brodkin, *How Jews Became White Folks, and What That Says about Race in America* (New Brunswick, NJ: Rutgers UP, 1998); Matthew Frye Jacobson, *Whiteness of a Different Color: European Immigrants and the Alchemy of Race* (Cambridge, MA: Harvard UP, 1998); David R. Roediger, *The Wages of Whiteness: Race and the Making of the American Working Class,* the Haymarket Series, eds. Mike Davis and Michael Sprinker (London: Verso, 1991).

Theodore W. Allen and Alexander Saxton make similar arguments on larger scales in their two-volume study *The Invention of the White Race* (London: Verso, 1994).

5. The term *racial formation* comes from Michael Omi and Howard Winant's groundbreaking recognition that race is not a stable subject but one that is constantly shifting. Taking their cue from Gramsci's formulation of class formation, Omi and Winant ("By the Rivers of Babylon: Race in the United States, Part One," *Cultural and Literary Critiques of the Concepts of "Race,"* ed. E. Nathaniel Gates [New York: Garland, 1997]) define racial formation as "the complex process, at once political, economic, and ideological, by which racial meanings are developed and applied, both to individual identities and to institutions" (70).

6. Juan Perea, in "The Black/White Binary Paradigm of Race" (*The Latino/a Condition: A Critical Reader*, eds. Richard Delgado and Jean Stefancic [New York: New York UP, 1998]), among many others, speaks to the pressure this false binary places on racial identification and attempts at understanding all people of color.

7. This sentiment is echoed more recently in the title of Dreama Moon's essay, "White Enculturation and Bourgeois Ideology: The Discursive Production of 'Good (White) Girls'" (*Whiteness: The Communication of Social Identity*, eds. Thomas K. Nakayama and Judith N. Martin [Thousand Oaks, CA: SAGE, 1999]).

8. Frye coins the term *whitely* to describe white behavior so that it can be separated from white people, in the hope that, much as *males* can choose not to act *masculine, whites* can choose not to act *whitely.*

9. Mason Stokes, in *The Color of Sex: Whiteness, Heterosexuality, and the Fictions of White Supremacy* (Durham: Duke UP, 2001), investigates precisely this relationship in white supremacist fiction in nineteenth-century America.

10. As Frye has noted in "On Being White: Thinking Toward a Feminist Understanding of Race and Race Supremacy," *The Politics of Reality: Essays in Feminist Theory*, the Crossing Press Feminist Series (Trumansburg, NY: Crossing, 1983), this focus has traditionally been associated with women of color rather than white women: "Feminists have commonly recognized that the pressure of compulsory motherhood on women of color is not just pressure to keep women down but pressure to keep the populations of their races up: we have not so commonly thought that the pressures of compulsory motherhood on white women are not just pressures to keep women down, but pressure to keep the white population up" ("On Being White" 123). Anna Davin's essay "Imperialism and Motherhood" (*History Workshop* 5 [1978]) documents the targeting of white women as mothers in the United Kingdom, particularly during wartime, through public education campaigns during the late nineteenth and early twentieth century. On a similar note, Allison Berg traces the rhetorical association between motherhood and race/nationhood in U.S. fiction of the early twentieth

century in *Mothering the Race: Women's Narratives of Reproduction, 1890–1930* (Urbana: U of Illinois P, 2002). She cites as exemplary of this type of rhetoric Theodore Roosevelt's 1906 presidential speech reproaching middle-class white women for their sterility and accusing them of fostering "national death, race death" (qtd. 1).

11. Lieberman notes that Barbie's inventor Ruth Handler was married to the cofounder of Mattel. She named the doll after her daughter, Barbara; her son, Ken, was the inspiration for Barbie's "boyfriend." Mattel's investment in Barbie's asexual sexuality resulted in a recent lawsuit against an artist whose "photos often depicted Barbie dolls placed in sexually provocative positions." See "Mattel Must Pay Artist over Barbie Lawsuit," *Washington Times* 30 June 2004, 29 October 2004 <http://washingtontimes.com/business/20040629–092636–8203r.htm> (last accessed 3 March 2007).

12. Suzanne W. Jones, ed., *Crossing the Color Line: Readings in Black and White* (Columbia, SC: U of South Carolina P, 2000); Faye Moskowitz, ed., *Her Face in the Mirror: Jewish Women on Mothers and Daughters* (New York: Beacon, 1994); Mirta Yáñez, ed., *Cubana: Contemporary Fiction by Cuban Women* (Boston: Beacon, 1998); Ann Louise Bardach, ed., *Cuba* (Berkeley: Whereabouts, 2002).

13. "Alyce Miller," *Indiana University Creative Writing Program*, 2001, Indiana University, 29 July 2004 <http://www.indiana.edu/~mfawrite/miller.html> (last accessed 3 March 2007); Alyce Miller, "Alyce Miller, Associate Professor of English," Mark Swanson, 29 July 2004 <http://mypage.iu.edu/~almiller/> (last accessed 3 March 2007). None of Miller's biographical information provides dates by which her age may be gauged; by the number of degrees listed on her homepage, though, one can surmise that she is, at the very least, approaching forty, or else a student prodigy. (Miller lists, in addition to her BA at Ohio State University, a K-12 teaching credential from Berkeley, MAs in both film and English from San Francisco State, an MFA in Writing from Vermont College, and a JD from Indiana, which she earned in 2003.)

14. Philip G. Cavanaugh, "The Present Is a Foreign Country: Lore Segal's Fiction," *Contemporary Literature* 34 (1993); Lawson, Peter, "Lore Segal," *Dictionary of Literary Biography*, vol. 299: *Holocaust Novelists*, ed. Efraim Sicher (Ben-Gurion University of the Negev: Gale, 2004), 304–309; "Segal, Lore (Groszmann)," *Contemporary Authors, New Revision Series*, ed. Ann Evory, vol. 5 (Detroit: Gale Research, 1982).

15. Most of the writing on mixed-race marriages and children that I encountered either acknowledges or assumes a black husband/father and white wife/mother. Presumably, this is because it is the more common configuration. See, for example, Ruth McRoy and Edith Freeman, "Racial-Identity Issues among Mixed-Race Children," *Social Work in Education* 8 (1986); Maureen T. Reddy, *Crossing the*

Color Line: Race, Parenting, and Culture (New Brunswick, NJ: Rutgers UP, 1994); Jane Lazarre, *Beyond the Whiteness of Whiteness: Memoir of a White Mother of Black Sons* (Durham, NC: Duke UP, 1996); James McBride, *The Color of Water: A Black Man's Tribute to His White Mother* (New York: Riverhead, 1996); France Winddance Twine, "Brown-Skinned White Girls: Class, Culture, and the Construction of White Identity in Suburban Communities," *Displacing Whiteness: Essays in Social and Cultural Criticism*, ed. Ruth Frankenberg (Durham: Duke UP, 1997); Jennifer A. Reich, "Building a Home on a Border: How Single White Women Raising Multiracial Children Construct Racial Meaning," *Working Through Whiteness: International Perspectives*, ed. Cynthia Levine-Rasky (Albany: State U of New York P, 2002). While many of these accounts offer relatively neutral or even positive portrayals of relationships between black men and white women, Terri Hulme Oliver's essay on black men's autobiographies, "Prison, Perversion, and Pimps: The White Temptress in *The Autobiography of Malcolm X* and Iceberg Slim's *Pimp*" (*White Women in Racialized Spaces: Imaginative Transformation and Ethical Action in Literature*, eds. Samina Najmi and Rajini Srikanth [New York: U of New York P, 2002]), finds that white women have an emasculating effect on their black male sexual partners.

16. Although Fanon, in *Black Skin, White Masks*, trans. Charles Lam Markmann (New York: Grove, 1967), writes about the experience of blacks in the Antilles, his theories have been widely appropriated by writers discussing other postslavery and postcolonial nations, including the United States.

17. Fanon considers lynching a kind of revenge on blacks for their (supposed) superior virility; similarly, he says that any black man who wants to sleep with a white woman "clearly [has] a wish to be white. A lust for revenge, in any case" (159, 16).

18. Fanon also quotes Michel Cournot's *Martinique* (Paris: Gallimard, 1948), 13–14: "The black man's sword is a sword. When he has thrust it into your wife, she has really felt something. It is a revelation. In the chasm that it has left, your little toy is lost. Pump away until the room is awash with your sweat, you might as well just be singing. . . . Four Negroes with their penises exposed would fill a cathedral. They would be unable to leave the building until their erections had subsided; and in such close quarters that would not be a simple matter" (qtd. 169).

19. This word originally meant *to blacken* and has since evolved into a synonym for *disparage*, a fact that I only learned during my research for this chapter.

20. Gregory Howard Williams attests to this fact in his memoir *Life on the Color Line: The True Story of a White Boy Who Discovered He Was Black* (New York: Dutton-Penguin, 1995). As a young boy, Williams grew up in a white community in Virginia, never having occasion to question his racial identity, but when his parents divorced, his father took him and

his brother to live with his family in the black section of Muncie, Indiana. Williams was constantly at the mercy of both black and white bullies because of his white looks and black heritage; whites, including his mother's side of his family, shunned him, and so did most blacks.

21. Tonya associates darker skin tones with enhanced sexual appeal, as she reveals in two remarks. She laments the chilly weather to Olivia as they wait in the car, saying, "When I go to college, I'm going to move some place warm. I want to have a tan and feel warm all the time" (78). While this comment is innocuous enough, and probably echoes the sentiments of any northerner in winter, when it is coupled with another remark, it gains meaning. When Olivia first shows Tonya the Polaroid snapshot of Wilma, Tonya's reaction is first to ask whether Olivia's mother knows and then to observe, "She sure is pretty. God, what I'd give to have skin like that. I get so white in the winter" (74). In Tonya's mind, dark skin is attractive and desirable, associated with warmth, comfort, and sexual magnetism. Paleness is associated with discomfort, with cold and ice, and perhaps even with frigidity. Tonya's association of whiteness with the cold north is analogous to broader American ideas about Canada as the ultimate in whiteness. With its chilling weather, its polite and respectable citizens, and its vast spaces, the Midwest of this story becomes a parallel to American conceptions of Canada as a dominion of whiteness. See George Elliott Clarke, "White Like Canada" (*Transition* 73 [1997]).

22. As Jane Lazarre remarks about her own marriage to a black man in *Beyond the Whiteness of Whiteness,* "I am more clearly a white woman with a Black man" (105).

23. James McBride, in *The Color of Water,* for example, quotes his mother, Ruth McBride Jordan, on the status of Jews in the first decades of the twentieth century; even Jews considered themselves distinct from the white race. Ruth recalls that her own Jewish mother "never spoke about Jewish people as white. She spoke about them as Jews, which made them somehow different" (87).

24. As Charles Chesnutt presciently understood, though, immigrant populations were vastly more successful at integrating themselves into the social fabric of the United States than were African Americans: "Every other people who come to this country seek to lose their separate identity as soon as possible, and to become Americans with no distinguishing mark. For a generation they have their ghettoes, their residence quarters, their churches, their social clubs. For another generation they may still retain a sentimental interest in those things. In the third generation they are all Americans, seldom speak of their foreign descent and often modify their names so that they will not suggest it. They enter fully and completely, if they are capable and worthy, into the life of this republic. Are we to help the white people to build up walls between themselves and us to fence in a gloomy back yard for our descendants to play in?" ("Race Prejudice: Its Causes and Its

Cure," *Charles W. Chesnutt, Selected Writings*, ed. SallyAnn H. Ferguson [Boston: Houghton Mifflin, 2001], 91–92).

25. Gilman here refers to light-skinned Jews, who may share many visible characteristics with "whites" ("The Jew's Body: Thoughts on Jewish Physical Difference," *Too Jewish? Challenging Traditional Identities*, ed. Norman L. Kleeblat [New York and New Brunswick, NJ: Jewish Museum and Rutgers UP, 1996]). This group would include the characters in Segal's story. As Fanon puts it, "[T]he Jew can be unknown in his Jewishness. He is not wholly what he is. . . . He is a white man, and, apart from some rather debatable characteristics, he can sometimes go unnoticed" (115).

26. Jacobson also discusses the case of Leo Frank, a Jewish plant manager in Atlanta tried and convicted of the 1913 murder of a fourteen-year-old white girl whose body was found in the basement of the plant. When his sentence was commuted in 1915 by the governor of Georgia, a mob broke into the prison where Frank was being held and lynched him. Frank's conviction was based primarily on the testimony of an African American janitor; Jacobson performs a fascinating reading of the ways in which Frank's conditional whiteness and the janitor's blackness fluctuate during the course of the trial (62–68), demonstrating the ways in which Jews and blacks could occupy the same liminal social status.

27. Dyer, in *White* (New York: Routledge, 1997), characterizes the Holocaust as the ultimate statement of whiteness: "It seems to represent the bringing to bear of the very thing that whites claim as their special virtue, civilisation, to wholesale human destruction. It was precisely the values of orderliness, systematicity and hidden ugliness that were used to expunge from Europe the Jews and other human 'dirt' (that is, the perceived sullying borders of whiteness)" (210).

28. While the story must be set in 1946 or later (since Flora was present for the end of the war in Germany in April 1945, and the story begins in February), there are few clues that identify precisely when its events occur.

29. Portions of this story reappear in Segal's later novel *Her First American* (New York: Knopf, 1985). The final words of the novel emphasize both Ilka's Jewishness and her racial alliance with Carter as she tells the story of Carter's interpretation of her name: "Carter said my name was a joke also. I told Carter Weissnix means 'Knownothing,' but Carter said it meant 'Notwhite,' because I am a Jew" (287).

30. Segal has commented on the meaning of the burglars (albeit in the novel version rather than the story) in an interview: "The burglars are evil. They're evil and they are disaster; they're true disaster. Those are the things you might not be able to bear, that you cannot bear, that's what they are. They are for real. They're Nazis, they're cancer, they're war. They're the things that do not fall into the category of things you can bear. . . . The burglars are the true nightmares. They're the

concentration camps. And they're also the things that attack you from within your own body" (qtd. in Cathy Earnest, "Lore Segal: A Conversation," *Another Chicago Magazine* 20 [1989]: 165).

31. Were there any doubt that Carter is talking about sex here, it is removed when he asks Ilka two lines later, "When did I last make love to you?" (38). In the version of the story published in Moskowitz's anthology, there are few major changes from the original publication in the *New Yorker* other than one sizable cut (of material that is clearly meant for the novel) and a few small ones, but this line has been revised to "When did I last fuck you?" (It is quite possible that this line existed in the initial version of the story, but the magazine's editors prohibited its publication.) What is interesting is that Carter's use of coarse language here would further stereotype him as poor, uneducated, etc.—in other words, not white.

32. For an examination of the ways in which the image of African American men as "black beasts" has functioned in American literature in the first half of the twentieth century, see Andrew Leiter, "Literary Figurations of the 'Black Beast' in the Harlem and Southern Renaissances (Dissertation, University of North Carolina at Chapel Hill, 2004). Leiter's argument is especially pertinent in this case, since it is not simply Carter's sexual prowess but his sexual magnetism vis-à-vis white women in particular that is foregrounded. His characterization by Fishgoppel as "the wrongest man in America" seems to stem from exactly this issue.

33. In the novel *Her First American*, Carter's character is much better fleshed out: he is an intellectual and a teacher who has published books and traveled extensively. In fact, Guy Stern, in "The Theme of Exile in the Works of the American Successor Generations" (*Die Resonanz des Exils: Gelungene und Misslungene Rezeption Deutschsprachiger Exilautoren*, ed. Dieter Sevin [Amsterdam: Rodopi, 1992]), remarks that the novel is unique in that it may be the only instance of an immigrant's Americanization through affiliation with the black intellectual community. Carter's resume as an intellectual in the novel is balanced, however, by the fact that his sexual prowess is also magnified from the level of the story; he acknowledges to Ilka in the novel that he has had hundreds of lovers before her. Philip G. Cavanaugh attributes the success of the novel's portrayal of black-white relationships to the "extraordinarily involving character" of Carter Bayoux (497). Cavanaugh also notes that Carter Bayoux appears as a character in Segal's earlier autobiographical *Other People's Houses* (New York: Harcourt, 1964). Although he observes that Segal's epigraph to that book does cast some doubts on Carter's facticity, he concludes that Bayoux "was a real person, occupying the world of autobiography and, to some degree at least, verifiable" (489).

34. This would probably not have been an uncommon sentiment at the time. McBride's *The Color of Water* traces the departure of his mother,

Ruth McBride Jordan, from the Jewish faith; she says of her experience leaving home to wed a black man in the early 1940s, "My family mourned me when I married your father. They said kaddish and sat shiva. That's how Orthodox Jews mourn their dead. They say prayers, turn their mirrors down, sit on boxes for seven days, and cover their heads. It's a real workout, which is maybe why I'm not a Jew now" (2). Although Ruth's family lived in Virginia, where racism may have been more overt and acceptable than New York City, Ruth's expulsion from her family and from Judaism is not made to seem an exceptional response to her choice to marry an African American.

35. Indeed, in the novel he dies of alcoholism.

36. The fact that dominant norms of American whiteness are actually reinforced rather than challenged by the presence of immigrants in the stories by Segal and Obejas may be explained by Lauren Berlant's observation in "The Face of America and the State of Emergency," *The Queen of America Goes to Washington City: Essays on Sex and Citizenship*, Q Series (Durham, NC: Duke UP, 1997): immigration "is proof that the United States is a country worthy of being loved. That is, after all, the only imaginable context in which the United States can be coded as antipatriarchal. Come to America and not only can you choose a lover and a specially personalized modern form of quotidian exploitation at work, but because you can and do choose them, they must be prima facie evidence that freedom and democracy exist in the United States" (196).

37. Antonio Benítez-Rojo has suggested in *The Repeating Island: The Caribbean and the Postmodern Perspective* (trans. James Maraniss, Post-Contemporary Interventions, eds. Stanley Fish and Fredric Jameson [Durham: Duke UP, 1996]) that one source of Cuban nationalism can be found in the cult of the Virgen de la Caridad del Cobre, who, according to legend, appeared to save three men whose boat was about to sink in a storm. The men of this myth were named Juan Criollo, Juan Indio, and Juan Esclavo, representing the European, American Indian, and African origins of the nation. The fact that all the men were, quite literally, in the same boat signifies a national hope for harmony among the three races as they live together in Cuba, writes Benítez-Rojo (52).

38. De la Fuente's remark can be read as a criticism of Fernando Ortiz's position in the 1940s that Cuba had reached what he termed an "integration" phase of dealing with race. Fernando Ortiz ("For a Cuban Integration of Whites and Blacks," *Afrocuba: An Anthology of Cuban Writing on Race, Politics and Culture*, eds. Pedro Pérez Sarduy and Jean Stubbs [Melbourne: Ocean, 1993]), an ethnographer who used Martí's writings on race in Cuba as a foundation for his own theories, argued that Cuba was reaching the last possible stage in its racial development in the decade before Castro's revolution. It hardly seems possible that Cuba could already have reached a racial utopia, however,

given that Castro made racial equality his own agenda soon after taking power in 1959.

39. He also notes that blackness and Afrocubanismo were presented as ways to combat foreign influence—as novelist Alejo Carpentier called them, "antidotes to Wall Street" (qtd. 188).

40. De la Fuente adds in *A Nation for All: Race, Inequality, and Politics in Twentieth-Century Cuba* (Envisioning Cuba Series, ed. Louis A. Pérez, Jr. [Chapel Hill, NC: U of North Carolina P, 2001]) that by 1962 "[r]acism was identified with social groups subservient to imperialist interests: the white, pro-Yankee, antinational bourgeoisie that had fled the country. Thus, not only was racism anticommunist or counterrrevolutionary; it was also antinational and a perilous sign of ideological 'backwardness'" (278).

41. In fact, the number of white refugees who took part in the exodus from Cuba was so great that it left Cuba virtually a different country, demographically and socioeconomically, by the 1980s, according to Pedro Pérez Sarduy and Jean Stubbs ("Introduction: The Rite of Social Communion," *Afrocuba: An Anthology of Cuban Writing on Race, Politics and Culture*, eds. Pedro Pérez Sarduy and Jean Stubbs [Melbourne: Ocean, 1993], 10).

42. Although in this story Obejas plays on the assumption that all Cubans are Catholic, Obejas herself has Jewish Cuban ancestry, as she recounts in "Writing and Responsibility" (*Discourse* 21.3 [1999]) and fictionalizes in the novel *Days of Awe* (New York: Ballantine, 2001).

43. One of the threads that runs through this story is a subtle questioning of the way in which perception and recall shift as one moves forward and backward in narrative time. For example, it seems unlikely that a ten-year-old girl would immediately recognize a transvestite as such when she sees one through her hotel window. Similarly, the narrator's recollections are consistently informed by the power of hindsight, as in her description of the processing center's presidential portrait of Kennedy, "which will need to be replaced in a week or so" (114), foreshadowing his assassination just days after her arrival. The narrator's temporal position is not just backward-looking, however; at one point she says that her mother will outlive both her father and herself, predicting her own demise and alluding to a diagnosis of cancer later in life.

44. The one physical attribute that signals the narrator's inability to completely pass for white is her hair texture: "[W]hen we couldn't find an apartment, everyone's saying it was because landlords in Miami didn't rent to families with kids, but knowing, always, that it was more than that . . . [like] a North American hairdresser's telling my mother she didn't do her kind of hair" (123). Casandra Badillo ("'Only My Hairdresser Knows for Sure': Stories of Race, Hair, and Gender," *NACLA Report on the Americas* 34.6 [2001]) has suggested that hair color can be read as a racial attribute in a way that makes the name of

the color reflect the perceived skin color: "It is of minor importance whether the hair is black or brown: If it's bad it's bad. In the Dominican Republic, a white woman's hair is described as blonde. Whether it is curly or straight, black or brown, it is said that she is blonde. About the 'others' it is said that they have bad hair and that's all—bad hair has no color" (36). While Badillo writes about the Dominican Republic rather than Cuba, her observation may shed light on the narrator's sense of connectedness with the doll, as well as her sense of separation from her while her blonde hair is still in place.

45. Such material success is typically both associated with and furthered by whiteness, as George Lipsitz has documented in "The Possessive Investment in Whiteness: Racialized Social Democracy and the 'White' Problem in American Studies" (*American Quarterly* 47 [1995]).

46. Cherríe Moraga has noted in "From a Long Line of Vendidas" (*Loving in the War Years* [Boston: South End, 1983]) that mothers' importance in Chicano culture rests primarily on their role as mothers of sons. Daughters are less valued, says Moraga, and must constantly prove their love and fidelity to their mothers, whereas sons are loved for being male. While critics are still arguing over whether Cuban American literature should be included in the category Hispanic/Chicano literature, it seems in this case that a similar idea may be guiding the mother's wish for her daughter to have sons. On the debate over the inclusion of Cuban American literature, see, for example, Nara Araújo, "I Came All the Way from Cuba So I Could Speak Like This? Cuban and Cubanamerican Literatures in the US," *Comparing Postcolonial Literatures: Dislocations*, eds. Ashok Bery and Patricia Murray (New York: St. Martin's, 2000).

47. Ruth Behar (*The Vulnerable Observer: Anthropology That Breaks Your Heart* [Boston: Beacon, 1996]) and Coco Fusco ("El Diario De Miranda / Miranda's Diary," *Bridges to Cuba = Puentes a Cuba*, ed. Ruth Behar [Ann Arbor, MI: U of Michigan P, 1995]) are two among many Cuban Americans who have written about the reactions of their friends and family upon hearing the news that they are planning a return to Cuba. As Fusco puts it, the "decision to reestablish contact with Cuba is often looked upon as an act of treason—we are traitors to the exile community's extremists, and ungrateful to our parents, who saved us from the Caribbean 'gulag'" (200).

48. Carla Golden ("Diversity and Variability in Women's Sexual Identities," *Lesbian Psychologies: Explorations and Challenges*, ed. Boston Lesbian Psychologies Collective [Urbana: U of Illinois P, 1987]), among others, has argued that there is no necessary correlation between sexual behavior and identification. For example, her interviews uncovered women who identified as lesbians even though all their sexual interaction had been with male partners. For this reason, it is risky to draw conclusions about the narrator's identification based on her sexual behavior.

49. Julia Alvarez, a light-skinned writer whose family members were political refugees from the Dominican Republic, has described a similar sense of growing connection with American whiteness in her biography. After graduating from college, which she attended during the Vietnam War era (like Obejas's narrator), she found herself increasingly distanced from her native culture: "Adrift from any Latino community in this country, my culture had become an internal homeland, periodically replenished by trips 'back home.' But as a professional woman on my own, I felt less and less at home on the island. My values, the loss of my Catholic faith, my lifestyle, my wardrobe, my hippy ways, and my feminist ideas separated me from my native culture. I did not subscribe to many of the mores and constraints that seemed to be an intrinsic part of that culture. And since my culture had always been my 'color,' by rejecting these mores I had become not only Americanized but whiter" ("A White Woman of Color," *Half and Half: Writers on Growing Up Biracial and Bicultural,* ed. Claudine Chiawei O'Hearn [New York: Pantheon, 1998], 145–146).

4 ECONOMIES

1. George Lipsitz, in "The Possessive Investment in Whiteness: Racialized Social Democracy and the 'White' Problem in American Studies" (*American Quarterly* 47 [1995]) describes many of the roots of the reasons that black Americans have had to rely on government assistance—as well as the myriad ways in which government programs have explicitly discriminated against African Americans.

2. Indeed, the families themselves don't appear to care about the amount, type, or product of the sexual activity going on within their ranks. There are so many family members that one loses count; the narrator of "River of Names" (*Trash*, New York: Firebrand, 1988) relates that in the course of one year she lost eight cousins: "We were so many we were without number and, like tadpoles, if there was one less from time to time, who counted? . . . They died and were not missed" (14).

3. Although *Story* magazine is no longer published, it was for many years an important outlet for short story writers because it printed only stories. Founded in 1931, the magazine saw fits and starts in print, with a hiatus between 1967 and 1989, before it was revived for ten years, during which time its circulation reached up to 40,000. For an overview, see Sylvia Yu and Heather Shannon, "Archives of *Story* Magazine and Story Press, 1931–1999: A Finding Aid," *Princeton University Library Rare Books and Special Collections* 15 August 2006, Manuscripts Division, Department of Rare Books and Special Collections, Princeton University Library <http://libweb.princeton.edu/libraries/firestone/rbsc/aids/story/> (last accessed 3 March 2007).

4. While the four major theorists whose work I investigate in this chapter are French and thus come from different economic systems than that of the United States, all of them write in response to capitalism and their thinking, at least in its broad contours, remains useful to understanding problems in American fiction.

5. Irigaray is more strongly associated with Lacanian psychoanalysis than Freudian psychoanalysis, partially because of the famous story of her expulsion from Lacan's Ecole Freudienne de Paris. In the essays I have chosen to discuss here, however, her critiques of Freud are foregrounded.

6. Irigaray's use of the female body as the foundation for her revision of concepts such as economy has earned her the label of "essentialist" by such critics as Toril Moi, while others, including Naomi Schor, have defended Irigaray's method as what Gayatri Chakravorty Spivak might call strategic essentialism. Toril Moi, *Sexual/Textual Politics: Feminist Literary Theory* (London: Routledge, 1985); Naomi Schor, "This Essentialism Which Is Not One: Coming to Grips with Irigaray," *Engaging with Irigaray*, eds. Carolyn Burke, Naomi Schor, and Margaret Whitford (New York: Columbia UP, 1994).

7. Spivak makes a similar move when she suggests that female sexuality should be understood as organized around the clitoris because it has no reproductive function. By eliminating society's (and Freud's) focus on the vagina as the salient sexual organ of women, Spivak argues, women can undo economies that see them only as vessels for reproduction in what she calls "uterine social organizations." A new understanding of female sexuality is, for Spivak, one way to upset masculine ways of determining women's value. Gayatri Chakravorty Spivak, "French Feminism in an International Frame," *In Other Worlds: Essays in Cultural Politics* (New York: Methuen, 1987).

8. Catherine Porter translates the second title as "Commodities among Themselves" in *This Sex Which Is Not One* (Ithaca: Cornell UP, 1985); I am using the first version to appear in English, and thus most familiar to readers, published in *New French Feminisms: An Anthology*, eds. Elaine Marks and Isabelle de Courtivron (New York: Schocken, 1981).

9. Claude Lévi-Strauss, *The Elementary Structures of Kinship*, trans. James Harle Bell, John Richard von Sturmer, and Rodney Needham, rev. ed. (Boston: Beacon, 1969). For another important feminist revision of Lévi-Strauss, see Gayle S. Rubin, "The Traffic in Women: Notes toward a 'Political Economy,'" *Toward an Anthropology of Women*, ed. Rayna Reiter (New York: Monthly Review, 1975).

10. Hélène Cixous, "Sorties: Out and Out: Attacks/Ways Out/Forays," trans. Betsy Wing, *The Newly Born Woman*, Theory and History of Literature, Vol. 24 (Minneapolis: U of Minnesota P, 1986), 80.

11. Founding her notion of the gift on women's potential for giving birth is a trouble spot in Cixous's theorization, for not all women can give birth or desire to be mothers, as Alan D. Schrift points out. Later, Cixous seems to recognize this issue, noting that women should not be forced to have children. Alan D. Schrift, "Introduction: Why Gift?" *The Logic of the Gift: Toward an Ethic of Generosity*, ed. Alan D. Schrift (New York: Routledge, 1997).

12. Women's writing, further, is central to what Cixous envisions as the disruption of masculine economies, as she develops in "Castration or Decapitation?" as well as "Laugh" and "Sorties."

13. Mutual recognition is also the keystone of Jessica Benjamin's revision of Freudian approaches to the mother-child relationship in *The Bonds of Love: Psychoanalysis, Feminism, and the Problem of Domination* (New York: Pantheon, 1988).

14. Jean Baudrillard goes further, in "When Bataille Attacked the Metaphysical Principle of Economy" (trans. David James Miller. *Bataille: A Critical Reader*, eds. Fred Botting and Scott Wilson, Blackwell Critical Readers [Oxford: Blackwell, 1998]), characterizing Bataille's approach as going "straight to the *metaphysical* principle of economy" (192).

15. Georges Bataille, *Visions of Excess: Selected Writings, 1927–1939*, trans. Allan Stoekl, Carl R. Lovitt, and Donald M. Leslie, Jr., ed. Allan Stoekl (Minneapolis: U of Minnesota P, 1985), 118. Contemporary warfare, however, is no longer a good example of the kind of glorious expenditure that Bataille envisioned, argue Fred Botting and Scott Wilson in "Introduction: From Experience to Economy," *The Bataille Reader*, eds. Fred Botting and Scott Wilson (Oxford: Blackwell, 1997), 22–23.

16. Benjamin Noys (*Georges Bataille: A Critical Introduction*, Modern European Thinkers, ed. Keith Reader [London: Pluto, 2000]) describes Bataille's search for examples that would perfectly demonstrate his notion of *dépense* as one that is impossible, for "Bataille is attempting to present a thought of that which is without example. This is a thought that cannot be contained within any framework or even within thought itself" (104).

17. Bataille does not seem interested in the immense human cost of the Aztec society's sacrifices except in their significance as expenditures; he also chooses to ignore the fact that potlatch necessarily implies reciprocation, believing that the ideal form of potlatch would be unanswered. In these respects, Bataille's hope for a return to the values of *dépense* seems rather naïve.

18. That said, my grouping of Bataille with two feminist writers is not meant to suggest that Bataille's writing is generally considered feminist. As Roland A. Champagne (*Georges Bataille*, Twayne's World Authors Series No. 872 [New York: Twayne, 1998]) puts it, speaking primarily of Bataille's work in fictional genres, "Bataille's attraction to tantric

cults and the virile motifs of his writing do not make an especially attractive feminist voice. . . . [D]espite the claim that Bataille is presenting a more frank view of human eroticism, the word 'clitoris' is absent from his presentations of women's sexuality" (95). He notes, however, that "Bataille does offer affinities to feminist interests, especially those radical feminists interested in creating a psychoanalytical space for women" and comments that Bataille is often compared with Cixous in terms of their common interests (96).

19. Louis Menand observes, however, that there has been careful attention to separating the editorial from the business staff at the magazine, to avoid any impression that the content has been purchased by advertising dollars ("A Friend Writes: The Old *New Yorker*," *American Studies* [New York: Farrar, Straus and Giroux, 2002], 127–128).

20. Katrina Kenison, the general editor of the Best American Short Stories series since 1990, describes her experience of reading short stories in the *New Yorker* as a constant competition for her attention from the many objects on the page: "My gaze wanders off to the ad for a Jamaican villa on the opposite page, or to the Roz Chast cartoon in the lower righthand corner. The magazines in which most of us encounter our short fiction are full of distractions that lure us away from the written word. There is way too much to read anyway, too much to look at, too much to take in." Katrina Kenison, Foreword, *The Best American Short Stories 2000*, eds. E. L. Doctorow and Katrina Kenison (Boston: Houghton Mifflin, 2000), x.

21. Prizes for individual stories are practically nonexistent, beyond recognition in magazine competitions (like those in *Seventeen*, for example) or inclusion in the O. Henry Prize Stories. In order for a story writer to merit a major prize—the National Book Award or PEN, for example—he or she must present a story as part of a larger single-author collection.

22. William Abrahams, writing of the literary scene in 1984, says, "Rare indeed is the author's collection of stories, being brought out in book form, that does not carry an appropriate acknowledgement to the various magazines in which the stories—all or most of them—first appeared. Even rarer is a book of stories of which none have been previously published. It would seem that without the pedigree or seal of approval that magazine publication represents, gaining for the writer some degree of recognition and the nucleus of an audience, publishers hesitate to take on the very real financial risk, especially as costs keep rising, that goes with bringing out a collection." William Abrahams, Introduction, *Prize Stories 1984: The O. Henry Awards*, ed. William Abrahams (New York: Doubleday, 1984), ix. Abrahams's comments seem no less appropriate today since recent collections widely cited as successes by reviewers have generally held to this formula, even demonstrating that most writers need at least one story published by a large-circulation magazine in order to find a major house to publish them. Jhumpa Lahiri's *Interpreter of Maladies*

(New York: Houghton Mifflin, 1999), the most generally critically acclaimed collection of at least the past decade, contains two *New Yorker* stories. (Lahiri won the PEN/Hemingway Award for the collection, as well as the 2000 Pulitzer Prize; the last Pulitzer for stories went to John Cheever in 1979.) Nell Freudenberger published one story in the *New Yorker* (and one in *The Paris Review*) before collecting them in *Lucky Girls* (New York: Ecco-HarperCollins, 2003), which contains only five stories. In the case of Nathan Englander's *For the Relief of Unbearable Urges* (New York: Knopf, 1999), one story is from the *New Yorker*, one from *Atlantic Monthly*, and three from *Story*. Among the four most frequently cited collections, only Adam Haslett's *You Are Not a Stranger Here* (New York: Nan A. Talese-Doubleday, 2002) contains no stories previously published in one of the four "large" magazines; five of them were originally printed in small ones.

A recent survey of the collections displayed at a major chain bookstore presented few challenges to this general principle. Among the few story collections on display, shoppers could choose from Ahdaf Soueif's *I Think of You: Stories* (New York: Anchor, 2007); Janet Peery's *What the Thunder Said: A Novella and Stories* (New York: St. Martin's, 2007); Ben Fountain's *Brief Encounters with Che Guevara: Stories* (New York: Ecco, 2006); and Olaf Olafsson's *Valentines: Stories* (New York: Pantheon, 2007). Soueif's collection contains only previously published stories, with the oldest dating to 1983 and the most recent from 1996. The collection is clearly an attempt to capitalize on the success of Soueif's more recent novels (the front book jacket of the story collection touts her success as the bestselling author of *The Map of Love*). Peery's collection includes a note that the material within appeared in a different form in a number of publications, including the *Best American Short Stories of 1993* as well as the *Kenyon Review, Shenandoah*, and *Black Warrior Review*. The extensive list of previous publications suggests that almost all of the stories have seen previous appearance elsewhere. Similarly, of the eight stories in Fountain's collection, seven have seen print before—one in *Harper's* and three in *Zoetrope*. Only Olafsson's stories appear to claim a majority of new material, with a single story previously published in *Zoetrope* and the rest new. Olafsson's collection, the obvious exception to Abrahams's rule, may be supported by his three previous English-language novels (one of which, the story collection cover touts, is about to begin filming under Liv Ullman's direction). Few publishers seem to be willing to gamble on stories previously unpublished—let alone writers who haven't before appeared much in print.

23. Nadine Gordimer ("The Flash of Fireflies," *The New Short Story Theories*, ed. Charles E. May [Athens, OH: Ohio UP, 1994]) notes

that inclusion in such anthologies is also financially beneficial to writers, since royalties for stories published in them can continue for years beyond the original publication (267). Yet writers who aren't yet known before their inclusion in the story annuals will likely "never be heard from again," as Raymond Carver put it in his introduction to the *Best American Short Stories 1986* (xix). Recognition is therefore no guarantee of a future career.

24. Laura Miller writes that most editors will acquire a short story collection only if it comes with a novel attached, claiming, in their defense, that readers prefer the longer form. Even their friends, say editors, are disappointed at the gift of a short story collection. Richard Burgin, himself a writer of both short stories and novels, confirms that agents are not interested in story collections by young (new) writers but are always on the lookout for novels. Miller and Burgin's sentiments are representative of most other critics. Gayle Feldman, on the other hand, arguing in 1987 that there was a short story boom, quotes an editor at Viking Penguin who asserts that the publisher can sell just about as many books by an unknown story writer as by an unknown novelist. Even Feldman recognizes that this is a minority opinion, though, for her other sources confirm that it is generally necessary for writers of story collections to sign on for a novel as well in order to get a contract. Laura Miller, "Long Story Short," *New York Times Book Review* 2 November 2003: 35; Erin McGraw, Lorrie Moore, and Richard Burgin, "The State of the Short Story," *Boulevard* 17 (2001): 4; Gayle Feldman, "Is There a Short Story Boom?" *Publishers Weekly* 25 December 1987: 27–28.

25. Louis L'Amour and Stephen King have also had story collections on the bestseller list, but few critics include their work within the rubric of literary fiction. Charles McGrath, "The Short Story Shakes Itself Out of Academe," *New York Times*, 25 August 2004: E1. *ProQuest Direct.* NC Live. University of North Carolina at Chapel Hill Libraries <http://proquest.umi.com> (last accessed 3 March 2007).

26. Martin Arnold, "Story Ideas from Coppola," *New York Times* 17 February 2000: E3, *ProQuest Direct*, NC Live, University of North Carolina at Chapel Hill Libraries, <http://proquest.umi.com> (last accessed 3 March 2007).

27. Feldman breaks these categories down even further, asserting that there are seven different "packages" in which short stories can be found: large-circulation magazines, literary magazines, books by small presses, annuals (the Best American Short Stories series, the O. Henry Prize stories, and the Pushcart Prize collections), anthologies from large houses, and collections by mainstream writers published by commercial presses (25).

28. By 1929, the disparity between Fitzgerald's earnings from novels and those from stories had grown even wider; that year, he earned $27,000 from the sale of eight stories to the *Saturday Evening Post*

but only $31.77 in book royalties—including a meager $5.10 from *Gatsby* (Arthur T. Vanderbilt II, *The Making of a Bestseller: From Author to Reader* [Jefferson, NC: McFarland, 1999], 10).

29. See, for example, Herschel Brickell, "What Happened to the Short Story?" *Atlantic Monthly* September 1952; Falcon O. Baker, "Short Stories for the Millions," *Saturday Review* 19 December 1953. Here the *New Yorker* is a notable exception to the rule, according to Menand. During World War II, the editors developed a "pony" version of the magazine with scaled-back content and no advertisements and made it available to soldiers on the front. By the conclusion of the war, the "pony" edition outsold the original. In the ensuing postwar middle-class boom, then, the *New Yorker* had an established readership (Menand 137).

30. Vince Passaro includes *GQ* and *Playboy* in this list, a fact indicative that there is some shifting of critical sentiments on the "best" commercial outlets for short stories. Vince Passaro, "Unlikely Stories: The Quiet Renaissance of American Short Fiction," *Harper's Magazine* August 1999. See also, for example, Arnold, "Story Ideas from Coppola"; John Updike, Introduction, *The Best American Short Stories 1984*, eds. John Updike and Shannon Ravenel (Boston: Houghton Mifflin, 1984).

31. The shrinking field of commercial outlets for short stories echoes larger trends of consolidation in the publishing industry, especially during the late 1970s and early 1980s, motivated by a drive for profitability over all other concerns, as Thomas Whiteside documents in *The Blockbuster Complex: Conglomerates, Show Business, and Book Publishing* (Middletown, CT: Wesleyan UP, 1981)—a book that, ironically enough, originated as a series of articles in the *New Yorker*.

32. Because they're published in commercial outlets, the stories would not be eligible for inclusion in the Pushcart Prize anthologies.

33. Indeed, a recent edition of NPR's *The Connection* touted studies that found that men preferred nonfiction books to fiction. "Buy the Book," narr. Michael Goldfarb, *The Connection* (National Public Radio, Boston, WBUR, 23 June 2004).

34. *Mademoiselle* is by far the frontrunner, with six appearances in the annuals between 1978 and 1987; *Redbook* stories are recognized three times (but limited to the O. Henry Prize stories), while the others are represented once apiece.

35. He concludes the 1984 introduction by remarking that feminists would do better by lobbying for more fiction by excellent women writers, of whom Abrahams sees many, in such magazines rather than worrying about soft-core pornography in publications targeted toward men: "Dare one suggest that if the women's movement wanted to raise its consciousness to the high level where it belongs, it begin by acquainting women with writers of whom they could justly

be proud and whose work they seem not to know at all, rather than worry about the tits-and-ass fiction and photographs that turn up in men's magazines that are themselves superannuated survivors of the 1950s" (xii).

36. In his 1984 introduction, Abrahams contrasts the readership of little magazines with that of larger commercial ones, calling them "discriminating readers whose taste is away from gossip (a kind of creeping *People*-ism now rife in the land) and the short-order read (a kind of creeping *USA*-ism) and who accepts without protest writing that is intelligent, free of stereotypes, and even at times difficult" (xi).

37. Between the large-circulation commercial magazines such as the *New Yorker*, *Esquire*, and the *Atlantic Monthly* and the little magazines—the literary journals and quarterlies with very small circulation numbers—there are a few medium-circulation magazines that do not neatly fit into either category. The newest and best known of these are *McSweeney's*, edited by Dave Eggers, and Francis Ford Coppola's *Zoetrope: All-Story* (whose title is slightly misleading, for the magazine has actually been known to devote an issue to one-act plays). For the purposes of the Pushcart Prize editors, both are considered among the "small presses," but their circulation numbers—30,000 and 40,000, respectively—put them in a slightly different league than the smallest of the "little magazines," of the type that Bishop catalogues. Their status as newcomers, though, makes it difficult to accurately assess their impact on the market.

Zoetrope publishes both unsolicited fiction and commissioned stories based on Coppola's ideas, which are then sent out to writers by the managing editor; the magazine's biggest success thus far has been Bank's *The Girls' Guide to Hunting and Fishing* (New York: Viking, 1999), which began with a commissioned story. Coppola's involvement with the magazine, he insists, is not to merely create a kind of development office for filmmaking, but Bank's collection was optioned by Disney because of its success. By 2001, in the magazine's fourth year of publication, there were already seven stories in some phase of movie production. Authors who sell their stories to *Zoetrope* sign contracts that give the magazine rights in all media, in perpetuity, globally.

Charles McGrath, former fiction editor of the *New Yorker*, calls Eggers "the [George] Plimpton of his generation," comparing him to the founder of the *Paris Review* ("Does the *Paris Review* Get a Second Act?" 4.14). Eggers has spun the success of the magazine (which operates in the black) into a publishing imprint with twenty-five books, a teaching foundation, and a spin-off devoted to reviews called *The Believer*. *McSweeney's* has become a kind of brand name, in short, for hip, intellectual reading. On *Zoetrope*, see Arnold, "Story Ideas from Coppola"; Lynda Richardson, "A Calm Presence in a

Tense, Tight-Deadline World," *New York Times* 14 December 2001: D4, *ProQuest Direct*, NC Live, University of North Carolina at Chapel Hill Libraries, <http://proquest.umi.com> (last accessed 3 March 2007). On *McSweeney's*, see Charles McGrath, "Does The Paris Review Get a Second Act?" *New York Times* 6 February 2005: 4.14, *ProQuest Direct*, NC Live, University of North Carolina at Chapel Hill Libraries, <http://proquest.umi.com> (last accessed 3 March 2007); "Ironic Tendency: McSweeney's," *The Economist* 8 January 2005: 72, *ProQuest Direct*, NC Live, University of North Carolina at Chapel Hill Libraries <http://proquest.umi.com> (last accessed 3 March 2007).

38. Passaro contends that the *New Yorker* editorial policy for fiction is too close to being a promotion department for publishers, often choosing stories from forthcoming collections or, worse, merely excerpts from novels rather than stories proper. His complaint is not widely echoed, however (82).

39. Indeed, the question of exactly what might constitute a "*New Yorker* story" prompted a Princeton senior to conduct a statistical analysis of the stories published between October 1992 and September 2001 for content and character representation. See David Carr, "A Princeton Student Does the Math on a Magazine's Choices," *New York Times* 1 June 2004, *ProQuest Direct*, NC Live, University of North Carolina at Chapel Hill Libraries, <http://proquest.umi.com> (last accessed 3 March 2007). Leitch has traced the origins of the term "*New Yorker* story" to the late 1930s, but even then critics weren't willing to define exactly what they meant by the phrase. Paradoxically, the magazine was so new at that time that there was barely enough of a sample of the short fiction published by the *New Yorker* to lump it together under a phrase like "*New Yorker* story." Leitch comments that the label eventually served as a kind of self-fulfilling prophecy: "[E]ven though recognizable examples of *New Yorker* fiction date back almost to the magazine's beginnings, the label existed before there were more than a few particular examples of the form, as if it had a meaning and use that preceded and predicted the appearance of the stories themselves." Thomas M. Leitch, "The *New Yorker* School," *Creative and Critical Approaches to the Short Story*, ed. Noel Harold Kaylor, Jr. (Lewiston, NY: Edwin Mellen, 1997), 126.

40. In contrast to the previous theorists I have discussed, Bourdieu's approach to the flow of capital is decidedly antirevolutionary, most critics agree. While his accounts of the way in which cultural, educational, and symbolic capital can be transformed into economic capital provide a historical understanding of the reasons that things came to be the way they are, they do not suggest the means by which the current conditions might be changed. For a good review of these kinds of critiques, see Richard Harker, Cheleen Mahar, Chris Wilkes, Henry

Barnard, John Codd, Ian Duncan, and Ivan Snook, "Conclusion: Critique," *An Introduction to the Work of Pierre Bourdieu: The Practice of Theory*, eds. Richard Harker, Cheleen Mahar, and Chris Wilkes (New York: St. Martin's, 1990). In addition, I use Bourdieu's theories to account for market phenomena in the United States, despite the fact that Bourdieu has sometimes been said to have a theory of capital without capitalism, a statement that may account for the relatively chilly reception that Bourdieu's work has found in the American academy, as John Guillory has speculated. John Guillory, "Bourdieu's Refusal," *Modern Language Quarterly* 58 (1997).

41. "[T]he literary field is the economic world reversed; [it establishes] . . . a negative correlation between temporal (notably financial) success and properly artistic value" (Pierre Bourdieu, "Field of Power, Literary Field and Habitus," trans. Randal Johnson, *The Field of Cultural Production: Essays on Art and Literature*, ed. Lawrence D. Kritzman, European Perspectives [New York: Columbia UP, 1993], 164).

42. Terry Eagleton (*Criticism and Ideology: A Study in Marxist Literary Theory*, Verso Classics [London: Verso, 1998]) uses the word *ideology* where I am using *ideas* to express the message or content of the text, a notion that reimbricates society into the formation of the text through the author's lived experience in that society. In other words, to use Eagleton to revise Bourdieu, every text is, in some ways, made three times over: the society (in a limited way) creates the individual, the individual creates the text, and the society re-creates the text.

43. See also William O'Rourke, "Morphological Metaphors for the Short Story: Matters of Production, Reproduction, and Consumption," *Short Story Theory at a Crossroads*, eds. Susan Lohafer and Jo Ellyn Clarey (Baton Rouge: Louisiana State UP, 1989), 203.

44. Some writers may even rely on stereotypes as shortcuts to invoke a particular type of character. Jane Tompkins has written that this is a highly effective way to communicate with a broad audience: "Stereotypes are the instantly recognizable representatives of overlapping racial, sexual, national, ethnic, economic, social, political, and religious categories; they convey enormous amounts of cultural information in an extremely condensed form" (xvi). In the past, though, this has been a problem in short stories, as the Writers' War Board of 1945 demonstrated. As Bill Mullen documents, the Board found that among all popular genres, including radio, advertisements, novels, and drama, short stories were by far the most guilty of relying on stereotypes—and usually harmful ones—to portray their characters. Jane Tompkins, *Sensational Designs: The Cultural Work of American Fiction, 1790–1860* (New York: Oxford UP, 1985), xvi; Bill Mullen, "Marking Race/Marketing Race: African American Short Fiction and

the Politics of Genre, 1933–1946," *Ethnicity and the American Short Story*, ed. Julie Brown (New York: Garland, 1997), 25.

45. *Habitus* is a key term for Bourdieu, and it takes on nuance and complexity as his writing continues. For my purposes, it might be defined as "the system of dispositions to a certain practice . . . an objective basis for regular modes of behaviour." Pierre Bourdieu, *In Other Words: Essays towards a Reflexive Sociology*, trans. Matthew Adamson (Stanford: Stanford UP, 1990), 77.

46. As John Codd points out, the class habitus is probably even more important to the individual's encounter with a work of art than his or her education, since the "best" kinds of taste are those that seem to come naturally to the observer or reader, rather than being the result of study. (Ergo a wealthy patron's instinctive appreciation of a work of art is a better indicator of good taste than a secondary teacher's knowledgeable assessment.) John Codd, "Making Distinctions: The Eye of the Beholder," *An Introduction to the Work of Pierre Bourdieu: The Practice of Theory*, eds. Richard Harker, Cheleen Mahar, and Chris Wilkes (New York: St. Martin's, 1990).

47. Chris Wilkes ("Bourdieu's Class," *An Introduction to the Work of Pierre Bourdieu: The Practice of Theory*, eds. Richard Harker, Cheleen Mahar, and Chris Wilkes [New York: St. Martin's, 1990]) explains Bourdieu's use of the term *class* as indicating social practice rather than simply a category or a lifestyle. It encompasses dispositions, structures, and social options, which combine and recombine dynamically (125).

48. During the 1930s, Menand remarks, the *New Yorker* capitalized on its distinction by limiting its subscriber base; the phone number for the business office was unlisted, which kept the magazine's target audience exactly where the editors wanted it (137).

49. As O'Rourke puts it, the short story is unusual among literary genres in its ability to target a particular audience: "[B]ecause of the nature of the short story—given the fact that its place of publication assumes a particular audience—it is still audience directed. Much more than a serious novelist, a short story author can envision the reader of the story: the demographics are more clear-cut" (200).

Works Cited

Abrahams, William. Introduction. *Prize Stories 1979: The O. Henry Awards.* Ed. William Abrahams. New York: Doubleday, 1979. 9–12.

———. Introduction. *Prize Stories 1984: The O. Henry Awards.* Ed. William Abrahams. New York: Doubleday, 1984. ix–xii.

———. Introduction. *Prize Stories 1986: The O. Henry Awards.* Ed. William Abrahams. New York: Doubleday, 1986. ix–xi.

———. Introduction. *Prize Stories 1993: The O. Henry Awards.* Ed. William Abrahams. New York: Doubleday, 1993. xi–xiii.

Abramson, Jane B. *Mothermania: A Psychological Study of Mother-Daughter Conflict.* Lexington, MA: Lexington Books-D. C. Heath, 1987.

Adams, Alice. Introduction. *The Best American Short Stories 1991.* Eds. Alice Adams and Katrina Kenison. Boston: Houghton Mifflin, 1991. xiii–xvii.

Adams, Parveen. "'Mothering.'" *m/f* 8 (1983): 40–52.

Alcoff, Linda Martín. "Is Latina/o Identity a Racial Identity?" *Hispanics/Latinos in the United States: Ethnicity, Race, and Rights.* Eds. Jorge J. E. Gracia and Pablo De Greiff. New York: Routledge, 2000. 23–44.

Alcoff, Linda, and Elizabeth Potter, eds. *Feminist Epistemologies.* New York: Routledge, 1993.

Allen, Theodore W. and Alexander Saxton. *The Invention of the White Race.* London: Verso, 1994.

Allen, Walter. *The Short Story in English.* Oxford: Clarendon, 1981.

Allison, Dorothy. "'The Meanest Woman Ever Left Tennessee.'" *Trash.* New York: Firebrand, 1988. 23–31.

———. "River of Names." *Trash.* New York: Firebrand, 1988. 13–21.

Alvarez, Julia. "A White Woman of Color." *Half and Half: Writers on Growing Up Biracial and Bicultural.* Ed. Claudine Chiawei O'Hearn. New York: Pantheon, 1998. 139–149.

"Alyce Miller." *Indiana University Creative Writing Program.* 2001. Indiana University. 29 July 2004 <http://www.indiana.edu/~mfawrite/miller.html> (last accessed 3 March 2007).

Anzaldúa, Gloria. *Borderlands/La Frontera: The New Mestiza.* San Francisco: Aunt Lute Books, 1987.

Aptheker, Bettina. "Tapestries of Life." *Tapestries of Life: Women's Work, Women's Consciousness, and the Meaning of Daily Experience.* Amherst: U of Massachusetts P, 1989. Rpt. in *Feminist Frameworks: Alternative Theoretical Accounts of the Relations between Men and Women.* Eds.

Alison M. Jaggar and Paula S. Rothenberg. 3rd ed. New York: McGraw-Hill, 1993. 85–93.

Araújo, Nara. "I Came All the Way from Cuba So I Could Speak Like This? Cuban and Cubanamerican Literatures in the US." *Comparing Postcolonial Literatures: Dislocations.* Eds. Ashok Bery and Patricia Murray. New York: St. Martin's, 2000. 93–103.

Arcana, Judith. *Our Mothers' Daughters.* Berkeley: Shameless Hussy, 1979.

Arnold, Martin. "A Big Anomaly in Short Stories." *New York Times* 19 February 1998: E3. *ProQuest Direct.* NC Live. University of North Carolina at Chapel Hill Libraries. 24 February 2005 <http://proquest.umi.com> (last accessed 3 March 2007).

———. "Story Ideas from Coppola." *New York Times* 17 February 2000: E3. *ProQuest Direct.* NC Live. University of North Carolina at Chapel Hill Libraries. 27 January 2005 <http://proquest.umi.com>.

Asch, Solomon. *Social Psychology.* Englewood Cliffs, NJ: Prentice Hall, 1952.

Atwood, Margaret. Introduction. *The Best American Short Stories 1989.* Eds. Margaret Atwood and Shannon Ravenel. Boston: Houghton Mifflin, 1989. xi–xxiii.

Babb, Valerie. *Whiteness Visible: The Meaning of Whiteness in American Literature and Culture.* New York: New York UP, 1998.

Badillo, Casandra. "'Only My Hairdresser Knows for Sure': Stories of Race, Hair, and Gender." *NACLA Report on the Americas* 34.6 (2001): 35–37.

Baker, Falcon O. "Short Stories for the Millions." *Saturday Review* 19 December 1953. Rpt. in *What Is the Short Story?* Eds. Eugene Current-García and Walton R. Patrick. Rev. ed. Glenview, IL: Scott, Foresman, 1974. 118–123.

Baldwin, James. "On Being White . . . and Other Lies." *Essence* (April 1984): 90–92. Rpt. in *Cultural and Literary Critiques of the Concepts of "Race."* Ed. E. Nathaniel Gates. New York: Garland, 1997. 2–4.

Bank, Melissa. *The Girls' Guide to Hunting and Fishing.* New York: Viking, 1999.

Bardach, Ann Louise, ed. *Cuba.* Berkeley: Whereabouts, 2002.

Barthes, Roland. *The Pleasure of the Text.* Trans. Richard Miller. New York: Hill and Wang, 1975.

Bataille, Georges. *The Accursed Share: An Essay on General Economy, Vol. I: Consumption.* Trans. Robert Hurley. New York: Zone Books, 1988.

———. *Visions of Excess: Selected Writings, 1927–1939.* Trans. Allan Stoekl, Carl R. Lovitt, and Donald M. Leslie, Jr. Ed. Allan Stoekl. Minneapolis: U of Minnesota P, 1985.

Bates, H. E. *The Modern Short Story: A Critical Survey.* 1941. 2nd ed. London: Michael Joseph, 1972.

Baudrillard, Jean. "When Bataille Attacked the Metaphysical Principle of Economy." Trans. David James Miller. *Bataille: A Critical Reader.* Eds. Fred Botting and Scott Wilson. Blackwell Critical Readers. Oxford: Blackwell, 1998. 191–195.

Baym, Nina. "The Madwoman and Her Languages: Why I Don't Do Feminist Literary Theory." *Tulsa Studies in Women's Literature* 3 (1984): 45–59.

Beattie, Ann. "Find and Replace." *New Yorker* 5 November 2001: 84–89.

———. *Follies: New Stories*. New York: Scribner, 2005.

———. Introduction. *The Best American Short Stories 1987*. Eds. Ann Beattie and Katrina Kenison. Boston: Houghton Mifflin, 1987. xi–xviii.

Beauvoir, Simone de. *The Second Sex*. Trans. H. M. Parshley. New York: Vintage, 1989.

Behar, Ruth. *The Vulnerable Observer: Anthropology That Breaks Your Heart*. Boston: Beacon, 1996.

Bell, Pearl K. "Literary Waifs." *Commentary* February 1979. Rpt. in *The Critical Response to Ann Beattie*. Ed. Jaye Berman Montresor. Westport, CT: Greenwood, 1993. 42–44.

Benítez-Rojo, Antonio. *The Repeating Island: The Caribbean and the Postmodern Perspective*. Trans. James Maraniss. Post-Contemporary Interventions. Eds. Stanley Fish and Fredric Jameson. Durham: Duke UP, 1996.

Benjamin, Jessica. *The Bonds of Love: Psychoanalysis, Feminism, and the Problem of Domination*. New York: Pantheon, 1988.

Benjamin, Walter. "The Storyteller: Reflections on the Works of Nikolai Leskov." Trans. Harry Zohn. *Illuminations*. Ed. Hannah Arendt. New York: Schocken, 1968. 83–109.

Berg, Allison. *Mothering the Race: Women's Narratives of Reproduction, 1890–1930*. Urbana: U of Illinois P, 2002.

Berlant, Lauren. "The Face of America and the State of Emergency." *The Queen of America Goes to Washington City: Essays on Sex and Citizenship*. Q Series. Durham, NC: Duke UP, 1997. 175–220.

Bernard, Jessie. *The Future of Motherhood*. New York: Dial, 1974.

Bishop, Edward. "Re: Covering Modernism—Format and Function in the Little Magazines." *Modernist Writers and the Marketplace*. Eds. Ian Willison, Warwick Gould, and Warren Chernaik. Houndmills, Basingstoke, Hampshire: Macmillan, 1996. 287–319.

Bloom, Amy. *A Blind Man Can See How Much I Love You*. New York: Vintage, 2000.

———. *Come to Me: Stories*. New York: HarperPerennial, 1993.

———. "The Story." *A Blind Man Can See How Much I Love You: Stories*. New York: Vintage, 2000. 145–161.

———. "When the Year Grows Old." *Come to Me: Stories*. New York: HarperPerennial, 1993. 145–161.

Bloom, Lynn Z. "Heritages: Dimensions of Mother-Daughter Relationships in Women's Autobiographies." *The Lost Tradition: Mothers and Daughters in Literature*. Eds. Cathy N. Davidson and E. M. Broner. New York: Frederick Ungar, 1980. 291–303.

Botting, Fred, and Scott Wilson. "Introduction: From Experience to Economy." *The Bataille Reader*. Eds. Fred Botting and Scott Wilson. Oxford: Blackwell, 1997. 1–34.

Bourdieu, Pierre. *Distinction: A Social Critique of the Judgment of Taste*. Trans. Richard Nice. Cambridge, MA: Harvard UP, 1984.

Bourdieu, Pierre. "The Field of Cultural Production, Or: The Economic World Reversed." Trans. Randal Johnson. *The Field of Cultural Production: Essays on Art and Literature.* Ed. Lawrence D. Kritzman. European Perspectives. New York: Columbia UP, 1993. 29–73.

———. "Field of Power, Literary Field and Habitus." Trans. Randal Johnson. *The Field of Cultural Production: Essays on Art and Literature.* Ed. Lawrence D. Kritzman. European Perspectives. New York: Columbia UP, 1993. 161–175.

———. *In Other Words: Essays towards a Reflexive Sociology.* Trans. Matthew Adamson. Stanford: Stanford UP, 1990.

———. "A Sociological Theory of Art Perception." Trans. Randal Johnson. *The Field of Cultural Production: Essays on Art and Literature.* Ed. Lawrence D. Kritzman. European Perspectives. New York: Columbia UP, 1993. 215–237.

Bowen, Elizabeth. Introduction. *The Faber Book of Modern Short Stories.* London: Faber & Faber, 1936. Rpt. in *The New Short Story Theories.* Ed. Charles E. May. Athens, OH: Ohio UP, 1994. 256–252.

Brickell, Herschel. "What Happened to the Short Story?" *Atlantic Monthly* September 1952. Rpt. in *What Is the Short Story?* Eds. Eugene Current-García and Walton R. Patrick. Rev. ed. Glenview, IL: Scott, Foresman, 1974. 110–114.

Brock, Lisa, and Bijan Bayne. "Not Just Black: African-Americans, Cubans, and Baseball." *Between Race and Empire: African-Americans and Cubans before the Cuban Revolution.* Eds. Lisa Brock and Digna Castañeda Fuertes. Philadelphia: Temple UP, 1998. 168–204.

Brodkin, Karen. *How Jews Became White Folks, and What That Says about Race in America.* New Brunswick, NJ: Rutgers UP, 1998.

Broner, E. M. and Cathy Davidson, eds. *Mothers and Daughters in Literature.* Spec. issue of *Women's Studies* 6.2 (1979): 123–234.

Brooks, Cleanth, and Robert Penn Warren. *Understanding Fiction.* New York: Crofts, 1943.

Brown, Norman O. *Life against Death: The Psychoanalytic Meaning of History.* Middleton, CT: Wesleyan UP, 1959.

Burgan, Mary. "The 'Feminine' Short Story in America: Historicizing Epiphanies." *American Women Short Story Writers: A Collection of Critical Essays.* Eds. Julie Brown. Wellesley Studies in Critical Theory, Literary History, and Culture. Vol. 8. New York: Garland, 1995. 267–280.

Butler, Judith. "Gender Trouble, Feminist Theory, and Psychoanalytic Discourse." *Feminism/Postmodernism.* Ed. Linda J. Nicholson. New York: Routledge, 1990. 324–340.

"Buy the Book." Narr. Michael Goldfarb. *The Connection.* National Public Radio. WBUR, Boston. 23 June 2004.

Caplan, Paula J. *The New Don't Blame Mother: Mending the Mother-Daughter Relationship.* New York: Routledge, 2000.

Carr, David. "A Princeton Student Does the Math on a Magazine's Choices." *New York Times* 1 June 2004. *ProQuest Direct.* NC Live. University of

North Carolina at Chapel Hill Libraries. 4 June 2004 <http://proquest.umi.com>.

Carter, Susanne, ed. *Mothers and Daughters in American Short Fiction: An Annotated Bibliography of Twentieth-Century Women's Literature*. Westport, CT: Greenwood, 1993.

Carver, Raymond. Introduction. *The Best American Short Stories 1986*. Eds. Raymond Carver and Shannon Ravenel. Boston: Houghton Mifflin, 1986. xi–xx.

Cavanaugh, Philip G. "The Present Is a Foreign Country: Lore Segal's Fiction." *Contemporary Literature* 34 (1993): 475–511.

Centola, Steven R. "An Interview with Ann Beattie." *Contemporary Literature* 31 (1990): 405–422.

Chambers-Schiller, Lee, ed. *Mothers and Daughters*. Spec. issue of *Frontiers* 3.2 (1978): 1–80.

Champagne, Roland A. *Georges Bataille*. Twayne's World Authors Series No. 872. New York: Twayne, 1998.

Charters, Ann, ed. *The Story and Its Writer: An Introduction to Short Fiction*. 6th ed. New York: Bedford, 2003.

Chesnutt, Charles W. *The Conjure Woman*. Boston: Houghton Mifflin, 1899.

———. "Race Prejudice: Its Causes and Its Cure." *Charles W. Chesnutt, Selected Writings*. Ed. SallyAnn H. Ferguson. Boston: Houghton Mifflin, 2001. 85–94.

———. "What Is a White Man?" *Charles W. Chesnutt, Selected Writings*. Ed. SallyAnn H. Ferguson. Boston: Houghton Mifflin, 2001. 24–32.

Chevigny, Bell Gale. "Daughter's Writing: Toward a Theory of Women's Biography." *Between Women: Biographers, Novelists, Critics, Teachers and Artists Write about Their Work on Women*. Eds. Carol Ascher, Louise DeSalvo, and Sara Ruddick. Boston: Beacon, 1984. 357–379.

Chodorow, Nancy J. "Reflections on *The Reproduction of Mothering*—Twenty Years Later." *Studies in Gender and Sexuality* 1 (2000): 337–348.

———. *The Reproduction of Mothering: Psychoanalysis and the Sociology of Gender*. 1978. 2nd ed. Berkeley: U of California P, 1999.

Chodorow, Nancy J., and Susan Contratto. "The Fantasy of the Perfect Mother." *Rethinking the Family: Some Feminist Questions*. Eds. Barrie Thorne and Marilyn Yalom. Rev. ed. Boston: Northeastern UP, 1992. 191–214.

Cixous, Hélène. "Castration or Decapitation?" Trans. Annette Kuhn. *Signs* 7.1 (1981): 41–55.

———. "The Laugh of the Medusa." Trans. Keith Cohen and Paula Cohen. *New French Feminisms: An Anthology*. Eds. Elaine Marks and Isabelle de Courtivron. New York: Schocken, 1981. 245–264.

———. "Sorties: Out and Out: Attacks/Ways Out/Forays." Trans. Betsy Wing. *The Newly Born Woman*. Theory and History of Literature. Vol. 24. Minneapolis: U of Minnesota P, 1986. 63–132.

Clarke, George Elliott. "White Like Canada." *Transition* 73 (1997): 98–109.

Codd, John. "Making Distinctions: The Eye of the Beholder." *An Introduction to the Work of Pierre Bourdieu: The Practice of Theory*. Eds.

Richard Harker, Cheleen Mahar, and Chris Wilkes. New York: St. Martin's, 1990. 132–159.

Cohen-Sandler, Roni, and Michelle Silver. *"I'm Not Mad, I Just Hate You!": A New Understanding of Mother-Daughter Conflict.* New York: Viking, 1999.

Coleman, Sheila Schuller. *Between Mother and Daughter.* Old Tappan, NJ: Fleming H. Revell, 1982.

Collins, Patricia Hill. "Black Feminist Epistemology." *Black Feminist Thought: Knowledge, Consciousness, and the Politics of Empowerment.* 2nd ed. New York: Routledge, 2000. 251–271.

Conley, Dalton. "Universal Freckle, or How I Learned to Be White." *The Making and Unmaking of Whiteness.* Eds. Birgit Brander Rasmussen et al. Durham: Duke UP, 2001. 25–42.

Contributors' Notes. *The Best American Short Stories 1998.* Eds. Garrison Keillor and Katrina Kenison. Boston: Houghton Mifflin, 1998. 283–296.

Cortázar, Julio. "Some Aspects of the Short Story." Trans. Aden W. Hayes. *Arizona Quarterly* 38.1 (1982): 5–18. Rpt. in *The New Short Story Theories.* Ed. Charles E. May. Athens, OH: Ohio UP, 1994. 245–255.

Cory, Herbert Ellsworth. "The Senility of the Short-Story." *Dial* 3 May 1917. Rpt. in *What Is the Short Story?* Eds. Eugene Current-García and Walton R. Patrick. Rev. ed. Glenview, IL: Scott, Foresman, 1974. 62–65.

Cournot, Michel. *Martinique.* Paris: Gallimard, 1948.

Culler, Jonathan. *Structuralist Poetics.* Ithaca: Cornell UP, 1975.

Dally, Ann. *Inventing Motherhood: The Consequences of an Ideal.* London: Burnett, 1982.

Dalton, Harlon. "Failing to See." *Racial Healing.* New York: Random House, 1995. Rpt. in *White Privilege: Essential Readings on the Other Side of Racism.* Ed. Paula S. Rothenberg. New York: Worth, 2002. 15–23.

Davidson, Cathy N., and E. M. Broner, eds. *The Lost Tradition: Mothers and Daughters in Literature.* New York: Frederick Ungar, 1980.

Davin, Anna. "Imperialism and Motherhood." *History Workshop* 5 (1978): 9–65.

de la Fuente, Alejandro. *A Nation for All: Race, Inequality, and Politics in Twentieth-Century Cuba.* Envisioning Cuba Series. Ed. Louis A. Pérez, Jr. Chapel Hill, NC: U of North Carolina P, 2001.

———. "The Resurgence of Racism in Cuba." *NACLA Report on the Americas* 34.6 (2001): 29–34, 46.

Deleuze, Gilles, and Fèlix Guattari. *Kafka: Toward a Minor Literature.* Trans. Dana Polan. Theory and History of Literature. Vol. 30. Minneapolis: U of Minnesota P, 1986.

Delgado, Richard, and Jean Stefancic. Introduction. *The Latino/a Condition: A Critical Reader.* Eds. Richard Delgado and Jean Stefancic. New York: New York UP, 1998. xvii–xix.

Derrida, Jacques. "Différance." Trans. Alan Bass. *Margins of Philosophy.* Chicago: U of Chicago P, 1982. 3–27.

———. *Of Grammatology.* 1976. Trans. Gayatri Chakravorty Spivak. Corr. ed. Baltimore: Johns Hopkins UP, 1998.

Deutsch, Helene. *The Psychology of Women: A Psychoanalytic Interpretation.* Vol. I. New York: Grune & Stratton, 1944.

DiMaggio, Paul. "Social Structure, Institutions, and Cultural Goods: The Case of the United States." *Social Theory for a Changing Society.* Eds. Pierre Bourdieu and James S. Coleman. Boulder, CO: Westview P, 1991. 133–155.

Dinnerstein, Dorothy. *The Mermaid and the Minotaur: Sexual Arrangements and Human Malaise.* New York: Harper & Row, 1976.

Doctorow, E. L. Introduction. *The Best American Short Stories 2000.* Eds. E. L. Doctorow and Katrina Kenison. Boston: Houghton Mifflin, 2000. xiii–xvi.

Donadio, Rachel. "Truth Is Stronger Than Fiction." *The New York Times Book Review* 7. Aug. 2005: 27.

Du Bois, W. E. B. *The Souls of Black Folk: Essays and Sketches.* Chicago: A. G. McClurg, 1903.

duCille, Ann. "The Shirley Temple of My Familiar." *Transition* 73 (1997): 10–32.

Dunn, Maggie, and Ann Morris. *The Composite Novel: The Short Story Cycle in Transition.* New York: Twayne, 1995.

DuPlessis, Rachel Blau, ed. *Toward a Feminist Theory of Motherhood.* Spec. issue of *Feminist Studies* 4.2 (1978): 1–202.

Duster, Troy. "The 'Morphing' Properties of Whiteness." *The Making and Unmaking of Whiteness.* Eds. Birgit Brander Rasmussen et al. Durham: Duke UP, 2001. 113–137.

Dyer, Richard. "White." *Screen* 29 (1988): 44–64. Rpt. in *Cultural and Literary Critiques of the Concepts of "Race".* Ed. E. Nathaniel Gates. New York: Garland, 1997. 6–26.

———. *White.* New York: Routledge, 1997.

Eagleton, Mary. "Gender and Genre." *Re-Reading the Short Story.* Ed. Clare Hanson. New York: St. Martin's, 1989. 55–68.

Eagleton, Terry. *Criticism and Ideology: A Study in Marxist Literary Theory.* Verso Classics. London: Verso, 1998.

Earnest, Cathy. "Lore Segal: A Conversation." *Another Chicago Magazine* 20 (1989): 153–167.

Éjxenbaum, B. M. "O. Henry and the Theory of the Short Story." Trans. I. R. Titunik. *Readings in Russian Poetics: Formalist and Structuralist Views.* Ed. Krystyna Pomorska. Cambridge: MIT P, 1971. 227–270.

Englander, Nathan. *For the Relief of Unbearable Urges.* New York: Knopf, 1999.

Fanon, Frantz. *Black Skin, White Masks.* Trans. Charles Lam Markmann. New York: Grove, 1967.

Feldman, Gayle. "Is There a Short Story Boom?" *Publishers Weekly* 25 December 1987: 25–29.

Ferguson, Suzanne C. "The Rise of the Short Story in the Hierarchy of Genres." *Short Story Theory at a Crossroads.* Eds. Susan Lohafer and Jo Ellyn Clarey. Baton Rouge: Louisiana State UP, 1989. 176–192.

Fields, Barbara J. "Ideology and Race in American History." *Region, Race, and Reconstruction: Essays in Honor of C. Vann Woodward.* Eds. J. Morgan Kousser and James M. McPherson. New York: Oxford UP, 1982. 143–177.

Foley, Neil. "Becoming Hispanic: Mexican Americans and the Faustian Pact with Whiteness." *Reflexiones 1997: New Directions in Mexican American Studies.* Ed. Neil Foley. Center for Mexican American Studies. Austin: U of Texas P, 1998. Rpt. in *White Privilege: Essential Readings on the Other Side of Racism.* Ed. Paula S. Rothenberg. New York: Worth Publishers, 2002. 49–59.

Foucault, Michel. *The History of Sexuality. Volume I: An Introduction.* Trans. Robert Hurley. New York: Vintage, 1990.

———. *The History of Sexuality. Volume II: The Use of Pleasure.* Trans. Robert Hurley. New York: Vintage, 1990.

———. "The Subject and Power." *Critical Inquiry* 8 (1982): 777–795.

Fountain, Ben. *Brief Encounters with Che Guevara: Stories.* New York: Ecco, 2006.

Frankenberg, Ruth. *White Women, Race Matters: The Social Construction of Whiteness.* Minneapolis: U of Minnesota P, 1993.

Fraser, Nancy, and Linda J. Nicholson. "Social Criticism without Philosophy: An Encounter between Feminism and Postmodernism." *Feminism/Postmodernism.* Ed. Linda J. Nicholson. New York: Routledge, 1990. 19–38.

Freud, Sigmund. "Civilization and Its Discontents." 1930. *The Standard Edition of the Complete Psychological Works of Sigmund Freud.* Ed. James Strachey. Vol. 21. London: Hogarth, 1968. 64–125.

———. "The Ego and the Id." 1923. *The Standard Edition of the Complete Psychological Works of Sigmund Freud.* Ed. James Strachey. Vol. 19: 3–66.

———. "Female Sexuality." 1931. *The Standard Edition of the Complete Psychological Works of Sigmund Freud.* Ed. James Strachey. Vol. 21: 223–243.

———. "Femininity." 1905. *The Standard Edition of the Complete Psychological Works of Sigmund Freud.* Ed. James Strachey. Vol. 22: 112–135.

———. "The Future of an Illusion." 1927. *The Standard Edition of the Complete Psychological Works of Sigmund Freud.* Ed. James Strachey. Vol. 21: 5–56.

———. "Jokes and Their Relation to the Unconscious." 1905. *The Standard Edition of the Complete Psychological Works of Sigmund Freud.* Ed. James Strachey. Vol. 8: 9–236.

———. "The Psychogenesis of a Case of Homosexuality in a Woman." 1920. *The Standard Edition of the Complete Psychological Works of Sigmund Freud.* Ed. James Strachey. Vol. 18: 147–172.

———. "Some Psychical Consequences of the Anatomical Distinction between the Sexes." 1925. *The Standard Edition of the Complete Psychological Works of Sigmund Freud.* Ed. James Strachey. Vol. 19: 243–258.

Freudenberger, Nell. *Lucky Girls: Stories.* New York: Ecco-HarperCollins, 2003.

Friday, Nancy. *Forbidden Flowers: More Women's Sexual Fantasies.* New York: Pocket-Simon & Schuster, 1975.

———. *My Mother/My Self: The Daughter's Search for Identity*. 1977. 2nd ed. New York: Delacorte P, 1997.

———. *My Secret Garden: Women's Sexual Fantasies*. New York: Trident, 1973.

Friedman, Ariella, Hana Weinberg, and Ayala M. Pines. "Sexuality and Motherhood: Mutually Exclusive in Perception of Women." *Sex Roles* 38 (1988): 781–800.

Friedman, Norman. "What Makes a Short Story Short?" *Modern Fiction Studies* 4 (1958). Rpt. in *The Essentials of the Theory of Fiction*. Eds. Michael J. Hoffman and Patrick D. Murphy. 2nd ed. Durham: Duke UP, 1996. 100–115.

Frye, Marilyn. "On Being White: Thinking toward a Feminist Understanding of Race and Race Supremacy." *The Politics of Reality: Essays in Feminist Theory*. The Crossing Press Feminist Series. Trumansburg, NY: Crossing, 1983. 110–127.

———. "The Possibility of Feminist Theory." *Theoretical Perspectives on Sexual Difference*. Ed. Deborah L. Rhode. New Haven: Yale UP, 1990. 174–184.

———. "White Woman Feminist, 1983–1992." *Willful Virgin: Essays in Feminism, 1976–1992*. Freedom, CA: Crossing, 1992. 147–169.

Fusco, Coco. "El Diario De Miranda / Miranda's Diary." *Bridges to Cuba = Puentes a Cuba*. Ed. Ruth Behar. Ann Arbor, MI: U of Michigan P, 1995. 198–216.

Gallop, Jane. "The Phallic Mother: Fraudian Analysis." *The Daughter's Seduction: Feminism and Psychoanalysis*. Ithaca: Cornell UP, 1982. 113–131.

Gardiner, Judith Kegan. "On Female Identity and Writing by Women." *Critical Inquiry* 8 (1981): 347–361.

Gerlach, John. "The Margins of Narrative: The Very Short Story, the Prose Poem, and the Lyric." *Short Story Theory at a Crossroads*. Eds. Susan Lohafer and Jo Ellyn Clarey. Baton Rouge: Louisiana State UP, 1989. 74–84.

———. "Through 'the Octascope': A View of Ann Beattie." *Studies in Short Fiction* 17 (1980): 489–494.

Gilman, Sander L. "The Jew's Body: Thoughts on Jewish Physical Difference." *Too Jewish? Challenging Traditional Identities*. Ed. Norman L. Kleeblat. New York and New Brunswick, NJ: Jewish Museum and Rutgers UP, 1996. 60–73.

Golden, Carla. "Diversity and Variability in Women's Sexual Identities." *Lesbian Psychologies: Explorations and Challenges*. Ed. Boston Lesbian Psychologies Collective. Urbana: U of Illinois P, 1987. 19–34.

Gonzalez-Pando, Miguel. *The Cuban Americans*. The New Americans. Ed. Ronald H. Bayor. Westport, CT: Greenwood, 1998.

Gordimer, Nadine. "The Flash of Fireflies." *Kenyon Review* 30 (1969). Rpt. in *The New Short Story Theories*. Ed. Charles E. May. Athens, OH: Ohio UP, 1994. 263–267.

Grillo, Evelio. *Black Cuban, Black American: A Memoir*. Recovering the U.S. Hispanic Literary Heritage. Houston: Arte Público P, 2000.

Guillory, John. "Bourdieu's Refusal." *Modern Language Quarterly* 58 (1997): 367–398.

Gullason, Thomas H. "The Short Story: An Underrated Art." *Studies in Short Fiction* 2 (1964): 13–31.

Gwynn, Frederick L., and Joseph L. Blotner, eds. *Faulkner in the University.* New York: Vintage, 1965.

Halberstam, Judith. *Female Masculinity.* Durham: Duke UP, 1998.

Hall, Stuart. "New Ethnicities." *Black British Cultural Studies.* Eds. Houston A. Baker, Jr., Manthia Diawara, and Ruth H. Lindeborg. Chicago: U of Chicago P, 1996. 163–172. Rpt. in *Cultural and Literary Critiques of the Concepts of "Race."* Ed. E. Nathaniel Gates. New York: Garland, 1997. 373–382.

Hammer, Signe. *Daughters and Mothers. Mothers and Daughters.* New York: Quadrangle, 1975.

Hanson, Clare. " 'Things Out of Words': Towards a Poetics of Short Fiction." *Re-Reading the Short Story.* Ed. Clare Hanson. New York: St. Martin's, 1989. 22–33.

Harding, Sandra. "Feminism, Science, and the Anti-Enlightenment Critiques." *Feminism/Postmodernism.* Ed. Linda J. Nicholson. New York: Routledge, 1990. 83–106.

Harker, Richard et al. "Conclusion: Critique." *An Introduction to the Work of Pierre Bourdieu: The Practice of Theory.* Eds. Richard Harker, Cheleen Mahar, and Chris Wilkes. New York: St. Martin's, 1990. 195–225.

Harris, Joel Chandler. *Nights with Uncle Remus: Myths and Legends of the Old Plantation.* Boston: James R. Osgood, 1883.

Hartigan, John, Jr. "Locating White Detroit." *Displacing Whiteness: Essays in Social and Cultural Criticism.* Ed. Ruth Frankenberg. Durham: Duke UP, 1997. 180–213.

Haslett, Adam. *You Are Not a Stranger Here.* New York: Nan A. Talese-Doubleday, 2002.

Hearn, Charles R. "F. Scott Fitzgerald and the Popular Magazine Formula Story of the Twenties." *Journal of American Culture* 18.3 (1995): 33–40.

Hemingway, Ernest. "Hills Like White Elephants." *The Complete Short Stories of Ernest Hemingway.* Finca Vigía ed. New York: Scribner's, 1987. 211–214.

Herman, Nini. *Too Long a Child: The Mother-Daughter Dyad.* London: Free Association, 1989.

Hernández-Truyol, Berta Esperanza. "Building Bridges: Latinas and Latinos at the Crossroads." *The Latino/a Condition: A Critical Reader.* Eds. Richard Delgado and Jean Stefancic. New York: New York UP, 1998. 24–31.

Hill, Robert W., and Jane Hill. "Ann Beattie." *Five Points* 1.3 (1997): 26–60.

Hirsch, Marianne. *The Mother/Daughter Plot: Narratives, Psychoanalysis, Feminism.* Bloomington: Indiana UP, 1989.

———. "Mothers and Daughters." *Signs* 7.1 (1981): 200–222.

Horne, Philip. "Henry James and the Economy of the Short Story." *Modernist Writers and the Marketplace.* Eds. Ian Willison, Warwick Gould, and Warren Chernaik. Houndmills, Basingstoke, Hampshire: Macmillan, 1996. 1–35.

Ignatiev, Noel. *How the Irish Became White*. New York: Routledge, 1995.
———. "The New Abolitionists." *Transition* 73 (1997): 199–203.
Ingman, Heather, ed. *Mothers and Daughters in the Twentieth Century: A Literary Anthology*. Edinburgh: Edinburgh UP, 1999.
Irigaray, Luce. "And the One Doesn't Stir without the Other." Trans. Hélène Vivienne Wenzel. *Signs* 7 (1981): 60–67.
———. "This Sex Which Is Not One." Trans. Claudia Reeder. *New French Feminisms: An Anthology*. Eds. Elaine Marks and Isabelle de Courtivron. New York: Schocken, 1981. 99–106.
———. "When the Goods Get Together." Trans. Claudia Reeder. *New French Feminisms: An Anthology*. Eds. Elaine Marks and Isabelle de Courtivron. New York: Schocken, 1981. 99–110.
———. "Women on the Market." Trans. Catherine Porter and Carolyn Burke. *This Sex Which Is Not One*. Ithaca: Cornell UP, 1984. 170–191.
"Ironic Tendency: *McSweeney's*." *The Economist* 8 January 2005: 72. *ProQuest Direct*. NC Live. University of North Carolina at Chapel Hill Libraries. 23 February 2005 <http://factiva.com> (last accessed 3 March 2007).
Jacobson, Matthew Frye. *Whiteness of a Different Color: European Immigrants and the Alchemy of Race*. Cambridge, MA: Harvard UP, 1998.
James, Henry. "The Art of Fiction." *Longman's Magazine* September 1884: 502–521. Rpt. in *The Art of Criticism: Henry James on the Theory and the Practice of Fiction*. Eds. William Veeder and Susan M. Griffin. Chicago: U of Chicago P, 1986. 165–183.
Jones, Suzanne W., ed. *Crossing the Color Line: Readings in Black and White*. Columbia, SC: U of South Carolina P, 2000.
Kaplan, E. Ann. *Motherhood and Representation: The Mother in Popular Culture and Melodrama*. London: Routledge, 1992.
Kartiganer, Donald. "An Introduction to the Last Great Short Story." *The Oxford American* May/June (1995): 51–53.
Kearns, Caledonia, ed. *Motherland: Writings by Irish American Women about Mothers and Daughters*. New York: HarperCollins, 1999.
Kenison, Katrina. Foreword. *The Best American Short Stories 2000*. Eds. E. L. Doctorow and Katrina Kenison. Boston: Houghton Mifflin, 2000. ix–xii.
Kenison, Katrina, and Kathleen Hirsch, eds. *Mothers: Twenty Stories of Contemporary Motherhood*. New York: North Point P-Farrar, Straus and Giroux, 1996.
Kincaid, Jamaica. "Girl." *At the Bottom of the River*. New York: Farrar, Straus & Giroux, 1983.
Kingsolver, Barbara. Introduction. *The Best American Short Stories 2001*. Eds. Barbara Kingsolver and Katrina Kenison. Boston: Houghton Mifflin, 2001. xiii–xix.
Kingston, Maxine Hong. *The Woman Warrior: Memoirs of a Girlhood Among Ghosts*. New York: Knopf, 1976.
Koppelman, Susan, ed. *Between Mothers and Daughters: Stories across a Generation*. Old Westbury, NY: Feminist, 1985.

Koppelman, Susan, ed. "Between Mothers and Daughters: Stories across a Generation; The Personal Is Political in Life and in Literature." *Women's Studies International Forum* 16.1 (1993): 47–56.

———. "A Preliminary Sketch of the Early History of U.S. Women's Short Stories." *Journal of American Culture* 22.2 (1999): 1–6.

Kothari, Geeta, ed. *Did My Mama Like to Dance?* New York: Avon, 1994.

Kristeva, Julia. "Motherhood according to Giovanni Bellini." *The Portable Kristeva*. Ed. Kelly Oliver. New York: Columbia UP, 1997. 301–307.

———. "Stabat Mater." Trans. Arthur Goldhammer. *Poetics Today* 6 (1985): 133–152.

Lahiri, Jhumpa. *Interpreter of Maladies*. New York: Houghton Mifflin, 1999.

LaPlanche, Jean, and J.-B. Pontalis. *The Language of Psycho-Analysis*. Trans. Donald Nicholson-Smith. New York: Norton, 1973.

Lawson, Peter, "Lore Segal." *Dictionary of Literary Biography*, vol. 299: *Holocaust Novelists*. Ed. Efraim Sicher. Ben-Gurion University of the Negev: Gale, 2004. 304–309.

Lazarre, Jane. *Beyond the Whiteness of Whiteness: Memoir of a White Mother of Black Sons*. Durham, NC: Duke UP, 1996.

———. *The Mother Knot*. New York: Dell, 1976.

Leitch, Thomas M. "The *New Yorker* School." *Creative and Critical Approaches to the Short Story*. Ed. Noel Harold Kaylor, Jr. Lewiston, NY: Edwin Mellen, 1997. 123–149.

Leiter, Andrew. "Literary Figurations of the 'Black Beast' in the Harlem and Southern Renaissances." Dissertation. University of North Carolina at Chapel Hill, 2004.

Lévi-Strauss, Claude. *The Elementary Structures of Kinship*. Trans. James Harle Bell, John Richard von Sturmer, and Rodney Needham. Rev. ed. Boston: Beacon, 1969.

Lieberman, Rhonda. "Jewish Barbie." *Too Jewish? Challenging Traditional Identities*. Ed. Norman L. Kleeblat. New York and New Brunswick, NJ: Jewish Museum and Rutgers UP, 1996. 108–113.

Lipsitz, George. "The Possessive Investment in Whiteness: Racialized Social Democracy and the 'White' Problem in American Studies." *American Quarterly* 47 (1995): 369–387.

Litt, Jacquelyn S. *Medicalized Motherhood: Perspectives from the Lives of African-American and Jewish Women*. New Brunswick, NJ: Rutgers UP, 2000.

Lohafer, Susan. *Coming to Terms with the Short Story*. Baton Rouge: Louisiana UP, 1985.

Lohafer, Susan, and Jo Ellyn Clarey, eds. *Short Story Theory at a Crossroads*. Baton Rouge: Louisiana UP, 1989.

Lorber, Judith et al. "On *The Reproduction of Mothering*: A Methodological Debate." *Signs* 6 (1981): 482–514.

Lott, Eric. "White Like Me: Racial Cross-Dressing and the Construction of American Whiteness." *Cultures of United States Imperialism*. Eds. Amy Kaplan and Donald E. Pease. Durham, NC: Duke UP, 1993. 474–495.

Lowinsky, Naomi Ruth. *Stories from the Motherline: Reclaiming the Mother-Daughter Bond, Finding Our Feminine Souls*. Los Angeles: Jeremy P. Tarcher, 1992.

Lukács, George. *The Theory of the Novel*. Trans. Anna Bodtock. Cambridge: MIT P, 1971.

Lynn, David H. "Editor's Notes." *The Kenyon Review* 26.4 (2004): 1.

MacDonald, Susan Peck. "Jane Austen and the Tradition of the Absent Mother." *The Lost Tradition: Mothers and Daughters in Literature*. Eds. Cathy N. Davidson and E. M. Broner. New York: Frederick Ungar, 1980. 58–69.

Manguel, Alberto, ed. *Fathers & Sons: An Anthology*. San Francisco: Chronicle, 1998.

———, ed. *Mothers & Daughters: An Anthology*. San Francisco: Chronicle, 1998.

Mann, Susan Garland. *The Short Story Cycle: A Genre Companion and Reference Guide*. New York: Greenwood, 1989.

"Mattel Must Pay Artist over Barbie Lawsuit." *Washington Times* 30 June 2004. 29 October 2004 <http://washingtontimes.com/business/20040629–092636–8203r.htm> (last accessed 3 March 2007).

Matthews, Brander. "The Philosophy of the Short-Story." *Pen and Ink: Papers on Subjects of More or Less Importance*. New York: Longmans, Green, 1888. Rpt. in *The New Short Story Theories*. Ed. Charles E. May. Athens, OH. Ohio UP, 1994. 73–80.

May, Charles E. Introduction. *The New Short Story Theories*. Ed. Charles E. May. Athens, OH: Ohio UP, 1994. xv–xxvi.

———. "The Nature of Knowledge in Short Fiction." *Studies in Short Fiction* 21 (1984): 327–338. Rpt. in *The New Short Story Theories*. Ed. Charles E. May. Athens, OH: Ohio UP, 1994. 131–143.

———, ed. *The New Short Story Theories*. Athens, OH: Ohio UP, 1994.

———. *The Short Story: The Reality of Artifice*. New York: Twayne, 1995.

McBride, James. *The Color of Water: A Black Man's Tribute to His White Mother*. New York: Riverhead, 1996.

McGrath, Charles. "Does the Paris Review Get a Second Act?" *New York Times* 6 February 2005: 4.14. *ProQuest Direct*. NC Live. University of North Carolina at Chapel Hill Libraries. 23 February 2005 <http://proquest.umi.com> (last accessed 3 March 2007).

———. "The Short Story Shakes Itself Out of Academe." *New York Times* 25 August 2004: E1. *ProQuest Direct*. NC Live. University of North Carolina at Chapel Hill Libraries <http://proquest.umi.com> (last accessed 3 March 2007).

McGraw, Erin, Lorrie Moore, and Richard Burgin. "The State of the Short Story." *Boulevard* 17 (2001): 1–27.

McKinstry, Susan Jaret. "The Speaking Silence of Ann Beattie's Voice." *Studies in Short Fiction* 24 (1987): 111–117.

McRoy, Ruth, and Edith Freeman. "Racial-Identity Issues among Mixed-Race Children." *Social Work in Education* 8 (1986): 164–174.

Menand, Louis. "A Friend Writes: The Old *New Yorker*." *American Studies*. New York: Farrar, Straus and Giroux, 2002. 125–145.

Miller, Alyce. "Alyce Miller, Associate Professor of English." Mark Swanson. 29 July 2004 <http://mypage.iu.edu/~almiller/> (last accessed 3 Macrh 2007).

———. "A Cold Winter Light." *The Nature of Longing: Stories*. Athens, GA: U of Georgia P, 1994. 61–86.

Miller, Laura. "Long Story Short." *New York Times Book Review* 2 November 2003: 35.

Miller, Sue. Introduction. *The Best American Short Stories 2002*. Eds. Sue Miller and Katrina Kenison. Boston: Houghton Mifflin, 2002. xiii–xviii.

Millier, Brett. *Elizabeth Bishop: Life and the Memory of It*. Berkeley: U of California P, 1993.

Minh-ha, Trinh T. *Woman, Native, Other: Writing Postcoloniality and Feminism*. Bloomington: Indiana UP, 1989.

Moi, Toril. *Sexual/Textual Politics: Feminist Literary Theory*. London: Routledge, 1985.

———. *What Is a Woman? And Other Essays*. Oxford: Oxford UP, 1999.

Moon, Dreama. "White Enculturation and Bourgeois Ideology: The Discursive Production of 'Good (White) Girls.'" *Whiteness: The Communication of Social Identity*. Eds. Thomas K. Nakayama and Judith N. Martin. Thousand Oaks, CA: SAGE, 1999. 177–197.

Moore, Lorrie. Introduction. *The Best American Short Stories 2004*. Eds. Lorrie Moore and Katrina Kenison. Boston: Houghton Mifflin, 2004. xiv–xxii.

———. "People Like That Are the Only People Here: Canonical Babbling in Peed Onk." *Birds of America*. New York: Knopf, 1998. 212–250.

———. "Which Is More than I Can Say about Some People." *Birds of America*. New York: Knopf, 1998. 26–46.

Moraga, Cherríe. "From a Long Line of Vendidas: Chicanas and Feminism." *Loving in the War Years*. Boston: South End, 1983.

Morgan, Jill, ed. *Mothers & Daughters*. New York: Signet, 1999.

———, ed. *Mothers & Daughters: Celebrating the Gift of Love with 12 New Stories*. New York: Penguin, 1998.

Morrison, Toni. *Beloved*. New York: Plume-Penguin, 1987.

———. *Playing in the Dark: Whiteness and the Literary Imagination*. New York: Vintage, 1992.

Moskowitz, Faye, ed. *Her Face in the Mirror: Jewish Women on Mothers and Daughters*. New York: Beacon, 1994.

Mukherjee, Bharati. "A Wife's Story." *The Middleman and Other Stories*. New York: Grove, 1988. 25–40.

Mullen, Bill. "Marking Race/Marketing Race: African American Short Fiction and the Politics of Genre, 1933–1946." *Ethnicity and the American Short Story*. Ed. Julie Brown. New York: Garland, 1997. 25–46.

Mullen, Harryette. "Optic White: Blackness and the Production of Whiteness." *Diacritics* 24.2–3 (1994): 71–89. Rpt. in *Cultural and Literary Critiques of* the Concepts of *"Race."* Ed. E. Nathaniel Gates. New York: Garland, 1997. 41–59.

Nagel, James. *The Contemporary American Short-Story Cycle: The Ethnic Resonance of Genre.* Baton Rouge: Louisiana State UP, 2001.

Naylor, Gloria. "Kiswana Browne." *The Women of Brewster Place.* New York: Viking, 1982.

Neisser, Edith. *Mothers and Daughters: A Lifelong Relationship.* Rev. ed. New York: Harper & Row, 1973.

Nelson, Lynn Hankinson. "Epistemological Communities." *Feminist Epistemologies.* Eds. Linda Alcoff and Elizabeth Potter. New York: Routledge, 1993. 121–159.

Newitz, Annalee, and Matt Wray. Introduction. *White Trash: Race and Class in America.* Eds. Matt Wray and Annalee Newitz. New York: Routledge, 1997. 1–12.

Newitz, Annalee, and Matthew Wray. "What Is 'White Trash'? Stereotypes and Economic Conditions of Poor Whites in the United States." *Whiteness: A Critical Reader.* Ed. Mike Hill. New York: New York UP, 1997. 168–184.

Noys, Benjamin. *Georges Bataille: A Critical Introduction.* Modern European Thinkers. Ed. Keith Reader. London: Pluto, 2000.

Oates, Joyce Carol. "Where Are You Going, Where Have You Been?" 1966. *Where Are You Going, Where Have You Been? Selected Early Stories.* New York: Ontario Review P, 1993. 118–136

Oates, Joyce Carol, and Janet Berliner, eds. *Snapshots: 20th Century Mother Daughter Fiction.* Boston: David R. Godine, 2000.

Obejas, Achy. *Days of Awe.* New York: Ballantine, 2001.

———. "We Came All the Way from Cuba So You Could Dress Like This?" *We Came All the Way from Cuba So You Could Dress Like This? Stories.* Pittsburgh, PA: Cleis, 1994. 113–131.

———. "Writing and Responsibility." *Discourse* 21.3 (1999).

Oboler, Suzanne. "Hispanics? That's What They Call Us." *The Latino/a Condition: A Critical Reader.* Eds. Richard Delgado and Jean Stefancic. New York: New York UP, 1998. 3–5.

O'Connor, Flannery. "Good Country People." *The Complete Stories.* New York: Noonday P-Farrar, Straus and Giroux, 1946. 271–291.

O'Connor, Frank. *The Lonely Voice: A Study of the Short Story.* Cleveland: World Publishing, 1963.

Olafsson, Olaf. *Valentines: Stories.* New York: Pantheon, 2007.

Oliver, Terri Hume. "Prison, Perversion, and Pimps: The White Temptress in *The Autobiography of Malcolm X* and Iceberg Slim's *Pimp.*" *White Women in Racialized Spaces: Imaginative Transformation and Ethical Action in Literature.* Eds. Samina Najmi and Rajini Srikanth. New York: U of New York P, 2002. 147–165.

Olsen, Tillie. "I Stand Here Ironing." *Tell Me a Riddle and Yonnondio.* London: Virago, 1990. 13–25.

Omi, Michael, and Howard Winant. "By the Rivers of Babylon: Race in the United States, Part One." *Socialist Review* 13.5 (1983): 31–65. Rpt. in

Cultural and Literary Critiques of the Concepts of "Race." Ed. E. Nathaniel Gates. New York: Garland, 1997. 61–95.

Ong, Walter J. *Orality and Literacy: The Technologizing of the Word.* New Accents Series. London: Methuen, 1982.

———. *The Presence of the Word: Some Prolegomena for Cultural and Religious History.* New Haven: Yale UP, 1967.

O'Rourke, William. "Morphological Metaphors for the Short Story: Matters of Production, Reproduction, and Consumption." *Short Story Theory at a Crossroads.* Eds. Susan Lohafer and Jo Ellyn Clarey. Baton Rouge: Louisiana State UP, 1989. 193–205.

Ortiz, Fernando. "For a Cuban Integration of Whites and Blacks." *Afrocuba: An Anthology of Cuban Writing on Race, Politics and Culture.* Eds. Pedro Pérez Sarduy and Jean Stubbs. Melbourne: Ocean, 1993. 27–33.

Overstreet, Bonaro. "Little Story, What Now?" *Saturday Review of Literature* 22 November 1941. Rpt. in *What Is the Short Story?* Eds. Eugene Current-García and Walton R. Patrick. Rev. ed. Glenview, IL: Scott, Foresman, 1974. 87–91.

Park, Christine, and Caroline Heaton, eds. *Close Company: Stories of Mothers and Daughters.* New York: Ticknor and Fields, 1987.

Passaro, Vince. "Unlikely Stories: The Quiet Renaissance of American Short Fiction." *Harper's Magazine* August 1999: 80–89.

Patchett, Ann. Introduction. *The Best American Short Stories 2006.* Eds. Ann Patchett and Katrina Kenison. Boston: Houghton Mifflin, 2006. xv–xxii.

Peery, Janet. *What the Thunder Said: A Novella and Stories.* New York: St. Martin's, 2007.

Perea, Juan F. "The Black/White Binary Paradigm of Race." *The Latino/a Condition: A Critical Reader.* Eds. Richard Delgado and Jean Stefancic. New York: New York UP, 1998. 359–368.

Pérez, Louis A., Jr. "The Circle of Connections: One Hundred Years of Cuba-U.S. Relations." *Bridges to Cuba = Puentes a Cuba.* Ed. Ruth Behar. Ann Arbor, MI: U of Michigan P, 1995. 161–179.

Phillips, Shelley. *Beyond the Myths: Mother-Daughter Relationships in Psychology, History, Literature and Everyday Life.* London: Penguin, 1991.

Piper, Adrian. "Passing for White, Passing for Black." *Transition* 58 (1992): 4–32.

Plath, James. "My Lover the Car: Ann Beattie's 'A Vintage Thunderbird' and Other Vehicles." *Kansas Quarterly* 21.4 (1989): 113–119.

Plath, Sylvia. "Daddy." *Collected Poems.* London: Faber, 1981. 222–224.

Poe, Edgar Allan. "The Philosophy of Composition." *Graham's Lady's and Gentleman's Magazine* April 1846. Rpt. in *Great Short Works of Edgar Allan Poe.* Ed. G. R. Thompson. New York: Harper & Row, 1970. 528–542.

———. "Review of 'Twice-Told Tales by Nathaniel Hawthorne.'" *Graham's Lady's and Gentleman's Magazine* May 1842. Rpt. in *Great Short Works of Edgar Allan Poe.* Ed. G. R. Thompson. New York: Harper & Row, 1970. 519–528.

————. *The Works of E. A. Poe*. Ed. John H. Ingram. Vol. IV. London: A. & C. Adams, 1901.

Porter, Carolyn. "Ann Beattie: The Art of the Missing." *Contemporary American Women Writers: Narrative Strategies*. Eds. Catherine Rainwater and William J. Scheik. Lexington: UP of Kentucky, 1985. 9–28.

Pratt, Mary Louise. "The Short Story: The Long and the Short of It." *Poetics* 10 (1981): 175–194. Rpt. in *The New Short Story Theories*. Ed. Charles E. May. Athens, OH: Ohio UP, 1994. 91–113.

Quiroga, Horacio. "Horacio Quiroga on the Short Story." Trans. Margaret Sayers Peden. *University of Denver Quarterly* 12.3 (1977): 45–53.

Rapaport, Herman. "Deconstruction's Other: Trinh T. Minh-ha and Jacques Derrida." *Diacritics* 25.2 (1995): 98–113.

Reddy, Maureen T. *Crossing the Color Line: Race, Parenting, and Culture*. New Brunswick, NJ: Rutgers UP, 1994.

Reich, Jennifer A. "Building a Home on a Border: How Single White Women Raising Multiracial Children Construct Racial Meaning." *Working Through Whiteness: International Perspectives*. Ed. Cynthia Levine-Rasky. Albany: State U of New York P, 2002. 179–208.

Reid, Ian. *The Short Story*. Critical Idiom. Ed. John D. Jump. Vol. 37. London: Methuen, 1977.

Rich, Adrienne. "Compulsory Heterosexuality and Lesbian Existence." *Powers of Desire: The Politics of Sexuality*. Eds. Ann Snitow, Christine Stansell, and Sharon Thompson. New York: Monthly Review, 1983. 177–205.

————. *Of Woman Born: Motherhood as Experience and Institution*. New York: Norton, 1976.

Richardson, Lynda. "A Calm Presence in a Tense, Tight-Deadline World." *New York Times* 14 December 2001: D4. *ProQuest Direct*. NC Live. University of North Carolina at Chapel Hill Libraries. 23 February 2005 <http://proquest.umi.com> (last accessed 3 March 2007).

Richardson, Michael. *Georges Bataille*. London: Routledge, 1994.

Richman, Michèle H. *Reading Georges Bataille: Beyond the Gift*. Baltimore: Johns Hopkins UP, 1982.

Risech, Flavio. "Political and Cultural Cross-Dressing: Negotiating a Second Generation Cuban-American Identity." *Bridges to Cuba = Puentes a Cuba*. Ed. Ruth Behar. Ann Arbor, MI: U of Michigan P, 1995. 57–71.

Rochette-Crawley, Susan. "Award Winning Trends in the Contemporary Short Story." *Literary Magazine Review* 14.3 (1995): 43–48.

Roediger, David R. *The Wages of Whiteness: Race and the Making of the American Working Class*. The Haymarket Series. Eds. Mike Davis and Michael Sprinker. London: Verso, 1991.

Rothman, Barbara Katz. *Recreating Motherhood: Ideology and Technology in a Patriarchal Society*. New York: Norton, 1989.

Rubin, Gayle S. "The Traffic in Women: Notes toward a 'Political Economy.'" *Toward an Anthropology of Women*. Ed. Rayna Reiter. New York: Monthly Review, 1975. 157–210.

Ruddick, Sara. *Maternal Thinking: Toward a Politics of Peace*. 1989. Boston: Beacon, 1995.

Sarduy, Pedro Pérez, and Jean Stubbs. "Introduction: The Rite of Social Communion." *Afrocuba: An Anthology of Cuban Writing on Race, Politics and Culture*. Eds. Pedro Pérez Sarduy and Jean Stubbs. Melbourne: Ocean, 1993. 3–26.

Saroyan, William. "What Is a Story?" *Saturday Review of Literature* 5 January 1935. Rpt. in *What Is the Short Story?* Eds. Eugene Current-García and Walton R. Patrick. Rev. ed. Glenview, IL: Scott, Foresman, 1974. 79–81.

Schapiro, Barbara. "Ann Beattie and the Culture of Narcissism." *Webster Review* 10.2 (1985): 86–101.

Schor, Naomi. "This Essentialism Which Is Not One: Coming to Grips with Irigaray." *Engaging with Irigaray*. Eds. Carolyn Burke, Naomi Schor, and Margaret Whitford. New York: Columbia UP, 1994. 57–78.

Schrift, Alan D. "Introduction: Why Gift?" *The Logic of the Gift: Toward an Ethic of Generosity*. Ed. Alan D. Schrift. New York: Routledge, 1997. 1–22.

Segal, Lore. "Burglars in the Flesh." *New Yorker* 16 June 1980: 32–42.

———. *Her First American*. New York: Knopf, 1985.

———. *Other People's Houses*. New York: Harcourt, 1964.

"Segal, Lore (Groszmann)." *Contemporary Authors, New Revision Series*. Ed. Ann Evory. Vol. 5. Detroit: Gale Research, 1982. 482–483.

Segrest, Mab. "'The Souls of White Folks.'" *The Making and Unmaking of Whiteness*. Eds. Birgit Brander Rasmussen et al. Durham: Duke UP, 2001. 43–71.

Seshadri-Crooks, Kalpana. *Desiring Whiteness: A Lacanian Analysis of Race*. London: Routledge, 2000.

Sexton, Anne. "Housewife." *All My Pretty Ones*. Boston: Houghton Mifflin, 1962. 48.

Shaw, Valerie. *The Short Story: A Critical Introduction*. London: Longman, 1983.

Silberman, Charles E. *A Certain People: American Jews and Their Lives Today*. New York: Summit Books, 1985.

Silko, Leslie Marmon. *Storyteller*. New York: Seaver Books-Grove, 1981.

Soueif, Ahdaf. *I Think of You: Stories*. New York: Anchor, 2007.

Spivak, Gayatri Chakravorty. "French Feminism in an International Frame." *In Other Worlds: Essays in Cultural Politics*. New York: Methuen, 1987. 134–153.

Stern, Guy. "The Theme of Exile in the Works of the American Successor Generations." *Die Resonanz des Exils: Gelungene und Misslungene Rezeption Deutschsprachiger Exilautoren*. Ed. Dieter Sevin. Amsterdam: Rodopi, 1992.

Stevenson, Lionel. "The Short Story in Embryo." *English Literature in Transition* 15 (1972): 261–268.

Stevick, Philip, ed. *The American Short Story, 1900–1945: A Critical History*. Boston: G. K. Hall, 1984.

Stoekl, Allan. Introduction. *Visions of Excess: Selected Writings, 1927–1939*. Ed. Allan Stoekl. Minneapolis: U of Minnesota P, 1985. ix–xxv.

Stokes, Mason Boyd. *The Color of Sex: Whiteness, Heterosexuality, and the Fictions of White Supremacy*. Durham: Duke UP, 2001.

Synge, J. M. *The Playboy of the Western World*. Dublin: Maunsel, 1907.

Tompkins, Jane. *Sensational Designs: The Cultural Work of American Fiction, 1790–1860*. New York: Oxford UP, 1985.

Tong, Rosemarie Putnam. *Feminist Thought: A More Comprehensive Introduction*. Boulder, CO: Westview, 1998.

Torres, Maria de los Angeles. "Beyond the Rupture: Reconciling with Our Enemies, Reconciling with Ourselves." *Bridges to Cuba = Puentes a Cuba*. Ed. Ruth Behar. Ann Arbor, MI: U of Michigan P, 1995. 25–42.

Twain, Mark. "How to Tell a Story." *How to Tell a Story and Other Essays*. New York: Harper & Brothers, 1897. 1–12.

Twine, France Winddance. "Brown-Skinned White Girls: Class, Culture, and the Construction of White Identity in Suburban Communities." *Displacing Whiteness: Essays in Social and Cultural Criticism*. Ed. Ruth Frankenberg. Durham: Duke UP, 1997. 214–243.

Updike, John. Introduction. *The Best American Short Stories 1984*. Eds. John Updike and Shannon Ravenel. Boston: Houghton Mifflin, 1984. xi–xxii.

Updike, John, and Katrina Kenison, eds. *The Best American Short Stories of the Century*. Boston: Houghton Mifflin, 1999.

Vanderbilt, II, Arthur T. *The Making of a Bestseller: From Author to Reader*. Jefferson, NC: McFarland, 1999.

Wagner-Martin, Linda. *Telling Women's Lives: The New Biography*. New Brunswick, NJ: Rutgers UP, 1994.

Walker, Alice. "Everyday Use." *In Love and Trouble: Stories of Black Women*. Harcourt Brace & Company, 1973.

———. "In Search of Our Mothers' Gardens." *In Search of Our Mothers' Gardens: Womanist Prose*. San Diego: Harvest-Harcourt Brace Jovanovich, 1983. 230–243.

Walker, Warren S. "From Raconteur to Writer: Oral Roots and Printed Leaves of Short Fiction." *The Teller and the Tale: Aspects of the Short Story*. Lubbock, TX: Texas Tech P, 1982. 13–26.

Washington, Mary Helen, ed. *Invented Lives: Narratives of Black Women 1860–1960*. Garden City, NY: Anchor-Doubleday, 1987.

Watt, Ian. *The Rise of the Novel: Studies in Defoe, Richardson, and Fielding*. Berkeley: U of California P, 1957.

Weaver, Gordon, ed. *The American Short Story, 1945–1980: A Critical History*. Boston: G. K. Hall, 1983.

Weisskopf, Susan Contratto. "Maternal Sexuality and Asexual Motherhood." *Signs* 5 (1980): 766–782.

Welty, Eudora. "Why I Live at the P. O." *The Collected Stories of Eudora Welty*. London: Penguin, 1980.

Wenzel, Hélène Vivienne. "Introduction to Luce Irigaray's 'And the One Doesn't Stir without the Other.'" *Signs* 7 (1981): 56–59.

Wharton, Edith. "Roman Fever." *Roman Fever and Other Stories*. New York: Collier Books-Macmillan, 1964. 3–22.

Whiteside, Thomas. *The Blockbuster Complex: Conglomerates, Show Business, and Book Publishing*. Middletown, CT: Wesleyan UP, 1981.

Wideman, John Edgar. Introduction. *The Best American Short Stories 1996*. Eds. John Edgar Wideman and Katrina Kenison. Boston: Houghton Mifflin, 1996. xv–xx.

Wiegman, Robyn. "Whiteness Studies and the Paradox of Particularity." *Boundary 2* 26.3 (1999): 115–150.

Wilkes, Chris. "Bourdieu's Class." *An Introduction to the Work of Pierre Bourdieu: The Practice of Theory*. Eds. Richard Harker, Cheleen Mahar, and Chris Wilkes. New York: St. Martin's, 1990. 109–131.

Williams, Gregory Howard. *Life on the Color Line: The True Story of a White Boy Who Discovered He Was Black*. New York: Dutton-Penguin, 1995.

Williams, Sherley Anne. "The Lawd Don't Like Ugly." *Between Mothers and Daughters: Stories across a Generation*. Ed. Susan Koppelman. Old Westbury, NY: Feminist, 1985. 242–264.

Winnicott, D. W. *The Family and Individual Development*. London: Tavistock, 1965.

Wodak, Ruth, and Muriel Schulz. *The Language of Love and Guilt: Mother-Daughter Relationships from a Cross-Cultural Perspective*. Amsterdam: John Benjamins, 1986.

Woolf, Virginia. *A Room of One's Own [and] Three Guineas*. 1929. New York: Harcourt Brace Jovanovich, 1992.

Yáñez, Mirta, ed. *Cubana: Contemporary Fiction by Cuban Women*. Boston: Beacon, 1998.

Yu, Sylvia, and Heather Shannon. "Archives of *Story* Magazine and Story Press, 1931–1999: A Finding Aid." *Princeton University Library Rare Books and Special Collections*. 15 August 2006. Manuscripts Division, Department of Rare Books and Special Collections, Princeton University Library. 12 February 2005 <http://libweb.princeton.edu/libraries/firestone/rbsc/aids/story/> (last accessed 3 March 2007).

Zahava, Irene, ed. *My Mother's Daughter: Stories by Women*. Freedom, CA: Crossing, 1991.

Index